TRACKERS

More from Avalon Press by Clancy Weeks:

The Zzkritti Imperative

Sleepers

Trackers

Filters (new in 2021)

Paths of Destiny

The Maker's Son (new in 2020)

The Stone of Tantalus

The Ward

Anodyne Dreams

Anodyne Dreams 2 (Sept. 2020)

TRACKERS

CLANCY WEEKS

Published in U.S.A. by Avalon Press.

Copyright © 2019 by Clancy Weeks

First edition: 2020

Title: Trackers
Names: Weeks, Clancy, author
Descriptions: First edition. | Tomball: Avalon Press [2020]
Identifiers:
 ISBN-13: 978-1-7321220-6-2 (paperback) |
 ISBN-13: 978-1-7321220-7-9 (e-book) |
Subjects: | Thriller | Science Fiction. | Suspense Fiction.

AVALON PRESS

*To all my friends and family who think I write them into my
stories under assumed names... I do, just not the heroes.*

.

How messed up is that?

PART ONE

We are all so much together, but we are all dying of loneliness.

—Albert Schweitzer

PROLOGUE

November 12, 2015

DENNY GOODMAN RATTLED SHUT THE DRIVER'S side door of his store's one and only delivery van and slogged toward the rear. White where the rust still hadn't reached, the faded red and yellow logo of *Denny's Maxi Mini-Mart* flaked from years of oxidation. He ran his hand along the side as he walked, fingers feeling the rough and worn surface, shoes squelching in the icy mud. *About time to trade the old girl in. Next bundle of cash from the crazy professor should make a nice down-payment.*

There was no bundle of cash in his future, nor was there ever any in his past. The memory, like his actions, programmed and implanted over a year ago.

Denny took the gloves from his back pocket and tugged them onto half-frozen fingers, then pulled the rear doors open. Even in the whirling frigid air, the odor drifting from the nearby ground strangled the breath from his throat, and he threw a corduroy covered arm over his mouth and nose to filter the stench. Months ago, an entirely different smell from buried embers drifted over the grounds. The delivery entrance was a pile of rubble black with soot, the heavy oak door reduced to metal hinges and ash, but Denny never noticed.

He removed the three heavy boxes of groceries and supplies and placed them on the ground, stacking them neatly among the others. There were so many he couldn't reach the door even if it still existed and would have vomited from the stench if he had. Thirty-six boxes of food delivered from his store lay rotting in the shadow of the old asylum—rats, cockroaches, and flies feasting on what remained; an entire ecosystem grew and thrived on the forgotten deliveries.

Denny set the last box in place and smiled at his handiwork, the steam from his breath billowing great clouds as his chest heaved. *The old man's a good customer. Never complains and always pays on time.* He slammed the doors shut and strolled to the front. *Wish all my customers were like him.*

He climbed inside and closed the door. The snow was just starting to fall again, and the tires spun a second before the van lurched ahead. He slewed to the left, then righted his aim as the tires bit into the gravel road, and he drove away from the charred bones of the old asylum.

Behind him, the stray dogs left the safety of the trees, apex predators of the new ecology.

CHAPTER 1

BLOOD WAS EVERYWHERE—FLOOR, WALLS, CEILING—thin lines painting every surface; a monochromatic Jackson Pollock. Tiny flecks, ricochets from the stream striking the wall, dried where they fell as glittering horror. Sheets of paper stuck to the floor, glued there with drying blood. Evan Barrow, National Registry Paramedic, pealed one up, flipped it, and was rewarded with a happy crimson butterfly—a gruesome Rorschach inkblot. Everything about Evan was average—right down to his shoe size—but his blue eyes saw nothing average about the ambulance. It was his turn to clean the bus, and it *would* have to come on the night Willie clipped a curb just as Evan was checking the vic's mainline.

"Looks like a fuckin' murder scene in here, Willie," he said, not even trying to hide his disgust. "I could use a little help, bro."

"Hey, I don't remember you offering any the night the lady's colostomy bag ruptured," Willie Alford said, sitting on the diamond-plate bumper, a half-smoked cigarette dangling from his bottom lip. A little too fat for a man in his line of work, he ran one hand through his thick mop of greasy dark hair. He crossed his arms and leaned back against one closed door, arching a woolly eyebrow at Evan. "My goddamn hair stank like shit for three whole days."

Evan grinned and set the box of cleaning supplies into the back of the ambulance. "No, Willie, you always smell like that."

Willie chuckled, took a long drag, then tossed the butt to the ground, crushing the life out of it with a booted toe. "And here I was ready to help you out." He stood and faced Evan. "Now I'm just gonna go home and bang my girlfriend." He grabbed his crotch. "She's been itchin' for this for a couple of days."

3

"She seemed pretty satisfied when I left her this morning," Evan said with an impish grin.

"Oh, hardy har, har," Willie said, smirking. "You're a real funny man."

The truth was Evan didn't like Willie all that much. The two had been assigned the same shifts for the past year, and Evan had never warmed to the man. *Besides, the cab always smells like stale cigarettes and sweat by the end of the shift.* More than that, Evan's own clothes and hair were a magnet for the odors. Both his mom and dad were heavy smokers, and it was his father's death from emphysema-predicated pneumonia that motivated Evan to become a paramedic. Stubborn to the end, his dad refused to stop smoking even after his diagnosis.

"Every man's gotta die of somethin'," he told his son before taking a long drag on the cancer stick, blowing acrid smoke from barely functioning lungs. In the end, it was ignorance that killed the old man.

Willie tapped the last smoke into his hand, then crushed the pack in his fist. He shoved the crumpled pack into his jacket—*At least he doesn't litter*—then expertly flipped the last cigarette into his mouth.

"You really ought to quit, you know."

"I do," Willie said with a grin. "Every time I stub one out."

"Cute," Evan said, then sighed. "Go home, Willie. I got this." As distasteful as this task was, he knew it was infinitely better doing it without Willie tugging on a smoke beside him. *Then there's the added benefit of bragging rights.* He got on his hands and knees, pulled a sponge from the bucket, squeezed out the antiseptic cleaning fluid with both gloved hands, and bent to work. Annie, his shift supervisor, always chided him for starting at the bottom, but he hated walking through the muck while tackling the upper areas first. Willie muttered something inaudible and sauntered away, and Evan's shoulders loosened. He scrubbed with both hands on the sponge, rinsing in the second bucket before dipping into the cleaner again, working from the back of the bus to the front, attending to every drop and splatter, and paying careful attention to where floor plates joined. Annie would check the whole thing over with her beady hawk-eyes, even sniffing the floor and cabinets.

Evan was so engrossed with his task, he didn't notice the soft buzzing. By the time he did, the sound had risen in volume and pitch, a dentist's drill shoved into his ears. He dropped the sponge, spine stiffening as he sat straight up on his haunches and grabbed the sides of his head with both hands, a scream gathering in the back of his

4

throat. The breath he drew to power that scream caught in his chest, then piteously sighed out like a rapidly deflating balloon, his eyes rolling back. He toppled backward, a tree felled by an unseen axe, and banged his head against the floor. His mind flickered like modem lights before the first bounce, the hardware ready for a fresh install.

The dreams were vivid and haunting, fractured images through shattered crystal. Here a man bent over a patient—a small boy of perhaps six or seven—there a tall man in dark clothing, a glowing item in one gloved hand. The pictures, some moving, some not, swirled around Evan's head like being trapped in the center of a carousel, his hands pressed against the mirrored glass as the world flew by. He pounded the glass, but no sound emerged, and no one on the other side took notice. And there *were* people on the other side.

Some were not people at all.

They peered into the mirror from the other side, seeing only themselves, preening and posing. One, an old man drew Evan's attention to him as a scampering mouse draws a cat's glare. Wild white hair covered by a dark tweed fedora crowned his head, and below bushy eyebrows piercing eyes stared. The old man looked right at him. He rested both gnarled hands against the glass, fingers splayed, then in one swift motion plunged bitter fingers through, reaching for Evan's throat. Evan scuttled back on hands and haunches, bumping against something solid in the thick blackness surrounding him. The fingers ached to grasp living flesh, but could not close the distance, only brushing the tip of Evan's nose.

The old man withdrew his hands and tipped his hat, grinning like a cheap department store Santa Claus. Santa spun and was shot in the forehead by a screw-faced man, rage boiling off him like live steam. Brains and chunks of skull flew from the yawning chasm at the back of Santa's head, a hot jet of blood spraying from the tiny hole marking death's entry. The scene repeated now on an endless and silent loop; Evan squeezed his eyes shut, fists pressed tight against his lids.

A sound like a hammer on an anvil, tiny and rhythmic, reached his ears. The sound grew with each strike, more distinct with every iteration.

Jack. Jack. Jack.

The tink of metal against metal became a pounding drumbeat, the pressure threating to rupture his eardrums.

5

JACK. JACK. JACK.

The man with the gun stopped killing Santa, turned to Evan, and peered through the mirror as Santa had. He stepped forward, ignoring the pile of bodies at his feet, and leaned close, nose pressing against the glass. There was no longer raw, seething anger there... only grim determination. Evan held his breath and waited for the gun to poke through and end the nightmare, but the man only stood, then turned back to his gruesome task.

Another Santa fell.

Evan opened his eyes to a black sky dotted with stars, sat up, and rubbed the back of his head. A large lump there screamed in pain, and he jerked the hand away, checking for blood. There was none, and his heart slowed its frantic pace. He looked around and frowned. No longer in the parking lot, he sat not in the back of the ambulance, but on the greasy wet concrete of an alley between two ancient brick buildings. The stench from the overflowing dumpsters hung in the damp air like a shroud, clinging to his skin and clothes; his gorge rose, but he guessed his concussion may have had more to do with that.

He was sure he had a concussion, and could even recommend the optimum treatment, but had no clue where he had come by the information. His name was Evan Barrow—he was sure of that, too—but could no longer remember where he lived or even the names of his parents.

"Retrograde amnesia due to traumatic brain injury," he mumbled, frowning. It was the most obvious cause, but he couldn't say how he knew. The phrase had simply popped into his mind as if waiting for the question.

Evan levered himself to his feet, then wiped both hands on the legs of his uniform. The same uniform still caked in dried blood from the unfortunate vic he and—

He stood in the middle of the alley, head swimming as he tried to remember the name of the man he worked with, when his eyes widened and he doubled over, emptying his stomach to the damp pavement. Steam rose from the puddle of vomit at his feet, and he stepped away from the mess, holding himself vertical with one hand against a sooty brick wall. A rat, nose twitching beneath shining predator's eyes, edged from beneath the dumpster a few feet ahead and to the right, and Evan backed away.

6

Where there is one, there are always more. He looked around for the exit and found it about forty feet to his rear. Evan fled, rubber-soled shoes slapping against wet pavement, and managed a half-dozen steps before the pain flared in his head, a white-hot poker cauterizing his brain from back to front. This was not the goose-egg on the back of his skull throbbing—oh, no. This was *inside* his skull, a rat eating its way out. The agony—less than what caused his blackout, yet somehow worse—almost drove him to his knees. With a massive effort, he continued moving, staggering to the end of the alley and the street beyond. Sounds of traffic heartened him, drawing him forward, a catfish on a hook.

The searing heat in his brain lessened, replaced by millions of ants. Crawling, digging, burrowing—but most of all, *building*; it was as if they tore apart pieces of Evan to create something new—something *not* Evan. Tears streamed down his cheeks, and he stumbled into the open, a gust of wind washing over him like a cleansing bath, driving away the stink of the alley. He breathed deep and the last of the pain fizzled. What remained was a high-pitch whine that grew or faded depending on which direction he faced. Something told him the sound would lower in pitch the closer he got to... wherever it was he needed to be.

Across the street a Wells Fargo Bank branch loomed, gloomy staid seriousness in the middle of a street awash in garish light and romp. Cars zipped by left and right, all but ignored by pedestrians filling the sidewalks or crossing the street in glorious violation of the law. Most wore loose coats against that last chill of Spring, and Evan—or what passed for Evan, now—looked up at the moon. Brighter than the back-lit panes shining from hundreds of windows above, it outshone the few stars visible in a light-polluted city.

Evan took a deep breath, let it out slowly, and grinned. He tugged the wallet from his back pocket and stepped off the curb to cross the street. If there were enough ATM's nearby, he could empty the man's bank accounts one withdrawal at a time. With luck, there was enough available balance on the credit cards to be useful. An image of a large house filled his head, one he had never seen before, but felt was his destination.

He didn't know who he was now, where he was going, or what he needed to do when he got there, but he guessed the information would present itself. Evan furrowed his brow and pursed his lips. *Something went wrong.* He didn't understand much, but he understood one thing for sure: He was a failsafe. A backup plan.

"Nice to know you're the one who gets called when things go in the shitter," he said and shoved the debit card in the slot.

❧

Six-thousand dollars and change stuffed into the small duffel on his lap, Evan sat in the back of the vibrating Greyhound bus, rethinking his choice of seats. Between the diesel fumes and the chemical toilet two feet away, his stomach twisted with every jostle and bump. It didn't help the driver was apparently prone to epileptic seizures every time he took a corner. The bus hadn't been full when Evan boarded, but that sound in his skull led him all the way down the aisle as if a gun were pressed against his spine. Each time he considered moving, his head hummed like a beehive.

The high-pitched whine had already lowered in pitch an octave or two, telling him he was getting closer to his goal. What that goal was, other than an image of a big house on a corner lot, had become no clearer, only that it was somewhere around Washington, D.C.

I'm going to see the primary. He frowned. *Where the hell did that come from?*

In the sixteen hours since he'd awakened in the alley, thoughts like that had bled into his consciousness, driving him to do things that often made no sense. He pulled the battered Atlanta Braves cap down with a snap, shading his eyes, and leaned against the window, away from the godawful odor on his right; the cloud of liquid stench followed his nose, hovering like a cat begging for food.

"I should have taken a plane," he grumbled, then closed his eyes. *But we must be careful with our spending*, that voice sitting atop his brain like a bull-rider whispered. It wiggled its ass, settling into the crevice between the left and right halves, straddling the corpus callosum. It buried thin, bony fingers into the gray matter on either side, taking greater control of the meat-machine it piloted. *Money will come later*, it said. *For now, we must spend wisely.*

The voice whispered in Evan's ear like a lost lover—comforting, cajoling, a wide-vista contentment calming his jangled nerves; it rang like a deep-throated church bell, smelled of fresh tobacco and old sweat, and Evan drifted into a cotton-headed slumber. What dreams followed he wouldn't remember, the last pieces of his psyche swept away by cold, cleansing sleep. The ants went to work yet again, remaking old into new, re-wiring and re-writing, editing and deleting, the second draft well and truly begun.

If death were nothing more than a dreamless eternal sleep, Evan died that day. If death were sleep, the dead could wake.

The trip from Sacramento took four days, including transfers and rest stops. When the battered old bus dumped him out at Union Station in D.C., Evan was so near his quarry the pitch sounding in his head was a thrumming bass-baritone; his mother had been partial to Paul Robeson, and "Old Man River" spooled out in his ears, an eight-track tape on a single-play loop. The memory was clear, and if enough of Evan had been left to wonder over it, the knowledge might have frightened him. But this was the new and improved Evan, body still a hair shy of thirty, with a mind only days old. The process would take many months to complete, and huge chunks of data presented as gaps in long-term memory, a few scrambled beyond repair, but most just gone. The heavy work near completion, the voice now had near-total control.

Yet... something of the Evan that was remained. He hid behind the mirrored panels of the carousel, eyes wide in panic, dark hair slick with sweat, back pressed so tight against the cold wall his vertebrae ached, hugging his knees to his chest with both arms. The old man piloting his body allowed him glimpses of the world as if it were an IMAX movie.

The bus rolled to a stop, brakes hissing, and disheveled passengers on either side of the aisle stood and stretched, backs popping and crackling like wet firecrackers on a hot and hushed 4th. A young couple, the wife so pregnant Evan wondered how she hadn't popped already, gathered their meager luggage from the overhead. On his right, a mother corralled her two small boys, a harbinger of the young wife's life-to-be. Others performed their own little dance farther ahead, each conscious of the others only as data points for their onboard avoidance systems. Evan watched it all with the detached disinterest of an entomologist dissecting larvae.

One by one, two by two, passengers departed, trudging the grooved and sticky walkway toward the door. Evan waited, gripping the duffel tight in both hands like a lifeline. He wandered forward, a step behind the pregnant woman, who he realized couldn't be more than seventeen. Her partner stopped short ahead of her, allowing the mother and her sons access, and the young woman stumbled. Evan's hand shot out before the old man could even pull the correct lever, and he gripped her elbow, steadying her as she recovered. She began to thank him, a self-conscious smile playing below shining green eyes, then her brow furrowed, and she swung away without a word. Evan released her arm and his reflection in the window. Face slack and ashen, it was as if the muscles had forgotten to hold everything in place. It was the face of a stroke victim—one with damage to both sides of his brain.

The old man chuckled in Evan's head, pulled at a lever or two, and the muscles in his face tightened to something approaching human. He watched everyone ahead disappear through the open doors, shambling single file like cattle to slaughter. The bus driver, nearly as old as the man driving Evan, his dark face crowned with a tight afro shot through with cotton-white strands, one gleaming gold tooth highlighting a wide and infectious smile, nodded and tipped his cap to each passenger as they passed. Evan had never seen a man so happy simply doing his job, and the corners of his mouth pulled up in sympathy. It was an instinct as old as man, and one not easily erased.

The young couple reached the front, and the girl beamed at the driver—*Carl*, the name stitched on his shirt said—before turning to the door.

"It'll work out," Carl said to her, touching her elbow with two fingers. He said it like an invocation.

"Pardon?" she said, pausing on the steps.

"Just, ya know... in general." He beamed. "I have a good feelin' 'bout you two." He nodded at the boy who stood at the foot of the steps outside the door. "He's a good boy. Don't know much 'bout manners, but a good boy." He squinted at the boy who looked at the ground and shuffled his feet, then nodded. "Yes'm. He'll do just fine."

The girl scrunched up her face, then grinned. "Thanks, I guess," she said, then exited the bus.

Evan moved forward, ignoring the driver. Iron fingers tightened around his upper arm, a vise-like grip holding as surely as if chained to the floor.

"*You*, on the other hand," Carl said, eyes hooded, face darkening further. "Things aren't gonna go so good for you. Nosir. Not good at all." He gave his head a sad shake before turning loose of Evan's arm. "I don't always drive this bus, son." He squinted hard into Evan's eyes. "Others take a turn at the wheel from time ta time, but I know I can always take 'er back when I'm of a mind." He nodded, then smirked as if he'd said something profound. "You remember

10

that, Evan." Carl shooed him out, closing the doors with a swift clank behind him.

Evan was almost out of the parking lot when he realized Carl had used his name.

How did he know my name?

The question played over and over in his head ever since he'd left the bus station, his legs propelling him forward on autopilot. It was impossible anyone recognized him, and the few memories left said he'd never been to D.C.

With a word, it all comes undone. No one had tracked him; he knew that much.

He'd hiked northwest on Massachusetts Avenue in a driving rain for perhaps two hours, following the directional beacon inside his head. Evan felt he wouldn't—*couldn't*—get sick, but that didn't stop his amygdala from seeking shelter. His eyes darted left and right as he stood on the corner gawping at the brick edifice hunched over the manicured lawn. He couldn't shake the feeling the strategically placed cameras were all pointed at *him*, watching with great concern for his next movement. Soaked and cold, he stood there swaying in the wind, looking for a way inside.

I don't need a way in. Only a way to get close. To whom wasn't clear, but he had a fair idea. *Somewhere in there is what I need.*

Now he'd found the place, the beacon fell silent, its absence as keenly felt as its grating presence had been. It was as if he had surfaced after a long dive in an endless ocean, and he grinned, blinking away fat raindrops.

The homeowner also owned a business. *Seven miles east, to be exact. Across the Anacostia River.*

It no longer mattered how he knew this. Evan threw the duffel's strap over one shoulder, shoved his hands into his pockets, and turned east. The company offered hard work for hard men, and surely there were some among the employees for whom a tight wad of cash would be more than tempting. Anything and anyone in D.C. could be bought for the right price.

I can be patient, he told himself. *There is time.*

Evan tugged at his tie, unused to the constriction around his neck, and shook hands with the foreman.

"There's not much to tell, really," he said, answering the question from the big man in the small chair. "I was a paramedic in California, but the wife got a job offer here in D.C. she couldn't refuse." He shrugged, affecting an air of fatalism. "Figured I'd try something new."

The man arched an eyebrow over a craggy face. "Workin' iron ain't like patchin' a boo-boo, friend."

"No," Evan chuckled. "I guess not." He let the retort lay between them like an old hound dog. Men like Eldon Carmichael preferred to assess job candidates with a hard stare; Evan had known men such as this his whole life.

Eldon took a deep breath through his nose, the sound a semi-truck hauling to a stop. "Still, a man with your skills could be an asset 'round here." He grinned and winked. "Iron work is a dangerous business, an' it's best ta deal with accidents in-house." The man lowered his head, his face darkening, and leaned forward, placing both elbows on the cluttered desktop; the chair groaned a long complaint. "If ya know what I mean."

"Sure do." There was no point in elaborating. Every company cut costs wherever they could, and this one was no different—just more callous. Evan suppressed a smile. *The sort of men I might need should be easy to come by in a place such as this.*

Eldon stared at him, beady eyes almost hidden behind fat cheeks and thick lids, then nodded. "Guess you'll do, then," he said. "Remember Doomsday over at one of the welding stations we passed?"

Evan had met many workers on the short tour of the building, but that one stood out. Short, twitchy, and always talking, even when he knew nothing of the subject. "I think so," he said with a nod.

"Go find him. He'll get ya fixed up." Eldon grabbed a pencil and paper, dashing off a quick note. He folded it once and held it out for Evan. "Give this to 'im." Evan took the folded paper, but did not open it. "I'm gonna start ya out as a sweeper fer now, but we'll train ya on the bending machines as ya go. Minimum wage at first, an' the pay goes up as ya train." He cocked an eyebrow. "Fair 'nuff?"

Evan, six grand still in the duffel hidden in his motel room, and even bigger plans near-term, simply nodded. He smiled, stood, and turned for the door.

"Hey," Eldon shouted as he reached for the knob. The fat man pointed at the hook beside the door. "Don't ferget yer hardhat."

"Sorry," he said, and grabbed the yellow hat. He pressed it down on his head, then opened the door in search of the little man with the long cornrows—the one the others laughingly called Doomsday.

"I'm tellin' ya," Double-D said, hand around his mug, leaning on the bar, already three sheets to the wind. "The bastard don't come down there more'n once or twice a month." He took a drink, slopping half on the bar and his sleeve. "Too afraid of gettin' his loafers scuffed."

After only a few days, Evan had found his patsy, and was one of the first men he'd met. Doomsday—or Double-D, as Evan preferred to call him—was a loudmouth and a provocateur, but harmless for the most part. He was the sort of man everyone described as "gentle" and "quiet" afterward, shocked he was involved in such a crime.

And a crime is necessary, now. Twelve days in, and the first thing he'd learned was the owner rarely visited the Works, and *never* the shop floor. Evan's first choice all along had been to confront the man and take the list from him, but now he realized that wasn't possible. What he still didn't know was what was on the list, why this man had it, or even how Evan knew about it. There were still too many holes in his memory. *I need to get close to him.*

Evan swirled the beer in his mug, then drained it before setting it down. "What are your plans for the next few days?" he asked casually, staring into the empty mug.

"I'm off for two more, but back on for seven." They'd both been on the same schedule since Evan's hire, so he wasn't surprised.

"You up for making some quick cash?" he asked, almost whispering. "I mean... a *lot* of cash." He knew the answer even before the man spoke.

"Sure," Double-D said with a snort. "Who ain't?" He raised an eyebrow, bloodshot eyes making him look for a second like a Black Christopher Lloyd. "Difficult or just illegal?"

"Definitely not difficult," Evan said with a tight grin.

Double-D lifted the mug to his face, tilted it, the spoke before the beer touched his lips. "Anyone gonna get hurt?"

"Depends."

Double-D finished the motion and his beer, set the mug down, and wiped his face with his sleeve. He spun on the barstool and faced Evan, already sobering. "What we gonna do?"

Two weeks at the Iron Works had robbed Evan of all patience. The home of the Vice President of the United States was so close he imagined he could smell it. *Number One Observatory Circle*, he thought, wondering where that tidbit of knowledge came from. More than a stone's throw, but well within walking distance. *So close—but it might as well be light-years.* He giggled a little at that, and the boy beside him whimpered. The other man, knife against the throat of the boy's father, sat on a stool happily munching a cold slice of pizza. He tossed the half-eaten piece into the box and stood, the knife's keen edge glinting; it never left the father's neck as he stepped around to stand behind. The father struggled against his bonds and gag while the mother softly sobbed.

"C'mon, dude," the twitchy little man said, eyes darting from window to door. "Let's just take the jewelry and cash and get the fuck out."

"I told you," Evan said with exaggerated calm, "first he needs to give me the list." His face split into a thin smile, more Joker than Grinch. "*Then* we can go."

"Yeah," Double-D said, waiving the knife in the air. "You keep talkin' about this list," he made little air-quotes with his fingers, "but a list of what?" He snorted once. "And why do you need it?"

Even if I knew, I wouldn't tell you. The truth was, when Evan woke two days ago, the idea of the list just popped into his head. He knew where to get it, but not what was on it, nor even *why* he needed it. But the urge to possess it was strong. Oh yes. Stronger than the need to eat, sleep, or fornicate. When Mr. High-and-Mighty over there refused his initial request, claiming no knowledge of such a list, Evan realized it would come to this.

The worst part was it was all so unnecessary. The man across from him, bound and gagged, fearing for his son's life, should have been the one to wake first.

Whatever that means. There was so much useless and disjointed information bounding around in his mind—rabbits running from a hunt, they skittered and scattered, each slipping from his grasp every time he drew near enough to examine one. *This man has means, proximity, and opportunity.* For what, he still didn't know, but he hoped the list would at least point him in the right direction. He now knew waking the father now was no longer an option.

Evan sighed, stood, and grabbed a handful of the boy's hair, jerking his head back with a sharp tug. The terror in the ten-year-old's eyes radiated in waves so strong Evan felt it straight through to his bones. He wanted nothing to do with any of this—until a month ago, he'd been a *paramedic, fer Christ's sake*—but want and need were two very different things. Early morning light poured in through the hastily drawn window curtains, the sounds of a waking neighborhood leaking through. *Time's up*, he thought, and reached for the glowing fireplace poker, pulling it from the hot coals. The boy's eyes, impossibly, grew wider, flicking around the room for a place to run. Tears streamed from the corners, running down the sides of his face into his ears. Evan gripped the boy's hair tight, holding the head steady.

The father, bloody and bruised, fought against his bindings, working with all his might to free himself. Double-D cut a thin slash across the father's face, then pointed the knife's bloody blade at the mother seated next to him. Mr. High-and-Mighty got the hint and settled down, squeezing his eyes shut.

"Now, I don't want to do this," Evan said, his voice as bland as a television newsreader. "But I need you to understand I'm serious." A thin voice in the innermost sanctum of his mind screamed *No!*, but Evan—this Evan—pushed it down with brutal force. *Now is not the time to be squeamish. We're way past that.* The voice he remembered as his own had grown weaker over the past month, while the new took command as if driving an old tank—clumsily at first, but with confidence building with each turn of the wheel.

He held the poker over the boy's head, then before he could think about it, pushed the glowing tip into his right eye. The cornea sizzled for a fraction of a second, then the eyeball swelled and burst as the child screamed. The odor of cooked sclera wafted to Evan's nose and the old version of himself gibbering in the corner of his mind retched and choked. The Evan driving the tank just looked on with detached indifference as the vitreous humor bubbled and oozed from the smoking socket. The mother screamed, but the father sat still as stone, his face reddening so brightly Evan feared he would stroke out.

The boy's strangled scream died, and he passed out from the pain and fear.

"Now I have your attention," Evan released the boy's hair, and the head lolled forward. "You will give me what I need." He strode forward with the poker in hand, its end still sizzling with cooked meat, and bent at the waist, his nose almost touching the other man's. "This ends when I have what I—"

Evan's eyes widened at the blood oozing from the slash on the man's face. So dark it was nearly black, the blood sparkled and glinted dully in the fireplace's glow. Like a thin film of oil on water, light refracted and reflected from its iridescent surface. Evan lifted a finger as if to touch it and drew back in shock when the blood reached for *him*.

"What?" Double-D tilted his head like a new puppy.

"Nothin'." Evan stood between the father and Double-D, but the old man at the controls barely contained his glee. He pulled levers and tugged nerves, and Evan reached out again, *touched* the streak of blood, allowed it to flow to him. It grabbed his finger like a leech, covering first the joints, then swarming his hand. That tiny part of Evan still alive screamed and flailed to fling the horrifying mass away, but the meat-Evan stood perfectly still, reveling in the sensation.

The father slumped forward, dead or unconscious, Evan neither knew nor cared which. The wife screamed through her gag, and Double-D laughed. He hadn't seen the horror climbing up Evan's arm.

While he watched, the blood that was surely not blood, faded as his skin absorbed it all. His mind exploded in pure white light, a million images flung at him at once, overloading mental retinas, locking every muscle. He stood that way for perhaps three seconds, an eternity, absorbing wave after wave of raw data, so much he thought he would drown.

When the onslaught subsided, he understood there had been no list. The *man* was the list. *He* was now the list. *The transfer had been a success, but the process interrupted.* Bits of him hid within dozens of people, and if he was to complete his mission, he must retrieve and integrate each piece of the code. He looked around at the mansion, then locked eyes with the father. *A pity I could not have awakened in you.*

"There's something I need to get, Double-D." He pulled the father's cell phone from his pocket and tossed it to the little man. "When he wakes, have him call an employee to bring you all the cash you think you can get, then try to disappear." The man was too stupid for that, even if he hadn't already programmed the fool to forget he had an accomplice. "Don't leave any witnesses."

Double-D coughed a cruel laugh and shoved the cell into his pocket. "Can I burn the place?"

"Whatever you want, buddy." He went up the stairs to the master bedroom, found the safe, and punched the code. The three bundles of cash totaling over fifty-thousand dollars would have to do for now. He pulled the velvet box from the back of the safe and opened it. Inside glittered several diamond rings and a diamond necklace. Once he'd removed the stones, he could fence them for enough cash for the next phase. He shoved everything into a white paint bucket he had taken from the garage and whistled as he descended the stairs toward the back entrance, passing a set of Porsche keys hanging on a hook. He raised an eyebrow, grabbed the keys, and pulled the hood of his jacket over his head, taking the ugly lime-green construction vest hanging beside it for good measure.

Evan Barrow stepped into the alley and strolled past a dumpster in search of the car, Dieter Braun at the wheel.

CHAPTER 2

August 2016

I T HAD BEEN A LONG, HOT, STICKY summer, and the car Sohrab drove was pretty much the same. He'd had no luck finding a cheap mechanic to repair the air conditioner in his wife's car, and fares in DC had been few and far between of late. The silly season was upon them, clinging to every pillar and branch like a swarm of horny cicadas, many legislators out of town for meet-and-greet with the folks back home, or raking in piles of last-minute donor cash; most locals were glad to see their backside. *Don't let the door hit ya on the ass on the way out.* It became a collective cry of frustration for the city, and most would celebrate when the clock struck midnight on this weird and wonderful election year.

Sohrab had given in to inevitability and decided to drive for Uber. His wife liked the fact he could set his own hours—and after fifteen years driving a cab, he knew the best times—and that he got to rate the *passengers* even as they rated him.

"There's something decidedly democratic about that," she had said, standing by the stove, the long-handled wooden spoon in hand as if directing an orchestra.

"Yes, but our best auto is yours, and even that needs repair," he told her for perhaps the hundredth time. "I will not get good reviews driving people around in this heat with no air conditioner."

The vanilla-colored Ford Edge she drove was clean and unblemished for the most part, and fully repaired, the car would fetch a premium in pricing.

Today, Sohrab drove west on highway 66 toward Groveton. His neighbor told him about a local mechanic—a *shade-tree* mechanic he'd called him—who worked cheap and had a good reputation with his customers.

"Such people are scarce around here," he muttered. He had developed the habit of talking to himself since the events of last year, and nothing had gotten him to stop. Even for a man with his experience, sleep was rare the first few months. *Some images never fade.*

Nearly as horrifying were his dreams of the aliens he had never seen. They appeared every so often, waking him in an icy sweat, manifesting as everything from giant insectoids to amorphous blobs. They were apparently responsible for every major war, catastrophic events—possibly even every pandemic—and political upheaval over the last six-thousand years. It was why Sohrab had stopped listening to the news—he imagined alien intervention behind every event of consequence. When even his wife commented on his growing paranoia, it was time to pull the plug.

I refuse to believe they're responsible for Trump, though. Humans were perfectly capable of fouling their own nests and had been since long before the alien influence. *We don't need their intervention for that,* he mused, combing his short beard with thin fingers.

Marie convinced him to trim the beard, fearing America's growing intolerance for anyone who even *appeared* Muslim—the weight he'd lost on his own; a combination of exercise, better diet, and fear-induced lack of sleep melting kilograms of fat over the last eighteen months. His face, leaner and more angular now, could pass for Greek if he stayed out of the sun. He'd also adopted a British accent when speaking to customers. Even though he'd abandoned his faith decades ago, he despised hiding who he was.

It is a lie, but Marie no longer frets for me, now.

A midnight-blue Mercedes sped past, the driver casually flipping him off, and Sohrab checked his speed. *Yes, twenty miles under the speed limit will anger many in this country.* He'd been doing that, too, a lot lately—slowing as he mulled and stewed. He pressed down on the accelerator and the car obliged, picking up speed to match the flow of traffic. "At least now the crazy Americans won't run me over," he grumbled.

Two miles outside of Groveton, he passed a Lilliputian shack of a barbecue joint, a place so world-weary the chipped paint was all that held the boards together, and his mind turned to Mason. He hadn't known him long, but some people burrowed in and made a home for themselves, no matter the time spent together. Sohrab grunted and spun the wheel, pulling off at the intersection, then taking the pock-marked feeder back to the crossroad where the place huddled beneath a stand of trees. Thick smoke poured from a rusted stand-pipe chimney in back like a tornado tethered to a fencepost, the aroma of hardwood-grilled meat wafting through the car's open windows. The driveway was dusty gravel, and the tires crunched happily as he slid to a stop. At ten in the morning, the only cars in the lot likely belonged to the owner and their employees, but the buzzing red neon *Open* sign by the door was a good omen.

Sohrab's stomach growled, an operatic rumble lasting a full five seconds including aftershocks, and he laughed. His laugh had grown smaller in the last year, but the heart powering it was still strong. He unbuckled his shoulder harness and opened the door, still chuckling.

"Barbecue is life," he said, quoting the lost friend, standing beside the open car door. He stepped away and closed it behind him, windows still open to the world. "Maybe if I eat like Mason, I can put some weight back on." He grinned, shoved his keys into his front pocket, and followed his nose.

"I don't know 'bout this country, no more," the older man said, wiping his hands on his grease-stained coveralls. The tight curls of silver in his hair were the only things remotely white about him; his skin was so dark it was almost blue. When Bud Redcliffe smiled, his face shined like a lighthouse; straight, white teeth glowing in a wine-dark sea.

His face wasn't shining now.

"That bit in Orlando really shook the missus," he said, shaking his head. Sohrab had grown used to these conversation starters—sincere men with their sincere concerns bringing up terrorist acts in a sincere effort to show him they held no grudge. *I'm one of the good ones, after all*, he thought bitterly. Sometimes they did it simply to gauge his reaction—see if he *was* one of the good ones. As always, Sohrab bit his tongue and kept his opinions to himself. He learned early on it was pointless to either argue or agree—his words fed their bias regardless of what he said. *And it will only worsen.* Racists crawled from beneath every rock these days, stretching in the sunshine as if after a long hibernation, smiling with needle-sharp teeth, their time come at last. *Maybe it has. America is a great country that often forgets what made it great.*

"Do you know what's wrong with it?" Sohrab could have been talking about the country, but Mr. Redcliffe answered the obvious after a long squint.

"Eh... nothin' that a can o' Freon won't fix." He shrugged. "She just needs chargin'. You might have a leak in the line somewhere, but I ain't found one." He snatched a dirty rag from the front bumper, rubbing the last of the grease from his fingers. "Happens to these models sometimes after a long hot summer." He raised his head and squinted into the sun. "This 'un's sure been one o' those."

"Indeed," Sohrab nodded, happy to have something with which to agree.

"Got a can in back." Bud gestured toward the interior of the large metal building he used as a working garage—no shade tree required. "Jes be a sec." He trundled off, walking with a slight, but distinct limp, favoring the right leg. *An old injury*, Sohrab thought, observing and cataloging with an instinct honed by years of training. *Medial collateral of the knee. A single sweep of the leg will incapacitate.* He shook his head, short and violent, clearing the thoughts. It was getting difficult to do that ever since...

Ever since Bill Montgomery dissolved right before my eyes.

He had seen many disturbing things in his years with the Mukhabarat—some on par with what happened to Bill. *Some I was responsible for, myself.* Dead was dead; the method unimportant in the grand design. *To the dead, it never matters.*

The older man appeared from the darkened interior, pushing a hand-truck with a large canister strapped tight. He held a hose with an in-line gauge attached in one hand, the end swinging freely as if he meant to use it as a whip; Sohrab balanced on the balls of his feet and waited.

Redcliffe stopped, settled the wheeled canister against the bumper, and grinned at Sohrab. "Have ya fixed up an' back on the road in a jiff." He leaned into the engine compartment to attach the hose. "I'll test the lines again once pressure's up."

The best time to test any system, Sohrab thought, the corners of his mouth turning up. *Always when the pressure is highest.*

The horizon was an angry bruise, fading to lavender overhead, fed by a fiery red sunset at his back. The sun was hot on his neck even through the tinted glass of the rear window, but the air blowing on his face was arctic. For the first time in a month, Sohrab drove with the windows up, and the noise outside faded like twilight. The radio held no interest for him now; he intended to make full use of the blissful silence surrounding him. Traffic slowed to a crawl as he neared Capital Beltway, drivers to-ing and fro-ing in a chaotic dance of heavy metal and exhaust fumes. He smirked with the satisfaction of a man locking most of the effluvium out, preserving an air-filtered oasis for a party of one.

Sohrab reached out to his smartphone, cradled in its dash-mounted holster, and woke it with a tap the screen. He swiped through to Marie's number and hit dial, realizing only when it began to ring he'd forgotten to turn on the car's sound system for the phone's audio. He poked at the button and the thing connected just as his wife picked up on the other end.

"How'd it go?" she asked. *Right to the point. It's what I love most about her.*

"I think I need a parka," he said, his smirk projecting through the phone's microphone.

"It's about damn time. I was getting tired of driving the kids to school in my swimsuit." She laughed, a sound as hearty as his used to be. He could forgive her for that—she had not seen the things he had. "Are you gonna make it home for supper?" Her voice held a faint touch of fatalism; she recognized what was coming even before he said it.

"I think I will try to earn back the money I just spent," he said, forcing humor into his words he did not feel. "I should be home by ten."

The pause was longer than usual, then she sighed. "See that you are. I'm not sure I remember your face anymore."

He glanced into the mirror, taking stock of the sunken cheeks and close-cropped beard. *Not sure I do, either.* It didn't matter. None of it did. He had to drive, and Marie knew it as much as he. Money was tight, and things always seemed to go wrong when that happened. Before the car, it was the water heater, and before that, Marie's appendicitis. The copay for the emergency room alone had eaten the last of their savings. *As poor as healthcare is here, at least it's better than Iraq.* That was true both before *and* after the American Invasion in 2003.

"Are you... okay?" Marie's voice was hesitant. She had never asked the details of his time with Jack and Mason, and he had avoided the subject whenever conversation swung in that direction. Still...

she had always known something had shaken him, and she kept a watchful eye out for changes in his mood.

"Sure, sure," he said with as much cheer as he could. "You know how I hate to spend money." She laughed again—not the true laugh he had grown to love, but a nervous titter that told him she didn't trust a word he said. It didn't help he didn't believe it either. They had fallen into a graceful rhythm over the years—him avoiding distasteful aspects of his former life, and her pretending it didn't matter. In most marriages dishonesty was the kiss of death, but in theirs even the dishonesty was pretense; it strengthened both, a shield against the worst parts of life each used to protect the other.

"Let me know when you're close to home," she said, an unasked question hidden inside simple words—*Will you return, body and soul?* He had no idea if he would ever be what he was a year ago, but the man of twenty was gone for good. Watching Bill die convinced him of that. *No one is the same forever. And if I am not the same as before, who am I now?* It was as if he were three different people over the course of his life, each with their own personality, tastes, and desires, if not for his DNA, no one could say he wasn't.

"Of course, Marie," he said, scratching his beard. "As always."

They said their goodbyes, and he ended the call before she could question him further. Their dance only worked when neither pushed too hard. For now he led, and that was enough. He tapped the icon for the Uber app on his phone and waited, driving inside the loop toward DC's sticky interior. By the time he reached the outskirts of Arlington, the app had already pinged with his first fare.

"Hello, there, Donna K," he said, accepting the job with a tap on the screen. From the looks of it, the ride was a short one, ending at Georgetown University. He didn't mind—there were always more college students nearby in need. With luck he could pick up a few going both ways and end his night early. Luck had been a seldom-seen visitor in his home, but that could change. *And why not? Everything else changes.* He checked for the best route, exited the highway at Fort Myer Drive, and drove north across the Potomac.

Amber sat on the corner of the concrete planter, rubbing the sole of one foot while Donna and Janelle waited for the car on the sidewalk. The two young women waved at passing cars, grinning to one another like the cheerleaders they once were, and giggling with the alcohol frothing in their veins. She sighed, removed the other shoe, and kneaded on the arch.

I don't know why I agreed to dinner with these two. She shook her head and dug into the knot in her foot. *I'm nearly a decade older, and a lifetime...* She wanted to say wiser, but that wasn't right. *What do you call someone who has lived through the horrors I have?*

Donna had invited her to dinner and a bit of club-hopping, but Amber begged off from clubbing as soon as she saw how much the other two were drinking during the meal. Not a single member of the staff bothered to check an ID, but if they had, would have sent the party packing after seeing the sad little fakes the two carried. Their beauty and bubbly personalities hid an abundance of flaws—not the least of which was their youth—and Amber remembered a time not so long ago when she wasn't far removed from their like.

Killing two men has a way of focusing one's priorities.

The single glass of wine she'd had with dinner had warmed her throat, if not her spirit, but the glow faded an hour ago, leaving her clear-headed—and perhaps somewhat envious. One driver honked at the waving young women as he passed, and both bounced and clapped. Amber sneered and put her shoes back on. *The only thing worse than being stupid drunk, is having to watch it when you're sober.*

She stood on aching feet and gazed at the lights of the capital. The top of the Washington Monument was all she could see from her vantage, but the lights of government burned with a happy glow, ignoring the turmoil of the campaigns rolling across the country. She wondered how much of that was alien interference, then banished the prospect from her head. *You'll go nuts looking for conspiracy behind every bush and tree.*

"Hey!" Donna said over the noise of the street. "I believe that's our car." She pointed back the other direction and waved at the cream-colored SUV headed their way. She wrinkled her nose as the car pulled to a stop a few feet away. "Ugh. He looks Middle-Eastern." She leaned closer to her tipsy companion. "Prolly a *Mooslum*," she stage-whispered so loud several people nearby snorted in disgust.

"No... he's not," Amber said as she watched Sohrab's eyes widen in recognition. "At least not anymore." Nothing like the man she remembered, he looked like those guys who lost weight by giving up carbs—leaner, skin sagging in places, a deep growling hunger in their eyes like bears waking after a long winter's hibernation. Without the car, she wouldn't have recognized him.

25

"How would *you* know?" Janelle said, sneering. *Donna may be a racist, but she is not the least likable of the two.* Janelle had thrown money around since the evening began; she knew full-well Amber's funds were limited, but she made it a point to pick a restaurant far out of Amber's price range.

"He's a friend of mine," Amber said with a shrug, gathering her purse and walking to the front passenger door. She beamed at the man in the driver's seat, opened the door, and climbed in before the others had a chance to choose. She scooted over in the seat, then reached across and gave Sohrab a big kiss on the cheek, giggling as his face reddened. Donna and Janelle piled into the back seat, bodies as limp as their intelligence, laughing at some unspoken joke. *I've had quite about enough of these two*, Amber realized, still smiling as if she cared what they thought. A broad, happy smile in the face of stupidity was one of the first skills she learned as a flight attendant, and it still served her well.

"Where to, ladies?" Sohrab said, his own face beaming with surprise and joy. Amber saw the sadness hiding behind dark irises, a bottomless well of pain, fear, and anger plastered over with cheap clown makeup—a familiar image plucked from her own mirror.

"Darnall Hall to drop off Miss Wet Blanket up there," Donna said, the words spilling out of her head like beer through a tap. "Then you're taking me and Janelle to Club 24." She giggled again and leaned against Janelle, pressing her to the door on the other side.

Sohrab gave Amber a wry grin, arched an eyebrow, then addressed Donna. "I don't think they will allow you ladies inside," he said. "They're very good at checking ID's. Perhaps Town Danceboutique, instead."

"*Ugh*," Donna scoffed, while Janelle heaved an overly dramatic sigh. Amber almost choked from the smell of alcohol. "Our ID's are just *fine*, thank you," Donna sniffed, then waggled the fingers of one hand at him. "Take us where we want to go."

Sohrab shrugged as if to say *it's your nickel*, and faced the front, winking at Amber. "Buckle up!" he said with a laugh and shot from the curb as if fired from a canon. The two girls fumbled for their seat belts, thrown to one side before they could buckle up, and Sohrab chuckled under his breath.

Headlights flashed past from oncoming traffic, lambent fans piercing the dark street, bathing the Iraqi's face in alternating bands of shadow and light, each crawling up and over his features like raising a window shade. He kept his eyes studiously forward, never glancing in her direction once the car lurched into traffic, not once checking the map on his phone; she knew he would never ask the one question on his tongue. She glanced back, Donna and Janelle in close conversation. Neither appeared to be listening to the other, much less Amber or Sohrab.

"I guess you're wondering why I'm in DC," she said. He gave her a look that said he knew the answer but said nothing. "After... last year," she began, then hesitated. Where do you start the story of your life when the beginning is a horror movie? She had never felt fear in Sohrab's presence, but fear and reticence born of insecurity were two different things. *Guess I can thank my mom for that.* Clichés existed for a reason. "After everything that happened, I realized I wanted to do more with my life than serve alcohol to flying drunks," she said, shrugging. "When the cops returned the cash they took during the investigation, I emptied my savings and applied for a bunch of schools." She grinned, remembering the day the letter arrived. "For some reason, Georgetown offered me a full ride."

Sohrab nodded. "Ah. I thought maybe..." He shook his head and frowned.

"You thought maybe, what?"

"Nothing." But it wasn't nothing; she recognized that, if nothing else. He turned at the intersection with a deft spin from decades of practice. "So... have you heard from Jack?"

There it was. The one question she felt he wanted to ask most. The one for which she had no good answer.

Amber cut her eyes to the girls in the back seat, but they were oblivious. "Not since, you know... that day," she said, leaning closer to Sohrab. She sighed and picked at an imagined thread on her skirt. "He wouldn't even open the door the last time I went to his apartment."

"I understand," he grunted. "It was a bad time for him." He drummed his fingers on the wheel, then blew out a long breath. *There's something he's not telling me.* She wouldn't push, though. Heaven knew she'd had her fill of that from her mom. Few former coworkers had checked up on her, but her mom made up for all of it—and then some. *And it would have been worse if I'd told her more than what she'd seen in the news.*

Amber touched the tiny gold cross hanging around her neck. She hadn't believed in a God since that day, but there were times she wished it was all true. *Better the manipulative force you know than the one you don't.* The rules had all changed when she wasn't looking, space folding around her like a Russian nesting doll, wheels within wheels; it was easier when everything happened by chance.

But nothing has ever happened by chance, it's just now you have proof.

"Here we are," Sohrab said, sliding to a smooth stop in front of the dorm.

"That was fast," Amber said.

"Not fast enough!" Donna squeaked from the back seat. "C'mon, *Apu*, happy hour's gonna be over before we get there."

"Donna!" Amber choked, but Sohrab placed a gentle hand on her arm, forestalling a nasty explosion. He narrowed his eyes and gave her an almost imperceptible shake of his head.

"Here," he said, fishing a card from his shirt pocket and handing it over. "Call me whenever you need a lift. No charge." He winked and smiled warmly, and Amber felt her ire at Donna's overt racism abating in spite of herself.

"Thanks," she said, smiling back. "But I'll pay. Everyone's gotta make a living, right?" He grunted approval, and she opened the door to get out. She stuck her head back inside and nodded at the two. "If they give you too much trouble, let me know," she said, an evil grin on her face. "We have a communal bath, so there are plenty of ways I can get them back."

"What makes you assume I still have your number?"

Amber snorted and arched an eyebrow. "Because you're the kind of guy who hangs onto things just in case." She blew him a kiss and closed the door, then watched him drive away.

"Coincidence," she whispered to the dwindling taillights, and a shiver crawled up her spine. "That's all."

But she no longer believed in coincidence. Not really.

Evan stood in the doorway of the empty apartment, the smell of drying paint tickling his sinuses, the lemon scent of industrial cleaner clinging to the Formica counters; the place felt as uninhabited as if recently completed. More than a year since his awakening, this was the one place that called to him—beckoning him, luring him to a broken building in Atlanta sporting a fresh coat of paint. *This was* his *apartment.* Anger welled, a slow burn deep in his chest. *The man who killed me.* He closed the door behind him, lest the manager notice his presence, the lock picked and useless for its intended purpose.

In the past year, Evan had killed and gathered the knowledge of three others since that first in DC, but he had come no closer to his murderer than the name Jack and this place. And he *had* been murdered—that much was burned into his psyche, even if little else was. How he had come to live again, who his murderer was, why he returned, and what the future held for him were as opaque as the wine-colored wall he faced. Somewhere in his list of receptacles rested the piece that would lead him to Jack. Somewhere among all the others were the remaining pieces of his mind waiting for recovery... waiting for him to give them meaning.

"I am immortal," he whispered into the void of empty space around him. More than statement, it was revelation. If he was not *the* God—and he was sure he was not—he was certainly *a* god, far removed from the creatures scurrying about as if they were the masters of this planet. The part of the old Evan that remained, tucked away in an inaccessible corner of his mind, rebelled at the idea; he shrank from the concept as if burned.

There are other creatures who would deny me. Demons of air and darkness. He was above them, too. Weak, now, they held no hope of controlling him as they once had. This information he had gained from his second kill, the skinny Argentinian succumbing after the first thrust of the knife, dying quietly in the darkened alley in Bariloche, iridescent lifeblood pouring from the gash in his neck. It irked Evan the old man offered nothing beyond a thin foreboding, the word *demon*, and a helping of contempt. He could not ignore them, but he need not fear them. *I am immortal. I fear nothing.*

Still, he felt old. Far older than the body he controlled.

How old am I? Old enough to have accumulated a small fortune in gold coins and gems. These he gained access to after the third kill, the location of the cache revealed complete with GPS coordinates. The blackened bones of the abandoned building hunched in the field at the end of the drive like the Athenian Acropolis, tumbled stone littered the ground and ghosts called from somewhere deep inside. He was thankful he hadn't had to go inside the remains. The football-sized cask was buried beneath a rotting oak near the stone fence. *If only the fool driving the old delivery truck realized the information he carried inside his veins.* Of course, if he had, Dieter might drive that man instead.

"This will do," he said, nodding. As a base of operations, the apartment wasn't the best choice, but he wanted to be near Jack's last known location when he gathered the last piece he needed: his killer's last name. *And perhaps the girl.* Her face haunted his dreams, but no name came with it. *There is time. It will come.* He grinned like a predator, lips skinning back from straight white teeth.

Evan left the apartment in search of the office and the building manager, pulling the wallet stuffed with crisp new bills from his jacket. Perhaps the manager was the sort he could bribe.

CHAPTER 3

C ARS ROLLED BY IN A NEVER-ENDING PARADE of imported plastic, steel, and aluminum. Some rumbled in deep-throated guzzle, belching noxious fumes that hung in the air like a wool blanket, others humming in well-tuned perfection. A fair few slipped past propelled by the high, near-silent whine of electric motors, their magnetic fields in quiet opposition, the sound of rubber on asphalt a grinding overlay of nostalgia. Tourists, a dozen strong, half-helmed examples of new-age white bread, zoomed through an intersection on Segways, ducklings trailing a mother tour guide. The morning was both warm and sticky, and Jack Montgomery stared at the Belgian waffle on his plate, upended the bottle of maple syrup, and filled every cup with its own sticky goodness.

The little sidewalk cafe was a favorite haunt for breakfast, midway on his daily bicycle ride between home and work. He'd given up the motorcycle when he moved to DC and his new job at the Department of Health, and even though he missed it, the exercise from pedaling the ten miles round-trip every day had done wonders for both his health and his psyche. *When the weather's good, that is.* When the weather was rotten—as it often was this close to the coast—*Well, I've got Sohrab for that, don't I?*

The boot up the ladder this spring had been a surprise, but the pay boost was a revelation of biblical proportions, and the move to DC had offered him the chance to leave all his bad memories behind—a clean slate ready to fill with new memories. *Or at least better ones.* He flipped through the news on his phone while he ate, catching up on the doings of the world, but *sometimes...* Sometimes he looked for the telltale fingerprint of the Shadowman—*Thirteen.* He didn't know what he was looking for, only that he—like Potter Stewart and pornography—would know it when he saw it.

That's the rub, isn't it? You're not supposed *to see him—or his masters.* He sometimes wondered if both had gone to ground, waiting for an ideal opportunity to push humanity in a new direction. "Ain't no better time than right now," he grumbled, then snorted. He refused to believe even *they* would stoop to using someone like Trump to further their cause; the man was too unpredictable, and too easily manipulated by actual humans. "Stranger things have happened." He flipped to another pointless news article.

He ate with the absentminded abandon of everyone in DC. For most, food was merely fuel, a brief respite from the grind of political life. Soon he stared at an empty plate, an amber glaze of syrup coating the surface. His phone danced on the wrought-iron table. *Speak of the devil.* He picked it up and tapped the answer button.

"Hey, Sohrab," he said, eyebrows knitting. "If you're calling *me* for a ride, the only space I got is on the handlebars." He grinned. "But if you're up for it—"

"Jack," Sohrab interrupted, then hesitated. One word was all Jack needed to hear. Something was wrong. Something alien. *Or at least related to it.* "Do you have time for lunch?"

"Um…" He almost said *Let me check my schedule*, but that was the default response for business meetings. Sohrab was a friend. "Sure. I can move some stuff around." He checked his watch. "How does one o'clock sound?"

Sohrab chuckled softly. "I drive a cab, Jack. Anytime's good for me."

"It's a date, then." He waited for a response, but none came. "What's this about, anyway?"

"It is nothing worrying, but I'd rather discuss it in person."

"Gotcha. Not bad, just stuff." Jack narrowed his eyes. "Seems legit."

"I'll pick you up at one," Sohrab said, then ended the call without a goodbye.

Jack held the phone in front of his face like it had grown a mustache. "Well, that's just rude." An overreaction, for sure. Sohrab was many things—precise, cheerful… *fucking deadly*—but he was never rude. Jack pocketed the phone, paid his usual with cash, grabbed the canvas messenger bag he used as a briefcase, and slung the strap over his neck. He smiled at the hostess, Jenny, then left the outdoor seating area and mounted his bike. The wind was picking up and his light jacket flapped in the breeze. *Storm's brewing southeast.* He watched clouds gather and pile atop one another. *Might be a nasty one soon.*

Jack dropped the bag on his desk, old-growth oak polished to a brilliant sheen; he kept the top swept clean of his usual chaos, the surface too beautiful to hide. His office, large and glass-walled on two sides, was a far cry from the closet he'd inhabited back in Atlanta. The carpet was new, the remaining two walls—still bare of the requisite "I love me" shrine—freshly painted in warm, if muted earth tones, and he had not once sniffed even a hint of the old industrial cleaner odor so omnipresent in his old digs. The ceiling, fourteen feet above the floor if it was an inch, was bordered in old-world plaster crown molding, and sported an intricate carved medallion above the pendant light fixture.

His leather chair's springs squawked as he settled into the seat, and he pulled his laptop from the bag and dropped it into the docking station atop the desk. A few seconds later, his wide monitor opened its eye, and he dragged the keyboard closer, opening a browser window with a tap. Jack rested his chin in one hand, elbow propped on the desk, and lazily typed search terms with the other. Four months on the job and he still didn't know exactly what his employers expected of him. They had placed him into a position well above his education level, given him a shiny new office, an expense account, unrestricted access to any level of information in the archives—up to, and including, *Eyes Only*—then promptly left him alone. They had given him no assignments, no directives, and no instruction. The one Org chart he'd seen upon arrival didn't even list a supervisor.

I may have been born at night, but it wasn't last night. It was the Zzkritti. It had to be. They had ignored his refusal to serve them and maneuvered him into accepting a position where they could monitor and use him as needed. *And I fucking fell for it, hook, line, and sinker.* Not immune to vanity, the offer had flattered him at first; he recognized too late the hand of the alien puppeteers. *I'm probably being paranoid. This is DC, after all—everyone here rises to the level of their incompetence. I just found mine with my first real promotion.* It was as sad a thought as he could imagine, and might even be worse than the idea the aliens were shepherding his career.

"Either way," he grumbled, "I'm stuck here."

Without instruction or a clear mandate, Jack reverted to what he knew best. Most days he sat behind his desk, typing in one keyword after another, fruitlessly looking for unusual patterns in disease outbreaks world-wide. Many were garden-variety flu epidemics, but a fractional few drew his attention like flies to manure. The Zika virus was an ever-present threat, spiking during the last few months, but there was nothing unusual about that—it correlated to mosquito population and migration. Much of what he saw was related to issues of basic sanitation or extreme poverty and were the kinds of things easily cured by the world's best-known medicine—money.

Everything he saw was already well in hand by either the World Health Organization, or the CDC. Earlier than usual, he clicked on the little picture of a cartoon man dressed in red and white stripes with a matching cap sitting at the lower left corner of his screen. The "Waldo" program it activated popped up over the browser, the cartoon character smiling his stupid smile and waving at the single text box in the center. Before ever hearing about this job, Jack had called Maribel Vargas, a friend of Mason's and self-professed hacker, and paid the woman to write a custom web-crawler. In hacker's terms, the bot was extremely polite, indexing information rather than scraping data, with such a small footprint it was rarely flagged for blocking. With a single search term, Jack could release the bot to gather information on any topic from any source connected to the Internet, whether they had a front-facing web presence or not. It was fast, secure, and offered the results Google could not.

It was also quite illegal.

Over the last few months, Jack had used the web-crawler to investigate every popular conspiracy theory gaining traction among the wired populace. *Mason would be proud*, he thought, a wan smile tugging the corners of his mouth. He typed "GMO" into the text box and hit enter. Waldo responded by twirling his finger around one ear in the universal sign for crazy, and the program went to work. Jack minimized the window and watched it disappear entirely from his screen. The longer he let it run, the more stories it found, but it didn't only find disparate articles and make a list for later perusal—this bot categorized stories by connection to real-world scientific research, then looked for connections, regardless of how tenuous.

Maribel had Mason's taste for conspiracy theories, and like him, only for entertainment.

"You're not really a *believer*, are you?" she had asked with obvious trepidation. "I'm only doing this because Mason…" she choked on the name and the silence had stretched between them, a gossamer thread of shared pain and loss.

"No," he said, lowering into the squeaking chair beside her. The room was dim, most of the light coming from the three monitors on the desk. Dust hung in the air, a thin curtain that moved with unseen air currents blown from the vent near the back wall of painted cinder block. Various posters were taped there in a haphazard pattern, some overlapping, others askew, all flaking crisp and crunchy corners curled away from the damp walls. A single, small, double window set high in the wall opposite the stairs completed the tableau of the quintessential hacker's lair. "I'm not a believer, but some of these crazy theories have a tiny kernel of truth." He took a long breath and let it out slowly through his nose. "And hiding somewhere in those truths are the people responsible for Mason's death."

She had gasped, covering her mouth with one hand, her twenty-something eyes suddenly looking much older. Jack knew those were the magic words. The hows and whys wouldn't matter to her. He had left a plot-hole large enough to drive a truck through, but she would never look at it. Her head was already too far into the opening.

Maribel put the final touches on the code, then saved and compiled everything into an executable file. They each ran simple search tests and compared results. When she was satisfied with her work, she saved everything to a thumb-drive and handed it to him.

"The installer executes automatically when you plug this in. It will install exactly once, then self-destruct on the thumb-drive, so make sure you place it on the exact computer you need." She smiled, then winked, her eyes returning to their former youth. "Replacements will cost you."

Jack pocketed the drive. "Don't worry. I'll be careful."

She brushed a spray of dark hair over one ear, brown eyes widening. "Mason, um, told me you were divorced..." She lifted her chin a tick, as if preparing for something. He'd seen this look before—especially in the months after the funeral.

"Not exactly," he said, standing. "My wife and daughter died a couple of years ago."

"I'm so sorry," she said, shrinking into her chair. "I didn't—"

"It's okay. No reason you should know." He drew his lips thin and tight, then patted the pocket with the drive. "This will help a lot. Thanks." He had turned for the stairs and left before she could gather her courage for another attempt.

35

Jack stood on the expansive stone courtyard outside the Hubert H. Humphrey Building, facing Second Street and leaning on the full bike rack. He checked the chain on his, making sure the lock was secure. There hadn't been a bike stolen from that rack since he'd started working in the building, but a man could never be too careful. He snorted. *It's not like the damn thing's expensive.* It was, in fact, the cheapest adult model at Walmart, and by far the ugliest of the lot chained to the rack. He'd toyed with the idea of calling it Betsy in memory of Mason's truck but couldn't bring himself to do it. *Besides, she looks more like a Patty.*

Traffic was sparse for lunchtime, cars passing sporadically, each on their way to somewhere Very Important. Most were probably tourists, August being prime time, the primary mode of transportation for them an SUV. Not exactly on the list of must visit tour destinations, the cars cruising by rarely slowed as they passed the stone edifice, and the passengers never glanced in the old girl's direction.

Jack's phone vibrated once in his pocket. Waldo had finished his search and pinged him with a text message. "I guess he didn't find anything of value on this one," Jack muttered, pulling at his bottom lip. A search yielding useful results took as long as a full day to run, and he hadn't seen one worth checking that ran in under two hours. He could reply to the text with a new search parameter but decided to wait until he was back in the office. He thought about calling Sohrab for an ETA, but the time glowing on his phone's screen showed two minutes to one. As if on cue, the vanilla Edge Sohrab drove turned onto Second and slowed to a stop in front of the bike rack. The heavily tinted passenger window slid down, a thin and bearded face appearing in the frame.

"Get in before someone thinks I am here to bomb the place," Sohrab said with a grin. Jack snorted once, then opened the door and climbed inside. He sat, waiting for the car to pull away, but Sohrab just raised an eyebrow.

"Oh, right," Jack said, pulling the shoulder harness across his body. "Forgot about your rule."

"It is not *my* rule, Jack," Sohrab said, chuckling. "And you always 'forget'." He said the last making little air quotes with his fingers. He faced forward and slipped the car in front of a delivery truck, the driver of which, not impressed by the maneuver, gave two short blasts with his horn. Sohrab grinned and waved in his rear-view mirror as if the driver could see.

"Where to for lunch?" Jack asked, already knowing the answer.

36

Sohrab's eyes twinkled. "McDonald's."

"Thought your people didn't eat beef."

"That's Hindu, Jack. I'm Muslim." The smile melted from Sohrab's face. "Or, at least, I used to be." He sat in silence as he made the block, then brightened again. "Besides, a friend told me the one on Wisconsin Avenue has the McRib." Jack could have sworn a tiny dab of drool formed at the corner of the man's mouth.

"Isn't pork a no-no, too?"

Sohrab, laughed, not as hearty as Jack remembered from their first meeting, but something approaching normal. "If there is any actual pork in that thing, I will eat this car."

Jack watched the world slide by his window, the car's air conditioner blasting icy wind in his face. The sky was crystal, a shade he liked to call hard-blue. If he ignored the women in shorts and tank tops, the air blowing in his face could convince him it was winter. *Might as well be winter, with the chill I've been feeling.* After a momentary sulk, his brow furrowed, and he faced Sohrab.

"Hey... I know the place you're talking about," he drawled. "It's way up past Georgetown."

Sohrab gripped the wheel tighter, his eyes glued to the road. "Why, so it is."

"I don't think I have enough time to—"

"Come, Jack," Sohrab sneered, "we both know you may come and go as you please." He let that hang in the space between them without further comment. There was no need; they both knew the score. Sohrab relaxed his grip on the wheel and shrugged. "I think you will be happy you came, regardless."

Jack realized his friend had something besides an imitation pork sandwich waiting for him at the end of this rainbow, but he would neither guess nor pry for the answer. Sohrab wouldn't tell him in any case. Years of tradecraft had trained him well, and not even torture could wrest the information from him if he chose to remain silent. And silence had become the word of the day—ever since Bill's death. *His murder.* It seemed the only place silence never took root was his own head; the voices there chided and complained, warned and scolded. More than anything, they blamed. A man could run from many things, but guilt stalked with cunning and relentless determination. Guilt was the Jason Voorhees of emotion.

They rode the arteries of the city like that for a time, each waiting for the other to fill the silence, Sohrab's face growing darker and more troubled with every turn. On Wisconsin Avenue, Jack watched the man flick his eyes to the left repeatedly as they passed George-town University, its compact campus barely larger than the capitol itself. At last, they passed the campus and Sohrab heaved a sigh, tiny beads of sweat glistening on his temple like stardust.

"Ready to tell me what—"

"I saw Amber last night," Sohrab blurted.

Jack paused, closing his mouth with a click. He pursed his lips, then tilted his head and arched an eyebrow. "Here? In DC?"

"Yes, of course here," Sohrab said with obvious, though mild, pique. "Did you think I drove to Atlanta?"

Jack opened his mouth to ask the first of many questions, then glanced back along their path and closed it again. "She's a student at Georgetown."

"Yes."

"How long?"

"Truly, I do not know." He kept his eyes on the road, lips pursed. "I do not believe she knows you have moved here," he said, his voice pensive.

"No reason why she should. We didn't exactly stay in touch af-ter..."

"That is what she said." He grinned, then his face relaxed, emo-tion draining. Jack imagined that face as the one some people saw at moment of their death. "I also do not think she wanted me to tell you where she is," he said, his tone flat. "I especially believe she did not wish for me to tell you she lives in Darnall Hall." His face found life again, and he winked. "It is important you not know this."

Jack snorted amusement. *Exactly the sort of matchmaking Mason would have tried.* If he were being truthful with himself, he didn't know what he should do with the information. *Our time has passed. Its funeral pyre lit the sky above Bill's tomb.*

He would not seek her out today. Or tomorrow. *Maybe some-day. After she has forgiven me.*

A noxious cloud of gas hung in the air, wet and thick, eyes and nose assaulted by the putrid fumes of half-digested McRib. Jack, nose scrunched, waved the belch away, peered into the screen on his desk, and muttered words spoken the world over: "Never again." Another wad of gas climbed up his throat, and he swung his head quickly to expel it away from the screen.

As he had expected, Waldo found no hidden connections among the hundreds of articles and studies on genetically modified organisms. Other than the obvious and all-too normal corporate shenanigans. With all the Zzkritti's work in human genetic modification and nano-technology, Jack was sure he'd find something in GMO research and development, but this was yet another dead-end. The sad part was Jack knew without a doubt he could simply ask them what their plans were. While he didn't know where they were, all he had to do was pick up any phone, dial any number, and ask to speak to Thirteen.

They monitored him as surely as he tried to monitor them.

He accepted it as one accepts the sky is blue, water is wet, and corporations cannot be trusted. It was two people noticing one another across a crowded restaurant, one of them doing their best not to be noticed. Jack didn't care if they watched him, but their whole power lay in not being seen. He knew how crazy it all sounded—there were people pounding on padded walls for this very reason—and the deeper he dove, the greater the lunacy.

"It's time I took that away from them," he said, fingers drumming on the desk. He typed in a new set of search parameters, one looking for odd or unusual murders, and this time he added the keyword *tabloid*. Jack had been loath to include yellow journalism; most tabloids made up their stories out of whole cloth, while others were filled by reporters willing to believe any loon with a good narrative. *Sometimes crazy is just a point of view.* He knew what he would get most would be animal mutilations, unsolved serial murders, and strange disappearances, but his day was already shot, and some tales were often good for a laugh.

Another belch rose, the McRib laying at the bottom of his stomach like a rock, and he spewed the foul air toward the doorway. Eyes half-lidded, the screen blurred as he hit the enter key, and Waldo spun his finger and went to work. Jack minimized the program, it faded the way his eyes were now fading, and he leaned back in his chair, propping his feet on the desk. *What I need right now is a good, long nap.* The clock on the wall told him he still had two hours before he could reasonably call it a day, and he struggled to keep his eyes open. *Maybe just a short one*, he told himself, eyes already closing, lids dropping like a garage door.

He was half-way to Oz when Waldo pinged with his first hit.

Jack's eyes snapped open like a sprung window shutter, and he dropped his feet to the floor. Waldo had never returned results this fast.

"Okay, boy," Jack muttered, tapping the key combination to bring Waldo's window front and center, "let's see what's got you so hot and bothered."

It wasn't much—just a list of three names, men murdered in the last year in three separate countries—but it was the circumstances of those deaths arousing Waldo's interest. *Exsanguination.* Each of the men had sustained massive blood loss resulting in their deaths. As Jack read the data—some of it, not surprisingly, reported in the *National Enquirer*—Waldo updated, adding a fourth victim. Two might be an anomaly, but three was significant—and four suggested a pattern. The summary for each showed a striking similarity in the cases, but the most recent stood out for the strangest, and most telling, of reasons: there were no wounds on that body. None. Not even a nick from shaving that morning.

Massive loss of blood with no wound?

If that didn't scream alien, nothing did. *Of course, it's in the Daily Mail...*

Maribel Vargas sipped tea from the mug in one thin-fingered hand, the brew now tepid after a long session of debugging the code now compiling on the screen to her right. Her hair pulled back in a thick ponytail, horn-rimmed glasses perched on the end of her nose, she absently scrolled through her Twitter feed with her right hand, waiting to see if anything of value caught her eye. The service had long ago given itself over to the advertising gods, her feed crammed with earnest people desperate for attention, each with a product to sell. Once in a great while a nugget of real information or comment of value slipped through, but most was an unending tableau of unabashed begging. Most of her peers spent their time scanning the sea of the dark web looking for new hacks or black-box code they could use, but Maribel was more of a coder purist, preferring to roll her own. The joy for her was in the elegance of a thing created, or the ferreting out and smashing of a particularly pernicious and elusive bug. Her father, a former math professor at Universidad Del Comahue Bariloche in Argentina, had taught her the pure beauty of an elegant proof.

Her face heated. *There a math professor, but here a common plumb-er.* "One should always remain on the side of whichever party is in power," he had once said in between lessons. It was a maxim he failed to follow only once. *And once is enough, ain't it Poppa?* He and her mother had fled to the US, barely escaping with the clothes on their backs. Maribel had been born here, a citizen, and that, coupled with their certain death should they return, allowed them to live and work in this country. Along with mathematics, though, her father had also given her a healthy distrust of all things government.

She took another sip of tea, now cold, and sighed. It was not even three in the afternoon, and she was already tired and bored. What once was a joy in her life had become—horror of horrors—a fucking *job*, sucking it dry of the lifeblood that drove her to find shorter and cheaper algorithms, clean dirty and tangled lines of code, and solving the myriad puzzles involved in creating the one perfect solution to an intractable problem. Her clients compensated her well for her efforts, but money was never the point.

A single ping interrupted her pity party, drawing her attention to the screen on her left. That one was devoted to important commu-nications and promised real intrigue. The odd little program she had written at the request of Mason's friend, Jack, had just notified her of a successful search. She had felt bad about including the back-door and notification subroutine in an executable written for a friend, but not bad enough to turn down the wad of cash the mystery customer had offered. His request was simple, but she made it clear she didn't make it a habit to undermine another customer's work. "It's bad for business," she'd told him. He was adamant, however, and browbeat her with endless messages until she relented and took the money.

"Sauce for the goose," she muttered, remembering the extra bit of code she'd included along with the requested hack.

Maribel tapped a key and opened the message, arching an eye-brow as she pushed the glasses up the bridge of her nose. One name on the short list had died close to her father's former place of em-ployment. She shrugged at the coincidence, then dutifully forwarded the data to the email account the old man had provided.

Within minutes, her bank account fattened by a factor of two.

Jeff looked at the screen held in his talon, scratching at the patch of fungus on his tail with the other. He read the glyphs three times to be sure.

"This came from her?" he asked, looking up into the mismatched eyes of Thirteen.

He nodded. "I received it only moments ago." The man's hand shook with tiny, barely perceptible tremors as he took the tablet back from the Zzkritti. "I believe it is worse than we feared."

The gill slits in Jeff's abdomen vibrated annoyance. *This one has a habit of stating the obvious.* "Of course it is worse than we feared," he hissed. "Where humans are concerned, that is the default setting." One hooked claw at the end of his striking talon tapped the floor in staccato frustration. It was another affectation Jeff had absorbed from his contact with humans, only adding to his discomfiture. "Our resources are already stretched wing-tight keeping the Americans from destroying their own government."

Thirteen shrugged, an annoying habit *he* had picked up from his association with Americans. "They will do what they will do," he said, so calm he appeared dead. "Their union will survive, but it may take a dark turn for a time." He reached across and scratched his left forearm, and Jeff sensed in the man's mind he didn't even know why he'd done it. The Zziikriti had offered to remove the tattoo, but a young Thirteen had angrily refused. Decades older, he resisted still.

The stone beneath Jeff's feet was too cold; he needed the desert sun to warm his chitin and ease his mind. More than that, he must absorb and store enough heat for the next phase of his duty as the Chosen. He finally noticed the tapping claw and willed it to stop.

"I have spent enough time with human generals to have learned a maxim: never present a problem without a solution already in your talons." Jeff gazed into the other's eyes, the nictitating membrane clearing fine grains of sand from his own with two quick flicks. "Do you have a solution?"

Thirteen shrugged again. "There is not enough data," he said with that same infuriating calm.

"When will you have enough?"

"When he makes his first move against us, I would think."

Air exploded from Jeff's gills in exasperation. "So your solution is to wait until he attacks?" He stalked to the doorway, motioning for Thirteen to follow. In the long tunnel, carved a century ago through the stone mountain, Jeff walked the upward grade. Other Zziikriti moved swiftly aside to allow their Chosen to pass, each chittering and snapping beaks begging his pardon. "Do you have any notion why he is killing these people?"

"I have no direct proof he has killed anyone, but the nature of the last death..."

"Yes," Jeff nodded. "I saw that as well." He stopped at the large door to the external airlock and rounded to Thirteen. "Dieter never murdered indiscriminately. Are you sure this is him?"

"Quite," Thirteen said without hesitation. "The deaths are on more than one continent; two are only days apart. I detect no pattern."

Jeff waved his talon over the airlock control and the inner door opened with a hiss and a flurry of dust. "I cannot commit any of my kind to this." He stepped through the opening. "I have found over the last six-thousand years, humans hunt humans best when there is a personal involvement." He activated the airlock controls on the other side and the door began to close, Jeff inside the lock, and Thirteen still in the tunnel.

Thirteen looked across the gulf between them, his eyes dull and empty. It wasn't mere distance that separated them now, but the wide expanse of genetics, the millions of years of evolution; more than that, it was the difference in thought. Jeff was learning to think like a human, but he could never be one.

"Am I still human?" Thirteen asked in that rumbling whisper, head inclined.

"You must deal with this alone," Jeff said as the door slammed shut. He rested on his tail, wondering what they all were becoming. *Am I still Zzkritti? And if not, what will I become when the Quickening is complete?*

43

CHAPTER 4

THERE WERE DAYS WHEN JACK MARVELED AT the wonders of modern technology—smartphones with access to petabytes of information, earphones without wires, electric cars with ranges now in the hundreds of miles—but in the cool dark of sunless morning, he'd give it all up for a few more minutes of sleep. He relinquished his hold on the dream and reached from beneath the covers, pawing at the phone jittering and dancing on the nightstand. It had buzzed an alert every two or three minutes for the past half-hour, waking him from a dead sleep. *I really must learn how to set the quiet hours on this damn thing*, he thought, blinking the sleep from his eyes as he woke the phone. He scrolled through the notifications and rubbed his eyes with his free hand for a moment or two before the import of what he saw socked him square in the jaw.

"What the fuck?" Jack sat straight up in bed and read the list of names and locations of the unexplained deaths Waldo compiled. *All in the last goddamn year.* He ran a finger down the list, counting. *Ten. Only ten.* He blew a breath between clinched teeth. *When did ten murders become an "only"?* It wasn't the number of deaths that shook him so much as the sheer randomness of it; the killing spree covered five countries and three continents, and there was no connection between any of them beyond the manner in which each had died.

Jack set the phone on its charger and climbed out of bed, heading toward the little bathroom. He relieved himself, flushed, then stepped into the shower for a quick wash and rinse. As the water cascaded over his head, Amber's face floated behind his eyelids. Was her presence in DC at this particular moment mere coincidence? He didn't think so; he'd stopped believing in such things as coincidence and fate the day he met Jeff the Zzkritti. Would they bother with such worthless pieces on their chessboard? Jack snorted and brushed the water from his face. *As chess-masters go, they do love to sacrifice their pawns.* He grabbed the soap from the dish and lathered up, scrubbing behind his ears like his mother taught him. *Old habits die hard.*

He finished his morning ritual, dried his hair, and scrutinized the man in the mirror with a detachment generally reserved for his job. Relatively healthy for a man of thirty-six, his skin had that waxy sheen of a recovering drug addict, and his hairline had begun the long march back along his scalp. Jack didn't mind that so much as the wrinkles at the corners of his eyes. Really, when it came down to it, what would a woman like Amber see in him? He was a battered and creaky tractor—one held together with duct tape, chicken wire, and daily affirmations.

While he dressed, Waldo found another death, the phone pinging a teeth-itching pitch. Jack lifted the phone from the wireless charging stand on the dresser and unlocked the screen. His hands shook as he read the details: Denny Goodman, age 48, Homer, GA, d. 11/12/15. *Homer*, he thought, eyes widening, spots forming in his vision. Jack sat on the edge of the bed, his legs little more than jointed noodles. This was no coincidence. The sleepy little town of Homer was near where Bill had breathed his last. Poor Mr. Goodman, pillar of the community, dying from an extreme lack of blood barely six months later.

It was clear the deaths all had one thing in common: Dieter. It did not explain what that connection was, nor did it offer Jack any clues about what to do, only presenting him with more questions.

"What are you up to, Thirteen?" Jack muttered through trembling lips. "And why did you wait so long?"

Sohrab prowled the streets around the National Mall, occasionally glancing at the Uber app running on his phone. The app hadn't notified him of any requests this morning, but he'd already ferried three sets of passengers from one end of the Mall to the other just by stopping and asking if anyone needed a ride. This time of year, tourists filled the Mall to overflowing, and the closer it got to noon, the more those on foot searched for transportation of any kind. These fares he kept off the books by having them pay in cash.

He saw a young couple with a small child sitting on a bench, the father holding a map, the mother looking tired and forlorn as she bounced the child on her knee, and was about to pull over next to them when the app alerted him of a fare. Sohrab reluctantly sped up, passing the possibility of payment for the surety of the app. He tapped through the screen and found the details, his heart skipping a beat from old and inbred bigotry and hatred when he read the fare's name: Josef Dunkelmann.

"Jews usually take real cabs," he murmured to himself, then pushed that side of himself away. "A fare is a fare." This one promised a big payout, too, the pickup way out at Joint Base Andrews. "Surely, there are closer...*ah*," he said, scrolling through the information. This passenger had requested him. It wasn't unheard of, and for Sohrab, not even that unusual. "Repeat customers are the best." He didn't recall the name, but he'd carried many passengers over the years.

The traffic in DC waxed and waned throughout the day; it ebbed and flowed like pouring real maple syrup over snow. The mid-morning wane had given way to a brunch-time waxing, cars and delivery trucks clogging the roadways like plaque filling an artery. There were any number of routes Sohrab could take, but he ignored the app and relied on his knowledge of the streets and their traffic patterns, twisting and turning through side streets and the occasional alleyway. By the time he entered the ramp for Suitland Parkway, he'd shaved five minutes from his ETA.

"Allah is good," he said, a lopsided grin on his face. For a heretic, Sohrab had noticed a great many religious words and phrases creeping back into his speech. It was the same among his atheist friends who were former Christians. *I suppose it is an American thing.* He grinned at the idea he was becoming more American. *I would wash everything Iraqi from my soul, if I could.* The grin disappeared, buried by the memories of his life before coming to the US. *That is all behind me, now.*

The thought offered little comfort. He knew the things behind you were often the most dangerous.

Waldo finally stopped updating the list after eleven names, now churning away as it looked for interconnections touching every victim on the list. The progress bar still read only one percent completed by the time Jack left the office for an early lunch. Several of his coworkers gave him the side-eye for leaving so early, but as he'd been in the building since sunrise, he felt justified. *I think they're more bugged that no one can touch me.* The talk of the building, guessing the nature of Jack's status as untouchable had become everyone's favorite game. The whispering stopped the instant he drew near any gathering of two or more people, their pitiable attempt at chit-chat more telling than the looks he got.

The only person who didn't seem to care one way, or the other was the receptionist, Janice Watson. She greeted him cheerily every morning and bade him a happy goodnight when he left. At least, when he wasn't arriving obscenely early or leaving ridiculously late. She was untouchable too, but for entirely different reasons: she performed a job well no one else wanted. He'd heard the job had gone unfilled for almost a year before the office manager hired her.

She smiled at him as he approached, toothy and far too wide, it somehow added to her attractiveness rather that subtract. A true blonde, golden hair paired with blue eyes and fair skin, she could have modeled in her youth. Those days were long behind her, but even for a woman in her sixties, she managed to keep trim and fit. The average visitor could not tell by looking at her, perched in the well of an elevated circular desk, but she was quite tall—six-foot two if Jack had to guess. He had no idea which would win in a tussle, if it came to that.

He grinned and nodded as he passed, and she stood, purse already in hand.

"Mind if I join you for lunch?" Her voice practically boomed off the walls. Shy was not a word Jack would use to describe her. He almost sighed, but restrained himself, and stopped near the door.

"How do you know I'm going to lunch?" he asked, arching an eyebrow.

"That's your usual 'going to lunch' walk," she said through puckered lips, her eyes dancing, as if the thing were self-evident. She exited through the back of the well and stepped down from the platform. "And the question still stands," she said as she made her way around the desk and walked toward the door.

Jack was caught, and he knew it. Of all the people working in this building, Janice had apparently made him her pet project, each morning finding a way to make him laugh with a joke or a wink, every night offering a warm smile to lift his sagging spirits, now moving to the next level—joining him for lunch for an afternoon of small talk. He knew she thought of him as overly dour, an acidic tomato soup needing just a *pinch* of sugar; he only wanted to be left alone to stew. *Why is it so hard for people to get that?*

Rather than argue, Jack offered a sweeping bow and opened the door for her.

"Such a gentleman." She passed him by as if he were a hotel doorman. Jack got the impression she'd had a lot of practice at that. He chuckled into his fist, disguising it as a cough when looked askance at him, then followed her into the sun.

"What I want to know is," she said, hands clasped at her chin over the remains of her Veal Oscar, "how come you have neither supervisor, nor any direct reports?" Her face, clear and almost wrinkle-free, was open and earnest. Playing the part of the priest in a confessional, she would have earned an Academy Award. It wasn't a facade; Jack knew from the moment they first met there wasn't a dishonest bone in the woman's body.

"To be perfectly honest, Janice, I haven't a clue," he said, his mouth in a tight line. The restaurant she had insisted upon was a tad out of his price range, but he had mentally shrugged and splurged for a change. She wasn't a glutton by any means, but had not only ordered one of the more expensive items on the menu, she had also ordered a pricey bottle of wine to go with it. He groaned inwardly at the thought of what this simple lunch would cost him.

"Oh," she laughed, bells ringing, "neither one of us believes that, Jack." He started to protest, but she held up a palm. "I can see it in your eyes."

"How about 'I don't know why'. Does that work for you?"

Janice lay her hands primly on the table in front of her, pushing the plate away as she did. "Not in the slightest." She pursed her lips and arched an eyebrow, then sighed. "But I guess that's as good as I'm going to get today."

"I'm really not trying to be opaque here," he said, wondering why he felt the need to justify himself. "It's just... I honestly don't know anything for sure." He sat back and tossed his napkin over a plate scraped clean of every last delicious morsel. *If I'm gonna pay this much, I'm damn well gonna eat it all.* "And I'm sure anything I say will end up being wrong when it all shakes out."

Janice stared at him for a long time, eyes narrowing. She was trying to read him, and he knew exactly when she gave up. "Jack, you have got to be the most pessimistic human I have ever met." She leaned forward and tapped the table for emphasis. "Keep in mind the town we're in." She sat like that a moment, then leaned back in her seat, a mirror-image of Jack. She brushed her shoulder-length hair back on one side with delicate, perfectly manicured and unadorned fingers; the only jewelry she wore was a simple gold wedding band, and a few thin gold bracelets on each wrist. The pearl earring she uncovered with that single swipe was as understated as the rest of her ensemble, right down to the simple cream-colored, boat-neck sleeveless dress she wore; it matched the string of pearls around her neck. Jack couldn't help thinking Jackie Kennedy must have made quite the impression on a young Janice Watson.

"Why are you so interested?" She tilted her head and shrugged, then looked around suspiciously before leaning closer. "There's a bit of a betting pool. Two, actually. One is we have to guess how you landed in our midst." She leaned back again, stroking the strand of pearls.

"And what's your guess?"

"Oh," she waved her hand as if brushing away a cobweb, "I've got you down as an international spy. A man of mystery chasing down a master criminal."

A bit too on the nose for comfort. He raised an eyebrow and forced a laugh. "Oh, nothing so sinister as that, I assure you." He glanced around for the waiter, but the man was nowhere in the room. "What's the second?"

Janice chuckled and her fingers returned to her pearls, a sly smile on her face. "Someone must get you to open up about why and how you came to us. I hoped to get you to talk over lunch." She grimaced, eyes narrowing. "Mostly I just don't want that nasty Mary Hopkins to win." She shuddered but said no more.

Jack chuckled. Interoffice politics had usually swirled around without ever touching him, and it was amusing to be the subject for a change. *Mary Hopkins? I've heard the name, but...* "Is she the one in Human Resources with, um..." he held his hands in front of his chest as if holding a beach ball.

"The giant boobs?" she said, laughing. "Yes, dear. That's the one."

He laughed at her lack of inhibition. "I'm still trying to under-stand the physics of how she stands and walks without falling on her face—especially in those stilettos."

"I *know*," she exclaimed, slapping the table and leaning forward, eyes wide. "It's maddening. I get dizzy watching her."

People at nearby tables stopped talking to watch Janice laugh, some laughing in sympathy, some turning up their nose in dis-dain. Jack didn't care. Watching her—tears squeezed from the cor-ners of shining eyes, a full-throated guffaw bellowed from her thin frame—filled his heart with a joy he hadn't felt in a long time. He scanned the room for their waiter, then pulled his over-stuffed wallet from his back pocket.

"Jack," she snapped. "What in the world do you keep looking around for?" She asked with such sincere curiosity, it was a moment before he realized it was for show.

"Our waiter seems to have forgotten us," he said, opening the wallet.

Janice shook her head, a sad gesture of quiet exasperation. "Put that away, dear boy," she said, waving at the offending envelope of soft leather. "It's already been taken care of." She winked and grinned. "I did ask you to lunch, after all."

"Janice, I can't allow you to—"

"Hush," she snapped like a mother scolding her son. "I'll hear no more talk about it."

"Yes, ma'am," he said with a chuckle, folding the wallet and shoving it back in his pocket. He pursed his lips and arched an eyebrow. "When did you...?" But he knew exactly when—he'd just been too preoccupied with Waldo to take note. The hostess had shown in like she owned the place, the manager and head waiter buzzing around her like flies. After she huddled a moment with the manager, the chef had come out and personally taken their order. At first, the attention flattered him, assuming all the fuss was for him—as if they'd known about his status, somehow.

"I'll let you in on a little secret," she said, a practiced conspiratorial look on her face. "I'm a lot more well-off than I let on." She nodded once, as if that said everything.

"I'm not gonna even ask," he said, laughing. He pushed out his chair and stood, then walked around the table and helped her up. She beamed up at him, a proud mother treating her son to lunch, then patted his cheek.

"My, my... you *are* a gentleman."

"Don't tell my mom," he whispered. "She still thinks I'm incorrigible." He presented his arm, and she took it without hesitation.

"Well... you can be both," she said, allowing him to walk her to the exit.

Jack tapped the eraser of his pencil on the notepad, hunched over his keyboard, one elbow on the desk, chin resting in his hand, and stared glassy eyed at the screen. Waldo had given up looking for connections, claiming the problem unmanageable. *Too random even for him, I guess.* He condensed the list to names, date of death, and location, zooming out for the big picture. He input each location into a mapping program, then displayed the map on the screen.

"They really are as random as I thought," he muttered. Waldo had made only a single connection to an unrelated murder in DC a year prior, but none of them had died in the manner of the members on the list. The link appeared coincidental, the death on the list occurring one day after, the victim a business acquaintance.

"I don't believe in coincidences," he said, his voice stronger.

On a hunch, he searched for flights from the US to each of the five countries where a murder occurred within days of the murders in DC. Jack changed the window to a single day when he noticed one pair of deaths in two separate countries had taken place within that time-frame. The list of airlines and flights was extensive, and he soon had filled several pages of the notepad. *There could be more than one killer, you dope.* That made any connection tenuous at best. He snorted and shook his head. "Nope, the only chance I have is to assume it's one guy." Adding even a single killer made the problem more difficult by orders of magnitude. The courses he'd taken in statistics had taught him the regression analysis formula for two independent variables was difficult, and anything over two was intractable for him.

Besides, I already know who the one guy is.

Whatever Thirteen was doing, he had gone to great lengths to disguise his movements. The one case where two murders were fewer than two days apart was the one in Argentina, followed by another in Texas. Jack homed in on those in hope of a clue. One light overhead sputtered and died, the room dimming, and he found he liked it better. *It's the little things*, he thought as he read the detailed reports for both cases.

The one in Argentina happened near a university in Bariloche, while the one in Texas was in The Woodlands near Houston. "Been there," he shivered. "The way they're pouring concrete over everything, it might as well *be* in Houston."

He tapped the screen, then his notepad. These two were the key—he was sure of it. Argentina had accepted the Nazis after World War II, and that was *no* coincidence; the fact the Zzkritti had allied with Nazi scientists made the connection that much stronger.

"Bariloche... Bariloche," he muttered, tapping the pencil on his bottom lip in rhythm with the word. "Where have I...?"

Jack performed a quick search in another browser window and soon found what he sought. One of his very first cases after joining the CDC, they had sent him to Argentina in 2009 because of the H1N1 flu pandemic gripping the country. The little town was next to a lake, nestled in a broad valley in the southern half of the Andes Mountains. They had sent him to Bariloche because it was the city in Rio Negro province with the largest number of infections, and Sally had wanted to know why. Jack now suspected she might have been testing him; she wanted to see how he got along with local health organizations. The fact Bariloche was where the Union of South American Nations held their summit only added to the fun—the most heated topic being Columbian military bases used by US forces. The one thing he remembered about that trip was the one and only airline flying in and out at the time was Aerolineas Argentinas, a South American partner of—

"*Delta*," he hissed. "And whose hub just happens to be in Atlanta." Jack narrowed his eyes and searched the web for Delta's hub map. "*Bingo!*" He slapped the desk, breaking the pencil. He was in full-bore, ignore-the-world, hyper-focused work mode, leaning forward and pounding out searches on the keyboard, following links and jumping from one thread to another; a bomb could detonate outside his door and he wouldn't hear it. Three other deaths matched his search parameters for the one-day window, each route offering nonstop service. *So*, he thought, scratching his chin, *Thirteen's flying out of Atlanta. But why?* More importantly, the next murder in the chain after Bariloche had been the one in Texas—the friend of the family killed in DC.

"There's my link." He leaned back in the chair. Every muscle in his body ached, each pulled tight as piano wire, and he willed himself to relax before something popped. A suspect who went by the creative moniker "Double-D", or sometimes "Double D", had been charged in the brutal murder and was currently residing in the Central Detention Facility in DC. His defense attorney claimed the man had been framed, and even the police believed at least one other person was involved. "Well Double-D," Jack said placing both hands behind his head and propping his feet on the desk, "looks like you're about to have a visitor."

❧

Sohrab checked his mirrors for perhaps the hundredth time in case his fare approached from the rear, then back to the exit he *should* have stepped from over an hour ago. He checked his watch again to be sure—also for the hundredth time—and drummed his fingers on the wheel. As a former field operative, he was accustomed to doing nothing on a stakeout, but this was no stakeout—it was wasting time waiting for a fare. Time he could use to service other paying customers. *Repeat customer or not, the tip better be good.* He sneered at his own thought. Tips were never good in cases like these; most people treating help this way did it out of a sense of entitlement, and never dreamed compensation should be involved.

"I'd settle for an apology," he grumbled, scratching his beard.

The sentry at the gate had given him a hard time at first, glaring at the obvious *mooslem* under the brim of his hat, eyes narrowed in suspicion, but as soon as Sohrab told him his fare's name, the young man waved him right through. Military bases the world over functioned much the same—wary doubt and distrust at strangers until the right name was uttered, then immediate action. *Sometimes that action is a bullet to the brain...* The sentry at the door, on the other hand... he hadn't come close enough to Sohrab's car to hear the magical name, trusting any man granted access to the base must be safe. Still, he watched the car, and its driver, his scrutiny closer and more concerned with every passing minute. Sohrab stared back, his eyes flat and unfocused, face slack and unconcerned, until the man with the uniform and gun looked away. He shifted his attention back to the door, mild surprise that he had sprinted through action scenarios to incapacitate the sentry the whole time.

He wondered if he would ever be free of such thoughts.

The right back passenger door opened and closed, the car settling lower. *How did...?* Sohrab turned and looked at the man who had just entered his car, and his eyes widened in recognition.

"I remember you," he said, lips pursed.

"Indeed you do, Mr. Bazzi," the man's voice, deep and gentle, was barely above a whisper.

"But your name wasn't Josef then," Sohrab said, lips pursed as he tried to remember the last time he saw him.

"I have gone by many names, but you may call me Thirteen." He shrugged. "Or Shadowman, if you prefer."

Sohrab worked to keep the shock from showing on his face, then faced front, drumming his fingers on the wheel. *Why is the Shadowman here... now? I met him long before—*

"Might I suggest you put the car in gear?" the Shadowman said, a touch of humor in his voice. "We have much to discuss, and little time."

Sohrab frowned, put the car in gear, and pulled away from the building. He spun the wheel, turning in a tight circle, and drove out the way he entered, the stone-faced sentry at the door watching him the entire time.

CHAPTER 5

THERE'S A SPECIAL KIND OF DUST, MINUSCULE bits of dead trees mixed with lye, pressed and repressed, folded and bound, and left on shelves to wait and rot, here and there the acrid tang of tannin drifting; it floats through every library in every university in every country, a shared comfortable sameness greeting visitors to labyrinthine stacks of wonder. Each year, a new group of students discover not just the wealth of knowledge locked inside, but the intoxicating pleasure of the smells found here, and only here. A good library wasn't solely a place of stored knowledge. It was a place of *being*. Students huddled together at tables, engrossed in their search for understanding, most taking notes, but a few only reading. Librarians trolled the aisles, replacing books both large and small, rearranging misplaced titles, and quelling potential mischief—the new monks of the modern monastery.

Amber gathered her books and shoved them into the canvas messenger bag, pushed away from the table, and stood. She had sat so long her feet had swollen. The notes she had written for this assignment were tucked away in her bag, and she picked up the heavy reference books and prepared to replace them on the shelves. She turned and ran straight into a wall of muscle, bouncing back and nearly stumbling. There wasn't a *nearly* involved with the books, all three tumbling to the floor, the sound of elephants waltzing.

"Sorry," she said, kneeling to retrieve the books.

"Not a problem," the boy said with a voice like velvet. And he was a boy—no more than nineteen, big wide grin on a scruffy face, a thatch of blond-tipped brown hair atop his head; he was a jock straight from Central Casting. He bent and extended his hand to help her up. She raised an eyebrow and ignored the offer, rising with the books held tight to her chest.

"Next time I'll watch where I'm going."

"I didn't mind," he breathed, his pupils dilating. "In fact," he stepped closer, close enough she felt the heat from his body. "You're in my American History class. Been meanin' to get to know you."

Amber placed a hand on his chest and gave a gentle shove, succeeding only in pushing herself back rather than shoving him away. "Like I said, I'll be more careful next time." She spun toward the reference stacks and took a single step before she felt a meaty paw grab her elbow. She froze, and without turning, said, "Please don't do that."

He chuckled. It was not a pleasant sound.

"Why not?"

"Because I don't want to hurt you."

Now the boy laughed loud enough to disturb the few students studying at nearby tables. He twisted her toward him and pulled her close. "Hey, I'm just tryin' ta be friendly here." He cocked an eyebrow. "Don't you know who I am?"

Don't make a scene, don't make a scene. After the first few times in school, her mom drilled that into her head like a goddamn mantra. "Good Southern girls don't make a scene," she had said. "Those boys don't mean any harm… it's just how they flirt." Amber knew she was pretty—everyone told her so—but being pretty was both blessing and curse. Especially in the South. *Don't make a scene!* She stared hard into the moon-faced boy hovering over her, his eyes wide with lust, her own pooling, preparing for another round of groping; she felt eyes all around watching… judging. She knew what they were thinking. *Don't make a scene.* Her face heated while her eyes grew cold, iced backed by searing flame. *Ah, fuck it.*

She dropped the books on his shoes, startling him, then reached down and grabbed his nuts through his thin and loose slacks and twisted—*hard.* He dropped to his knees like a sack of wet cement, and she followed him down, maintaining an iron grip on the boy's manhood. She lifted his chin with her other hand, ignoring the gasps and whoops of the other students, and peered into his tear-filled eyes. "Don't ever, *ever*, grab someone like that again," she spat, just loud enough for him—and only him—to hear. "It's for your own good. The next person might have a gun." She forced a cheerful wink. "*I* might have a gun. And trust me on this, *boy*, I won't hesitate to shoot you." She gave the family jewels another hard twist for emphasis. "I've done you a favor today. Don't waste it."

Amber released him and he took his first, chest-heaving breath, then collapsed to the floor in a fetal position, holding his throbbing sack with both hands. She nodded, grinned, retrieved the books and stood, brushing her knees clean, then wiped her nut-twisting hand on her pants. The room was as quiet as, well... a library, and she lifted her chin, spun and strode away.

The big bad jock writhed on the floor behind her, while the women—even one librarian—quietly applauded.

What is *his name?* she thought as she escaped the building.

Thirteen watched Sohrab's eyes even as the man watched him. He detected neither concern nor anxiety, but the ancient device in his pocket—one of two—could handle him with ease if it came to that. *Much as it handles me, in fact.* The two had driven in silence for perhaps twenty minutes, no destination, no urgent arrival time; it was the first mission in sixty years they had left him to his own devices.

He wasn't sure that was better or worse.

"Hey... big guy," Sohrab said with what sounded to Thirteen like forced humor. "You hungry? I'm hungry. Sat in the car and drove right by lunchtime. Let's pull in here." He spun the wheel so sudden, Thirteen was caught off guard, bracing one hand against the door just in time. Sohrab took them across two lanes of traffic, smoothly weaving between a phalanx of cars, and onto the exit ramp. The car bumped and jostled as it entered the unkempt frontage road, then bounced again when the crazy Iraqi clipped the curb with a rear wheel as he pulled into the parking lot.

"Denny's?" Thirteen said, nonplussed.

"Of course," Sohrab said, his voice booming, then he laughed. "I've heard no one *plans* to go to Denny's—they just end up there." He shrugged when Thirteen offered no response. "It's the dead time between lunch and dinner, so we will not worry over too many ears." He turned, a wide grin on his face. "And their menu is extensive. Should be something to suit your alien-fed palate."

"I eat regular food, I assure you. The Zzkritti cannot metabolize left-handed proteins. They must synthesize theirs." He squinted, his only attempt at emotional display. "It is... not appealing."

Sohrab sat as still as a frozen video screen, blinked several times, then snorted. "Whatever. Let us eat and discuss your presence here in DC." He arched an eyebrow and his cheeks reddened. "And perhaps why you guided my team into an ambush."

Thirteen remembered that day. As he remembered every other moment in his life with crystal clarity—the device and the machines coursing through his body would not allow him to forget. The Zzkritti saw a perfect memory as a necessary tool in an operative's kit. To Thirteen it was a curse brought down upon his head for the myriad crimes he had been forced to commit. *There are no innocent hands in an evil act.*

"Yes, Mr. Bazzi. Perhaps we shall."

Sohrab killed the engine and climbed out. Thirteen sat motionless for a few seconds, then exited the car. He looked up at the bright yellow and red sign above the restaurant and sighed. *It is indeed human food...*

Dieter/Evan stepped into the gloom of the alley, tall buildings of brick and steel on either side creating a sunless artificial canyon, the cracked blacktop glistening with sweat from the runoff of rains past, too shaded to evaporate; it was the kind of place city planners might design for the occasional drug deal, shady people guarded by innocuous and unseeing stone. They moved with a listless grace, the sliding step of the exhausted.

The energy loss was so gradual they hadn't noticed at first, and it took them two days to realize the cause. The tiny machines harvested from the slain backups powered their mechanical bodies by stealing energy from Dieter/Evan, attaching themselves to mitochondria and siphoning off adenosine triphosphate. Normally this had little effect, but Dieter/Evan now carried ten additional colonies, each vying for the same energy source, robbing them not only of physical ability, but cognitive as well. Amphetamines were the answer, and they settled on Adderall as the most effective and easiest to acquire. Once they gained the last of Dieter, they could synthesize all the amphetamine they'd ever need, but that information and skill was still out there awaiting harvesting.

The immediate concern was obtaining a supply from the gentleman waiting at the far end of the alley. James "Boney" Watson had been the consensus choice of the drug users in the park across the street, and Dieter/Evan had one of them set up a buy.

Boney, as the name suggested, was a spare man. Softened and pushed through a pasta machine, he'd come out the business end both thin and hard. The clothing hung on his body like someone had tossed an extra-large hoodie atop a spindly coat rack. The hair, woven into the ever-popular dreadlocks, was a mutant tarantula lounging upon a skull sporting the largest forehead Dieter/Evan had ever seen.

"You can stop right there," Boney said, leaning on a wooden crate tucked up against the chain-link fence blocking the alley's exit. He frowned, then pursed his lips, head bobbing. "Nah, man. You smell like a cop."

"I can assure you, young man, I am no police officer."

Short, harsh laughter exploded from the man's face. "You don' sound like no cop, that's fer sure." He looked Dieter/Evan up and down, eyes half-lidded, taking his measure. The seeming disinterest didn't fool them—the eyes behind those sleepy lids were both sharp and preternaturally aware. Boney was in his element, a panther lounging on a tree limb, ready to strike without thought. Dieter/Evan watched the hand buried deep inside the left pocket of Boney's hoodie, waiting for movement. They had brought no weapons for this encounter and now wished they'd reconsidered.

"Do you have what I require?"

"We'll get to that in a sec, bro." Boney had a wide grin that never seemed to show in his eyes. "Show me your roll." Dieter/Evan tilted their head, then reached for the pocket of their jacket. "Nice an' slow, bro," Boney oozed.

Dieter/Evan stopped, then with obvious care used only thumb and forefinger to dip inside and pull out the thick roll of bills bound with a rubber band. They held it up for Boney to see, and the man took three lanky steps forward and snatched it from their hand. He tore off the rubber band and counted.

"It is all there," they said, maintaining a cool outer calm. Inside a battle raged, Evan railing against the illegal purchase and the stupidity of self-medication while Dieter fought for control, a bead of sweat forming on their temple.

Boney finished counting and looked at Dieter/Evan. "You don' look so good, bro." He dropped the cash in one pocket, then fished a large pill bottle from the other. He held the bottle up near his face and shook it, a rattlesnake warning. "Could be this is worth more'n I thought." Dieter/Evan stood still as stone, and just as silent. They both stood that way for another ten seconds, then Boney snorted. "Eh, a deal's a deal." He hesitated another beat, then tossed the bottle to

Dieter/Evan. They fumbled the catch but gained control before it hit the ground.

Dieter/Evan twisted the cap off and shook two tablets into a trembling palm. Dieter accessed Evan's memories about dosage, shrugged and popped them into their mouth. Both knew the drugs took over an hour to take effect, but the trembling stopped almost at once. *Probably only an emotional response.*

"Slow down, hoss," Boney said, chuckling. "You'll be back for more in a week at that rate." His eyes glowed with the avarice borne of another junkie on the hook.

"No," they said. "This should be sufficient." There were enough pills to last a month at the very least, and Dieter would be fully integrated long before then.

Boney's face fell, then darkened. "Then I guess we're done here," he said, the wary cat back at once. "Get out b'fore you scare off my next customer."

I should kill him, Dieter mused. *A boon to society at large.*

No, Evan whispered. *You may need him again.*

Not likely, but the possibility exists... however small.

They nodded to Boney and turned toward the street, both satisfied for once.

Sohrab pushed away from the table and leaned back, watching the Shadowman pick at his food. It was an odd sight. The old man was eighty years old if he was a day, but he ate like he'd never seen food. *At least not food like this.* The man had ordered several entrees and spent the whole time eating small portions of each, savoring some and turning his nose up at others.

"I thought you said you ate human food."

"I do, but I am rarely conscious for the event." The Shadowman took another bite of the apple pie, ignoring the prime rib sandwich in front of him. He saw the expression of confusion on Sohrab's face, swallowed, and grinned. "The Zzkritti kept me offline much of the time in between missions. I was an automaton, traveling where they desired, performing simple tasks they required, and refueling when necessary—all without conscious thought on my part."

"That sounds... horrifying," Sohrab said, shaken.

"It was not so bad, though they occasionally forgot to let me sleep or eat." He took another bite of pie. "You must remember the Zzkritti evolved from insectoids—they are more like ants than humans—and for much of their history, their drones functioned in much the same manner. Only the queens had autonomy."

Sohrab dismissed the idea with a wave of one hand. "Bah, monarchies are useless relics of the past."

"Perhaps," the Shadowman said, "but true democracies are messy and inefficient."

Sohrab thought about the current election cycle in America and had to agree. *Though I am sure I would take either candidate over a queen.* "If they are so perfect, why do they need my help?" The surprise on the Shadowman's face brightened Sohrab's day more than he would have thought possible. The man stopped mid-bite, fork poised at the edge of his lips, eyebrows knitting. He placed the fork on the dessert plate and laced his fingers in front of his face, elbows resting on the table.

"Why would you think I need—"

"Because you haven't killed me or even grilled me for information, and I have access to the one thing you don't."

"And that is?"

Sohrab leaned forward and tapped the table with a hard finger. "Jack."

The Shadowman nodded assent, then went back to eating his pie, a satisfied expression on his face. *Is that because I bested him, or is it the pie?* He finished every last crumb, scraped the plate of the last few laggards that had steadfastly refused to join the rest, then sat back with a soft grin on his lips. After a few moments, his brow furrowed, and he reached across and scratched his forearm—not like someone goes at an itch, but more like a violinist draws his bow.

"I must apologize for my behavior during the First Gulf War," he said at last. Sohrab saw it took something from the man, made him smaller, but he offered the apology with the same detached indifference with which he ordered his meal.

The same way in which he killed.

"You were so ordered, were you not?" Sohrab said, offering the olive branch.

The Shadowman gave him a single shallow nod. The scratching grew more pronounced. "Still, every soldier is always responsible for his actions."

"Human soldiers have a choice about following orders. Did you?"

"There are... ways—"

"Tell me this," Sohrab growled, tapping the table a second time, harder than the first. "Did you believe in the mission?"

63

The Shadowman closed his mouth with a click, tilting his head and frowning. He seemed to notice the scratching and drew the hand back, placing it on the table. "At the time."

"Then I accept your apology." Sohrab leaned back once again. "We will speak no more about it."

The tall man sighed, shoulders relaxing like a worn bellows, averted his eyes from Sohrab's hard gaze for a moment. "Thank you," he said, and locked eyes again with the man he'd wronged a quarter-century ago.

"So," Sohrab said, forcing a smile that cheered him in spite of himself. "What is so urgent you need my help?"

"As you said, it is Jack I need. I ask that you urge him to meet with me, and soon." The man's face grew stern and bleak. "I fear time is slipping away."

"Why do you need Jack? And what makes you think he'll agree to speak with you?"

The Shadowman leaned across the table and growled, "Dieter is back."

∞

Amber held her head high as she exited the library, her spine straight, a bounce in her step; she was the very model of a carefree freshman, the smile she held tight to her face never once threatening to slide. She rounded a corner, out of sight of the main entrance, unshouldered her pack, sat on a bench beneath an old oak and cried. Her hands shook as she held her face, the quiet tears morphing into great racking sobs, and she doubled over, practically nose to kneecap. She thought of all the times in her life she had been treated the way this boy felt he had the right to—the jocks in high school, the occasional teacher, an uncle who, thankfully, lived far away... even her first real boyfriend. It wasn't just annoying—it was assault. And it was constant.

She had enjoyed her job as a flight attendant for exactly two reasons: her looks were a plus, and aggressive passengers were handled immediately. Sure, she had to endure the occasional pinch or slap on her ass, and drunken businessmen had propositioned her more times than she could count, but if she couldn't handle it, there was always the Air Marshall or police ready to step in.

After a long time, Amber stopped crying so suddenly it seemed the tears crawled back into her eyes. She wiped her face and straightened. *Until today, I've always either put up with it, or allowed a man to*

64

handle it for me, she thought, frowning. She brushed hair from her face, then took a deep breath, inhaling the sweet decay of old, damp leaves beneath the oak. A slight breeze rustled the living tree, upper branches swaying in slow motion. Without conscious thought, her breathing slowed and matched the rhythm in that sway, the tree's own breath from the wind's push and pull. She closed her eyes and felt the wind on her arms, her face... felt the cotton of her shirt dance to the air's movement. When she had released the last dying vestiges of anger, hate, and self-loathing, she stood, smiling for real this time, and picked up her pack.

She strolled at a speed befitting the splendid day, and each time the boy's face intruded her thoughts, she batted it away as a cat paws an over-curious puppy. That made her smile, too. Even the thought of seeing him in class held no fear for her; she knew from experience the wounded puppy didn't soon return to the scene of his humiliation. Some might escalate, but she knew she'd put the fear of God into him. She'd seen it in his eyes. *From now on, I deal with it myself.* "I should get a Taser," she said, grinning. "Pepper spray at the very least." No matter what she'd told the boy, she had no gun, nor would she ever fire one again at a living thing, human or otherwise. *Twice in my life is more than enough*, she thought with a shudder.

The closer she got to the dorm, the more people crowded the walkways and unofficial paths. Georgetown University was not a large campus, but made up for it in stunning old-world architecture, impeccably maintained grounds and landscaping, and a manner of packing as many students as possible in a compact space without feeling crowded. The tail-end of the second summer session was never crowded on any campus, and Georgetown was no different, but this time of year saw more than its fair share of high school seniors and recent graduates taking their first tour.

And, of course, there were the jocks. Some, like the puppy in the library, came early and made up deficiencies for NCAA eligibility, while the main body had arrived for training. This was Amber's first summer on campus, and now as she jostled among the students for walking space, wondered how much more crowded it would be in the fall.

"*There* you are!" The voice behind her was as grating as it was cheerful. Amber sighed, shoulders slumping, and turned.

"Hey, Donna," she said, her recent good mood souring. They stood facing one another in the middle of the path, other students parting like water around a stone as they passed by, annoyance clear on their faces.

Donna held up her phone, the Uber app already open. "Your *friend* docked us on his review." She cocked an eyebrow at Amber, in the universal sign of *what are you gonna do about it?*

"What can I say," Amber shrugged. "He's ex-military, so his patience for inebriated teens is thin."

"We weren't *drunk*." Donna bit each word off, her face instantly dark. She brightened almost as quickly, a pixie grin on her lips. "Just a bit tipsy."

"Okay. If you say so."

"I do," she nodded with the last word. Donna cast her gaze to her feet. "Hey, um... did you wanna come to our room and study for the history final with me and Janelle?"

Amber knew what that meant—she'd spend the whole evening explaining to those two bubble-headed young women every detail of American History they'd neglected to learn. She knew the type—smart but without a lick of common sense. *They'll learn someday, but by then it may be too late.* She also knew that without her help, they had no chance of passing. Resigned to her fate, she sighed.

"Sure, but you guys come to my room."

"*That* empty ol' place?" Donna said, incredulous, placing one palm on her chest, eyes wide for effect. "You don't even have a TV."

"All the better to study by." Amber grinned. "I keep my place simple for a reason."

"Party pooper," Donna pouted.

"You have fun when the work is done," she said, then chuckled hearing her father's words come out of her mouth. That had been happening more and more often lately, culminating most recent-ly in her takedown of the puppy. "I've gotta go," she said, mov-ing away. "Come by after supper." She walked away before Donna could complain. "And bring your own book, highlighters, and your notes." She wanted to laugh at the frightened look on the girl's face at the word *notes*. *Well, she's got a few hours.*

The river of bodies carried her onward, swallowing a wide-eyed Donna beneath its waves. Amber followed the path, then stepped off for the well-trod unofficial path to her dorm. She roamed through shadows of looming buildings, a hodgepodge of old and new, the shoe-and-boot-plowed footpath arcing through the deepest parts of the shadows. The air was cooler and sweeter here, and all thoughts of the puppy, Donna, and Janelle were swept away, cleansed by the simplest acts of Mother Nature.

Amber rounded the last corner, her building in sight, and she slowed to a snail's pace, unwilling to trade sunlight for fluorescent lighting. People entered and left the building in a seemingly never-ending flow, like blood following the circuit of arteries and veins. As she drew near, she noticed one person never moved. Tall and thin, his back to her, he looked up the side of the building every few seconds. *Waiting for someone.* A chill crawled up her spine despite the heat.

He turned and her breath caught in her throat.

"Jack?"

"Hey, Amber." His tone was light, but smooth and resonant. "Can we talk?"

CHAPTER 6

THE FRIGHTENED ANIMAL NESTLED IN THE BASE of Sohrab's brain wanted to bolt, to run until his muscles burned, but his rational mind held the reins firm; it recognized what his instincts did not: the notion of Dieter's return was preposterous. He didn't know how long he sat, stone-faced and silent while the two parts of him fought for control, but it must have been a long time. He shook himself and looked up into the craggy face of the waitress, steaming coffee pot held in one hand, a look of patient consternation in her gray eyes.

"I'm sorry," he said looking from the pot to his cup and back again. "Of course. A refill would be nice. Thank you." She smiled; a motion so practiced he couldn't tell if it was genuine.

"That's okay, sweetie." The woman filled his cup, her hands trembling from age and arms too thin and weak to hold the carafe steady. "I get lost in my thoughts sometimes, too." She finished and hurried away to the only other occupied table in her territory.

I bet you do. Perhaps a bit unkind, but... He looked across the table at the Shadowman. That man was easily twenty years the woman's senior, but his mind was sharp—sharper than any man Sohrab knew—and his body was far from frail.

The frightened animal returned, and an icy shiver ran up Sohrab's spine.

"You cannot be serious. The man dissolved before my eyes. I watched Jack put a round in his head." He leaned forward, glancing at the waitress. "I set the fire that burned the place to the ground." He shook his head. "No one could survive that. I do not care what your alien science can do." Sohrab sat back against the worn cushion.

"All true," the Shadowman said, his face as bland as a bowl of oatmeal. "But none of that negates my statement." He splayed his hands on the table and cocked his head a tick. "Dieter is indeed back."

"How is such a thing possible?"

The Shadowman winced, the closest he had come to a show of emotion since he put down his fork. His lips tightened, and years of training told Sohrab he was either about to be lied to... or stonewalled.

"The means are... not important." There was pain behind that answer.

Stonewalled it is, then.

"They are if your intent is for me to believe what you say." Sohrab crossed his arms and waited.

The Shadowman's mouth bunched, and he cocked his head further, eyes now focused beyond the walls of the diner as if listening to something distant. *He most likely is*, Sohrab thought. After perhaps five seconds, the Shadowman nodded, blinked, and shifted his attention back to Sohrab.

"Far in the Zzkritti's past they toyed with artificial intelligence, the result a race of self-aware machines that almost destroyed the collective. Now, while they have many intelligent devices, they abandoned the idea of autonomous self-aware machines." He wrung his hands together, eyes drifting to the table. "A consequence of this research was learning to bond an individual's memories and consciousness with a computing device—what human theorists call the 'singularity'."

"So, Dieter is now what... a robot?"

"No." The wringing intensified. "The technology was not lost, so much as suppressed," he said as if recalling a recent event. "The Zzkritti had no idea Dieter had even learned—"

"What did he do?" Sohrab growled.

The Shadowman's shoulders slumped, and he spread his hands once again. "At some point before he died—most likely as a fail-safe borne of paranoia—he used his nanites to upload his mind into a human host. Probably one of his—"

"He did *what?*" Sohrab had raised his voice to where the other patrons stopped their mindless chatter and stared. He cast a hard glare about the room, forcing eyes to avert.

"He uploaded his mind—all of it—into one of his operatives, replacing the host's mind with his own."

"That is just... just—"

"Inhuman?"

"I was reaching for insane, but I defer to you." Sohrab pulled at his beard. If everything the Shadowman said was true, where to begin their search? He didn't even entertain the idea it would not involve him. "Do you have hard evidence this has happened?"

"None that would hold up in court." The Shadowman pursed his lips. "Call it hard *inferences*, if you will." He picked up his coffee mug and took a sip, scrunched his nose, then set the mug down. "There have been a series of murders over the past year in various locations all over the globe, and it is my belief they are connected."

"Bah," Sohrab said, waving his hand, "murders happen every second of every—"

"Not like these. The cause in every case but one has been exsanguination—most with no visible wound."

Sohrab frowned and pulled at his beard again. *No wounds?* So vampirism, as little as he understood of the practice, was out. *That leaves only magic and technology. And who has the best technology on the planet?*

"Jack will believe you are behind this. I am not sure *I* do not."

"Oh, I have no illusions he does not blame us."

"Does not?" *Why not 'will not'?*

"Jack discovered the pattern."

"You have been watching him." There was no question in Sohrab's voice, and his eyes stabbed with frozen daggers.

"We watch you all," the Shadowman said, the shrug evident in his voice, if not his shoulders.

"So access to Jack—"

"Is not what I require, *Colonel* Bazzi." The Shadowman spoke the rank in a hushed tone, but the meaning was unmistakable. "I have always had access—we provided his new position, after all. What I need is for Jack to believe—not only of our innocence, but of Dieter's return—and for that a friend must mount the argument. Someone he trusts."

Sohrab shook his head, a grim smile between mustache and beard. "Then it is not me you need. For that you want Amber."

"You could never trust me again." Amber watched Jack, hands in the pockets of his jeans, drawing circles in the dirt with the toe of his shoe. She had brought him to the only quiet place she knew—the bench beneath the great oak—sitting while he shuffled about in front of her. "I understood that, even if you didn't," she said, tears welling. *I won't cry, goddamn it. I won't.* "Jack, there's no way to apologize for what I did. No justification I can—"

"You've got it all backward," he breathed, his eyes never lifting to meet hers. "I came to apologize to *you.*" That one simple statement took so much out of him, like draining rainwater from a cistern, diminishing him in ways she couldn't yet comprehend. "I was angry... depressed. And I took it out on you." He lifted his chin and locked eyes with her. Where they once held only despair and anger, there was now resolve and determination. "It wasn't fair to you, nor even to me."

"I know what you saw when you looked at me, Jack," she said, voice quivering. How could she not? She saw it every time she looked in the mirror—Mason and Bill, both lives destroyed by her hand. "I took the two souls you cared for most and blew them out like candles." Amber buried her face in her hands, forcing the tears back. She listened for the calming breeze, the rustle of leaves in the canopy above her head, the chitter of squirrels as they scampered from branch to branch, but all she heard was the heavy drumbeat of her heart.

"Three," Jack whispered, kneeling in the dirt.

Amber sniffed once, pushing the tears away, and lifted her face, meeting his eyes once again. "What?"

"Three. Two of the three I care about." He reached for her hands, and she almost pulled away, but he settled his atop hers and held them in a soft grip. "Don't let me lose the third," he murmured. "At least don't let me lose you because I was too stupid and hurt to apologize." The corners of his mouth pulled up, and he sighed through his nose. "Besides, there are plenty of other reasons for losing someone... like forgetting their first kiss, or their first date, or—"

"Enough," she said, cutting him off. There was no heat in it, but he drew back regardless. His hands, though, never left hers. She pulled her right hand from beneath his, brushed a spray of hair over her ear, then placed her hand on his cheek. It heated at once under her fingertips, but she was determined. "I hope this doesn't sound cold, but... you have practice at losing people." She saw the look in his eyes and plowed ahead before the hurt grew. "But I *killed* people, Jack. Innocents." She shook her head, closing her eyes, tears leaking from the corners. "I will never get used to that. I don't *want* to." The tears spilled now, and she realized she no longer cared. "When I look in your eyes, I see it all over again."

He released her hand, stood, then sat beside her, draping a lanky arm around her shoulders. He held her as she lay her head on his shoulder, and she wept, squeezing the last bitter tears from her soul. *For now. There are more where they come from.*

"So," he said, looking into her eyes. "Friends from afar?" It wasn't a question, but an offering. A compromise where none could legitimately exist.

"Sure," she said, wiping her eyes. "I think that's for the best."

"Mind if we talk online once in a while?" His grin was genuine, and she smiled half-heartedly in return. "Sometimes I need to vent about my weird-ass job."

Amber pulled back and looked at him, puzzled. "How is it so different from your last weird-ass job?"

Jack snorted and shook his head. "Oh, honey, the things I could tell you."

Jack looked at the screen on his phone, the word *disconnected* bright as day staring back at him. It was the fourth time in as many hours he'd tried to call Sohrab, and each time it had gone to voicemail after two rings. *That means he's getting the call and hitting the ignore button.* He could see the man having a schedule busy enough he couldn't take a call, but certainly not for four straight hours on a workday. Sohrab hadn't even responded when Jack requested him on the Uber app; he'd had to settle for a college student who, apparently, lived by her GPS. Sohrab knew the roads better than any app, but this young woman was green in more ways than just youth. During her rapid-fire attempts at chit-chat, she'd told Jack about her family, her cats—Beth and Angel—and their various health issues, her complete degree plan in pre-med and its resultant financial strains on her parents, and the fact she'd only been driving for Uber for a couple of weeks.

"I name the cats after me," she said, spinning the wheel and pinning Jack against the door. "You know... Beth and Angel. My name's Bethany, so—"

"I think that's our turn up there on the left," he said, hoping she'd planned to change lanes, but knowing she hadn't.

"Yeah," she said, popping her gum and checking the app. She hit the brakes before missing the turn, and swerved across two lanes of traffic, earning one blaring horn blast and two birds in the process. "Sorry, sorry," she said through the window. She turned and winced at Jack. "I'm so sorry. I'm just worried about—"

73

"That's my stop," he said, pointing at the building they were passing.

"Oh, yeah. Right." She hit the brakes and pulled to the curb, the wheels complaining as the car skidded to a stop. She sighed, heavy and forlorn. "I don't think I'm very good at this."

Jack chuckled. "Don't worry. Like everything in life, the more you do it, the better you get." He patted her on the shoulder, and she faced him. "Besides, any landing you can walk away from, right?"

She smiled, sad yet warm. "Thanks. I'll get better."

Jack grinned back at her. "I know you will. I'll request you in a month or so. Bet you're a pro by then." He opened the door and stepped out, waving as she drove away. The phone still in hand, he opened the Uber app and added a generous tip. *I need all the good karma I can get.* He considered dialing Sohrab again but thought better of it and dropped the phone into his pocket. The Central Detention Facility building at his back beckoned, and he spun and walked toward the main entrance.

As soon as he'd noticed the link between the man known as Double-D and the other murders, Jack had called to schedule an appointment with the Department of Corrections. The gruff, gravelly voiced woman had given him flack about calling so late in the week, and how Double-D's lawyer had used up the man's visitation time, but as soon as she checked Jack's government ID number, she'd bent over backward to accommodate him. He could tell she still wasn't happy about it. *In DC, people are always doing things they're not happy about,* he mused, a wry grin on his face.

Outside, the detention facility looked much like a single-edifice community college, complete with a main entry foyer and windows that didn't open. *Probably find the same sort of people in each. Kids wanting to learn, trapped inside with others who couldn't care less, all overseen by indifferent and often belligerent administrators.*

Jack stepped through the doors and shook his head about how easy it was. They built jails and prisons to keep people *in*, not out; security in the latter was far less daunting than the former. A woman in uniform, so close to retirement she had its address and home phone number, waddled toward him with a fierce energy that screamed *I'm in charge* to anyone who cared enough to listen. Red cheeks beneath deep-set eyes brightened as she approached, throwing off waves of heat he could feel. Her hair never moved as she walked, plastered in place by a liberal application of her last can of lacquer.

"You must be Jack Montgomery," she said sliding one sausage-fingered hand forward.

"Sometimes I wish I wasn't," he said, taking her and pumped it twice. "Nice to meet you, um...."

"Sergeant Clark, if you don't mind." With a twinkle in her eye, she held his hand a bit longer, shaking it with a firm tug toward her. Surprised, he almost toppled over. *Ugh*, he thought, willing his eyes not to roll. *I fucking hate dominance games.* "I assume you're here to escort me... see to my needs?" Jack offered her a wide grin as he extricated his hand from hers. He might hate the game, but he played it better than most.

"Sure," she said through tight lips. "Of course. Right this way." The matronly woman stepped around him and led him down a long cream and gray hallway, fluorescent lights flickering and humming overhead—her soft-soled shoes sounded like a tiny mouse battle as she walked, while his clicked on the bland linoleum tile. "I've been told you require a private area for your visit, so I'm taking you to one of the smaller in-processing cells."

"Who told you to—?"

"Some bigwig in the DOC," she said with a dismissive wave of her hand. "I didn't take the call. Upper administration just passed the info along."

Shit rolls downhill. Guards, a couple both taller and wider than Jack, passed by in the opposite direction—*Shift change, most likely*—and to a man, each afforded Sergeant Clark a very wide berth. None held eye contact with her for long, and only one exchanged a greeting. Something about the way they looked at her booted his danger avoidance system, the hairs on his neck prickling enough he marked every turn as she led him deeper into the building. After more than a dozen turns and a few flights of stairs upward, she stopped before a massive putty-gray door. She grasped the thick handle—somehow, he knew there would be no twin on the other side—and levered it down, opening the door. It swung outward with a whisper on well-oiled hinges and she waved him inside.

"I'm afraid I don't have enough staff to guard your man while you two visit, but he'll be shackled hands and feet, so you should be fine." Clark grinned while Jack pondered the way she had said *should. This has gone beyond childish dominance games.* He kept the expression on his face as if painted there. She pointed at the panel beside the door. "Just press the call button when you're ready to go." With that, she stepped back and slammed the door closed with a boom that vibrated his teeth, and the heavy locks engaged with a thick clank before he had time to object.

Shit rolls downhill, he reminded himself. *And I think I'm standing at the bottom.*

Jack sat at the only table in the room, the hard aluminum chair barely moving when he lowered into it. Its twin stood empty on the other side. He'd seen a documentary on *60 Minutes* years ago about these chairs. First commissioned by the Navy for use on submarines during WWII, the bid called for an indestructible piece that would stay put in rough seas. *Now the goddamn things are everywhere.* They made perfect sense in a jail or prison, but he guessed in a riot the chairs made great weapons. *For anyone who can lift them.*

The light overhead snapped and buzzed, and he lifted his gaze. A basic panel of fluorescent tubes hung on chains screwed into the concrete, suspended a good fourteen feet above his head. The room was a very tall, very narrow, very spare box of dull putty-gray surfaces. The door on the opposite side of the room, like the one behind him, had no handle on this side.

Jack checked his watch. *Only fifteen minutes?* He bunched his lips, crossed one leg over the other, and sighed. *A man could go nuts in this room,* which had become the intent over the past fifty years. No more rehabilitation—only punishment and retribution. He bounced his leg, heel slapping against the tile, and checked his watch again. He was about to stand and begin pacing when the far door opened with a long, gritty scrape.

A guard stepped into the room and another escorted the prisoner inside. Jack noted the man wore no chains on either his wrists or ankles. *More games. An oversight... or something else?* He really didn't want to believe the *something else.* Dreadlocks tossing to and fro, Double-D glared first at the guard in front, then the guard behind. He thrust his chin out at Jack.

"This ain't my fuckin' lawyer."

"No one said he was, dipshit," the guard behind him growled. "Only said you had a visitor." The guard sneered at Jack, winked at his partner, then swung back to Double-D. "You gonna be a good boy?"

"Ain't I always?" He stepped away from the guards, brushed his dreadlocks back over his shoulders, pulled the chair away from the table, and spun it around and straddled it. He rested his arms on the back and stared at Jack. Both guards snorted and chuckled, then hustled out of the room, pulling the door shut behind with grim finality. Double-D didn't bother watching them leave, his interest was glued to Jack's face. "I don't know you, man."

Jack shrugged, a gesture he hoped the other would interpret as calm indifference. A year ago he *would* have been calm—at peace; no need to fear for your life when you didn't care if you woke up the next morning. Now he was nervous, and his only hope was this man didn't see it.

"No reason you should, Mr.—"

"Just call me Double-D," he snapped. "Never did like that slave name." He cut his eyes away from Jack's face when he said it.

Jack dropped his crossed leg and leaned forward, elbows resting on the table, pulling the man's attention back to him. "I need to ask you some questions about the murders you're accused of." He kept his voice level, but pictures of the aftermath of the crime flashed inside his mind.

Double-D narrowed his eyes. "You some kinda reporter?" He spit the last word as if the taste offended him. "I already told you people I ain't talking 'till my family sees some cash."

"No, sir. Not a reporter." Jack scrunched his mouth and tilted his head. "I'm sort of... an investigator."

"A cop."

"No, not a police officer. I'm with a branch of the Federal government."

"Right. A *federal* cop."

Jack was getting nowhere—there was no trust, no reason for him to cooperate—so he played the only card he had.

"I know you didn't commit the crime alone." He watched Double-D's eyes narrow a bit more. "I know it wasn't even your idea." Now the look was more cautious than mistrustful. "You were, in fact, *compelled* to do these things, and you probably don't even know why." Jack peered into the man's widening, fear-filled eyes and leaned back in his chair. *Got him!*

"How do you know this shit?" Double-D croaked out, his bottom lip trembling. "I ain't even told my lawyer."

Jack shrugged, shook his head, and snorted. "That's a long story, and more than half of it you'll think is crazy." He was no longer sure *anything* would seem crazy to him after the last year, but to someone who had never met a Zzkritti, everything he said from this point forward would sound crazier than a shit-house rat.

Double-D craned his neck forward tapped a hard finger on the table. "Try me."

∽

Amber sat at the desk in her room, an untouched meal beside her open laptop, tapping at the keyboard, transcribing notes from the morning's classes. The open notebook contained scribblings and equations, the margins filled with the random drawings and musings of the truly bored. The required course was beneath her, but as it was a prerequisite for the advanced math courses she needed, there was little she could do but endure.

Enduring had become her default setting.

She checked the time. *Almost six. Two more hours of peace before the bubbleheads arrive.* She finished the last of the notes, closed the file, then scrubbed her face with both hands and stretched her back. Her stomach complained, calling to the half-eaten sandwich on the plate, and she grabbed it with one hand and took a healthy bite. While she chewed, she opened the file containing the notes from her American History class. She kept her notes in single files, running the length of the course and in outline format; it made for an easy review before an exam. Amber printed the entire last unit, then took the stack of papers and her plate over to the bed. She hadn't made it past the first paragraph before the knock on her door.

Ah, hell. They're early. Amber frowned, tossed the notes aside, and stood. Irritated, she stomped to the door and threw it open.

"I said eight..." Her eyes widened, and she stumbled back, tripping over the desk chair and sprawling to the floor.

"It's okay, Amber," Sohrab said, taking a quick step inside, kneeling, and extending his hand. He nodded back at the man filling the door's frame; a shadow come to life. "He is not here to hurt you." Sohrab offered Amber an embarrassed grin. "In fact, he—*we*—need your help."

My help? What could they possibly need from...? She frowned. *Oh.*

Amber batted Sohrab's hand away and stood on her own, squaring her shoulders against them both. "No," she said as firmly as her jangled nerves allowed. "I've done my part—*more* than my part. You can't drag me back into whatever shit-storm you're involved in." She peered hard into the Shadowman's watery eyes, the grit in her voice growing with every second. "And I won't let you drag Jack down with you, either." She crossed her arms over her chest, glaring at both men.

"But Mr. Montgomery is already involved, Ms. Riley," the Shadowman said, head inclined, his voice a rumble as thick and sweet as molten chocolate. "May I?" he said, indicating the doorway with a casual flick of one hand. His expression so warm she almost forgot he was a stone-cold assassin. *Almost.* Sohrab stood and moved aside.

Is it like inviting a vampire in to your home? She cocked an eyebrow at Sohrab. "You presume too much," she said, breathing hard. She forced her shoulders to relax, then nodded at the scarecrow blocking her door. "Fine," she said, waving him inside. "It's not like I could stop you, anyway."

"Thank you." He removed his hat and stepped into the room, then pushed the door closed behind him.

"What do you mean Jack is already involved?"

The Shadowman cast a glance toward Sohrab and gave a slight nod.

"We'll, ah, get to that in a minute," Sohrab said. "First... have you, ah, heard from him recently?" To her he looked like the puppy after she'd gripped his balls.

"This afternoon, in fact," she said warily, then sat on the edge of her bed. "Why?"

"I cannot reach him by phone." Sohrab winced, then smiled crookedly. "I spent most of the day ignoring his calls, so..." He shrugged.

"You think he's ditching your calls because he's angry?" She shook her head. "That doesn't sound like Jack."

"No," he agreed. "It doesn't." He glanced at the Shadowman. "But could you call to be sure?"

"You think he might be in danger, don't you?" She was looking at Sohrab, but aimed the question squarely at the Shadowman.

Of course he's in danger. Why else come my door, literally hat in hand? Finally shed of the worst of her nightmares, here they were again standing in her dorm room. Her heart fluttered, and a knot formed in her stomach. *And if he's in the kind of danger even the Shadowman can't identify...* "Stop buying trouble," her father rasped in her ear, as clear as if he sat beside her. *This is not like worrying about the prom, Pop. Where assassins are involved, it's best to live in a constant state of worry.* Her father had no response to that.

Amber lifted her cell from the nightstand. She dialed, fully expecting Jack to answer, the tightness in her chest warning her he wouldn't.

The phone rang a long time before it went to voicemail.

Jack saw the determination and question on Double-D's face, the man's finger still planted firmly on the surface of the table. He had no clue how the man would react to the story, but that hardly mattered. What mattered—the only thing that mattered—was what he remembered. *More accurately,* who *he remembers.*

"Let's put aside my story for now," Jack said. "I'll answer all your questions as soon as you answer a few of mine."

Double-D glared at Jack, then lifted his hand and leaned back. He crossed his arms over his chest and grinned like the cat that swallowed the canary. That was one of his mom's favorite phrases when he was a boy, and Jack had never understood what that looked like until now.

"Go ahead," Double-D said, nodding. "I get how this works." He arched an eyebrow. "But it's tit for tat, brother. No tit, no tat."

Jack snorted. "Fair enough. I'll go first." He considered a moment, pulling at his bottom lip. Double-D's first question was likely one that would require mention of the Zzkritti, so Jack's initial question needed to get to the core before he lost all credibility. "What do you remember about that day?"

Double-D sighed and his face softened, eyes drifting to the table. "Frankly, not a whole hell of a lot. I remember waking up the morning a day before... having a drink that afternoon with a dude from work." He lifted his eyes to Jack's. "Then nothin'. Next thing I know, I'm standin' outside a burnin' mansion."

A day and a half wiped away. That certainly sounds like someone I know. It occurred to him the accomplice must have presented himself in the bar. Someone nearby, another customer... possibly even the bartender himself. *Nope. Simpler.*

"This friend—"

"Uh-uh," the prisoner said, shaking his head. "Tit for tat, remember?"

Jack sighed, checking the time on his phone. "Fine," he said. "Shoot."

"How did you know I didn't remember doin' nothin'?" The man's face was doughy, and his voice cracked from the emotion buried in that question. He was a man who'd spent the last year knowing no one would believe anything he said.

"Something very similar happened to me and my friends over a year ago." Jack leaned closer and frowned. "Does the name Jack Montgomery mean anything?"

Double-D pursed his lips, brow furrowing—Jack's mom would have said she could smell the wood burning as the man thought hard—then his eyes flew open wide. "*You're* the dude!" he said with unabashed respect. "There was a whole fuckin' nationwide manhunt for you."

"World-wide, actually," Jack said, nodding his head.

"How'd ya get outta that?"

"Sorry," Jack said, wagging a finger. "One question at a time. My turn."

"Go ahead, man. You've earned it."

I've earned nothing, except the right to be free of this. But he would never be free; he knew that with the same certainty he knew his own name. He was bound to the Zzkritti now and forever more, locked in an eternal battle for the soul of humanity. *Ah, don't make it more than it is. You just want the chance to stop them while you're still breathing.*

"This friend. What do you remember about him?"

"Not much. He—"

The locks on the doors, both in front and behind, clacked free, and the doors swung open with such force they slammed against the walls, the thunderous rattle shaking dust and flecks of lead paint from the ceiling.

"This interview is over!" The guard burst through the door behind Double-D in full riot gear, followed by five more just like him—a moving wall of meat and bone, melon heads perched on neck-less shoulders with rocks for brains.

"But—"

"But nothing, Mr. Montgomery." Sergeant Clark gripped his shoulder with surprising strength and pressed him down. She shifted slightly, moving her free hand toward his face. He watched the men drag Double-D from his chair, one drawing his weapon and calmly splashing the man's brains over the near wall, the sound of the single shot reverberating inside Jack's head, the pungent odor of nitroglycerin wrinkling his nose. The last supplanted by another, sweeter smell of berries, and then there really was nothing.

PART TWO

"Each friend represents a world in us, a world possibly not born until they arrive, and it is only by this meeting that a new world is born."

—Anais Nin

CHAPTER 7

AMBER TOSSED AND TURNED IN HER BED as the last of an interminably long day bled away, evening fading into night, night blurring into sunrise; she wondered if sleep would ever be as easy again as it was before she met Jack. Birds flitted back and forth among the branches of the tree outside her window, crowding the stage as they sang their good-mornings. She resisted the urge to grab her phone from the nightstand and dial Jack's number—the last fifty or so attempts had been unsuccessful, and there was no reason to assume number fifty-one would be any different.

Jack was gone. Not *incommunicado* as Sohrab reassured her; eyes told the tale even if words did not. The Shadowman, of all people, had offered a half-hearted attempt at assuaging her apprehension, but none of it convinced her. Jack may still be alive, but he was gone in every other sense. She felt it deep in her bones, like diving into an ice-covered lake, needle-sharp, numbing, and murderously cold. The only question left was, did he take himself out of the picture, or was he forced out? If the first, there was little she could do—any of them, really—not even the Shadowman, with all his skill and technology, could locate him, and that frightened her most of all. If the latter—and that seemed most likely in the harsh light of day—there was nothing she could do.

"At least nothing Sohrab and the Shadowman couldn't do better," she grumbled, turning over to the watch the birds. The east-facing window sparkled in brilliant sunlight, shadows of leaves waving and birds flapping dancing on the opposite wall. A crack in one pane split the light, painting the wall with a pastel spray of color—a backdrop for the shadow-dancers and the concert outside. She could lay in bed all day—wanted to, in fact—*But dead things just lay there*, she thought. A half-smile tugged the corners of her mouth, and she dragged herself out of bed, yawning and stretching. "Time to get moving." She grabbed a rubber band from the nightstand and tied her hair back, then dressed in jeans and a t-shirt. Before she'd finished tying her favorite pair of plain Converse All-Stars, her door rattled under a soft, but insistent knock. Amber sighed and stood. "I'd know that knock anywhere." A second knock came as she jerked the door open.

"Hey," Donna said, irritation pulling one corner of her mouth like a hooked trout. She pushed past and strode into Amber's room as if she'd paid for the right. "Glad to see you're still alive." She pouted and furrowed her brow. "I didn't appreciate you blowing me and Janelle off for those two old creepers."

"And I don't appreciate you calling my friends creepers," Amber said, looming over the girl. *Okay, the Shadowman's technically no friend, but that's beside the point.* Donna shied away, eyes widening.

"*Sor*-ry," she said, rolling her eyes. "But it still wasn't cool."

"No, it wasn't, but some things are more important than studying."

Donna's eyes fluttered and her mouth fell open. She stood there just blinking for several seconds, then giggled. "I was sure you'd say nothing was more important than studying."

"If you'd seen what I have..." *That wasn't fair, and likely to invite questions I can't answer.*

Donna stared as if mulling it over, then frowned and shrugged. "Think we can reschedule for Sunday? Or do you have church?"

Amber barked a short laugh before stifling it. *Unless Christianity explains the Zzkritti, my church-going days are far behind me.* "Why not tonight or tomorrow?" she asked before Donna dove farther down that rabbit-hole.

"*Ugh...* don't you know?"

Amber only inclined her head in a question.

"Sigma's throwing a big back-to-school party tonight," Donna said with a sneer. "And Saturday is for—"

"Clubbing," Amber finished for her. "I get it. I can't promise anything for Sunday, though." She began to feel she couldn't promise anything for the foreseeable future. Not to Donna. Not to anyone. "Give me a call Sunday morning and we'll see." She ushered Donna gently toward the door.

"I can't find my cell," Donna said, her face falling. It was the saddest Amber had seen her since they first met. "Daddy's gonna kill me if I've lost another one." She stopped at the doorway and turned moist eyes up, bottom lip quivering. Amber wanted to laugh, but knew that was cruel. Instead, she shrugged.

"Where's the last place you..." She frowned a moment, then raised an eyebrow. *Of course! Jack mentioned something about a meeting before he left yesterday.* Her first impulse was to call Sohrab, but she shook that off at once. *Thirteen needs him, and it's probably better for Jack if I found him first.* She realized her mouth was still open, mid-sentence, and closed it with an audible click.

"Are you okay?" There was real concern in Donna's eyes.

"Sure, sure," Amber said, pushing her out the door. "Start with where you saw it last. I'm sure you'll find it."

"Okay, well—"

Amber closed the door before she heard the rest. She tucked her shirt into her jeans, grabbed her purse and cell, then spun toward the door again. She waited a good thirty seconds to be sure Donna had left, then opened it and stepped toward the elevator. Her fingers flew over the cell's face, dialing for a cab as she waited for the doors to open. *No sense alerting Sohrab. Not yet.* The doors opened just as the phone began to ring on the other end. She stepped inside and the elevator began its descent qw someone picked up on the other end.

"Capitol Cab," the too-chipper voice said. "How can I help you?"

"Can you send a cab to Darnall Hall?"

"Of course. Your name?"

"Amber Riley." She engaged in conversation on autopilot, securing the driver without thinking. What she thought about instead was Jack. *I'll find you. If you need help, I'll help. But if you're just hiding—or worse,* drinking—*woe be unto you, Jack Montgomery.*

She hoped for the latter.

Amber paid the cabbie and stepped out of the car. The sounds of morning traffic behind her, she looked up at the building crowding the corner. It wasn't tall by modern standards, but fit right in with the DC skyline. Dull, monolithic, and massive, it was an architecture that came into style like a high fastball and left just as quickly. The cab pulled away from the curb and Amber strode with apprehension toward the glass doors. She pulled the handle and entered, the sounds of the street disappearing as the door sighed shut.

"Why, dear, you look lost as a lamb." The woman behind the desk spoke with a grandmother's demeanor, but something about the way she peered over her glasses told Amber the illusion only went so far. Amber ground to a halt and looked up at the woman. "Anything I can help you with, sweetie?" She winked, eyes sparkling behind the out-sized frames. "It's my job, after all."

"Um... Jack Montgomery..." Amber hesitated. She didn't know what his hours were, or if he even had an office here, but it was the only place she knew to start.

"Well, that can't be your name—you don't look anything like him."

Amber straightened her spine and crossed to the semi-circular desk. "I'm here to see Jack. If he's available, I mean."

The woman leaned forward, the world's skinniest owl. "And you are...?"

Amber cleared her throat and raised her chin. "Amber Riley. I'm a... friend of his."

The woman's eyes lit up, and a smile curled the corners of her mouth. "So *you're* the famous Amber." She practically giggled, covering her mouth with her palm. "I've heard a bit about you. I'm Janice... also a friend of Jack's." She beamed and waved toward the elevators. "Third floor, corner office."

"Shouldn't you let him know I'm coming?"

"I won't tell if you didn't," Janice said, winking again. "He has a secretary for that if you like." She tilted her head, a shadow falling over her face when she mentioned the secretary, then brightened again. "I haven't seen him today, but he may just not have arrived yet." Her brow furrowed, and she pursed her lips. "Though I can't say I've ever known him to come in this late."

Amber grinned up at Janice, forcing down her growing trepidation. "I'll let you know if I find him." She angled toward the elevators, pressed the call button, and waited. *He's not here,* she thought, brushing a stray strand of hair over her ear. She knew that even before she stepped into the building, but having it confirmed only made it worse. The elevator bay chimed, and one set of doors slid open, revealing an empty car—dim and smelling of old carpet and Murphy's Oil Soap, more coffin than conveyance. She pushed the button for the third floor, the door closed, and the car jerked into motion, her stomach turning a short flip.

When Amber stepped out, a bustle of activity covered the floor. Janice had said Jack's office was closest to the elevator, but not which one. She found the one secretary relaxing amidst the coordinated chaos calmly sipping a cup of coffee and strode to her desk.

"I'm here to see Jack Montgomery."

The secretary sputtered, sat up, set the mug on her desk, and frowned up at Amber, looking her up and down with that disapproving gaze women had given her since high school. "Not here," she said after clearing her throat. She squinted and rubbed the side of her nose "You know... I think you're the first visitor he's had since he started working here."

Of course I am, Amber thought with a smirk. *With no oversight, or even any duties, why would he have visitors?* "Do you know when he'll be in?"

"No. He's usually in by eight, or calls when he'll be later."

"When was the last time you saw him?"

The woman's face grew dark and bitter, her eyes hooded and her mouth puckering. "I'm sorry... *who* are you again?"

Amber couldn't blame her for being suspicious. Working in the government had gotten dangerous lately. "I apologize, Ms..."

"Hopkins."

"Yes, well, my name is Amber Riley," she said, extending her hand. The secretary scrutinized it, her mouth drawstring-tight, and after a moment's hesitation, took it in her own and gave it a half-hearted shake. When she released it, she dipped her hand below the desk. Amber kept her eyes from narrowing, knowing the woman was wiping her hand on her slacks. *Either germophobic, or she just doesn't like me. I choose the former.* She shifted and sat on the edge of the desk, watching the other woman's reaction. *Nope. It's definitely dislike.* "I'm a friend of Jack's, and I was hoping to find him here." She leaned closer, her voice conspiratorial. "I haven't heard from him since our conversation yesterday afternoon. He hasn't answered any calls, whether from me or another friend of his, and frankly... I'm worried."

Hopkins' eyes widened somewhat, and she took a deep breath and let it out deliberately. Rather than address Amber's concerns, she grabbed the handset from its cradle and dialed, letting it ring until voicemail answered. "Hmm..." She frowned, then turned to her computer and tapped the keyboard. "I'm sure he's fine, Ms. Riley," she said, her nose buried in the screen while she typed.

"He mentioned something about a meeting around five." Amber couldn't see the screen from her position, and she shifted for a better look."

"I'm sorry, but I have nothing in his calendar," Hopkins said, catching Amber's movement from the corner of her eye and closing the window with Jack's schedule. Her face softened in what looked to Amber as an attempt to appear sympathetic, but the obvious distaste hung in her eyes like a banner. "He'll check in when time allows." She stood and gently ushered Amber toward the elevators. "I'll be sure to let him know you stopped by when he does."

"But—"

"I'm sorry, Ms. Riley, but I must get back to my work. This office has been swamped recently." She grinned, a reptile basking in the sun, and waved Amber away. "You understand, of course."

I do, you obsequious little cunt. You just want to get back to lollygagging.

Sohrab wrinkled his nose and set his mug on the kitchen table. In all the years since arriving in American, he'd never gotten used to the weak brew his new countrymen called coffee. *There certainly must be more important things to worry over*, he thought, then thumbed through the day's headlines on his phone. Both campaigns for president had taken strange and unprecedented turns in the last few days, and he fought the urge to toss the phone across the room. *Americans do not understand what they have in democracy. They waste it with pointless bickering.* "Bah, there is nothing united about these states," he spat under his breath.

"Get off your phone, then," Marie said behind him. She swept into the kitchen like a whirlwind, grabbed a travel mug of coffee hastily prepared, and tossed the strap of her bag over one shoulder. She strode to the table, stood beside him, and looked down her nose like his mother used to when he'd been particularly recalcitrant. "Are you working today, or just me?"

"Can't," he looked away. "I must wait for his call."

"That man?" She said it like a cold shiver, though none of the emotion showed on her face. All that was there was stony displeasure at her husband's refusal to work today. "I don't like him." "He gives me the creeps."

"Then your intuition is functioning properly," Sohrab said, lifting the mug to his lips. He offered nothing more. He couldn't... not without worrying her further. The sip he took was just as bad as the last, and he wrinkled his nose again. He felt her eyes on him but refused to raise his. After perhaps ten seconds of dark silence, she sighed.

"At least wash the dishes while you wait." Marie swung to the doorway, took two steps, and stopped. "Do me a favor," she said, not looking back. "Don't leave your children fatherless."

It was a knife to his heart, and she raced away before he could say anything, the door slamming shut behind her.

"I'll do my best," he said when he was sure she could not hear.

Sohrab stood, drained the mug, and rounded to the sink. *How do we go through so many in one day?* The dirty dishes on one side of the sink were piled high, a wobbly arrangement that would topple from a strong glare. He glared at them now, wishing they'd wash themselves and trundle off to their respective cabinets, Disney-style. He set the mug in the empty half of the sink and ran the water until it was good and hot, then plugged the drain and poured in dish soap. The water frothed and suds rose, and Sohrab stared into the sink pulling his beard. He had mulled over yesterday's revelations, and still could not get beyond the truth that not even the Shadowman could locate Jack. Amber had been no help, and they'd only succeeded in worrying her.

Water spilled over the sides of the sink, shaking him from his thoughts, and he quickly shut off the faucet. He plunged his hand into the steaming water and pulled the drain plug while he grabbed a towel to soak the water from the floor. Before he could kneel, his phone rang, jittering across the table. He dropped the towel on the puddle and snatched his phone before it danced its way to a short fall and quick demise. The caller ID read *unknown*, and he narrowed his eyes before answering.

"Yes?" he said. He wasn't surprised at the smooth baritone that greeted him.

"Meet me outside in one minute," the Shadowman said and hung up.

Sohrab stared at the screen for a few seconds, then shoved the phone into the front pocket of his jeans. He admired the man's precise and business-like nature but still found it unnerving. The puddle on the floor would not clean itself, no matter how he wished for the powers of the Sorcerer's Apprentice, so he knelt and soaked up the rest of the spill with the towel. That task completed, he stood over the sink, wrung the towel out, and draped it over the faucet to dry. He looked at the pile of dishes and tipped an imaginary cap. "Another time, perhaps," he said, and swung for the door. He checked his watch, then stepped into the mid-morning light, timing his stride, and reached the Shadowman's car precisely sixty-one seconds after the man had hung up. The passenger-side window slid down and the Shadowman leaned across.

"You are late," he said without a hint of humor.

Sohrab grinned, opened the door and climbed in. "You have news of Jack?"

"Unfortunately, no." He put the car in gear and pulled away from the curb. "There is an asset nearby who may offer some insight."

"That is rather cryptic." Sohrab suppressed the sudden urge to chuckle. "Even for you."

"There is a programmer—I believe you would call her a hacker—we have used in the past," he said, his eyes never leaving the road. "The Zzkritti have given me permission to purchase her assistance." He inclined his head a tick. "She is... a talented individual."

The admission felt odd to Sohrab, and he was sure what the Shadowman deemed *talent* was likely true brilliance. "Does this hacker have a name?"

"She goes by the name Maribel Vargas, though I suspect that is a deeply embedded alias."

If he only suspects, she is indeed brilliant. To stymie the Shadowman—not to mention the Zzkritti... Jack had told him all about the device the Shadowman carried. How it could control not only human minds through the nanomachines, but any computer, laying any system open for him to peruse.

"You have never met her, have you?"

The Shadowman angled to meet Sohrab's eyes. "No. She guards her privacy, communicating only through intermediaries or a publicly available terminal." He faced forward again, grinding his hands on the wheel, a rare show of frustration. "Based on past communication, I have narrowed her location to a radius of two miles."

"That is still a rather large area to search."

"I have a plan."

Amber rode the elevator to the lobby, holding back hot tears of anger, frustration, and worry. Sometimes women treated her worse than men. *They never look past the surface to see the person. I'm nothing but a pretty face and hot ass to any of them.* She pounded her fist once on the wall, a hammer blow that did nothing to calm the rage building. Jaw clenched, her face burning, she pressed redial on her phone to call for a cab. *To where? I don't even know what to try. There's no one to ask... no one to help.* She pressed *end call* and pocketed the phone.

The elevator jerked to an abrupt stop, and the door rattled open. She stepped out and stalked to the exit.

"Did you find him, honey?" Janice called at Amber's back. Amber ignored her and pushed through the door, strode five paces on inertia alone, then stopped, her shoulders slumping as she tried to calm herself.

That was rude. Just because I got angry doesn't mean I have to pass it on. It's not her fault. In truth, it was no one's fault, really. Men were drawn to her, women dismissed her—or worse, hated her—and for the same reason. Society told them to. Three hundred years ago, it would have deemed her too skinny to be attractive. *Guess I was just born at the wrong time.* She pulled out her phone and hit redial for the cab company. She pressed the phone to her hear, then spun to go back inside and apologize to Janice.

"Are you okay, dear?" Janice stood in the doorway, holding it open with both hands, head tilted in concern. To Amber she looked like a porcelain Mary Poppins—tall, thin, and possessing a regal elegance that was both delicate and dynamic; she knew as surely as she knew her own name they wasted this woman behind a reception desk.

"No, ma'am. I am definitely not okay." A lonely fencepost, Amber stood forlorn and lost, her legs refusing to move in any direction. *I will not cry.* She gathered herself and straightened.

"No need to 'ma'am' me, sweetie." Janice stepped through and the door closed behind her. The woman raced to Amber in three long strides, heels clicking on the stone. She stopped less than two feet away, then reached out and took Amber in her arms. Janice pulled her close in a warm embrace. "You look like you could use a hug." As if she felt Amber's resolve weakening, she stepped back, both hands resting on the young woman's shoulders. "I'm taking an early lunch," she said, giving a gentle squeeze, then checked her watch. "Okay, early brunch." She smirked and turned Amber around. "And you're coming with me."

"But—"

"No buts, dear. We're going to put our heads together and see if we can figure out where Jack is." Janice wrapped one arm around Amber's shoulders as they strolled side-by-side. "I hear things." She shrugged. "People ignore the receptionist."

Amber snorted once and peered into the woman's eyes. "I have a hard time believing anyone ignores you."

Olinda Gutierrez slipped out of the apartment she shared with the father of her two children, tied her favorite scarf over dark hair, adjusted it to cover the ripening bruise on her cheek, and quietly closed the door, silencing the muffled snoring from the bedroom. She hurried down the dingy hallway, its frayed carpeting reaching to snag and trip unsuspecting feet. Most days Olinda shuffled in robotic silence through the lonely hall, lights flickering and buzzing overhead, but today she wore the new sneakers Alvaro had bought for her, and her feet practically bounced over the uneven flooring; she wouldn't even mind the long descent to the street, no matter that *pendejo* apartment manager had promised for over a year to repair the elevator.

Alvaro always bought nice things for her. Usually after a beating, coming home on bended knee with a gift and a promise of *never again*. She always accepted both gift and apology, but never inside—never where he couldn't see. There she dreamed of freedom. If not for her, then for Carlos and Alejandro. Her babies were all she had, though Carlos was no longer a baby. Ten years old and already becoming a man—a man who could no longer stand by while another beat his mother. While fending off Alvaro's meaty hand, Olinda had seen her boy balling his fists, his eyes filled with a slow-burning rage.

He will challenge his father soon... and Alvaro will kill him. For months she had worried, even confessing to the Padre. He had given her a phone number and a name, but had offered nothing else. Not even absolution for the sin of hate for her husband. *It is because he knows I deserve this.* She pushed through the barred door to the stairwell. *My boys do not, and they will be free of him.*

She reached into her bra and pulled out the paper with the address. The woman told her it was a safe place, but no place was truly safe. *Not from a man like Alvaro.* He thought she was working today. *He is as stupid as he is fat.* Olinda smirked, then winced at the pain it brought. She only had to take the boys out of school and bring them to the shelter. There was a small school there, so they wouldn't have to go outside for a while. Every dollar she had secretly saved was in her purse, but it would not hold them for long. Eventually she must return to work.

And he will be waiting.

But her boys would be free.

Olinda passed no one on the stairs this morning and would have found that odd if she hadn't been deep in her own worries. She rounded the last landing and descended the final nine steps to the bottom. Her shoes made no noise, and the silence was unnerving. Above her the sounds of the building filtered through heavy doors and she lifted wide brown eyes, watching the dust float on flickering light.

She didn't notice the presence behind her until it was too late. Before she could scream, he had a knife to her throat, then a knee in the small of her back, forcing her to the floor. On her knees, the keen edge of the blade reflected light from the door's tiny window into her eyes. *Alvaro could never move so fast...*

The man, pale as milk and thin as a reed, moved around her and knelt on the floor, his face so close she smelled the coffee on his breath. He had the wild eyes of an addict, but something else was hidden there. *Shame.*

"I d-do not have much money," she said, and that was the truth. It was still probably more than he needed for a quick fix.

"What I need from you is far more valuable than money," he said, his voice a hum, like the lights over her head. He leaned closer and raised his other hand to her face. In it was a small vial of clear liquid. He popped the top with his thumb, careful to keep the knife against her skin.

"What is th-that?"

He ignored her question and started to move the vial closer, stopped, squinted, and shook his head. "Shut up, Evan!" He muttered to himself for a moment, then his whole body relaxed.

"I will give you what I have," she pleaded, still hoping for a way out.

The man smiled a snake's smile, and he waved the vial around her like a priest with an incense pot. "Don't worry Olinda," he said, his voice like warm chocolate. "It's much easier now."

"What do—?"

That was as far as she got. A veil of heavy black gauze dropped over her eyes, the world fading with each beat of her heart. She felt as if sweat flowed from every pore of her body, her limbs turning to lead.

My boys will never be free...

CHAPTER 8

"GOD DAMN IT!" MARIBEL SLAPPED HER HAND on the desk, rattling even the heavy thirty-four inch monitor. "No way am I getting paid enough for this shit."

Her client had asked for a way to close any back doors into their data systems. The longer she worked on the problem though, the more she wondered. *Who could possibly need a back door into these guys?* The company her contact claimed to work for had to grow some to be considered small fry. She smelled organized crime, but asking questions was not something she did unless the buyer wanted her to dip her toe into illegal waters.

"Doesn't matter either way if I can't deliver." She tossed her pencil aside and ran cramped fingers through tangled hair, then grabbed the coffee mug from the desk and took a sip. "Ugh," she said, wrinkling her nose. She stood, stretched her back, then walked to the sink and emptied the tepid mug. The coffee maker beside the sink was old, but serviceable—the kind of appliance that was indestructible only because it was cheap. Anything more expensive and it would have broken after its first year of use, unless she'd purchased the extended warranty—then it would have lasted until the day after the warranty expired. She set the mug beneath the spout, dropped a new pod into the receiver and pressed brew. It coughed and sputtered, then dribbled black gold.

Maribel leaned back against the counter and crossed her arms. The project had stymied her at every turn, the last failure to tighten their security the most infuriating; she thought *this* time it would work. *At least the failure provided useful data.*

The machine at her side gurgled and hissed, trumpeting completion. She took the cup, poured a heavy dose of sugar, and a spoonful of cream inside and stirred. The computer quacked like a duck, signaling arrival of a message on the secure servers, and Maribel sighed, dropped the spoon into the sink, and pushed away from the counter. "As if I'm not busy enough already," she groused, then shuffled to her chair and set the mug on the desk, tapping out a complex pattern on the keyboard. She picked up her mug and sat back, putting her feet up to wait for her program to reassemble the message.

Maribel sat up at once, spilling her coffee when she saw what popped up on the screen. "Son of a bitch," she breathed, absently wiping the coffee from her clothes. The last time she'd done a job for this guy, she'd pocketed twenty grand, and that was less than a week ago. Her eyes goggled at the offer.

"Well, well, well." She tapped the number the screen with a short fingernail. "What kind of job pays a hundred grand in advance?"

"What makes you think she will answer so soon?" Sohrab sat at the terminal, randomly tapping keys and watching the door in the monitor's reflection. His skills as a field operative had grown rusty, but once learned they had become a part of him, like walking. He had almost backed out when The Shadowman produced the tiny transceiver that now lay deep inside his ear canal. A bio-machine, it had crawled there and attached itself to his eardrum. *I must admit even ten blocks away the reception is clear.*

"She knows my code and that I fulfill my end of any bargain," the Shadowman said inside Sohrab's head. "By now, she has decided the amount I promised is worth the danger the number implies." Sohrab heard keys tapping on the other end, the Shadowman playing the same part as he. "Or she may decline—although I doubt that. Either way, she must respond."

"And for that, she must come to one of these locations?"

"Yes. There are other options, but they are..." There was the squeak of a chair and the keys stopped clacking. "Hold, please."

"Is the target in sight?" Sohrab kept his eyes glued to the door.

"I believe so."

"How can you be sure?"

"I cannot—yet—but the device has mapped every terminal in this establishment, and as soon as she replies I will know which she uses."

He said the word *device* with some reverence, like he spoke of an honored ancestor; Sohrab wouldn't have thought it possible to impart such emotion on so sterile a word, but the Shadowman was capable of surprises. *Usually with a stiletto to the base of the skull.* The day may arrive when the Shadowman would come for him—he wasn't blind to the possibility—Sohrab's only hope was his family was not in the way.

"Once she's marked, do you still plan to follow her back to her home?" Sohrab hadn't been too keen on that part—a professional's home was sacrosanct, and this sort of business should never invade that space.

"I no longer see that as necessary."

"Why not?"

"Because she is standing in front of me."

Maribel stared up into the deep-set eyes of the old man. He was much taller than she imagined, and thin as a rail; the rumpled suit he wore hung from his shoulders as if on a wire hanger. He had a haggard look to him—craggy, yet clean-shaven face, clipped hair a trifle unkempt beneath a tweed fedora, shoulders rounded and stooped as if perpetually ducking doorways—and underneath it all, deep inside his core, radiated a profound sadness, a tender empathy; he was a grandfather who had never known children.

"Nice to finally meet you, Mr. Dunkelmann," she said, extending her hand. He took it, lifted it gently by the fingertips, clicked his heels, and kissed the back.

"You may call me Josef," he said in an Austrian-accented baritone, and released her hand. Too surprised to move, she let it hover there a moment before collecting herself and lowering it to her side.

"It's such a nice day," she said, still staring into his eyes. "Shall we take a walk?"

"Of course." He gestured to the door and offered her his arm. She shifted her pack to the other shoulder and locked arms with him.

"Tell your friend to meet us at Thirty-first and Main in five."

"He is on the way now."

Together they exited the cafe walking arm-in-arm, strolling along the sidewalk like old friends. Maribel felt no danger in his company, but there was no way she would allow them near her home. *My parents' home*, she reminded herself. She realized long ago that the longer she did this kind of work, the more likely it was the danger could end up on their doorstep. *Maybe it's time I get my own place.* A home of her own wouldn't be the worst decision in her life.

"You are worried," Josef said, lips pursed and eyes hooded. "I assure you we mean no harm." When she didn't respond, he arched an eyebrow. "I am interested in how you discovered my deception."

"Sorry, I don't reveal company secrets." She tapped her ear. "I've been listening in ever since I got in range." Her grin broadened when the old man stiffened at that revelation.

His brow furrowed. "That is not possible. The transmissions are encrypted and are not on a commonly used frequency."

"What can I say, big guy... I'm just that good."

"Indeed," he said with obvious respect. "I daresay even you do not know how gifted you are."

That stopped her. *Does he really trust his system is that secure?* True, it was far from child's-play to locate the frequency their radios used—even worse to decrypt the signal—but she had been doing that very thing since she was a kid. What she would never admit was she'd only had time to break the code for his end—the other still a mystery. She had mentally congratulated them both for using separate decryption for each, impressed by the raw processing power of the in-ear transceivers they used. *Cutting edge stuff, that's for sure. To do that in real-time...*

A cream-colored Ford Edge pulled up to the curb, stopped, and the front passenger door opened.

"Our ride," Josef said, waving her to the car.

Maribel narrowed her eyes at the swarthy man inside, then at Josef. "How about we just have a chat in the park across the street," she said, disengaging her arm from Josef's and pointing toward an unoccupied picnic table. The man in the car grinned—not like a predator, but more a jovial uncle—shrugged, and killed the engine. Josef closed the door as the other man exited. They strolled in silence, Josef at her side and his friend behind them, and blithely jaywalked their way to the park.

Sohrab sat next to the Shadowman on one side of the table, watching Maribel on the other. *She is far calmer than I might be.* Most hackers—at least those of the black-hat variety—were skittish to the point of paranoia. A healthy paranoia was necessary in a field operative, but only so long as it did not lead to mental paralysis. *This young woman...* He watched her jugular pulse its slow and steady rhythm, never climbing above eighty beats per minute, and wished he'd known such temperament at her age. He remembered being perpetually angry during that time, a cold fire burning in his belly he could never sate; it was an anger eradicated through months of harsh and bitter training. *And they used that rage to fuel my hunger for Qisās.* Only later did he realize they had taught him to seek legal retribution through extra-legal means. It was that, even more than his government's humiliating defeat, that led him to America.

"So... what is it you want me to do for an insane amount of cash?" She sat as if dropped on the bench, a rumpled pile of clothing pretending to be a woman, hunched over the bag in her lap. She rested her forearms on the table, hands clasped together, not even the strands of her dark hair blowing in the breeze hinting at femininity; she was everyone and no one, and it was a carefully cultivated and practiced image.

"We need you to locate someone," the Shadowman said. Maribel had called him Josef, but Sohrab still couldn't wrap his brain around that name. He would always be the Shadowman.

"For that amount, he must be important."

"Only to us," he said, glancing at Sohrab.

"Yeah, about that... I'm not really up for a threesome." She glared at both men, reserving most of her heat for the Shadowman.

"Unavoidable," he said with a shrug. "I could not be sure at which location you would appear."

"So if I went to the other, tall dark and olive here was supposed to nab me?"

Sohrab grunted. "No, I was to mark you and follow you home."

"Oh... I feel *so* much better now." She tapped the table in a random rhythm as she spoke, and both his ire and admiration grew; it was a standard technique for unnerving an interrogator. *Does she know this, or is it instinctive?* She turned back to the Shadowman. "So... who's the target?"

"I believe you know him. His name is Jack Montgomery, and he has been missing since yesterday."

Maribel looked at him as if tasting spoiled meat. "Have you tried calling the cops? They don't really do the forty-eight-hour thing anymore."

The Shadowman stiffened and raised on eyebrow. "I assure you, Ms. Vargas, if we could have found him through conventional measures, we would not be having this conversation."

"And Jack isn't the type to simply disappear," Sohrab interjected. *Not without a compelling reason, at least.* Those first months after he'd lost both Mason and his brother Bill were filled with a notable silence.

"Why do you need to find him so bad?" She narrowed her eyes. "Maybe he doesn't want to be found."

The Shadowman's lips drew tight, and he glared back at her. "I have no doubt you saw the information he found, even if you do not know its importance." His face softened, but only slightly. "I presume he saw connections within the data, and his pursuit of that may have led him into the hands of... an adversary."

"So the big number for such a small job?" she asked, looking from one to the other.

Neither spoke, but Sohrab inclined his head and arched an eyebrow.

"Ah," she nodded a paranoid's understanding. "Just searching will make me a target."

"Indeed," the Shadowman said with a nod. "But you have demonstrated ingenuity in remaining hidden."

"Yeah, well," she snorted and pointed at his chest. "*You* found me."

"I had an advantage in my ability to contact you." He frowned. "I have no such advantage with Jack."

"And you believe your, um... *adversary* has none with me." She pulled at her bottom lip. "Is that it?"

"Essentially."

"Belief is the ugly step-child of knowing." Her eyes looked far away... vacant. Sohrab knew that look. She was already calculating the angles, weighing them against the money waved in her face. Finally, she nodded once. "All right." She dug a battered laptop from her bag. "Give me everything you've got."

Janice watched the young woman across the table sip her tea. Amber held the tiny cup in one hand, forgoing the handle, the saucer held beneath in the other; she stared with hollow eyes into the black Earl Grey between sips. The longer she sat with Amber, the more convinced she was the young lady had seen far too much in her short life. Those eyes were haunted in ways only someone versed in life's true horrors could understand. She had seen that same look in Jack's from time to time, and every time Janice had inquired, he'd

batted her concerns away with a joke or, more often, a grunt of acknowledgment as he passed her on his way to the elevator.

"You know, I had lunch with Jack yesterday in this very restaurant," Janice said.

Amber stopped, cup poised for another sip, and looked up for the
first time since the waiter had cleared away the plates. "You did?" She
set both cup and saucer on the table and leaned forward. "Did he...
say anything?"

"About?"

"I don't know," Amber said, her face flushing. "What he's
working on, travel plans... his, um, life before he came to work here."

"No, dear. His life before I met him is quite the mystery, and I
guess it amuses him to keep it that way." Janice smiled and leaned
back in her chair. "He spoke of *you* on more than one occasion,
though, and I got the impression you are important to him." She
sighed, inclined her head, took the napkin from her lap, and tossed it
on the table. "He has the same look in his eyes as you, child—like you
share the same terrible story." She crossed her ankles and smoothed
her dress with both hands.

"Oh, Mrs. Watson... you don't know the half of it." Amber let
out a long breath, as if she released a lifetime's worth of secrets and...
Guilt, Janice thought. *There is so much guilt in her heart.*

"Janice."

"Excuse me?"

"You must call me Janice if we're to be friends," Janice said. "And
I expect you very much need a friend right now."

"You don't want to be my friend, Janice," Amber said, running
a hand through her hair, brushing it back. *Poor thing looks on the verge
of tears.* "My friends have a way of... getting hurt." She turned away,
refusing to meet Janice's eyes, and crossed her arms over her chest.

Janice's two daughters had acted the same when caught in a lie,
or they had something important to tell her—something they didn't
want to say. Her own mother did the same whenever she told a young
Janice her father slaughtered a favored lamb or calf. Growing up on a
farm, even one as small as her father's, taught her much about life,
love, and loss. *This woman has lost more than a friend.* It was clear to
Janice now, Amber had lost a piece of her soul, and if she didn't open
up about it soon, the strain may well take the rest of her.

"Why don't you let me worry about myself, dear," Janice said. It
wasn't difficult—she'd been doing the same for others most of her
life. "Fear isn't really my thing." She winked, but Amber still hadn't

met her gaze, so she reached out and patted Amber's arm. Her shoulders stiffened for a moment, then relaxed, and she finally shifted her gaze to Janice. "Jack told me the same about his past... that I would think he was crazy if he shared the whole story."

Amber snorted once, then took a shuddering breath. "I know it's all true, and even I think it's nuts." Her eyes were wild, like those poor lambs just before the bolt pierced their skulls, and a minor tremor rippled down her arms. "I know it's crazy, but it feels just like last time."

"Why don't you tell me about it," Janice said, patting Amber's arm, loosening it, disentangling it from the other. "I promise not to judge."

"Good luck with that." It was as close to a sneer as Janice was likely to see from her. "The story begins over six-thousand years ago," she said, clearly watching Janice for a reaction. When none came, she gave a thin, knowing smile, and nodded, waving her hand in the air. "But we can dispense with most of it for now." She leaned closer, locking eyes with Janice. "Jack's story really begins with the death of his wife and daughter."

CHAPTER 9

JANICE SAT, AS STILL AS OZYMANDIAS, LOOKING as if she would crack and tumble into weathered rubble as easily. *Give her points for not interrupting with questions, at least. Now she's wondering just how crazy I am—or worse—realizing it might all be true.* The woman had sat in stony silence throughout the entirety of Amber's tale, but a spiderweb of fault-lines formed in her foundation early in the telling, and only grown from there. When Amber finished, Janice's eyes were wide and vacant, one hand raised to her lips as if to hold back manic titters. Her eyes darted left and right, either looking for escape from the lunatic before her, or monsters watching from the shadows.

One thing Amber knew with certainty... Janice Watson's life would never be the same.

"I'm... speechless," she said at last, her mouth still obscured by the trembling hand.

"Keep talking," Amber said. "It helps. Trust me." She leaned away, a knot of muscle along her spine screaming from prolonged tension. She had told the story from beginning to end, filling in details with what Jack had told her about his meeting with the Shadow-man—only glossing over the deaths of Mason and Bill. *I doubt she'd still be sitting here if she learned the truth of that.* "Go ahead," she said, waving her hand in the universal *come along* gesture. "You've got questions. I'll answer what I can."

Janice moved her hand away from her mouth and brushed a stray strand of hair from her face and back over her ear where it belonged. "So... those *things*... are they still inside you?"

As a first question, it was definitely not what Amber expected, and told her two things: one, Janice might actually believe her, and two, she understood many of Amber's actions may have been programmed—out of her control. *Maybe I should have told her about Mason and Bill.*

"I believe they are, but I haven't tested for them," she said after a long pause. "I'm not really sure I want to know."

"But the... the... zz—"

"Zzkritti."

"Yes. They could take them out, correct?"

Amber shook her head. "I don't know that either, but I *do* know I'd rather not find out." Now it was her turn to shiver. Part of Dieter's programming had been a clear image of their true form, and the nightmares from *that* had taken almost as much time to fade as Mason's murder.

"Hmm..." Janice pursed her lips and drummed impeccably manicured nails on the tabletop. In the time it had taken Amber to tell her story, the restaurant had cleared the usual lunch crowd, and while the staff reset for dinner, none came within earshot of their conversation. In DC, where information was currency, such behavior was unusual. Janice caught her looking around and grinned. "One of the things I like about this place is their professionalism, dear," she said. "No worries—they will not come unless called."

"It's more than that, isn't it?"

"What do you mean?" Janice had a sly look in her eyes, as if she and Amber already shared a secret.

"I mean they know you here. You have some clout with the owner, or at the very least, the manager."

Janice held a straight face for perhaps two seconds, then laughed, covering her mouth as quick as a snake. "Jack never did catch on to that."

At the mention of Jack's name, Amber's face fell, all mirth drained in an instant. The humor in Janice's eyes shifted as quickly to concern, and she placed her hand over Amber's.

"We'll find him, dear."

"But *how?*"

"Any intractable problem can be solved by throwing enough money at it." She arched an eyebrow. "Besides, I can get what you couldn't from the lazy biddy guarding Jack's office."

She had no clue what the woman meant about money—Amber certainly had none to throw around—but she was grateful Janice was there to help with the secretary. She stood at once, offering Janice her hand.

"Let's get to it, then."

Maribel closed the lid on her laptop, sighed, and shook her head. The wretched thing's battery was two minutes from giving up the ghost, forcing her to stop.

"Nothin'," she said, patting the lid. Both men stared at her with frowns that said they expected more. "I've hacked into a dozen law enforcement systems, even tried to track him with traffic light cameras..." she held her palms out and open, "nothin'." Her face puckered, and she scratched the side of her nose. "The camera thing probably would have worked if more than half of them were operational in this stinkin' town." She tucked the laptop back in her bag, then leaned on the table with both elbows. "The best I could do was track him to Georgetown," she said, then shrugged. "After that?"

"Nothing," Josef finished for her. "Yes, Ms. Vargas... we understand."

"We already know he visited the campus," Sohrab said, pulling at his beard. The man didn't even look at her as he spoke, his eyes focused somewhere else. "It is where he went after that concerns us."

Maribel snorted. "You don't think I know that, Mr.?" Sohrab turned to her, his face devoid of emotion of any kind; an owl considering a mouse. She shivered inside, her nerves rattled under that cold stare. "I'm telling you, it's like he disappeared down a manhole."

"Well, he has literally done that once before," Sohrab said, the corners of his mouth curling. "Or, more accurately, up a manhole."

Glad to see a stone killer can still find humor. She realized from the first what this man was... at least in a former life. Josef, she had also pegged with his first communication—he was a known quantity—but Sohrab was more complicated. *He wouldn't kill for pleasure, nor on the order of a superior. To protect or defend, though... that was a different matter.* She looked into his eyes, searching for whatever motivation lay behind. *What would you fight and kill for, I wonder?* His eyes drifted back to the park, away from her penetrating gaze.

"I'm not beaten yet, guys," she said, pulling at her bottom lip. *They're not gonna pay me unless I deliver, but it's like every mention of the man has been scrubbed clean.* If she didn't give them something soon, she felt they'd walk. "Let me go home—no following—and with time I can access every surveillance camera in every building in town."

"How much time?" Josef asked, his face thrust forward, cold calculation hiding behind narrowed eyes.

"Two, three days at most," she said.

"Three days?" Sohrab exploded. "We do not have three days!"

"I said two or—"

"Call your master." Sohrab gripped the other man's shoulder, demanding his attention. "What was his name? Jeff?" He had a manic energy that fairly crackled. "Or use your device. Surely—"

"Jeff is... indisposed for the near term," he said, the calm eye of the storm of emotions flowing from Sohrab. "And the device only works where there is information to find." He peeled Sohrab's hand from his shoulder with less effort than peeling a banana.

"Uh, guys... what device?" Maribel asked, but they either ignored her or didn't hear.

"I entered the data stream as soon as I discovered Jack was missing, but found nothing," Josef said, still holding Sohrab's hand. "I had hoped Ms. Vargas knew of an approach I may have missed."

Entered the data stream? What the hell does he mean by that? And who the hell is Jeff? The questions flipped through her mind like cards on a Rolodex, and she ignored the rest of their conversation while her mind worked in overdrive. She had always been good at focusing on a problem, blocking out everything as she untangled the central knot. The one real piece of information was that Jack was last seen at Georgetown—they had even provided a window of time. If he had taken the subway to or from the campus, her search of the video during that window would surely have shown him either coming or going—all those cameras worked.

But there had been nothing. Which meant—

"How did he get there?" she mumbled to herself, still pulling on her lip.

"Excuse me?" Josef's face had drawn in on itself.

"Jack," Maribel said. "How did he get to Georgetown?"

"I assume the sub—"

"Nope. Ruled that out first."

"A cab?"

"No," Sohrab said, his voice booming over them both. "He only calls me for rides." He faced Maribel. "I drive for Uber." His brow knotted, each side fighting the other for dominance of the center, then his cheeks glowed cherry red and he slapped his forehead. "And I ignored his calls."

"Can you find his driver?" Josef asked Maribel.

"Easily," she beamed. "But the laptop is toast until I get to an outlet."

Sohrab stood at once and grabbed her by the hand. "Come," he said, and dragged her from the bench and out of the park.

"I didn't expect to be back here so soon." Amber stood on the corner and craned her neck looking up at the third-floor windows. "Do you really think she'll tell us anything?"

"Us?" Janice said with an innocent grin, then shook her head. "No, but me she'll talk to." She locked arms with Amber and led her to the door. "She thinks I have some sort of influence with her boss."

"My guess is she would be right." She had taken an instant liking to Janice, but there was more to it than simply a pleasant demeanor. *The woman is a force. Not wild and uncontrollable like a storm, but more a thoroughbred racehorse.* "Even if she's wrong, I bet you can play the part, anyway."

"I can, and I will." Together, they entered the building, but once inside Janice released Amber's arm and faced her. "I should go alone," she said, a stern expression on her face. "From what you told me, she's already formed an opinion of you, and it's not kind."

"That's an understatement." Amber raised an eyebrow. "I look forward to straightening her out someday."

"Hmm... of course, dear." Janice gave her a grandmotherly grin. "For now, why don't you wait here at my desk." She gestured toward the opening in the semi-circular well. "Feel free to surf the web on my computer... or whatever they're calling it now." She watched Amber walk around and step up on the platform. "I won't be long, dear." She spun at the ding of an arriving elevator, as if it came just for her, waited for the occupant to exit, and stepped inside. The doors closed, leaving Amber alone in the Foyer.

For the first few minutes, Amber did as Janice suggested, opening a browser window and scanning the latest headlines. There seemed no shortage of unhappy news in the world: here the latest from the Summer Olympics, there Russia launches airstrikes into Syria, and closer to home, an inmate at the local jail escapes. The one that caught her eye was the earthquake in central Italy.

Earthquakes are right up the Zzkritti's alley. She frowned at the screen. *I wonder if that one was on the list Jack had...*

She'd spent the past year wondering if every major event in the world were somehow tied to the aliens. There was no way to know for sure but that didn't stop her from imagining the worst. *Daddy said no one was ever taken by surprise by expecting the worst.* She snorted and smirked. "Daddy was always a 'glass is half-empty' kind of guy."

There was no point in obsessing over headlines—events would unfold as they were meant to; all that mattered was the here and now, and right now that was Jack. *The Shadowman said he may have encountered an adversary—but whose? An enemy of Jack's or the Zzkritti.* Of the former she knew only one, and he was dead. She didn't want to consider the latter. Anyone—or any*thing*—willing to take on the Zzkritti was too dangerous for Jack to handle.

"Where are you?" she breathed.

∞

Sohrab dragged Maribel into the nearest Starbucks, wrenching her wrist as he all but threw her into the padded leather chair.

"Plug your computer in and get started," he barked, then, his urgency seeming to melt away, gave her a half smile. "I'll get the coffee. What is your preference?"

My preference is that you shouldn't manhandle me, she thought, rubbing her sore wrist. She glared at him for a good five seconds before digging into her bag for the laptop and charger. "This isn't coffee," she said, unwrapping the cord and stretching behind in search of an outlet. "Let's stick with tea for now. Earl Grey, please. Hot and sweet."

He gave her an odd frown, then strode to the counter. She noticed he hadn't waited for Josef, either while he dragged her across the street, or while making his order. She glanced to the door when the tall man strode inside, his measured pace never changing—from their first walk to the park, to the mad dash here, he never hurried—and like a geriatric Michael Myers, he never fell far behind. While the computer booted, she looked around for a good source. There were at least three people on laptops of their own, but they were likely using Starbuck's gateway, and were not usable for her purposes. Maribel wanted to leave no footprint, even something as innocuous as dipping into the Uber server for a quick scan of their database. When her screen finally displayed her desktop, she launched her scanner, and three IP addresses popped up at once—one was the store's gateway, but the other two were from iPhones.

"Hell yeah," she muttered, then with four keystrokes, invaded one of the two and took over their data connection. In seconds she was online and untraceable. Before Sohrab had returned with her tea, she was inside. She held out her hand, still engrossed in the data

110

filling her screen, and allowed him to place it there while she continued to type with the other. She barely registered the movement when Josef sat the other chair across from her. "I'm in," she said, looking up at Sohrab, the man still towering over her. "What do you want to know?"

"Did Jack take an Uber yesterday, and where was he dropped off."

"That's easy," she said, sneering, then shredded the company's security on her stroll through their data. There were several Jack Montgomery's across the country, but only two in the DC area. "There are two to pick from," she said, not looking up. "But I think the one we're looking for is this guy." She angled the laptop so he could see. He leaned over, tapped the name on the screen as if waking a sleeping child.

"That is him."

Maribel spun the laptop back to her and drilled down through the data. "It looks like they picked him up at three forty-five at Georgetown and dropped off around four at... hmm."

"What?"

She smirked. "Jack's a hell of a tipper."

"Just tell me where the driver left him," he growled low and dangerous.

"Don't get your panties in a wad, big guy. Says here they left him outside the DC detention center." She looked up, frowning. "Any idea why he'd go there?"

"No," he said, stroking his beard. "Was he picked up again after?"

"Um... nope." She scrolled through pickups. "Nothing from the detention center, nor from a four-block radius for the rest of the night." She scrunched her face, her eyebrows meeting in the center. "Is it possible he gave himself up for some crime or something?"

"No," he said without appearing to even consider it. "They would still have processed him through a police station first. Prisoners are always delivered by police or federal marshals."

"You say that as if you are intimate with the details." Rather than get a rise out of him, he ignored her and shifted to Josef.

"Do you have people there? A reason for him to stay?"

"We have no operatives at that location. I would have been informed if we had. And as for 'turning himself in', I think we both know Mr. Montgomery has committed no crime."

"What are you guys talking about?" Maribel said. Both faced her but did not answer. She got the impression it was better if she didn't know, but her curiosity was kindled, and she'd always had problems ignoring a good mystery.

Sohrab nodded to Josef. "Then that is where we must begin."

"Indeed. The evidence suggests he may still be there."

"Don't bet on it," Maribel said, snorting derision. She blanched at the exasperation on their faces. "I mean he's either a prisoner—which you claim is unlikely—or someone has taken him." They stared at her as if she'd grown another head. "You know... *away.*"

Sohrab opened his mouth, but Josef spoke first with deadly calm. "Your logic is sound. Either way, that is where we must begin our search."

"Let me pack up and—"

"You are not coming," Sohrab said, slicing the air with his hand. It was the same motion her father used when refusing permission to go out with her friends.

Maribel snorted and unplugged her laptop. "Like hell I'm not." She shoved everything back in her bag and stood. "If he's still there, he may be in the system. If not, someone has spirited him away and there should be a record of comings and goings regardless of the reason." She grinned up at Sohrab. "In any event, you'll need me to get that information."

Both men gave the other a knowing glance, a twinkle of amusement in Josef's eyes. It was apparent neither believed she was useful beyond this point, but only Sohrab seemed to care if she joined them.

"Your services are no longer required," Josef said.

"But—"

"But... I believe you may still be of use. You may accompany us for now, but you assume all responsibility for any injuries you may incur."

Injuries! What the fuck? It really didn't matter, but curiosity drove her now, and her father warned her it would get her into trouble one day.

"Fine." She tossed her untouched tea into the trash. Josef led the way out, and she looked up into Sohrab's face as he waved her ahead. "Uber's seriously shorting you on your pay, you know," she said, wiping that superior look off his face. "I can fix that for you."

Janice loomed over Grace Ellison; a dominance tactic she'd learned long ago that worked well on bullies. And Grace was a bully, known for her merciless harassment of new staff—especially the younger and more attractive temps hired to do the work she always seemed too busy to perform. *If the woman's self-esteem weren't so low, she might notice attractiveness wasn't a competition.* Janice did her best to hide a smirk. *But then what excuse would she have for being so unpleasant?*

"I told you already." Grace leaned back in her seat and sipped hot coffee in a vain attempt to appear unintimidated. "Mr. Montgomery had no appointments on his calendar for yesterday afternoon." She took another sip from the *World's Greatest Secretary* mug that always seemed perpetually full. *I'd bet my last dollar she bought that for herself,* Janice mused, one corner of her mouth curling upward. "He left sometime after noon and never returned. I assumed he went home."

"Jack never leaves that early," Janice said, her mouth now turned down. "And especially without his laptop."

"What—"

"I can see it through the window on his desk, Grace," Janice said, pointing. Grace swiveled her chair and peered through the glass. "If that's still here, he was coming back."

"Huh..." Grace grunted, set the mug on her desk, and stood. She furrowed her brow, stepped to the door, unlocked it, and slipped inside. Janice followed, but Grace barred her with one hand. "I can't let you in here without Mr. Montgomery." She closed the door in Janice's face.

"One good dominance game deserves another," Janice muttered, and stalked back to the desk. She sat on the edge near the mug and crossed her arms. The main office space was surprisingly empty, with only a few secretaries—both male and female—bustling about on the opposite end of the floor. *Stop looking for the unusual. The building always empties early on Fridays. It doesn't take an alien invasion for that.* She still didn't know what to make of Amber's story, but was convinced the woman wasn't outright lying. *And if she's not lying, she's either crazy or telling the truth.* Janice shuddered at the thought, the room suddenly a few degrees colder. The door to Jack's office swung inward, and Grace stepped out.

"You're right," she said, a rare admission for her. "It looks like he planned to return." Her face closed in on itself, her eyes focused beyond Janice, and stepped toward her desk without closing the door behind her. "I'll inform security." She pulled out her chair and sat, still not looking up. "They can decide what to do from there."

Always the bare minimum with you, isn't it? Janice narrowed her eyes at the door, still ajar and unlocked, then set both hands at her sides on the desk. "Tell you what..." she began, pushed away from the desk, and in the same smooth motion brushed the *World's Greatest Secretary* mug of coffee into Grace's lap. Grace leapt to her feet, moving faster than Janice thought possible, the mug tumbling to the carpet as she wiped at her skirt.

"What the hell?"

"Oh, dear. I am so sorry." Janice grabbed some papers from the desk and wiped at the liquid soaking into the heavy tweed cloth. "I'm such a clumsy goof."

"Stop, stop!" Grace snatched the papers from her hand. "Those are the budget reports," she said, laying them on the desk and spreading them out. "Now I'll have to do them over."

"Let me get some towels from—"

"You've done enough," Grace snapped. "I'll go wash up—see if I can clean this off before it stains." She took a few steps away, then rounded. "Please be gone before I return."

"Of course," Janice said, stifling a snicker. "And again, I'm—"

"*So* sorry. Yeah, I got it." Grace spun and stormed off. When she was out of sight, Janice smirked and raced through the open door to Jack's office.

She knew she had little time—Grace may take a while cleaning up, but surely someone would pass by and see Janice in a place she didn't belong. The overhead light was off, but enough light streamed through the window to see. She stepped behind the desk and looked at the open laptop, hesitated, then touched the trackpad. The screen woke, but only offered the standard log-in box. She considered snatching it up and taking it with her, but so far she was only in an office without permission—taking the laptop crossed the line into felony theft.

"I don't have to go that far," she muttered. "Not yet." There were several loose sheets of paper on the desktop, but all were official memos or reports; none contained information remotely related to a meeting. *One may have prompted a meeting, but...* She slid a stack of papers aside near the laptop and uncovered a standard yellow legal pad. The top page was blank, but over half had been torn away. The wastebasket under the desk was devoid of yellow paper, so she assumed he'd taken them with him or thrown them away somewhere else. Impressions from covered the page below the tear.

"Okay, Ellery Queen, let's see if this really works," she muttered, then grabbed a sharpened pencil from the nearby holder and made a rubbing with the soft lead. Words and numbers appeared in negative relief, and two lines caught her eye at once.

"Darryl Dominguez," she said brow furrowing. "I've heard that name somewhere..." The second line brought it into focus. "Central Detention Facility..." Her hand flew to her mouth, covering a gasp. "Darryl Dominguez!"

Amber tapped her foot and checked her watch, then the Uber app on her phone for the fifth time. *Still five minutes out*, she fumed. *Same as the last time I checked. Is this guy driving a Segway?*

"Calm down, dear," Janice said. "It's only been a few minutes."

Amber checked the street, first one direction, then the other. "We could have walked there by now." She paced, holding the rubbing Janice had brought downstairs, and doing her best to decipher everything there. Some impressions were light and unreadable, but others were clearer. Among those was the name Darryl Dominguez, and the words *Central Detention Facility*. She had thought little of either, but Janice had been practically apoplectic when she presented the page to Amber. "Why are you so sure he went there?"

"You weren't here last year, so you may be forgiven your ignorance, but Mr. Dominguez is quite the infamous celebrity." Janice's face grew dark, a hot anger burning behind her eyes. "The way he murdered that family..." She shook her head. "Monstrous."

"I don't understand why Jack would visit a murderer," Amber said.

"That's just it... he wouldn't." Janice grasped Amber's arm as she passed, forcing her to stop her obsessive pacing. "Don't you see? It *must* have something to do with why he's missing."

"You're grasping, Janice."

Janice tilted her head and shrugged. "Maybe," she said, then gave a lopsided grin. "Do you have any better ideas?"

Amber frowned. "No, in fact, I don't."

Janice gently turned her and pointed to an ice-blue Civic Hybrid jerking to a stop at the curb. "Our ride."

The tinted window slid down, and a young woman leaned across the passenger seat. "Amber Riley?" she asked, chewing a thick wad of gum.

"Yes," Janice said. "And one." She pushed Amber to the door and leaned down. "We're going—"

"Central Detention Facility," the driver said, then tapped her phone. "It's all right here." She winked and snapped her gum. "Hop in."

Amber opened the rear door and climbed in, Janice following. The seating wasn't cramped, but both she and Janice had long legs—it took them a moment to sort out the logistics.

The driver grinned. "This car doesn't move until you're both buckled up."

"Of course," Amber said, and pulled the shoulder harness across. The instant she latched the mechanism the car lurched forward, leaping from a standing start to a pert thirty miles per hour like she drove an Indy car. Amber's head bounced against the headrest, and she checked to see if Janice was okay. Janice just grinned and rolled her eyes. "No need to hurry," Amber said, holding her need for speed at bay.

"Sorry. I've had a few narrow misses lately, and... well..." She shrugged and popped her gum several times in rapid succession. "Can't blame a girl for getting antsy."

"No, dear, I guess we can't," Janice said, winking at Amber.

"You know... this is the second trip in two days I've made to the jail." She turned her head toward Amber and grinned. "Is there a party or something?" She kept her head pointed in the wrong direction far too long for Amber's taste, chewing her gum and grinning like she hadn't a care in the world. *At her age she probably doesn't.* As Amber's discomfort faded, the import of what the young woman said hit her like ice water.

"You drove someone there yesterday?"

"Sure," she said, finally facing the road. "Guy named Jack Montgomery." She spun the wheel at the intersection, completely ignoring the state of the traffic light. Amber could only press hard on her imaginary brake and choke the life out of the door handle. "You don't forget a dude who leaves a fifty-dollar tip on a three-mile ride." She made another turn. "My name's Bethany, by the way... but everyone just calls me Beth." Amber half expected her to turn all the way around and try to shake hands.

"You drove Jack there yesterday," Amber said, more a statement than a question, then braced herself as Beth swerved, zipping in between two cars as she changed lanes.

"You know him?" This time she did turn, deep lines forming on her forehead.

Amber ignored the question. "Did you wait for him? Drive him somewhere else?"

Beth spun back in time to avoid hitting a pedestrian, then slammed on her brakes to stop at the light. "Nope. Just dropped him off about, oh, four o'clock, and left for another call." She pursed her lips, eyebrows meeting in the middle. "Last I saw of him, he was walking inside."

Amber didn't want to say more. *Too many people have been touched by this.*

"That's the last *anyone* saw of him, dear," Janice said.

Just great, Amber thought, glaring at her new friend. She knew where this was going even before the conversation played out, and her heart sank.

"What do you mean?" There was genuine concern in Beth's voice.

"No one's heard from him since you dropped him off," Janice said. "He hasn't been to work, or even answered a phone." She glanced at Amber. "He didn't go home, either, did he?"

"Not according to, um... his friends," she said in clipped tones. *Please, Janice... just shut up. Take the hint already.*

"Maybe he doesn't want to be found." Beth gripped the wheel in both hands and hunched closer. "Maybe he's some kind of spy. He had that look, you know. Like he knows stuff. Stuff he shouldn't talk about." The ever-increasing speed of the little car matched her rapid-fire delivery, the motor whining to keep up. She turned again to Amber. "Do you think he's in trouble?"

"It's too soon to—"

"I bet he is!" she said, her eyes widening. "You've got the same look, you know. Like you know stuff you can't talk about. Just not where he is or how to find him." She glanced at the road, then hit her blinker, pulling up to the curb. "Hey, I could help!"

"No!" both women screeched. Amber looked at Janice, her heart pounding in her throat, and mouthed the word *no*. "It's just that, well... we don't know anything right now. It may only be a misunderstanding."

"Sure," Beth said. "Of course." The girl seemed to calm, but she turned completely around in her seat, straining against the shoulder harness, and hooked a thumb over her shoulder at the sidewalk. "But then why did those three start heading this way as soon as the guy with the beard looked in our car?"

Amber finally noticed Sohrab, Thirteen, and a woman she'd never met walking their way. Sohrab shaded his eyes as he bent to peer inside.

Janice noticed as well, then pointed a thin finger at Thirteen. "Is that...?"

"Yes, it is." She watched Janice's eyes widen, but other than that, there was no fear. "Stay in the car while I chat with an old friend."

"I'll do no such thing, young lady."

Beth sheepishly raised her hand. "I will."

"No," Amber said. "You can leave us here."

Beth looked from Sohrab, now standing beside Amber's door, arms crossed over his chest, to Amber, then to Janice. "Nah," she said, drawing the word out and killing the engine. "I think I'll hang here in case you need me."

God damn it, Amber thought. *Just God damn it all to hell.*

CHAPTER 10

SOHRAB TAPPED ON THE GLASS, AND THE door swung open and Amber unfolded from the back seat. She looked haggard in a way that suggested more than a sleepless night, and his heart sank at the sight of her, then skipped a beat entirely when the other passenger door opened and a much older woman stepped out. The newcomer brushed strands of hair from her face in a losing battle with the wind, all the while staring at the Shadowman.

"Why are you here?" Amber stood, chin jutting forward in raw defiance.

"The same as you, I imagine. Jack's trail seems to have stopped right here."

"I thought I was clear." He leaned close, more heat in his voice than intended. "The Shadowman and I will find Jack. You were to wait until called."

Amber narrowed her eyes at him. "I don't do waiting very well." She nodded to the woman beside the Shadowman. "I see you picked up a friend."

Sohrab inclined his head toward her companion. "As have you." His eyes were hard, but there was no heat there. "You should have left her out of this."

Amber chuckled and stage-whispered, "*You* tell her. I think you'll find leaving her behind more difficult than it sounds."

Sohrab relaxed and cast a glance toward Maribel. "I wager mine is worse than yours." They stood that way, staring at one another for three seconds, then both burst out laughing. The tension broken, Sohrab's ire faded, and he gestured toward the Shadowman. "It seems we have reinforcements." The Shadowman merely smiled his annoyingly enigmatic smile. *It was always thus with him. Even in*

Iraq. There, the man's gloomy reticence hid another agenda, and one that had gotten Sohrab's men killed. *What is your agenda now? How many must die this time to protect your masters?* Sohrab's only goal now was to limit that number.

He appraised the building and mentally compiled a list of visible points of egress. *There will be others in back.* Service entrances, loading docks, employee checkpoints—weaknesses cataloged and prioritized before he'd even chosen a course of action.

He frowned at Amber and scratched his beard. "We cannot all go inside."

"Why?"

"Too many in the party will spook the officials—especially if they're responsible for whatever happened to Jack."

"I hate to break it to you, big guy, but men who look like you aren't exactly welcome in government buildings these days." She ducked her chin in shame. "Not since a fair fraction of this country slid into insanity."

Sohrab considered her words. That was something he should have thought of; he was far closer to it than Amber.

"Janice, you and Sohrab hang back and get to know one another," she said over her shoulder. "Maybe he can convince you to let Beth drive you home."

"Not a chance in hell," Janice said, eyes twinkling. "And not just because Beth is a terrible driver."

Amber watched Janice for a while, her whole face a frown, then shook it off and angled back to Sohrab. "I'm going to play the part of, um... assistant to Silent Bob the attorney over there." She leveled her gaze at the Shadowman. "You can do that, right?" He nodded in the affirmative. "And the mouse can be his secretary, or stenographer, or whatever."

"Hey!" Maribel said, softer than she meant. He ignored her, as did Amber.

"What use is she that I am not?"

"I don't think you brought her along to bake a cake," Amber said. "If she's with you two, she's got some skills—probably ones we'll need inside."

Sohrab couldn't find fault with her logic, though relegating him to the sideline was a little much for his ego. He certainly was not used to taking orders from women. *Well... women who aren't my wife.*

"What do you expect to find inside?"

"Jack, I hope."

"And if he is not there?"

"Oh," she said, looking past him to the Shadowman, "I'm sure you can get someone to tell us where he is."

"Did you have an inmate in mind, or should I choose one from their records?" Thirteen stood next to Amber, his voice a rumbling whisper. Other than he and the woman who introduced herself as Maribel, they were alone in the entry. A guard sat in his booth at the far end, but no one else was close enough to hear. Amber frowned at his question and did her best to appear unconcerned with her surroundings.

"Darryl Dominguez." She watched him zone out for a second, knowing he was communing with the device.

"Ah, the man who murdered who four people a year ago," he said, then inclined his head. "He was captured only recently." He leaned closer to Amber. "A shame the authorities could not have called me."

"Hey... a joke," Maribel said, one end of her mouth curling up. "I didn't know you could do that."

Thirteen ignored her. "I do not understand why Jack..." He got that faraway look again, then his eyes widened. "Of course. The father."

Amber hadn't a clue what he was talking about, nor did she care. "Make sure you're his new lawyer. The guard's looking at us funny... we should probably stop standing around looking guilty of something."

"Indeed," Thirteen said, then led their small troupe to the man behind the bulletproof glass.

Maribel fell in beside Amber. She pursed her lips, glancing toward her. "What did you mean 'make sure you're his new lawyer'?"

"Just watch and listen. I'll explain later if you need to know." *And I really hope you never do.* There were already too many people involved. She had wanted to send Sohrab home to his wife and kids, but that was a lost cause. She still held out hope this was nothing but Jack being Jack. *You know better than that, though, don't you? Thirteen is here, and Sohrab is worried; there's no better evidence things have gone seriously sideways.*

Maribel only grunted but asked no more questions. Thirteen reached the desk and tapped on the window, and the now annoyed guard looked up from whatever had so engrossed him a moment before.

"What's your business?" The guard's voice was as rough as his exterior, yet still professional somehow. He looked no more than thirty, but his gut was far past middle-age; it spread over his tight belt like someone had set a water-balloon on a fencepost. His wiry hair shorn high and tight, he looked like the before picture of an army recruitment poster, though there wasn't a branch of any service that would take him given the thickness of the glasses he wore.

"My associates and I are here to see my client," Thirteen said in a voice Amber could tell was accustomed to lying.

"Name, social security, or spin?" The guard waited with one hand poised over a keyboard.

"Darryl Dominguez."

The guard's mouth drew tight, and he tapped at the keyboard, then he pursed his lips and bent closer to the screen. "His visiting time is all used up this week," he said, still looking at the screen and cocking an eyebrow. "Come back Monday." The guard looked up, his face placid and unemotional. "Good day," he said, then went back to studying a magazine.

Amber covered a grin as Thirteen zoned out again for exactly two seconds. He stepped closer to the glass and pointed at the screen. "I have an appointment to speak with my client," he said, his inflection as flat as the guard's. "Please check again."

The guard rolled his eyes, sighed, and peered at the screen. His whole face frowned as he looked again at the data. "Huh," he said, absently tapping the screen, a rhythmic flashing reflecting from his glasses. "Looks like I was wrong." He reached across his desk, pressed a big red button, a loud buzzer sounded, and the locking mechanism on a door to their left clacked like someone racked a shotgun.

"Thank you," Thirteen said, and tipped his hat. "Come along," he called to Amber and Maribel.

"Just a second, please," a booming, gruff voice called. The owner of that voice chugged toward them huffing and puffing, a train jumping its tracks as it slid downhill. She walked as if one leg was shorter than the other, and she reminded Amber of an old and nearly blind bulldog she had as a child. "Leon," she called to the guard in the cage. "Lock that door, and open number three." Her request was followed by two more shotguns racking, the sound reverberating off the hard walls around them.

Thirteen narrowed his eyes at the newcomer. "I'm sorry, but I have an ap—"

"So I heard," the woman said, pulling to a stop. Her eyes widened a little, as if recognizing a long-lost relative. "Mr. Dominguez is currently unavailable. There's a... waiting room right this way," she said, leading him away from the reception area. "Once you get settled in, I'll come get you when he's ready."

I've got a bad feeling about this Chewy, Amber thought hard at Thirteen. *I hope you can read minds.*

"Where is he? Why can I not see him now?"

"There was an accident, and he's getting stitched up in the infirmary," she said, her face beaming. "Nothing serious." She took two waddling steps toward the door. "Please... come." She waved them along as if leading a tour. Amber frowned but complied. *I bet that's not far from the truth.*

They followed the stout Pied Piper, Thirteen ahead, Amber and Maribel shuffling behind. When he reached the door, he pulled up short, and Amber ran straight into his back. Even as tall as he was, she was sure the man couldn't have weighed over one-eighty, but he didn't move so much as a millimeter when she hit him.

He patted his coat pockets a few times, then turned to Maribel. "I'm sorry," he said. "Do you have my digital recorder?"

She looked at him with her face scrunched up and tilted her head. "Um... no?"

"Would you be so kind as to fetch it from the car?" he said, his voice sweet as molasses. He swung back to the matronly guard. "You'll bring her to us when she returns?"

"Oh... of course, sir," she oozed. "Hey Leon, give me a call when she comes back," she yelled to the guard. He gave a tight grin and waved.

Thirteen followed the woman through the doorway, but Amber held back. She looked at Maribel, attempting to convey urgency with her eyes. Maribel raised both eyebrows and shrugged. *Great,* Amber thought. *She doesn't get it, or has no clue what to do. Either way... we're fucked.* She snorted as she spun to follow Thirteen. He waited there patiently holding the door for her. *Well, maybe not him. Pretty sure he could wipe out this place.* She gave one last glance toward Maribel, now hurrying from the building as if chased.

Maribel hustled down the steps without looking back. *Something's hinkey with that woman.* The bag with her laptop slapped against her hip with each jostling step, and she nearly broke out into a flat run when she reached the bottom. *Don't run, don't run. I don't even know there's anything to panic about.* But something gnawed at the base of her brain like a horde of leaf-cutter ants, scraping bits of resolve and calm, chewing them up and passing them down the line. Her spine itched, as if her back drew every pair of eyes in the building.

The little Civic was still parked at the curb, a rhythmic thumping vibrating the windows. She didn't recognize the song, and it didn't get better the closer she got. Maribel yanked the handle on the back passenger door, threw it open, and climbed in before anyone had a chance to complain. She pulled her laptop from the bag, along with the travel charger, and tossed the business end to the driver.

"Plug this in, will ya?" She didn't wait for a response, opening the laptop and connecting the power cord. Neither of the two women spoke, too startled by her sudden arrival. She blocked everything out—including the horrid music—and quickly nabbed the internet connection from the driver's cell. Once connected, she killed the music, then dove straight for the county records database.

Janice shook off her surprise. "Where is Amber?"

Maribel ignored her. Getting past the so-called security was a breeze, but the whole database was massively disorganized. *Idiots need a new database designer—like twenty years ago.* They built the whole thing atop a creaky server system fully two decades out of date. *That's the government for you. Even the IR-fucking-S needs a complete overhaul.* She tried more than a dozen search terms before zeroing in on her quarry.

"There you are you little bastard," she said with a feral growl, punching the enter key hard enough to sound like a real keyboard. The file opened, and for once she was impressed. The entire set of blueprints for the detention facility had been dutifully digitized and packed inside a standard PDF file. She felt eyes on her and looked up, then into the front seat. "Hey... where's the big guy?"

"He left right before you came out," the Beth said with a shrug. "He said he was going to the garage to get his car. Said he had a bad feeling or something. I thought he might be sick, but he didn't look sick, just kinda—"

"Okay," Maribel said, her palm in the air to stem the avalanche of words. "I get it." She pursed her lips and furrowed her brow. "Why are you still here?"

Beth opened her mouth, but Janice beat her to the punch. "That's my doing," she said. "I had a bit of a bad feeling about this, too, so I've hired her for the rest of the day."

That can't be cheap, Maribel thought, though that didn't really answer her question. "Well, it seems you and Sohrab have a lot in common," she said, turning back to the blueprints. She traced a path on the screen with her finger. "Now that's just odd," she mumbled.

"What's that?" Beth said, leaning toward the laptop.

"Can't find a room, waiting or otherwise, on that side." She drew her finger back and forth over the area where she last saw Amber and Josef. "There's not even a door number three." She checked the date on the bottom. "And they updated these last year."

"What are you talking about?" Janice said, worry creeping into her voice.

Maribel looked at her for the first time. She noted the worry wasn't limited to just her voice—it had made it all the way to her eyes. "They went through a door that's not on these plans to a room that doesn't exist."

"What's on that side, then?"

"A whole lot of inmates in large cells." She checked the reports that accompanied the plans. "From what I can tell, that's the segregated unit."

"Like, by race and stuff?" Beth said, her face scrunched.

"No," Maribel said, shaking her head at the stupidity. "That's where they keep the rapists and pedophiles so the general population doesn't beat them to death." She tapped on the keyboard, then used the track pad to zoom in. There were several rooms, but it was still essentially a long hallway with guards at each end. *Plus the guard at the main entrance.*

"Are they in dang—"

"Shush," Maribel hissed. "I'm thinking." *If they're in trouble, and if they escape, and if Josef is as capable as I think he is, and if they're lucky...* It was too many ifs for her taste, but if the first case was true, then the others must be, or they'd probably go the way of Jack. She was already in deeper than she ever planned. *In for a penny, I guess.* She locked eyes with Beth. "Take us to E Street. There's a service entrance on that side."

"Why would we do that? The scarecrow said to wait here."

"I don't think they're coming back this way," she said, lowering her head back to the task at hand. "Just do what I tell you."

Beth popped her gum a few times, but Janice lay a hand on her shoulder. "Go on, dear. Do what she asks, please."

She popped her gum again, then shrugged. "You're the boss." She started the car and pulled away from the curb in a tight u-turn. "Then what?"

Maribel tapped on the keyboard, saved the blueprints to her laptop, withdrew from the county records, then dove into the Department of Corrections system. "I'm working on that."

The bulldog with the gimpy leg led Amber and Thirteen first down a long hallway, then through a series of twists and turns. Amber was sure the maze-like nature of the building was not a design flaw so much as a feature—any inmate escaping from a cell would become hopelessly lost after a few seconds of running. *That won't work with Thirteen, though.* She gave his back a grim smile. *You've cataloged every turn in that alien-modified brain of yours, haven't you?*

"What's a *spin?*" Amber asked, her confusion and curiosity finally getting the better of her. "The guard back there asked us for Darryl's spin."

The woman in front rounded and narrowed her eyes at Amber, then she snorted once. "A spin is short for system person number. We use them to keep track of the inmates. It follows them throughout the system, whether here or a permanent facility." She arched an eyebrow at Thirteen and harrumphed. "But a lawyer would know that, wouldn't he?"

"I do, indeed, Ms...."

"Clark," she said, turning away. "*Sergeant* Clark."

So far, none of the doors they'd passed resembled anything like what she would expect for a waiting room. Most were the same dull gray she'd seen in countless movies. Two had a wide purple horizontal stripe painted above the handle, and all held the same small glass and wire mesh windows. At the far end of this hallway was another booth on a raised platform, one meaty guard perched behind heavy glass, a microphone on a stand next to him; a fitter version of the guard in the foyer. Behind him an open door led to a break room where two other guards sat at a table sipping coffee. Sergeant Clark waddled up to the booth, her eyes barely clearing the lower half of the cinderblock wall, and peered up at the guard.

"Open number twelve." Amber watched the guard's eyes expand ever so slightly, but he did as ordered and pressed a button on the panel. A purple-striped door to their left clacked and rattled, then slid open. "You two wait in here," she said, waving them toward the open doorway. "I'll bring the inmate and your assistant as soon as I can."

Not *let you know when he's ready* or *come get you*, Amber noticed at once, but *bring them to you*. It was a minor slip as slips go, but an important one. *We're not meant to leave this room.* The look in Thirteen's eyes told her he caught it as well. Nevertheless, he didn't hesitate for a single breath before crossing the threshold. She watched him go as Clark and the guard watched her.

"If you would?" Clark said, placing one hand on the small of Amber's back and gesturing with the other. She gave her a less than gentle shove, and Amber resisted at first, then acquiesced and walked through the doorway.

I hope you know what you're doing.

The door slid shut behind her with a thunderous boom, and the lock engaged. She spun and gave Thirteen the stink-eye, but he put a finger to his lips, forestalling whatever comment dangled from her tongue. She had plenty to say—and even more to ask—but remained silent. Instead, she turned away and took inventory of their surroundings. The cavernous room appeared to be a common area. There were a couple of tables with chairs, a few cots lining the near wall, a vinyl sofa facing a small television bolted to one wall, and far across the room a low wall separating the main area from three shower heads mounted there. To her right was a metal open staircase leading to a second level of thick-barred cages lining the other three walls away from the door. On that second level, between two cages on the far side, was a second door—much lighter in construction than the others and sporting a standard doorknob.

"This isn't a waiting room, is it," she whispered.

"No, it is not." He scanned every nook and cranny of the space. *Can he see through walls like Superman?* "I believe this is a holding cell used for deviants after final in-processing."

"Deviants?"

"Rapists and the like." He strode to one table and lowered himself into a heavy aluminum chair.

"That's just great." She joined him and rested her elbows on the table. "A perfect end to a perfect day."

Thirteen closed his eyes for a few seconds, then opened them and gave her an appraising look. "We may speak freely now."

"Cool," she said with a slight sneer. "Now... what's your plan?"

He pursed his lips and furrowed his brow. "I have no plan," he said. "Other than to wait for their next move."

"Whose next move? Dieter's?"

He nodded. "Or his agents, yes. I believe the woman recognized me, and that is only possible if she is in Dieter's thrall."

"His thrall..." Amber shook her head. "Where did you learn to talk like that?"

"Argentina," he said without smiling. *If that's a joke, it's as dry as talcum powder.*

"Anyway... why not just kill us? Why bring us here?"

"I suppose he is curious how we followed Jack's trail here, and how best to cover his tracks now the Zzkritti know what I know." He shrugged and pointed one ear at the back wall. "They would find killing me difficult in any event." She noticed he didn't include her. "One thing we know is Jack is not here."

"How can you be so sure?"

"Because they would have simply given us a plausible story to turn us away at the door." He stared at the door high on the back wall. "He has Jack, and for whatever reason has not killed him yet." He glanced back and caught the look in her eye. "If he had, we would already know." Now she heard the sound he had been listening to—voices, dozens of them murmuring to one another, the volume inching ever upward.

"What's—"

Thirteen stood at once and moved away from the table, grabbing her by the wrist and pulling her with him. He kept his eyes on the door but leaned close. "Keep me between you and that door," he hissed. "They are here."

Before she could process what he'd said, the door on the catwalk exploded inward, bouncing and clanging off the wall on crying hinges. More men than she could count boiled through the opening, a driving onslaught like an ocean wave, dark and angry—each man sported a purple wristband, each carried a makeshift weapon, and each focused their eyes on her.

A perfect end to a perfect day.

Sohrab sat in his car and stared at the spot where the little Civic should be. *Allah be praised.* He wiped his brow. *At least those two had the good sense to go home.* In truth, he was both disappointed and relieved the pair had left. He had detected a strong resolve in Janice; she would be a formidable ally if she were not so old, but she represented one more person to protect when their plans inevitably broke down.

No battle plan survives contact with the enemy. The officer who trained him taught him that. He had claimed the phrase was his own, but Sohrab had known better even then. *No matter. The truth of it still lives, even if Colonel Nassar does not.*

The car's air conditioner was working overtime to dump the heat, but it wasn't fast enough for his taste, and he turned the fan all the way up as he waited for Amber, Maribel, and the Shadowman to return. The clock on the dashboard said they'd only been inside for twenty minutes, but it felt like hours, and he couldn't shake the feeling something bore down on them like a runaway train. It was a trepidation borne of long years of experience. *The Americans call it Murphy's Law... whatever bad* can *happen* will *happen.* For a field operative, they were words to live by, and for the first time, Sohrab understood the connection between Murphy's and Nassar's laws.

He took the cell from his pocket to check in with Marie, but the thing surprised him by waking on its own, the ringtone he'd assigned to unknown callers blaring. He frowned at the screen a moment, then pressed answer.

"Yes?"

"Hey big guy." The voice was Maribel's, but she sounded preoccupied—confused, even.

"How did you get this number?" he barked, already understanding how.

"Is that really the first question you want to ask?"

Of course. The question shouldn't be how, but...

"Why are you calling?"

"Josef sent me outside right after we entered," she said, breathless. "I think he believed something was wrong in there."

"Where are you? I will come to you."

"Exactly what I was thinking." He heard the relief in her voice. "We're in back on the southwest side of the building, off E street. There's a service gate, and we're already inside."

"Tell him about the door," another voice called out.

"What door?"

"Just get over here," Maribel said. "I'm pretty sure there's not much time, and we might need a distraction, if not the extra muscle."

"Is the gate guarded?"

"Of course. I had to cobble together an appointment and clearance on the fly." She whispered something to someone with her, a shushing sound as you would silence a child. "I don't know how long it will hold before someone comes over to check us again. Right now we're sitting in the car near an exit door."

"Can you do the same for me?"

"I... don't think so." He heard her tapping on her keyboard. "That was a one-off. Another intrusion and they'll know something's up."

Ah, Murphy's Law. He sighed resignation. There might be nothing to worry about, but either way Maribel had trespassed upon the jail's grounds. Extraction would be difficult regardless of her plans. *She said a distraction might be necessary.* He wondered what that might entail.

"All right. What do you need me to do?"

"Thought you'd never ask, big guy."

The men hesitated for only a moment, but in that moment Amber saw into the void behind their eyes. More animal than human, driven by instinct or raw animus, they neither reasoned nor felt, every muscle, sinew, and nerve taut as a watch-spring; their attack was both preordained and imminent. Amber gasped, and it was if someone opened a flood-gate. The men flowed toward the stairs on both sides of the room with the calm of a panther and the speed of a cheetah, the first halfway down before Thirteen sprang.

He took the first man to reach the bottom with ease, wrenching the short length of iron pipe from his hands as if he were a child, bashing him on the back of his head and sending him to the floor in a limp heap. He took the second with a blow beneath the chin, snapping his head back and putting the man instantly to sleep, then pivoted around the falling body to take the third with the pipe across his throat. That man dropped his bat, then fell to his knees, blocking the path of the remaining men on that side. Thirteen grabbed the bat, leapt from the stairs and dashed to the other side, catching the two men who had reached the floor with a whirling display of martial art worthy of Bruce Lee. It was fluid. It was beautiful. It was brutal.

Men fell unconscious at his feet left and right, and when that side was clogged with bodies he retreated and stood between Amber and the rest. One by one they went down, some getting one good swing in first, most not, and all bleeding. Amber heard crunching bones and snapping tendons, and her gorge rose at the thought of the sheer ferocity of Thirteen's display. *This is what they built him for.* It frightened her more than even the thought of his alien masters.

It was over in seconds, and when he was finished, he held the last of them up by the throat with a single arm, feet dangling in the air as the man struggled to breathe, his feeble attempts to tear that hand away pitiful and ineffective. He set the mindless beast down on quivering legs, but did not release his throat. *He's not even breathing hard.*

"Why did—"

"Quiet," Thirteen snapped, his battle fever not quite faded. He reached inside his pocket and pulled out the device Jack had described to her. Only this one was far different. Egg shaped and almost the size of his fist, the green gem on top glowed and pulsed like a living thing. Four sinister black claws emerging from its base reached up and over as if gripping the gem on top, and her eyes widened as she saw them writhe.

Thirteen held the green horror to the man's head, both his eyes and the other's growing wide. He leaned close, almost touching noses, and held that position for longer than it had taken to dispatch the horde. Twisting his head this way and that, peering deep in the man's eyes, he held them both frozen in time as the gem pulsed faster and faster, the light growing brighter with each pulse.

The inmate closed his eyes, and Thirteen released the man's limp body. It oozed to the floor like molasses and Thirteen faced Amber. "It's not Dieter!"

"What?"

He nodded at the lifeless husk at his feet. "This one suicided before I could delve further." He gestured at the scattering of bodies about the room. "But Dieter had nothing to do with this. Nor Jack's disappearance." The vein on his forehead that had been throbbing throughout the communion with the inmate slowed and faded.

"Then who could..." Amber feared finishing, the rest of her question catching in her throat. She didn't want to think about it. She *couldn't* think about it.

"I don't know," he muttered, and that admission frightened her most of all.

CHAPTER 11

THIRTEEN SAW THE LOOK ON AMBER'S FACE—a frightened rabbit ready to bolt—and pitied her. *She was never prepared for the horrors she has endured.* He considered trying with another of the inmates but dismissed it at once; there was movement all around the facility, and many of the minds inside moved in his direction. The only clear pathway was the door their attackers came through, and no time to consider other options.

"We must go," he said. "Now."

Amber, her mouth still agape from the aborted question moments before, surprised him for the second time that day. "I assume you already have the floor plans in your head." She looked up into his eyes with something approaching humor. "Lead on, Macduff."

He nodded and strode toward the staircase leading to the catwalk. Amber watched him with interest as he removed the unconscious men from where they had fallen, clearing a path up and out. In times past he wouldn't have bothered with concern for their well-being, but times had changed. *He* had changed. Jack had asked him to not harm any more humans in the Zzkritti's quest, and when Jeff acquiesced and removed the directive from his mind, it was as if he'd been reborn. Much of his lost humanity had returned that day.

I hope this is not a mistake. He lifted the last man in their path and set him aside. *Already I waste too much time.*

His hearing, keener than any human and most animals, detected boots headed their way—most from the hallway where he and Amber first entered, but a few coming from above. Amber was correct about the blueprints in his head, but they were incomplete. This room was not included; he had no knowledge of what was beyond. He moved as swiftly as he could but was cognizant of Amber's ability to keep up.

"Hold," he whispered when they reached the top of the stairs. Amber stopped at once and waited. "I do not know where this leads. It is not in the blueprints, but I do know distance and direction to the nearest exit." Thirteen communed with the device, stretching his mind paper-thin, delving into every computer and electronic system in the building. One command he sent to the nearest cell phone, then moved on to the next target, trusting the device to finish what he'd begun.

Amber shifted from one foot to the other as she waited for Thirteen to give a signal. He found what he needed seconds before the guard breached the door.

"Ignore what you hear." He grabbed her by the wrist. "It is important you keep pace." Before she could wipe the confusion from her face, the building's alarm blared like the world's largest cicada. It cleaved the silence, and in that seam Thirteen drove forward, dragging Amber along behind him. "I have opened all the cell doors on the other end of the building, disconnected power, and disrupted communications." He grinned back at her as they ran. "That should keep them busy for a while."

"Gave them a taste of their own medicine," Amber said, grinning.

"Indeed."

Two guards appeared around the first turn, billy clubs in hand, and Thirteen dropped them without slowing.

Sohrab pulled up just outside the gate, set the car in park, and waited. The engine idle felt rough, sputtering every second or so. *Of course it needs a tuneup*, he thought, his father's fatalism rearing its head. *Just when I've depleted our savings repairing the air conditioner.* There seemed no end to the parade of expenses in his life—the kids and their constant need for school supplies, the car, the house... it all added up so fast. There had also been the two months Marie was unable to work due to a broken ankle—an injury she got helping him repair the roof because they couldn't afford to pay someone to do the work. Now the credit cards were maxed from the medical bills and every extra penny went to servicing that debt.

"At least in Iraq we had medical coverage," he grumbled. It almost didn't matter he'd had to torture people to earn it.

Almost.

It wasn't as if he'd had a choice. Colonel Nassar had trained him, shaped him, broke him, then recommended him for the job. He'd also threatened Sohrab's family when he'd tried to refuse.

"You have a duty," Nassar said, his rotund and sweaty body poured into a uniform one size too small. He leaned across his desk, plucked the big cigar from his mouth, and used it as a pointer, flicking ashes and glowing coals at Sohrab as he spoke. "And if you do not do your duty, then what use are you? What use is the family that produced such a cowardly dog?"

Sohrab drummed his fingers on the wheel as he remembered the greasy lout. "And what happened to you in the war, fat man?" he grumbled. "Shot in the back by your own men and burned to ash before the battle had been lost." His only regret was he hadn't been there to pull the trigger. "*Cur*," he spat.

If he were being true to himself, he had to admit he'd liked it at first. Not just the power, but the respect that power brought him. It had taken the better part of two years to understand none of the respect resulted from anything other than blind fear. Even his own family feared him, and it was that fear in his mother's eyes that woke him from the long sleep.

Sohrab grunted, then grimaced. "It is better to be poor and unknown."

His phone chirped twice in his pocket with an incoming text message. He fished it out and frowned at the display. There was no identifier—not even the generic *unknown caller* displayed—but the message was simple and concise: *Be ready*. There were myriad ways to interpret that, but the most obvious presented itself the instant alarms rang out from the building in front of him.

He watched the guard at the gate turn toward the noise, hand poised on the butt of his holstered weapon, then said a quick prayer to an Allah he no longer believed in and threw the car into drive. Dollar signs filled his vision as he crashed through the barrier, sending the guard scurrying for the cover of his booth.

Marie's going to bludgeon me in my sleep.

"I still don't understand why we're back here." Janice screwed her mouth up just like when she used to scold her husband. "What if they come out the front?" There was much about this she still didn't understand. *Like, how does this woman know there's a problem? Or why she needs the other man to join us?* Janice didn't enjoy being in the dark and had told her husband as much when he'd first come to DC to begin his lobbying career. Even the secrets he *tried* to keep she eventually discovered.

"Look at it this way, ma'am," Maribel said, still tapping at her keyboard. "If they go out the front, all well and good. No harm, no foul." She looked up and Janice saw a hint of fear on her face. "But if they must leave any other way, *that's* a problem, and if they get to choose their path, the only likely candidate is through that door right there." She pointed at the little service entrance. It was the only door for perhaps two dozen yards in any direction. It had a red light over it and a large sign that read: *Authorized Personnel Only.* Janice was sure none of them, inside or out, fit that category.

"And if they're caught?"

"Then we turn around and scurry home before anyone suspects we're involved."

"Really," Janice said, her voice sucking the heat from the cabin. "You would leave your friends so easily?"

Maribel snorted and stopped typing. "First of all, lady, none of these people are my friends. Josef hired me to do a job. That's it." She looked down at the computer. "And second, I've already gone above and beyond. My only goal now is to get out undetected. Live to fight another day and all that." Janice watched Maribel's face flush as she spoke and wondered what sort of woman could be so cold about another human being. *Be fair. Maybe she doesn't know what's at stake. Maybe she doesn't know anything but what's in front of her on that screen.*

The silence thickened between them, and Janice leaned away as if avoiding an unpleasant odor. She'd known people like Maribel her whole life, but every one of them had been men. Every man she'd known had treated life as a contest rather than just lived. She'd grown up in a far different time and place, but right was still right no matter the era.

"You guys are funny," Beth chirped, then snapped her gum. She craned her neck, poking her head into the stew of condescension and derision. Her eyes shined like a cat's and she grinned at both women. "I'm driving this car, and I say what we'll do and won't do."

Janice glared at her. "I hired you to—"

"I can give you your money back if that makes you feel better," she said with some heat, still with that same impish grin. Her eyes were two gleaming stones, hard as diamond, and they said to Janice *don't fuck with me.* Taken aback, Janice studied the girl's face and re-assessed.

"What, then, is *your* plan?"

Beth gave her an honest and warm smile, softening the eyes. "We're gonna sit right here until something happens." She winked, the sound of it grinding on Janice's eardrums. It took her almost a full second to realize it was the grating sound of an alarm coming from the jail.

"Time's up," Maribel said, snapping the laptop closed. They all jumped when a car crashed through the gate behind them. "What now?" Maribel said to Beth. "Any plans for that?"

"What did you do?" Janice cried, grasping Maribel's arm for her attention."

"I didn't do anything, lady," she said, wiping Janice's hand off her arm. "That's got to be Josef on the move." She leaned forward and grasped the passenger seat ahead of her with both hands. Sohrab pulled to a sliding stop beside them, a cloud of dust enveloping both cars. "Shouldn't be long now."

Amber struggled to break free of Thirteen's grasp, but he held tight, pulling her up and over the bodies he left in his wake. So far, the only one to die was the one he'd attempted to question. He hadn't penetrated the man's mind far before the locks had fallen and the suicide imperative engaged. *The human will to live is strong.* It took a lot to overcome that will, and the Zzkritti rarely found it worth the cost. Thirteen acted as the failsafe in such situations, eliminating compromised operatives when necessary. The number of guards had dwindled the farther they ran, most now engaged with rounding up escaped prisoners. He encountered few of the latter since the common room, and none were modified.

Thirteen stopped at the next intersection, pulling himself and Amber tight against the wall. He used the device to dip into the surveillance system and look around the corner. His concern for Amber's well-being had forced him to use a caution he thought gone. For the last forty years his belief in the device's infallibility and the faith he had in his own skills and training had made such ventures almost too easy. Now there was someone else to consider, and that fact made him most uncomfortable. He would have exited the building long ago without the woman in tow.

The hall was unoccupied, so he pulled Amber away from the wall and lumbered toward a door across the way. He pushed against the bar and to door swung open, revealing a service hallway. Pipes carrying water and electrical wiring ran the length over his head, each color coded and tagged with an inspection number. He searched for a red-coded conduit, checked his orientation within the design, then turned, tugging Amber along.

"Let *go* of me!" She wrenched her arm away from his grasp. Thirteen widened his eyes in surprise. "I'm not a dog on a leash." She stood her ground, rubbing her wrist and panting.

He inclined his head and frowned. "Can you continue?"

Her breathing, and she narrowed her eyes as she rubbed her wrist. "You just try to leave me behind," she said, her voice husky.

"I can, but I will endeavor to allow you to keep up." He stood there a moment considering her strength—both physical and mental—before she waved him along.

"Get moving, then. I'm right behind you."

Thirteen shrugged, checked his direction again, and loped down the service hall; he gauged the rhythm of her footfalls, never allowing her to fall more than three steps behind. They ran through several twists and turns until they reached a narrow staircase. He hesitated, looking down the steps. *Jack is not here. But the answers are.* The staircase bottomed out a single flight below—that way was freedom. He craned his neck upward. *The answers are above.*

"C'mon," Amber said. "We're kinda sitting ducks here." She peered up, then frowned at the steps leading down. "That's got to be the way out, right?" She chewed on her bottom lip, shuffling from one foot to the other.

"If we leave now, I may never understand who is behind this."

"If we *don't* leave now, we may never get out." She took a step down, then another, turning back to implore him. "I have friends out there. If they're waiting for us, they're also in danger."

Thirteen looked deep in her eyes. He could compel her to follow, but to what end? His duty to keep her safe need not extend beyond this point, though something kept him at her side—or at least compelled him to keep her close to his. He'd blinded the sensors and cameras in this section of the building, unlocked every door blocking their escape, yet still he hesitated. Neither his masters nor Dieter had taken control of these people. *And they used Zzkritti technology to do it. Finding Jack is now secondary.* The realization surprised him. Above them, a door slammed open in the stairwell, and three sets of boots pounded the steps in their descent. Amber looked up, her eyes wild.

"Go," he said. "There is a door at the bottom to your left. It will take you outside." He took two steps up the staircase before Amber recovered enough to call out.

"Where are you going?"

"Go," he repeated. "Your friends are waiting." The guards were now only five flights above them. "I must know who is behind this, and there is one here who may have that information." His face heated. "There may never be a better opportunity." Thirteen began his climb, relaxing only when he heard Amber descend and open the door.

"Be careful." She leapt down the steps, leaving him to his fate.

"Care is unnecessary when you are prepared," he muttered before engaging the three guards.

Amber didn't want to leave Thirteen behind, not out of fear for his safety but for that of the guards. The speed with which he'd dispatched both prisoners and guards was a revelation. She'd always known the Zzkritti must have enhanced him, but until today never imagined the extent of those modifications. *Seems a long life with a healthy body wasn't enough.* She watched him bound up the stairway by twos. *They had to create an unstoppable killing machine.* She hadn't seen him kill today, but she held out no hope that would be the case for long. By the time he'd passed from her field of vision, the sounds of first combat filled the stairwell; it shook her from her reverie.

"Time to go." She bounded to the bottom and turning left. The stairwell opened into a short hallway, a series of doors lining the wall left and right. Each looked like they might open onto a storage room or supply closet, but there were no labels to hint at their contents, just numbers and letters in pure government-speak. None had the type of locks required to keep prisoners inside, and she bypassed them all in her flight to the end of the hall. There, like a beacon in the night, harsh sunlight poured in through a small window on a large metal door. Painted battleship gray, wide enough to allow two large men to pass through side-by-side, the inner surface sported no handle, only the standard push-bar. She hit the door at a run, trusting Thirteen to have disengaged all the locks and alarms, the bar clacking happily as the door lumbered open, tossing her into bright daylight. A small cloud of dust was just settling, revealing Sohrab's Ford parked alongside the little Civic.

"Come," Sohrab yelled through his open window, waving at her to run to his car. "Where is the Shadowman?"

Amber hesitated for only a second, looking at the passengers in each vehicle. She wanted to run to Sohrab—it was her first instinct—but something nudged her away, toward the Civic. "He's not coming," she said, reaching for the handle of the small car. Sohrab had an odd look on his face, but men were hustling their way there was and no time to talk. Some were guards, but most were not. "Trust me, he'll be fine." She gave him a last look that she hoped conveyed all she'd seen, then opened the door and flopped into the front seat beside Beth. She slammed the door closed just as two inmates reached the car. "Hit it!"

Beth didn't wait for an explanation—she just threw the car into reverse and stomped on the gas. The car's tires spun for a second, then grabbed the gravel and everyone but Beth lurched forward as the car backed away from the building as fast as its little wheels could carry it. They picked up speed heading for the opening in the gate Sohrab had provided, while everyone fought with their seat belts to buckle up. Beth faced backward, driving with one hand on the wheel and the other holding the lever for the emergency brake. No one spoke, least of all Beth—she just kept chewing her gum with casual indifference. There was a calm intensity in the way she stared through the rear window as she drove.

"Hang on." It was the only warning she gave, and almost an entire second before she did what every movie hero did in a high-speed chase. With a fluid synchronicity that told of many attempts, she jerked hard on the brake and spun the wheel. The car's wheels locked, and it skidded backward even as it spun. Before Amber processed the maneuver, before Maribel had stopped screaming, Beth released the brake and the wheel just as the nose of the car pointed toward the gate, shifting it back into drive at the same time. She floored it again and the car shot through without ever slowing. She executed another turn as they hit the street, throwing everyone to their right.

"Jesus, Mary, and Joseph," Janice cried, then laughed and clapped. "Where in the world did you learn to drive like that?"

Beth turned, a wide grin on her face. "Alabama," she said as if that told the whole story. She faced forward and placed both hands on the wheel again. "Grew up with four older brothers and a father who raced on the weekends."

Amber heard a gunshot and squealing tires, and Sohrab plowed through the gate, racing in the opposite direction. *He's leading them away. He knew the cops would chase the last one through the gate.* Sure enough, a police car with siren blaring blasted through the remains of the gate and followed him. Sohrab had already rounded the corner by that time, and Amber knew he could lead them on a wild goose chase for at least half an hour. *Maybe we can improve his odds.* She pointed at the laptop Maribel clutched to her chest.

"You any good with that?" she said, pointing at the laptop. The woman frowned, then cocked an eyebrow.

"Of course," she sniffed. "It's what Josef hired me for."

"Josef?"

"You know," she said, mouth tight. "The scarecrow."

Amber smirked, then grew serious. "Any chance you can pull the cops away from Sohrab? Scramble their ID on the car?"

Maribel shrugged. "Sure, but it's gonna cost you."

Amber opened her mouth, ready to threaten if necessary, but Janice stopped her.

"How much?" *So sweet you could ice a cake.*

Sazzaad, First Among Equals, turned the animal's head first one way, then the other, his worm-polished claws leaving deep impressions in the soft skin, a tiny bead of the thing's blood welling where one claw-tip punctured the surface. Coarse fur darkened the face below the eyes and around its mouth. *How have these things survived for so long without chitin?* He released the creature's head, allowing it to loll to the side against the cold steel table.

"Will it wake?" he asked the attendant. The sexless creature, half his size but with a larger head and longer claws, skittered to the table and passed a small scanner over the body.

The attendant stared at the device for a moment, communing with it, then looked up at the First. "He is deep in the Dream-Sleep, First," it said. "He will not wake until allowed."

"That is well." The First blinked. "It must be destroyed if it wakes here, and we have invested too many resources in this creature to dispose of it now."

"May this one ask its purpose?" The attendant detected the creature's status in the First's pitch modulation. It knew the First's disdain for the planet's dominant species and should have coded a reminder in its hind-cortex for future interaction.

"You may not," the First said, a buzzing susurrus of irritation emanating from its abdominal slits. He leaned close to the creature and poised a gleaming claw over its throat. *It would be so easy. Humans are weak. They do not deserve this world.* Every drone had thought this when they arrived so long ago—his opinion had never wavered, though many of his broodmates' had. The battle that followed Hive's new directive was brutal, winnowing all but the most hardy and resourceful, but the First never wavered in his commitment to the Endless Test. Those who did were an abomination to his faith—to the faith of all Zzkritti. *Those who do not endure the Test, must fertilize the path*, he thought, chanting the old *Kaazisstra*, the Arbiter's Lament.

He straightened and saw curiosity in the eyes of the attendant—it must have heard him murmur the chant aloud; the thing was not attuned to the collective. None of its caste were. He absently stroked the kasz-skin cloak about his carapace as he listened to the buzzing voices of the collective, choosing which to hear and which to ignore. The raiment of office he wore as his right as First, but the tradition was so ancient the knowledge of *why* was lost to time. *Regardless, tradition must be followed unerringly. Tradition draws order from chaos.*

"When will its programming be completed?" The First checked the rows of vials in the wall sconces.

"It... resists, First," the attendant said, scuffling back a step. The tip of its tail swept side to side in nervous fear, its barb gouging deep channels into the wall.

The First glared at the underling and fought back the desire to sacrifice it on the spot. This outpost, while growing, was still far too few to waste even the worthless.

"How long?"

"We first had to heal its old injuries to remove all the metal in its body so the—"

"How... *long?*" the First's voice boomed, shaking the very stone beneath the attendant's tail.

"Some humans are more pliable than others," the attendant blurted, its claws flexing in the air, the tail's twitch growing in amplitude. "This one, however..."

"It will break." The First caressed the primate's head. "They all do."

"But at what cost?"

"Your meaning?"

142

"It may not function afterward." The attendant hesitated. "Worse, it may malfunction only after we return it to the others."

The First considered this. "That is a risk all must take. You will continue until you succeed." He spun and scuttled away, leaving the attendant to wonder at its future.

Jack Montgomery writhed and moaned on the table, lost inside the Dream Sleep.

CHAPTER 12

BETH DROVE UNTIL THE SIRENS FADED, POPPING her gum in a rapid staccato. It was an old habit, and one which grew worse when she was under pressure. She scrunched her face, rolled the window down, and spat the wad to the pavement. Within seconds of rolling the window up, she already craved another. She relaxed the pressure on the accelerator and the car slowed to just above the speed limit. *No use getting away clean, then getting stopped by DC police.*

"Anyone got a destination in mind?" She glanced at Janice in the rear-view mirror.

"My place is as good as any, I guess," Amber sighed before Janice opened her mouth.

"Uh uh." Beth shook her head. "Pretty sure the cops made you as soon as you entered the building."

"Thirt... um, *Josef*, has already wiped those files, I think," Amber said, then pulled at her bottom lip. Beth noticed the vocal tick but didn't push.

"That's not possible," Maribel said, her face still nose-to-screen with her laptop. She had been tapping the keys with furious abandon ever since they had left the facility. "I'm not even in yet, and there's no way he—"

"Trust me." The ice in her voice dropped the cabin temperature ten degrees. "He's already done that job for you."

"Doesn't matter," Beth said. "Not unless your guy knows a way to wipe a person's memory, too." She looked at Amber as she spoke, and the flat, emotionless face staring back told her more than she wanted to know. *Damn, girl. What the hell have you gotten yourself into? She actually believes he can wipe a guy's memory.* Beth didn't know

145

what chilled her more, that there was a man who could work such miracles, or that someone sitting next to her believed he could.

Janice cleared her throat, drawing everyone's attention. "I think the only option is my place." Her voice soft yet firm. Maribel opened her mouth to argue, but Janice cut her off. "We can't go to your place for the same reason we can't go to Amber's... they've seen your face."

"I wasn't about to offer mine," Maribel said with a sneer. "No one goes to my place." She cocked an eyebrow. "And they won't find out anything about me from just my face—trust me." She nodded at Beth. "I was gonna suggest hers."

"Hey!" Beth said. "I'm not in this."

"Of course you are, dear," Janice said. Beth glared at her in the mirror and bit her lip. *Maybe I am, maybe I'm not. No one decides that but me.* Janice pursed her lips and looked at each person in the car, brow furrowing. "Didn't anyone else notice the camera above the door?" She snorted and shook her head. "Even if it couldn't make out the faces inside, it surely registered the license plate on this car."

"Son of a bitch!" Beth said, slapping the wheel.

"Indeed."

Beth took another turn, driving in what she hoped was a random pattern. *There's an oxymoron, if ever there was one.* She wanted to pull over and think it through—hash it out with the others if they were of a mind—but the need to keep moving was visceral. She felt as if they were being chased, and any stop—any hesitation—would lead to disaster. Her eyes wandered to the side mirrors, every black sedan becoming a predator intent on her capture. She shivered and gripped the wheel tighter.

"No," Janice said, "the only real option is my place. I have no connection to any of you, and I'm the one person in this car least likely to have been identified."

"Well, you can drop me off anywhere," Maribel said, closing her laptop. "I can't get into their system from here, anyway." She tucked the computer in her bag. "Keep your money, lady, 'cause Sohrab's on his own," she said, heaving a sigh. "I'm out."

"What about Sohrab?" Amber said, more to herself than Maribel.

"I only said I couldn't break into the system," Maribel said with a grin. "I never said I couldn't do anything. I did what I could... the rest is on him."

Beth held her breath, waiting for the inevitable full-on cat-fight, and no one dared to speak as time ground to a lumbering halt. Amber stared out the window, lost in thoughts she chose not to share, while

Janice and Maribel glared at one another. The moments dragged, and Beth took another random turn.

"How much?" Janice said through clenched teeth.

"Pardon?" Maribel arched an eyebrow.

"How much to stay on the job?"

"I'm not sure—"

"We may need your services a while longer, and I am willing to pay." Janice took a deep breath and visibly calmed herself. "So... how much?"

Maribel pursed her lips and tilted her head, then seemingly plucked a number from thin air. "Um... two grand," she said, eyes narrowing. "Per day."

Both Amber and Beth gasped, but Janice didn't even blink. Instead she patted Beth's shoulder.

"You won't be offended?" she asked.

Will I? That's almost ten times what I'll be making, Beth chuckled to herself. *Then again, what she's paying me is more than I could hope to see if I drove this thing twenty-four hours a day. Plus, anyone can drive a fucking car.* "Nah," she said. "Her thing has nothing to do with mine."

"All right, then," Janice said with a nod, then stuck her hand out for Maribel to take. "Deal."

Maribel took it at once and shook, then before releasing it, squinted up at Janice and tilted her head again. "You would have taken it even if I'd said ten a day, wouldn't you?"

Janice wagged a finger at her. "Ah, ah, aah... no backsies."

Everyone but Amber chuckled, the pressure released like lancing a boil. She continued to stare out her window as if contemplating her place in the universe. *We're all just bacteria under a microscope, lady.* Beth fished in her purse and rescued the pack of gum hiding there, took out another piece, unwrapped it, and popped it into her mouth.

"Okay, back to the original question," she said, chewing a moment, then making that first satisfying pop. "Where to?"

One by one the cars chasing Sohrab dropped behind, then with a suddenness that spoke of design, the last two screeched to a halt and spun in the opposite direction. They were the actions of men given a more pressing task. *What could be more pressing than a jailbreak?* He wasn't sure he wanted to know. This was DC, after all, and anything requiring men to abandon a high-speed chase likely had national security implications. *Either that or another senator got in an accident.*

The number of self-important, small-minded men in the city had doubled, and would double again before the election. Egos and fortunes waxed and waned with rhythmic regularity, and no amount of reality mitigated either.

"Down here at the bottom things are simpler," he grumbled. He had grown too accustomed to surviving on scraps thrown from the tables of the wealthy and powerful, but the predictability of it was seductive. "It is no wonder why tyrants maintain their rule. The people prefer oppression over chaos."

Something rattled in the engine compartment, and he noticed the engine's temperature had climbed.

"Speaking of chaos..."

Sohrab spun the wheel and pulled to the curb. Faint tendrils of steam drifted from the crumpled hood of the car, but he left the engine running and turned the heater as high as it would go to help relieve the buildup of waste heat. He popped the hood and strode to the front to verify what he knew was a punctured radiator. It took a series of loud grunts and three tries to wrench the hood up. The hole was small, but large enough. He had a few water bottles in the cargo area, so he gathered them all.

"I cannot plug the hole," he muttered and began emptying bottles into the steaming radiator. "But I know someone who can."

By the time he'd emptied the last bottle, closed the hood as best he could, and got back behind the wheel, the cabin was an oven, but the engine temperature had dropped below dangerous levels. He rolled down all four windows and opened the panoramic roof, then put the car in gear and pulled away from the curb. Once on the road, he took his phone from his pocket and dialed the newest number in his contact list. The phone on the other end rang for a long time before anyone answered, and he almost gave up, then remembered it was a landline and who he was calling.

"Ayup?" That voice was unmistakable, even if Sohrab had only once before spoken with the man.

"Mr. Redcliffe?"

"Yessir, that's me."

"You repaired my air conditioner a few days ago," Sohrab said, sure that was introduction enough.

"Yessir, I recall yer voice now. Anything wrong with it?"

"No... I have a hole in my radiator. May I bring it in now?"

"Sure. Bring 'er in an' I'll have a look-see." Sohrab heard the smile behind the words. "Long as ya don' mind waitin'."

Waiting there is safer than driving these streets. "That will be fine. I may have to stop a few times to fill it up, but I should be there in the hour."

"I'll be waitin'. You let me know if you need a tow."

"I will indeed." The beginnings of a smile played on his lips; the old man's cheer was infectious. He said his goodbyes and hung up, then limped his way out of town.

Janice listened for the first reaction and covered a smile when Maribel whistled softly beside her. When Beth turned onto the long driveway, the young woman practically giggled.

Maribel shook her head. "Lady, I seriously underbid on this project, didn't I?"

Janice waved dismissively, her hand scribing little circles in the air. "There is always a ceiling on any negotiation, dear. If it became necessary, I should have had no trouble finding someone else to do your job. You are a nice happenstance—that is all."

"Ouch," Maribel said with a genial snort. "That hurts." She showed her teeth. "It also happens to be false. You may find someone else who can *claim* to do what I can, but they would be lying."

"That remains to be seen." Janice's voice was full of ice.

"Girls, girls... you're both pretty," Beth said over her shoulder, then shook her head in disgust when there was no response. She braked in front of the garage, then killed the engine. "Seriously? You're telling me no one got that reference?" Both Janice and Maribel looked at one another, then back at her, shaking their heads and shrugging. "Ugh! You two need to get out more."

"Roxanne from Megamind," Amber muttered.

"Yes!" Beth cried in triumph, holding her fist out for Amber to bump. "Finally... someone with culture." Amber looked at the young woman's hand, furrowed her brow, opened her door, and climbed out.

"I need to pee," she said, then hurried toward the nearest entrance at the rear of the mansion. And mansion it was, in more than just name. The driveway, lined with hedges and rose bushes, was smooth cobblestone; it wound from the street, around the back of the main house, and ended at a five-car garage. The main house was three floors of chiseled limestone and brick, while the garage sported the popular "mother-in-law's" apartment on its spacious second floor. Massive marble columns of dark-veined alabaster reached the full three floors, protecting an equally tall entryway. The roof was a riot of peaks and angles, four tall chimneys sprouting from top and sides, lending a Gothic vibe to the place.

Beth looked out her window, up and up, eyes widening as they drifted skyward, then shrugged at Janice. "What she said." She popped her gum, opened the door, and got out, followed soon after by Maribel. The latter clambered out of the car with bag in hand, a pile of laundry on two legs. Janice shook her head at the lot of them and joined the march to the nearest entry, digging her keys from her purse.

She never had much use for the key-less entry system Paul installed when they first moved in. Even though he'd spent most of his long career as a lobbyist for the textile industry, his first and true love was technology. The house was lousy with gadgets and gizmos, each a constant reminder of the man she'd lost to cancer less than a year ago. Janice sighed, climbed the back steps, keys in hand, and unlocked the door.

"The house is quite empty." She watched the women enter as if they were invading a lion's den. She tossed the keys and her purse on the enormous marble-topped island in the center of the kitchen, then dropped into one of the tall chairs in front. "There's a bathroom around the corner and down the hall on the right, and another near the front entry." She waved toward the ceiling. "There are three more on the second floor, and another two on the third, but I'd have to draw you a map."

Amber didn't wait for the map, and strode straight to the one near the kitchen, while Beth made a beeline for the entry. Maribel watched them hurry away and tossed her bag atop the island, then climbed into the chair beside Janice.

"You live in this place alone?" She looked from the twelve-foot ceiling to the marble-tiled floor. Her eyes wandered back to Janice. "Seems a bit much."

"The very thing I told my husband when he showed it to me." Janice leaned back against the island and settled her weight on both elbows resting against the top. "I grew up on a farm. That house was large, too, but out of necessity." She sighed. *And I'd move back there now if it still stood.* She waved her hand. "This place is just for show. Paul insisted we needed all this to impress the congressmen and senators he feted."

"Buying politicians requires a bit of glitz, I hear," Maribel said, the sneer implied if not shown.

Janice narrowed her eyes at the young woman. She couldn't remember the last time she'd taken such a dislike to someone she'd only just met, but this woman had rubbed her the wrong way from the beginning. *And she does it with such ease. It's either carefully crafted, or so ingrained in her personality she doesn't even know she's doing it.* Janice suspected it was the former. In her experience, women like Maribel rarely did anything by accident. She stared at her for a few more seconds, then chewed her lip, holding her ire in check. At last she sighed and pushed away from the island.

"You want something to drink? I've got beer in the fridge."

"Huh," Maribel said, tilting her head. "I pegged you for a white wine type."

"Not until after six, dear." Janice opened the refrigerator and pulled two bottles from the rack.

"What happens after six?"

Janice twisted the caps from each and offered one to Maribel. "That's when civilized people sit down for supper."

Maribel took the offered bottle and nodded her thanks. "You know, I think you wear civilized society like a mask. You peel it off every night before you go to bed, and glue it back on every morning." She took a long drink, gulping like a fish on dry land, then wiped her mouth with her sleeve. "You're a country girl at your core—and not the middle class variety, either. I hear it in your voice. It hides behind your eyes." She grinned, a look of triumph on her face. "Your family may have lived in a big house on a farm, but they didn't own any of it. You worked for the owners like indentured servants, dirt poor and indebted beyond any ability to pay." She widened her eyes and raised both eyebrows. "Am I close?"

It had been years—decades—since anyone had spoken to her so plainly, and she didn't like it one bit. Since childhood, nothing in Janice's life had been by accident. She had worked hard to get away from that past, even if she still missed parts of it. The owners had taken her family in when her father had lost his own little farm, but small-town Texas was not the best place for poor children. People there blamed the poor for their own straits—even blaming the children for not being born to better parents—and kids could be the most cruel. By the time she'd reached sixth grade, she knew her place in the hierarchy of childhood cliques.

She also learned early to spot one of her own.

"My turn," Janice drawled. "Your family *came* from money and lost everything." She took a drink from her bottle and waved it like a pointer. "Your family depended on the kindness of strangers. Too proud to beg, your father took jobs far below his station and education to put food on your table, your mother taking a job outside the home for the first time in her life." She leaned closer, studying the young woman's rapidly heating face. "It's aged them beyond their years, too." She took another swig, warming up. "You left as soon as you found you had a marketable skill and haven't looked back, not even helping the people who gave up so much to clothe and feed you." She stepped back and held her bottle up in salute. "How am I doing?"

Maribel's eyes were a viper's slits, and she opened her mouth to speak but nothing came out. Before she gathered herself, Beth returned, stopping cold in the doorway when she saw the two women squaring off.

"Hey, this is an awesome place." She snapped her gum. "I bet there's a game-room somewhere, am I right? At least a decent media room?" She looked from one to the other, but neither moved.

"Everyone getting along okay?" Amber entered from the hallway, and her voice held the first hint of cheer Janice had heard since lunch.

"Just fine, dear," Janice said, turning away from Maribel. She placed an appropriate smile on her face and gestured toward the fridge. "Anyone else want a beer?"

Thirteen set the limp form of Sergeant Clarke on the battered metal table, her rotund body rolling to the side, threatening to fall the short distance to the stone floor. The only light in the room came from the soft glow of the device he placed by her head. He dared not use it to delve into her mind—he knew as soon as her eyes widened when she saw him approaching that she'd been compromised by Zz-kritti technology; she would suicide as soon as he established the link, just as the inmate had. No, he'd had to resort to more barbaric means to subdue her, cracking her on the head before carrying her down to this basement room. For every other encounter he had used the device, a trail of limp and unthinking bodies littering the hallways and stairways marking his path to the depths of the facility.

Most of the overhead lighting was nonfunctional in this section, leading him to believe the area was unused, if not forgotten. Somewhere past the massive metal door, now shut and barred, water dropped into a small pool, the steady drip of a cracked and neglected pipe. Beyond that, rats skittered and squeaked their displeasure at his presence. Two of these he set as watches at each end of the hallway, another sent to the upper landing—sentries only slightly less mindless than those on two legs two floors above. They, too, skittered about, squawking confusion and displeasure, calling to others and barking orders to inmates. Thirteen's lips skinned back from his teeth. Officious and self-important men in chaos always cheered him.

He leaned over the woman, his nose almost touching hers, and examined the lump on her head in the green glow from the device. The light cast garish shadows from her features, and lent a gray cast to her skin, draining it of color. *How long before she wakes?* He hadn't resorted to purely physical means in decades, and couldn't be sure the damage wasn't more severe than intended. The woman's carotid pulsed rhythmically, and Thirteen lifted first one eyelid and then the other. The pupils barely reacted in the dim light, but they did react. *She is a pawn. Perhaps not of Dieter, but someone.* He leaned back and loomed over her. *It is not her fault.* Thirteen had never considered culpability when following the orders of his masters; Jeff, intentionally or not, had given him that ability with his freedom.

One rat sentry squeaked, it's mind racing, and Thirteen stiffened before realizing the thing had simply found a cockroach. He disliked relying on such primitive measures, but he hadn't been able to take complete control of the building's computer or security systems. *Something other than human technology guards this place.* It had the unmistakable taste of the Zzkritti, but the flavor was... *different.* Like how apple pie from the Southern states always tasted different from those in the North; recognizable in either, but not the same.

Sergeant Clarke groaned, and Thirteen checked her breathing. It had slowed and deepened since bringing her inside. He located a metal chair laying on its side in one corner of the room, righted it, and dragged it to the table. Clarke's eyes fluttered open as he sat, and she groaned again, reaching with one hand to feel the lump on the back of her head. She began to sit up while still holding her head, failed, tried again, failed, then gave up. She turned on her side and rested on one elbow.

"You're gonna die in prison for this, ya know," she croaked.

"Who is your master?" Not *where is Jack*, or even *why did you take him*. Those questions were no longer important.

She looked at the device beside her on the table and her eyes widened slightly, then narrowed at him. "Who is yours?"

"I cannot use that to rip the information from your mind," he said, nodding at the device. "They programmed you to die if I do. I must use more direct methods." She didn't react to his words, but inched away from the glow. "I ask you again... who is your master?"

"Blow it out yer ass, Lurch." She stopped rubbing her head, swung her legs around, and sat up after the third try. "I have no master."

"You have too much autonomy for a mere mental slave." He rubbed his chin. "Therefore, you have met your masters—in one form or another—and know their desires."

"Don't know what yer talkin' about." She grinned back at him, wild and hot.

Thirteen sighed and stood. "I know you are immune to physical torture, and since I cannot use the device, I must resort to other means." He watched her resolve crack for a moment. *She is a recent recruit. Perhaps only newly trained and altered.* For the first time in his memory he pitied the person he must break.

But she will break. He'd had too much experience to believe otherwise.

He picked up the device and stepped to the door. "When I leave, the light will leave with me. I will send one rat a day for your nourishment. If you are quick, you will eat." Her eyes widened in horror as realization struck. "I will visit you again in a week."

"*No!*" She slid from the table to her feet, the struggle to stand would have been heartbreaking to anyone else.

He hesitated only a moment, then opened the door and stepped through. Dogging it closed behind him, the woman's screams muffled by stone and steel, he placed one palm on the rusted metal and bowed his head, whether in shame or prayer even he didn't know.

"Tomorrow." *Any longer and she may be too mad to question.* He turned and shuffled toward the stairwell, his legs leaden, his heart a stone. Behind him, the furious howling began.

CHAPTER 13

Evan Barrow, former EMT and owner/operator of the machine once known as his body, sat in a corner of a glass-walled room of his own making, knees clutched against his chest, and watched Dieter toss two pills into his mouth. The monster driving Evan's body chewed the bitter tablets, crunching noisily before swallowing. He drank cold and stale coffee from a stained cup to chase the pills into his gullet, then went to the sink and dropped it into the dirty water. Dieter strode into the tiny living room of the apartment once inhabited by a nemesis Evan had come to regard as mythic, sat on the stained sofa and waited for the drug to take effect.

It won't be long, now, Evan thought.

"It won't be long, now," Dieter said as if the thought were his own. Evan had perhaps thirty minutes before Dieter's head cleared enough to continue the assault on Evan's one-room fortress. Already, cracks had appeared in the glass—spiderwebs of fractal fracture spreading across the surface, each reaching for the other. Until recently, Evan had been able to repair most of the damage, but with each attack a few stubbornly refused to heal. *Days*, he thought. *Weeks, if I'm lucky. Then nothing left of me but the memories he decides to keep.*

Evan hated Dieter. He had never hated anyone in his life, but the hatred he had for this man was palpable—corrosive; he could taste it. Like a mouthful of ash, it choked and nauseated him. Anger, hate, revulsion... these were the only weapons of real power left to him, and he used them in defense of every incursion by Dieter, dipping into what seemed a bottomless well of dark emotion, knowing that even if the madman never destroyed him, his slide into darkness would. Whatever hope Evan retained, Dieter snuffed out like a guttering candle flame with the first mental swipe of his hand.

With each of Dieter's attacks, a gap in his own defenses opened for Evan to strike, and he targeted those responses with surgical precision. His latest triumph was ripping a memory the monster had worked so hard to secure: Jack Montgomery's new job and address. There were others, but the best by far was of someone Dieter knew as *Thirteen* or *Josef*. There were so many of this man, but Evan had time and energy to choose only one, he settled for the one perfect day in Dieter's life... the day Josef had slipped and called him father.

That one had stabbed deep into Dieter's heart, though the monster never realized why.

Evan felt the drug cross the barrier from blood to brain, Dieter's mental thunderstorm calming, focusing into crystal clarity. In moments the assault would begin anew, and Even girded for battle. He must repel every thrust, parry with his own, and hold his ground another day. He still had not seen the whole of Dieter's plans, but he had seen enough—the monster still missed one piece of his mental puzzle, and the space required to place it was currently occupied by one Evan Barrow. While Evan held out, Dieter could never be whole; he wouldn't have the necessary knowledge to bring his plans to fruition. Evan's only consolation was Dieter didn't know where that last piece was located.

I do, though, Evan thought, grim and determined. He had guessed its location from the bits and pieces of Dieter's final moments he'd stolen. *And when he destroys me, he loses that information.*

"All right," Dieter said, breathing deep, a too-satisfied smile crawling across his face. "Shall we begin?"

"You did *what?*" Marie's voice always rose an octave when angry, and Sohrab was sure when she heard the rest that only dogs would hear what she said next.

"I'm sorry." He held the phone away from his face just in case. It was the only thing he could say, and there was exactly zero chance it would mollify her. "There are now too many involved, and I had to do something; they would have been captured before we had even begun." His wife's breathing was heavy, but it slowed, and she was silent for a long time. Cars whizzed past on the highway fifty feet from where he stood, the road noise making it difficult to hear.

"So you decided to lead the cops on a merry chase around DC." Her voice was now dangerously calm. "You do realize their next stop is our doorstep."

"Possibly." He wondered if even he believed that. He knew she wouldn't. "It is also possible the records have been erased. They gave up the chase rather easily."

"Riiight..." She drew out the word, leaving no room for misinterpretation on his part. "These cops, in this atmosphere, at this time of the year, are gonna just ignore an Iraqi busting through a security gate at a prison."

"It is not a prison—"

"You know what I mean!"

He did but didn't respond. *She will do that for me.*

"So where are you now?" That wasn't the question she was asking; what she really asked was *are you all right?*

"I am fine," he said, answering the only one he could. "It is best I don't tell you where I am or my destination. There may be people listening already." He didn't believe it was possible so soon, but it was always better to be cautious. Marie sighed, but didn't argue the point. "I must dispose of this phone soon, but I will be in touch when I can."

"And when will that be?" Her concern leaked into her voice, and his heart ached. His thoughts drifted to Bill Montgomery and the wife and children he'd left behind. *I will not do that to mine.* As soon as the vow fluttered across his mind, a butterfly with a broken wing, he saw it was meaningless. Too much was at stake. He still didn't understand what was going on, but he recognized one thing—*whoever they are have shown their hand by taking Jack, and that is either a mistake of desperation, or part of a greater design.* Neither option boded well for his friends.

"Tomorrow, perhaps. Much depends on what happens today."

"Doesn't it always?" There was a hint of cheer in her voice. The exchange was a common one and had become a mantra of hope for them both over the years.

"Marie..." he began, then hesitated, not sure he wanted to say what came next. "I must empty our savings."

"I know," she said softly, as if he had just professed his love for her. In a way, he had.

"It may not matter, but I must do this. With luck, things will work out."

She chuckled, and he imagined her shaking her head. "Yeah... just like always."

Sohrab didn't intend to put any faith in luck; he never had before. *Luck favors the prepared.*

"I love you," he said, then closed the phone before she could respond. He scrolled back through the incoming calls and found the one from the Shadowman. *Was it only this morning?* It already felt like days. He tapped on the entry and opened a text message. He had no way to be sure the Shadowman would receive his plea for help, but the text wasn't for him, anyway.

Jeff Z.—Please take care of my savings account, he typed, thick fingers missing keys, forcing him to backtrack and re-type more than once. Simple and to the point. He knew the Zzkritti must monitor the Shadowman's phone, but that was no guarantee Jeff would respond.

"It does not matter." He tapped the send button. "What must be done, must be done." He tore the back from the phone, removed the SIM card, snapped it in half, then removed the battery and tossed everything into the nearby trashcan. He strode back to the car and finished filling the radiator from the hose at the convenience store where he had parked, then replaced the cap and closed the hood. On the other side of the parking lot was a Wells Fargo where his meager savings account resided, and he strolled toward the door, pulling the empty wallet from his back pocket.

Cars entered and left the parking lot, large trucks lumbered noisily down the busy highway, the occupants of each oblivious to the danger that threatened their world.

If only I were so lucky. He pulled the door open and sterile cold air blasted him in the face, then stepped through and it closed with the sucking sound of an airlock. An eerie silence dropped over him like a bell jar. A single unoccupied teller looked away from her screen and smiled. Sohrab smiled back, sighed, and stepped to the window, ready to cash in his dreams to battle a nightmare.

Amber sat on the over-sized leather sofa, legs curled beneath her, a bottle of beer in one hand and her phone in the other. *How can there not be a signal? We're right in the goddamn middle of DC.* Maribel sat at the far end, legs splayed, one arm draped across the back of the sofa, and drinking lustily from her second bottle. In moments she'd drained it, then wiped her mouth with the back of her hand. With the worn canvas messenger containing her laptop tucked between her hip and the arm of the sofa, she looked like a bear protecting her young. Beth, now chewing a new piece of gum, had finished her beer and was examining the pictures on the stone fireplace's mantle across the room. She wandered from frame to frame, her face so close to them she could lick the glass. She picked one up, her eyes twinkling.

"Your little girls are cute," she said, waving the simple wooden frame.

"Not so little anymore," Janice said, grinning. "They have children of their own, now." Her expression drooped, and she arranged her legs and shifted her weight in the wingback chair. "Jackie lives in Amherst, and Leslie moved to Los Angeles right after Paul passed." She lifted her beer from the coffee table and took a sip. Beth replaced the picture before wandering back to the matching chair at Janice's side.

"So you're all alone in this big house?" she asked, dropping into the chair's embrace. "I think I'd go nuts without someone to talk to."

"Well, dear, I've always been a private person." Janice shrugged and pursed her lips. "You get used to it. Being alone isn't so bad when you're comfortable with yourself."

"Hear, hear," Maribel muttered under her breath. She had curled her legs up on the cushion beside her, and stared at the floor, her mind plainly somewhere else. *Where have you wandered off to?* She had seen that look more than once on Jack's face when he was connecting the dots, his leaps in logic defying gravity. Her own mind now drawn back to the task at hand, she set her bottle on the coffee table and looked at Janice.

"I still need to find out what happened to Jack."

Janice frowned and tilted her head. "Isn't your friend still inside searching for him?"

"That's the thing... I can't see what he expects to find, but Jack is no longer at the top of his list." She pulled at a thread on the seam of her jeans and looked away when Janice's jaw dropped. "And Thirteen is not my friend."

"How is finding Jack *not* a priority?"

"Thirteen?" Beth said, her brow furrowed.

Amber ignored the question. "He doesn't think Dieter is involved in Jack's disappearance, and he knows the Zzkritti are not. He thinks there's another player—one powerful enough to stay hidden from his masters."

"Um... *Zzkritti?*" Beth had one eyebrow arched, her eyes wide and searching.

"Another...?" Janice began, then closed her mouth. Amber didn't blame her—the woman had only recently accepted the story of alien influence, and the thought someone—some*thing*—else with that kind of power was terrifying. *Worse, it means there's an invisible war between two or more superpowers. One of which, at least, is a fucking race of super-advanced aliens.*

Some days, it didn't pay to get out of bed.

"Hey!" Beth waved her hand in the air like a student in a crowded classroom. She leaned forward in her chair so far Amber felt sure the woman would topple over. "Who, or what, is a fucking Zzkritti? Or Dieter, for that matter?"

Janice forced a smile, reached across the space between them, grabbed the waving arm, and pulled it down. "A very long story," she said with a weary sigh.

"And one you don't need to hear," Amber cut in. She shook her head and chuckled. "You wouldn't believe it, anyway."

"So... aliens, then," Beth said, calming as if the revelation made complete sense.

Amber's eyes widened, but she refused to either confirm or deny Beth's lucky guess. *Or maybe she's one of those Reptilian conspiracy nuts.* Amber sighed. *Turns out those nuts were at least half right.*

"None of that matters." She brushed Beth's question aside. "Regardless of who is involved. Find Jack and you'll find the others."

"Save the cheerleader, save the world," Maribel muttered, still staring at the floor. She now pulled at her bottom lip, moving her head like a bird, as if conversing with herself.

"So how do we do that without Thirteen?" Janice asked, releasing Beth's arm.

Maribel sat up and looked at the others as if waking from a deep sleep. "I think I can find him," she said, rubbing her eyes, then scrubbing her face with both hands. "But I'll need more than this thing," she patted her bag, "to do it."

Janice stood and held out a hand for Maribel. "I think I have just what the hacker ordered."

Jeff stood before the crucible, arms, legs, and tail splayed, two talons of attendants scurrying around and over his body, applying the gelatinous secretions from their toothless beaks with care; they left no crevice untouched. A single talon of them worked inside the crucible, itself not much larger than a standard sleeping pod, spreading the catalyst. Others attended the First he'd chosen and Consecrated that morning. The entire process had been compressed, but the hive could wait no longer; they'd lost or sacrificed too many in the last few years. Numbers must be replenished, and as the Chosen, it fell to Jeff.

Will I carry that name with me when the transformation is complete? Will I still be me?

He hadn't been an individual long enough to miss the concept, but he found the prospect of losing his *self* terrifying. *How does the caterpillar cope?*

"By being simple-minded," his First said, abdominal slits fluttering in amusement.

"You find my fears humorous?"

"I find your fears unnecessary. And unbecoming." The First raised his arms and splayed his talons wide, the attendants shifting their attention there. "I also find this individuality... uncomfortable."

As well you should. He had raised the other to this level through the Consecration, drawing him from the collective just enough to stand outside. The First was usually chosen with greater care—most could not survive the transition from collective to individual. *How do the humans do it with such ease? It must explain why they work so hard at communication, and so value their friendships.*

"In time, and with the help of the Becoming, you will come to accept individuality. Embrace it, even."

"How did you do it?"

"I have not gone through the process."

"But you transitioned to individual long ago. The collective learned of your crime before even you."

"You still deem it crime when it has become the means of our very survival?"

The First tilted his head and considered. The collective had pardoned Jeff for the crime of individuality, then named him Chosen. *They* recognized this as the next step in their evolution, sweeping aside countless millennia of doggerel and blind tradition. With a bit of what humans might call retribution, or lesser intellects *irony*, Jeff had chosen his chief accuser as First. Together they would endure the Change, and together they would save their small hive.

The attendants finished at the tip of his tail and skittered away, leaving he and the First alone in the chamber. This phase, as was the one after the Becoming, was not meant for others to witness. Like a well-rehearsed dance, the motions were instinctive and immediate. The two Zzkritti closed the gap between them, their tails writhing in the air like snakes. When they stood a talon-length apart, both tails lashed out, slicing the chitin on the arm of the other, brownish-yellow ichor dripping from each crystalline barb. The tails slowed, then with a motion too fast to see, plunged deep into their own abdomen. Now joined unto death, they were of one mind, and after the Becoming they would mate but once.

For now, they turned away from one another and entered their crucible, each settling back and facing the opening. Jeff closed his eyes before the crucible closed like a healing wound, and entered the Dream Sleep while the catalyst and gel reacted and expanded, filling the remaining space around him.

I will still be me, he vowed as the mist of Dream Sleep swirled in his head. *I will just be Queen.*

"It's beautiful!" Maribel stroked the three huge monitors on the desk. Amber watched the woman's eyes goggle when she saw the computer tower beside the screen, but her strongest praise had been for the Internet connection.

"Paul called it a T-1, whatever the hell that is," Janice told her. "He once mentioned something about a ten-gig ring, but I left all that falderal to him." She beamed at the computer, the pride of a parent. "This was his baby. It cost him a pretty penny, too." She turned to Maribel, who was already in the chair and pulling up to the desk. "You think this will suit your needs?" *Of course it will.* Amber grinned. *And you know it, you smug old woman.*

Maribel only grunted as she started clacking on the keyboard, her fingers flying almost too fast to see. "Someone drag my laptop out of the bag and set it next to the tower here." She patted the open space beside her without looking away from the monitor. "Somebody bring me coffee!"

"Someone's in heaven," Janice whispered to Amber, though loud enough for everyone to hear.

"Coffee!" Maribel repeated with more force. "Cream and lot's of sugar."

"Right." Janice turned to Beth. "Get the girl's laptop, won't you?"

"Sure, ma'am," Beth said, grabbing the bag from where Maribel had dropped it by the door. She opened it, took out the laptop, lifted the lid and pressed the power button, then set it within Maribel's reach.

"Dig out a USB cable while you're at it."

Beth complied, and Amber watched as Maribel connected the two computers with the cable.

"I've got some dedicated software that should be useful," she said, opening a file manager in a separate window before turning back to the other computer. She stopped typing and focused her attention to the two women behind her. "I don't like people looking over my shoulder while I work. I'll call you when I have something—or when I need more coffee."

Amber snorted and turned to Beth. "I think we've been dismissed."

"Sounds like it." She popped her gum and took Amber's hand. "Let's go find that media room."

"I don't think I'm—"

"Stop thinking, then." Beth tugged Amber through the French doors of the office and into the open space of the den. She made a beeline toward the wide and open staircase leading to the second floor, dragging Amber behind.

"Hey!" Amber yanked her hand from the young woman's grip. "Why does everyone think I'm a dog on a leash?"

Beth stopped and faced her, laughing. "Lady, you may be many things, but a dog ain't one of them."

Is she seriously hitting on me? Aside from the fact she'd never considered the question of the girl's orientation—or her own—this simply wasn't the time. Beth must have seen something in Amber's eyes, because she grinned and winked.

"Don't worry," she said. "You're not quite my type."

"You'd be surprised at the number of people I'm not the type for."

"I would, indeed."

"Who's up for supper?" Janice entered from the kitchen, a steaming mug on a saucer in hand. She looked at Beth and held the mug out to her. "Be a dear and take this to Maribel. Amber and I will start cooking." Beth's smile faded, but she took the mug and saucer from Janice's hands. "Thank you, dear. Tell her to use the saucer."

Beth nodded and raced back toward the office. "I still want to see that media room," she called over her shoulder.

Janice leaned close to Amber. "I don't have the heart to tell her there isn't one," she whispered. "I do have a wonderful library, though."

Amber snickered and followed her to the kitchen. Now that cooking was a foregone conclusion, she took note of the space for the first time. The island she was well-acquainted with, but hadn't noticed the pot-rack hanging overhead filled with stainless steel cookware—nor had she noticed the gigantic Wolf stove-top and double oven adjacent to the refrigerator. *High-end stuff, for sure.*

"More of Paul's falderal?" she asked, waving at the stove.

"Oh, no, dear. This is all me." She hustled to the refrigerator and pulled out a heavy package wrapped in clean white butcher paper. "I'm a closet chef at heart." She held the package up. "Steaks okay?"

"Unless one of our new friends is vegan."

"Bite your tongue!" Janice dropped the package on the island and stepped into the pantry, then emerged with a bag of potatoes in hand. "You'll find a peeler and a knife in the drawer over there," she said, nodding to her left. "Grab one of those pots over your head and fill it with water first."

"Aye, aye, Cap'n," Amber said, saluting. She did as Janice asked, then pulled out a stool and sat at the island to peel and cut up the potatoes. Janice opened the wrapper, took out three slabs of meat so thick Amber would have called them small roasts, and began trimming them down to six eight-ounce steaks.

"Have you stopped to consider that you and I met for the first time this morning?" Janice mused as she cut with deft strokes. "We've known the other two for less than that, and here we are now, almost all friends."

"Yeah," Amber said. "What is it with you and Maribel?"

"I wish I knew." Janice seasoned each fillet with items from a spice drawer on her side of the island. She stopped and pursed her lips. "Ever have someone just rub you the wrong way?"

"I was a flight attendant," Amber said, tossing the potatoes into the pot.

Janice snorted. "Oh, dear... you do understand, don't you?" She took the pot from Amber and placed it on the stove, then ignited the burner and turned it up as high as it would go. She grabbed a box of salt from the cabinet beside the stove and poured in a copious amount, then took a large pan from the rack. "Hand me the olive oil, and grab a stick of butter from the fridge," she said, igniting another burner and turning on the oven.

"It's funny how life works," Amber said, handing Janice the items she'd asked for. "I met Jack on a plane, and in a blink was sucked into the plot of a sci-fi novel." She sat on the stool again and watched Janice work. "A year later and I'm sucked right back in again."

"Saving the world is a full-time job, isn't it?"

"Yeah, well... I've done my time. I just want to go back to the way my life was before I knew all this."

"You can't. Stop wishing for things that can never be, and deal with what *is*."

"I could walk away. Go home, go to school, and never look back."

"No, you can't." Janice poured oil into the pan, then cut up far too much butter and placed it inside as well. She let it heat, turning her back on it to confront Amber. "That's not how you're made. I've known you almost one whole day and I already know that."

"Maybe it's time I—"

"The hacker says to bring more coffee," Beth said, running into the kitchen breathless. "She also says she might have something if you're interested."

"Okay," Amber said, bending closer to the screen. "What exactly am I looking at?"

The video, pixelated and dark, was paused on a truck exiting the back of the detention facility in the dead of night. If the gate had not been so well-lit, she would have seen nothing. The angle indicated the camera was positioned off the property somewhere.

"I still can't quite get all the way into the system, but I've been able to get a few things," Maribel said. She tapped the screen with her finger, indicating the truck. "I couldn't get into the security system at all, so I searched for other web-enabled cameras in the area and got a hit on a building across the street." She grinned up at Amber. "Had to blow it up to see anything of value, but once I input the time frame, my search program found this."

"And what is it, exactly?"

"Just an unscheduled and undocumented shipment *from* the facility to parts unknown."

"What makes you think it's unscheduled?" Janice asked over Amber's shoulder.

Maribel sneered up at her, then spoke directly to Amber. "I couldn't get into the security system, but their schedule of deliveries and such are criminally unprotected."

"And you think Jack was in that truck," Amber said. There was no point making it a question—she already believed it.

"Yep. And that's not all." Maribel tapped a few keys, opening other windows with videos already cued up. "Three blocks away using a traffic cam... same truck." She clicked on another window. "Now here." Another. "And here."

"Were you able to track it to a final destination?"

Maribel snorted and rolled her eyes. "You pay for the best, you get the best," she said. "Our friend ended up at the airport." She brought up security footage from an airport camera. "This is where they load cargo for intercontinental flights."

Amber leaned closer and squinted at the truck. It was a basic box truck, painted black with no logos or lettering of any kind. If it had been a UPS or FedEx truck, no one would have noticed, but like this it stood out like a beacon. *It's like they don't understand how people think at all.* A cold and familiar chill ran up her spine.

"Do you know where he ended up?" Beth asked.

Maribel zoomed in on the airplane's tail, the numbers painted there fuzzy but readable. "This particular bird had one destination yesterday—Bariloche, Argentina."

"Then where?" Amber felt hopeful for the first time since Sohrab first walked into her dorm.

"Sorry," Maribel said, an honest sadness in her voice. "I lost him right after the plane landed. There just aren't that many cameras to lock onto there."

Amber tapped the image of the airplane on the screen, pursing her lips. The room was silent except for everyone's breathing. She felt everyone's eyes on her, their worries... their *pity*. To come so close...

I could walk away right here. No one would blame me. What else is there to do?

When there is nothing to do, do nothing, her father had said. He usually followed it with *in all other cases, keep moving forward.* She could pretend there was nothing more she could do, but it would always be a lie.

She heaved a heavy sigh, straightened, and crossed her arms over her chest. "Looks like I'm going to Argentina," she said, possibly the most surprised person in the room.

No one spoke at first, and she sensed each was gathering their forces to argue with her—talk her out of it. *Knock some sense into my head.* The biggest surprise of the day came next.

"Looks like I'm going with you, then," Maribel breathed. She sounded more exasperated than determined.

Amber shook her head firmly. "No. I'm going alone. There's no need for anyone else—"

"Speak Rioplatense, do you?"

"Excuse me?"

"It's a particular and peculiar dialect of Spanish spoken down there."

"You're Argentinian?"

"Worse," she said, bunching her lips. "Bariloche is my home town."

"I'm in," Beth said, snapping her gum and grinning. "I'd love to visit the place."

"Oh, no," Amber said, shaking her head more violently.

"What, you gonna trust just any old local if you get in a chase?" She batted her eyes, the innocent look falling far short of its mark.

"She's got a point, sister," Maribel said. "And they drive on the right down there, just like in the good ol' US of A, so she's good to go as far as that's concerned."

Janice sighed, and all eyes focused on her. "You'll need money, and someone used to dealing with authorities."

They had boxed her in and Amber knew it. She had made the call for herself, and only herself, but she could neither ask the others to join her nor tell them to remain behind. All she could do was bear the responsibility if any of them got hurt... or worse. The weight draped over her shoulders like a backpack full of lead. *Bear what you can, shed what you can't*, her daddy said. There was no shedding this—bearing it was her only option.

"Fine," she said at last. "But I don't think any of us should travel under our own names."

"Don't worry," Maribel said. "With a little help from Lady Mc-Moneybags here," she hitched a thumb at Janice. "I think I've got you covered."

CHAPTER 14

MORNING BRILLIANCE LANCED THROUGH THE HOLE IN the curtain, a laser-beam of visible light and hard radiation reflecting and refracting off Dieter's glistening forehead. Sweat boiled from every pore on his hijacked face, hair alternately slicked and matted, the muscles in his neck and jaw straining—he looked like a young Bruce Banner mid-change. He was something far more dangerous than a mere Hulk; the Hulk, even at his most angry, had never possessed the power to destroy a planet.

For now, the final piece he needed to create that power eluded him, and he released his tension—his hate and anger—and slumped forward.

"Fuck!" He wheezed hard after what seemed an eternity of struggle. It had, in fact, only been eleven hours. Eleven long hours in an attempt to pry the last pitiful pieces of Evan Barrow from the fortress he'd built inside his mind. Yes, he was trapped as well as protected, but even a prisoner could disrupt the smooth function of a prison.

"You can't hold out forever," Dieter croaked. A throaty and hollow laughter echoed inside his head. Evan had lived to fight another day, and as long as he survived, Dieter's plans were in doubt. *What are my plans, really?* He rose to his feet. Other than finding Jack Montgomery and killing him, he wasn't clear on the rest. He only knew they went far beyond one simple act of revenge. Worse, he remembered finding the man's location, but that and even the method of discovery had been taken from him—stolen by a desperate Evan.

"I can still prepare," he said, his voice stronger now. He took two more pills from the bottle, popping them into his mouth and swallowing. His throat was almost too dry to do the job. There were bits and pieces of Dieter's former plans still running through his memories like stray threads in a weave; none of them seemed to connect, their ends terminating in a central location like a bullet hole, but he'd stitch that closed soon enough. Until then, he performed the small tasks associated with each thread, gathering the materials and people he needed.

I can't gather every person, though, can I? Many he could pay or purchase—everyone from dog walkers to congressmen and senators were for hire in DC, but some required a more direct approach. An approach he couldn't remember how to perform. He knew it had to do with the nanomachines coursing through his veins, but lost the method of their use to his fragmentation. In a target's presence, he could command them to do anything he liked, and they followed his orders without fail, but once he'd moved more than twenty feet away, the effect dissolved like sugar in warm water. He'd surmised the machines crossed the physical gap to force others to do his bidding, but he couldn't control it at distance. Politician were too faithless and feckless to trust on their own without reliable motivation and guidance. Copious amounts of money did the trick for many, but there were that rare few for which no amount was motivation enough.

"Thankfully, there is a whole party devoted to the notion you can buy any politician."

Liberating money in large and untraceable amounts was one of the few bits of knowledge Dieter re-acquired after waking, and he'd been busy doing just that ever since he'd cleaned out Evan's savings. He hadn't found the millions of US dollars his former self had stashed in an offshore account until after he'd already made millions of his own. Most of it he'd used to create a Super-PAC, hiding behind several layers of shell corporations, then creating a quick web-site to take in donations from the gullible and uninformed voters.

Dieter looked around the tiny and dingy apartment and chortled. "Best place in the world to hide a millionaire." He stepped back to the desk where most people would have put a television, sat, grabbed the corporate checkbook, and opened the notebook at its side. A long list of names graced the first page, some with marks already beside them. He lifted a pen and began writing, graceful loops and sharp angles spelling out the name of another politician for hire.

❧

Amber rose on her elbows, tossed the covers from her legs, and crawled from the warm embrace of the cloud-like bed. She held her head as she stood, the blood pounding like war drums against the inner wall of her skull; they had all drunk too much for good sense before wandering off to separate bedrooms. The one she occupied was Jackie's, Janice's oldest daughter, and her taste in decorating, much like her mother's, was simple and understated—pale mint-green walls complimenting the dark hardwood flooring and sheer white curtains. The walls were adorned only with photographs of varying size in plain wooden frames.

She staggered toward the private bath and paused at the doorway, tilting her head at the picture hung there. It was of Jackie, Janice, and someone Amber assumed was Leslie, the youngest; it showed a happier time, a time before responsibility set in and crushed a person flat. Janice was no older than fourteen, and all three wore huge smiles as they posed on the ski slope for the camera. The day was crystalline, the powder at their feet as white as sunlight, each leaning over their skis, poles in hand as if ready to push off down the mountain. Amber assumed the photographer was Paul, his shadow falling over the women's skis like a dark blanket. She tapped the picture, then entered the bathroom to clean up.

By the time she finished and emerged, towel wrapped around her body, another encircling her head like a turban, there were fresh clothes laid out on the newly made bed. *Does that woman even sleep?* She lifted the clean, white t-shirt. *At least she knows my style.* A simple pair of bluejeans lay beneath the shirt. Amber knew the clothing was likely from one of her daughters, and knowing Jackie's preference for a low-key style, she guessed the items came from the dresser across the room. There was no bra among them, but her own would suffice—she doubted she and Jackie wore the same size, regardless. She removed the towels and dressed, then brushed out her hair and pulled it back into a ponytail. Both the shirt and jeans were snug, but not uncomfortably so, and she sat on the bed to pull her shoes on as the sounds of a waking house drifted through the door.

Maribel arranged for fake ID's and passports for all of them—including Jack—but the forger had needed twenty-four hours. She took photographs of each, sending them by encrypted email through what she claimed was an untraceable route. Jack's photograph was harder to come by, but Maribel found a usable image from an online news story about his accident. With nothing else to do until morning, alcohol had somehow appeared at the dinner table.

"I should know better," she grumbled, rubbing her temples. "Never mix wine and beer." She opened the door to the hall and was immediately assaulted by the aroma of cooking bacon. Her stomach growled in anticipation even as it turned over, nausea and hunger both fighting for control. "Can't throw up until I put something in you," she said to her belly, then descended the stairs to the kitchen.

Beth was there already at the island finishing up the last of a fried egg, chasing the last bits around the plate with her toast, and Amber's stomach rolled yet again. Janice stood at the stove, rescuing thick slices of cooked bacon from the frying pan before expertly flipping an egg in another.

"Nice to see you made it out of bed." Janice smiled sympathetically. "You have that 'dry toast breakfast' look." She winked and pointed with her grease-covered fork at the plate filled with thick slabs of toasted bread. "Help yourself."

"Got any mustard?" Amber stepped to the fridge. "I think I can handle a bacon sandwich. It's the eggs I can't take."

"Suit yourself," Janice said, flipping the egg over again, a perfect sunny side up. "Mustard's in the door."

"Thanks." She found the bottle just where Janice said, pulled it out, walked to the island, and sat beside Beth.

"You should really try the eggs," Beth said, licking the remains from her fork. "Perfect."

"I think I'd rather have the sandwich... with an aspirin chaser."

Beth reached inside her pocket, pulled out a small container of pills, and slid it over. "Pro tip... always pop a couple before bed when you've been drinking." She smiled wide and infectious. "Takes that morning edge right off."

"I'll keep that in mind." She quickly assembled her breakfast, hesitated, then took a nibble and swallowed. When nothing happened, she took a larger bite, chewing slowly. Before the next, she took two aspirin from the little tin and tossed them into her mouth. These she chewed and swallowed as well.

"Eewww," Beth said, watching her. "You know there's juice to wash them down, right?" She slid a glass and the bottle of orange juice across the island.

"That's okay," Amber said. "I kinda like the flavor of aspirin."

"That's just gross."

Amber smirked and took another bite. The bacon was that perfect blend of crispy and limp, chewy enough to feel substantial, but not fatty. *Raw fat is definitely not something my stomach wants right now.*

"Where's Maribel?" she asked, covering her mouth as she chewed.

"Still in bed," Janice said without turning, the words *the lazy bitch* added even if unspoken.

"She stayed up pretty late, I think," Beth said in Maribel's defense. "She mentioned something about boots on the ground."

Amber frowned. "What the hell does that mean?"

"Haven't a clue."

Janice rolled her eyes. "But I bet there's a price attached."

"There's a price attached to everything, lady," Maribel said, yawning and rubbing her eyes as she entered the kitchen. She looked as if she'd slept fully clothed, rumpled canvas jacket included, and Amber raised an eyebrow at Janice in an unspoken question.

Janice grinned and shrugged. "Didn't have anything in her size."

Maribel threw herself into an empty stool at the island, pulled the plate filled with bacon close, and tossed one strip after another into her wide mouth. She munched thoughtfully for a while, the others waiting. After the fifth or sixth piece, she filled a glass with juice and drank it down, then wiped her mouth with the back of her hand. She picked up another slice of bacon and waved it at Amber.

"Your boy Sohrab is in the clear."

Amber's brow furrowed. "You spoke to him?"

"Nah. He ditched his phone west of Arlington about an hour after we left the jail." She took a bite, then waved the end at Amber again. "I spent most of the night digging into the cops' database. There's nothing in there about him. At all."

"What about me?" Beth said.

"Oh... *you're* in there all right," Maribel sneered. "Lot's of traffic and parking violations, and one pretty good picture of your license tag behind the jail."

"Fuck."

"Oh yeah."

"Can't you... you know?" Beth wiggled her fingers as if casting a spell.

"Not without my system at home, and I'm not going back there soon." She looked Beth up and down and shook her head. "Besides... I doubt you have the cash for a job like that."

Janice cleared her throat and joined them at the island. "Excuse me, but I believe I'm paying you to use your skills to help us. Taking care of Beth's problem is part of that." She stood close to Maribel, looming over her, and slid the plate of bacon away. "Unless you think I should hire someone else."

Maribel chewed slowly, outwardly unperturbed, but Amber knew better. *I was pretty good at this game with my mom. And I always lost.* The two women, locked in a battle of wills, stared at one another, the heat between them warming the room. Maribel took another bite, tearing the bacon in two. "It's all good. I'll take care of her when we get back."

"Fine," Janice said, the room turning decidedly chilly.

"And on that note," Maribel said, sitting up. "Argus contacted me this morning. He says our papers are all ready."

Beth scrunched her face. "I thought he told you it would take twenty-four hours."

Maribel waved the question away. "Oh, he does that all the time. It preserves his image as a miracle-worker."

"When do we leave?"

"As soon as we're packed and ready, I guess." She looked at her clothes, then at the messenger bag over her shoulder. "Me, I'm ready right now."

"We'll need another car," Amber said.

Beth let out a pained sigh. "Yeah... can't take mine."

"That's okay, young lady." Janice winked, and in a voice mirroring Maribel's, said, "I think I've got you covered."

The door on the garage rolled up, silent and smooth, unlike every other garage door Amber had ever known. The morning sun was still low enough in the sky to shine through the opening, and they all had to shade their eyes from the light reflecting from the chrome bumper and flawless cherry red paint of the vintage '57 Chevy Bel-Air convertible. It lounged within like a mother bear in her cave; the nose pointed outward, it looked ready to pounce at a moment's notice.

"Oh my god!" Beth said before Amber or Maribel could get their mouths to work.

"I know, right?" Janice said, beaming. "I wanted one ever since I was a little girl, and Paul had this restored for me for our fiftieth." She stepped inside the garage and lay her hand lovingly on the hood. "He said he found it in a junk yard, if you can believe that."

"He could'a bought one on Ebay, you know," Maribel sneered, hitching her bag higher on her shoulder.

"Of course he could, but where's the fun in that?" She pulled a set of keys from the hook on the wall, and tossed them to Beth, who nearly fumbled the catch. The young woman's eyes widened at the keys in her hand.

"Really?"

"You're our driver, aren't you?"

"For life, I think." She opened the door and scrambling in. "We're doing this with the top down, right?"

"Is there any other way?"

Beth started the car; it rumbled to life with a throaty growl, and she stuck her head out the window. "What are you guys waiting for? C'mon already." Her head disappeared back inside, and she grumbled frustration for a moment, then the top slowly collapsed behind her. "Found it."

Everyone piled in, Janice in front with Beth, Amber and Maribel in back, then Beth grabbed the column shifter and put it in drive. She drove gingerly out of the garage and around her car, then stopped at the threshold of the street. She turned to Janice, a sheepish grin on her face.

"You sure about this?"

Janice laughed and patted Beth's knee. "Seeing the look on your face, I've never been more sure of anything."

"Okay," Beth said, then after looking both ways, drove the car onto the street. The suspension groaned as the car jounced from driveway to pavement, but quickly smoothed as Beth gunned the motor and rocketed away in the crisp morning air. Amber held the door handle in a white knuckled grip and wished for airbags. She found the seatbelt and fumbled with it for a moment before latching and tightening it across her lap. *How did people survive a wreck without shoulder harnesses and airbags?* The strap felt weird across her lap, like the seatbelt on an airplane. She had known since her first week as a flight attendant the belts were more for the passenger's peace of mind than real safety; in a catastrophic event they were less than useless, only there to keep the body in place for easier recovery. *That's why airlines always sprang for harnesses for their crews—we knew better.*

The car hit a shallow dip and bounced for several seconds, but with the wind flying through their hair, only Maribel seemed to care. Janice laughed and held her hand out the window, letting it ride the wind. Maribel huddled against her door clutching her bag to her chest, eyes wide and frightened. *She looks like a rabbit ready to bolt.* She got the impression the woman didn't get out much and probably hadn't gone on a joy ride since high school. *If even then. I doubt she had many friends outside her circle of like-minded nerds.* She shook off the unkind thought and grinned at her across the wide expanse of the leather bench seat. Maribel gave a sick nod back, and Amber counted that as progress.

Maribel took out her phone and consulted the screen for a moment. "Take a left at the next intersection," she said over the roar of wind and road noise.

"Just give me his address," Beth called over her shoulder. She pushed down on the lever for the turn signal and slowed the behemoth beneath them.

"We're not going to the man's house, for Pete's sake." Her mouth was tight and disapproving. "He's not stupid."

"Where, then?"

"Pentagon City Mall."

"Awesome." Beth spun the huge wheel left when the light changed. "I haven't been there in months."

"We're not going shopping, kid."

"Speak for yourself," Janice snapped and faced Amber. "We don't know how long we'll be in Argentina, and I think at least one change of clothes is appropriate."

"Then you should have packed a bag when I told you to," Maribel said, snorting once for punctuation.

"Oh, lighten up." Janice waved her hand. "My treat."

"Damn skippy your treat," Maribel grumbled, almost too soft to hear.

The car bounced again, jostling everyone from their seats momentarily, then leveled out as Beth increased their speed. Now she knew where they were going, it seemed she was in a hurry to get there. The ride was otherwise smooth, the sheer mass of the car lending it a feeling of luxury. *Like taking a yacht out for a cruise.* She relaxed and settled into her seat, resting her arm on the window sill, her hand surfing the wind like Janice's earlier. A warm—and considering the circumstances, inappropriate—humor welled in her heart. She hadn't been truly happy in over a year, but the short time she'd spent in the company of these women had cheered her like nothing else.

The weight of their mission grabbed her then, dragging her back to earth; it threatened to pull her into the depths of despair she hadn't felt since she'd murdered Mason. A chill crawled up her spine and her expression melted away. *Hang on, Jack. I'm coming.*

She refused to think about what she might find.

Sohrab sat on the edge of the bed and checked the alarm clock. *Nine-thirty. Already?* He had slept well into the morning, the cheap motel wrapped around him like a cloak of invisibility. The keys he'd thrown on the nightstand beside his wallet were not his own—they belonged to a beat up old Ford Ranger Redcliffe had loaned him.

"Yeah," he'd said as he inspected Sohrab's car. "You did a real number on 'er, that's fer sure." Redcliffe ducked his head beneath the front bumper, now hanging on by a single bolt and three metal clips, and whistled. "The radiator's punctured in two places, and one of 'em's too shredded to repair." He pushed out, rolling on the flat dolly, and sat up, grabbing a greasy rag from his back pocket and rubbing his hands. He stood and whistled again. "Yer grill is a lost cause, as is the hood I'm afraid, but I think I can save the bumper."

"How long?" Sohrab asked. Not *how much*; he'd pay regardless of the cost.

"Two, three days fer repairs," the old man said. "Maybe four if I can't find a compatible radiator at the junk yard." He squinted at the car, tilting his head. "If I'm lucky, I might find ya a new hood, too." He stepped back and leaned against the tree beneath which Sohrab had parked the car. "The real issue is paint," he said, rubbing his chin. His fingers, still greasy, left dark streaks where he scratched. "Got a guy a few miles down the road who'll match the paint no sweat, but he's pretty busy most days. I'm not sure he can get to it by the time I'm through."

"I am in no hurry." He should get back to work, but that could take weeks. "I will rent a car until you are finished."

Radcliffe pursed his lips, arched an eyebrow, and looked from Sohrab to the car and back again. He chuckled and shook his head. "No... I don't think ya will. That damage ain't from runnin' into another car." He grinned and pointed. "That there's from smashin' through one o' those pay garage arms or somesuch." He shrugged and chuckled again. "Me, I don't care much what ya did, but my guess is there's people lookin' fer this car."

This man is too smart for his own good. In the past, he would have simply eliminated the possible threat. *The past is the past... and good riddance.* He crossed his arms and waited.

"Tell ya what. Got me an old truck out back. She ain't much, but I'll rent 'er to ya fer ten bucks a day." He'd stuck out his hand. "Deal?"

Sohrab reached for his wallet, thanking Allah he wouldn't have to steal a car or take his chances with a rental.

"Nah," Radcliffe said, placing his hand over Sohrab's arm. "We'll settle up when I'm finished with yer car. Fair enough?"

"More than fair, Mr. Radcliffe," Sohrab said, taking the man's hand. "But do you not want a binder of some kind to ensure your vehicle's safe return?"

Radcliffe laughed hard. "Boy, just wait 'till you see the truck."

He'd almost changed his mind when he had. It had once been red, but where the paint wasn't faded it was simply missing, some places showing primer, others bare metal, and neither bumper was in much better shape than his own—and even though it was manual transmission with a clutch that slipped with every third shift, it ran well enough to carry him to the little roach motel in Arlington. It was the one place Sohrab knew took cash and asked no questions, frequented as it was by politicians accompanied by rough women with rougher pimps.

Sohrab showered and dressed, grabbed his wallet and the keys from the nightstand, and left the motel in search of a burner phone. He would text the Shadowman's number and wait. He was good at waiting; it was one of the few skills he'd been taught that hadn't faded from neglect. Amber and the others had gotten away safely, he was sure of that, and was a worry he could leave behind. *Jack would never forgive me if she were harmed.* A great weight had been lifted from his shoulders when the three women had sped away, the police ignoring them. He jerked the truck's door open and climbed inside. *The farther she stays from this, the safer she will be.* He got the engine to turn over on the third try, and he shifted into gear with minimal grinding.

"I will call her when we have found Jack." He guided the assemblage of rust and rubber out of the parking lot. "Until then, she can stay safely in the dark."

CHAPTER 15

"I TOLD YOU. ARGUS IS A PRIVATE DUDE. Skittish, in fact." Maribel stood beside the car, leaned on the open door, and hitched the strap of her bag higher on her shoulder. The look she saw on Janice's face was worth the discomfort she felt at meeting Argus alone. "If he sees the whole band coming his way, he'll likely bolt. Money doesn't seem to have the same importance for him as most, so he might not even agree to another meet." Maribel hadn't needed the greasy man's services more than a handful of times in the last four or five years, but each time he'd insisted on meeting with her alone. The possible reasons why were limited, and each elicited a shudder. He wasn't just slovenly, odorous, and disagreeable, but also *connected*. Good forgers always were. *The latter, at least.*

"Well," Janice drawled, the old bag's mouth a prune. "I'm the one paying, so I'll go along." She said it with the finality of someone used to getting her way. *Not this time.*

"Your precious money is safe with me. I won't run off to Aruba with it or anything." She scoffed and shook her head, then hefted the tight bundle of bills in her fist. "Besides, you and I both know this is little more than pocket change for you."

Amber laid a gentle hand on Janice's shoulder. "We can hit up a few shops for necessities while we wait."

"That sounds fun, doesn't it?" Beth said with a vigorous nod. She had bubbled and bounced the whole drive, and looked to Maribel like a new puppy staring at a rubber ball, tail wagging in anticipation.

Janice looked from one to the other, irritation playing across her face. *She doesn't want to come with me. Just another damn dominance game.* Amber bit her bottom lip and furrowed her brow, but Beth's wide-eyed stare was vacuous. Maribel suppressed a snicker. *Some people shouldn't be allowed off their leash.*

"Fine," Janice said at last. "We can start with purchasing small carry-on bags. I don't want to go through luggage check."

"Whatever," Maribel said, closing the car door. "I'll call you when I have the goods." She shifted the bag again and turned away. None called after her with even a *good luck*, or *see ya later*, but there was a haughty sniff from the old bag. Maribel knew she put people off, and that was fine with her—getting too close to anyone was dangerous in her business; most of her acquaintances were of the online variety.

The parking garage was busy, and she had to thread past several moving cars on her way to the mall's entrance, then stepped into the frantic bustle of the atrium. The Starbuck's where Argus said to meet him was on the Metro Level and wasn't far from where Beth had parked. She hadn't told them where the meet was, but since they could—and probably would—follow her, she wandered through several stores before doubling back. The Bag 'n Baggage they were likely to hit up first was on the third floor, so she sat on a bench with a clear line-of-sight to the store's entrance and waited. At the four minute mark, all three entered. Both Janice and Amber looked over the railing for a moment, scanning the mall floor, then turned and followed Beth inside.

"Guess they gave up sooner than I thought," Maribel muttered with a nod. "Pros they definitely are not." She sighed, stood, hitched up her bag, and turned toward the Starbuck's with dread. It wasn't far, but her legs refused to move very fast. Sooner than she liked, she was close enough to make Argus. He sat at a round table with a smaller circumference than his middle, no other customer sitting closer than ten feet. It was as if an invisible force field protected him from intruders.

"Yeah," she breathed. "That would be the smell." She prepared her nostrils for the eventual assault and stepped up to his table, pulled out a metal and wood chair with a grating screech, and flopped into the seat.

"Hello, Newman." Her nose wrinkling at once. The odor was pungent, distinctive, and mildly sweet—like rotting meat. "There's a store around here that specializes in soap. You should wander by there some time."

"I told you not to call me that," he squeaked, thick black hair flinging flecks of sweat as he cast furtive glances from side to side. "And I've also told you this is a condition, not a choice."

"Sure, sure, *Argus*. Only reminding you I know where you live, dig?"

"Believe me, Phoebe, I remember." His breathing was shallow and rapid, but it was every time she met with him. She chose to believe it meant nothing. "Are you ever gonna tell me your real name?"

"Not until our wedding night, sweetie," she said with a grin, eyelashes fluttering. *That's just mean.* His cheeks flushed cherry red. She watched him hover between fear and asking her out on a date, then his breathing slowed, and he reached under the table. His eyes never left her face, but he fumbled through his bag and withdrew a thick envelope, then placed it atop the table, one hirsute paw covering it protectively.

"Show me yours and I'll show you mine." He tried to waggle his eyebrows but succeeded in only making the two woollybears battle one another.

Maribel sighed, dug insider her bag, and withdrew the stack of hundred-dollar bills. She waved them in his face and his eyes widened in horror.

"Don't do that!" he cried, then snatched the bills from her hand. "You don't know who's watching."

"I'd think everyone in this town is used to it by now," she said with a sniff, then tugged the envelope from beneath his hand. She opened the flap and pulled out each of the documents, inspecting them with a practiced eye.

"Don't worry." He fanned the bills, giving them a sniff. "They'll pass."

"They'd better." The implied threat made him stop, and he looked over the top of the bills directly into her eyes.

"It's a bit late to start questioning my work, isn't it?" His voice shifted instantly level and low, and Maribel realized she'd crossed a line. No matter the games they played with one another, she recognized he always held the best hand. *At least the best hole-card.*

"Sorry," she muttered, stuffed the documents back inside the envelope, and shoved it into her bag. Argus wasn't really a bad sort, but a girl could only take so much. "Thanks."

"I enjoy doing business with you. You're a good customer."

She smirked at him, nodded, and stood, pushing her chair back, then took her phone from her jacket and dialed Janice's number. It rang only twice before the old woman answered.

"You have them?"

"Yes. Where do I meet you?"

"Third floor. Bag 'n Baggage."

"Be right there." Maribel grinned down at Argus again for reasons she couldn't comprehend.

"Oh," Janice said before Maribel hung up. "While you're there, could you get us each a latte?"

"Ah, fuck." Maribel snapped the phone closed. "I hate it when customers get cute."

Argus arched an eyebrow at her. "Don't we all."

The attendant scuttled around the table where the human lay in its Dream Sleep, the scanner in its talon scraping out the soothing tones. Two others monitored vital signs, but this one was First for its tiny workforce. Not like the *true* First, *praise be his name*, but at least nominally in charge.

This one was pleased. The human had accepted the mites without complication, and the little machines had long-since finished the arduous task of replacing the bits of surgical metal with human bone. There was no reason to believe those now administered to the animal's brain would not perform as satisfactorily. The more pressing concern was the dearth of new mites available to the hive. The growing vats all belonged to *the others*, with no hope of recovery.

The First was overdue for his visit, and this one worried there had been little progress since his last. *What will he do?* Firsts became erratic as their term of autonomy stretched into decades, requiring sacrifice and replacement, and this First had been autonomous for a *very* long time.

This one wandered over to a small growing vat it had cobbled together after the splintering and looked down past the gel to the single K'zzetti seed growing within. This one had escaped with it during the final battle with *the others* and had spent decades encouraging its growth. The raw materials were rare on Earth, but it had found enough. Soon the hive would have a functioning K'zzetti Scritt, the one device upon which all their plans rested. It would take decades yet to grow into a Mother, but its utility even at this stage was more than enough to penetrate the pitiful computing machines and their masters on this planet.

The First will be pleased with the progress on the seed, it thought. It hoped. Its back itched with worry, and its tail swished from side to side. The other attendants in the room mirrored their leader's projected emotions, unconscious of the act as they busied themselves with assigned tasks. It noticed the motion of their tails and willed itself to calm. *It makes no sense to heal the human only to slice off its head with a random slash. The First would sacrifice us all.* It wouldn't matter if attendants were in short supply, either—not for such an egregious error.

The door irised open, and the First strode through, cape billowing behind. He went directly to the table with the human, crossed his arms over his thorax, and tapped a single claw on the stone floor with a steady, slow, staccato rhythm.

"Why is this animal not in programming?" His abdominal slits vibrated in sympathy, a buzzing accompaniment to his voice. "You were told to have him ready." The First turned and loomed over the attendant, his abdomen pulsating.

It took a step back. "The mites were implanted this morning after this one was sure we had eliminated the last of the metal in its skull." The First was still close enough to strike, but the attendant had given itself enough room to parry.

Not that it would dare, regardless of the genetic imperative for survival.

"Do you think me a fool?" the First said, closing the gap.

"No, First. This one would never imply—"

"Then stop your excuses and complete the task."

"We must give The mites time to integrate with the human's central nervous system, First. It may develop a resistance if the process is begun too soon."

"Another excuse," the First bellowed. He paced, his tail's barb coming dangerously close to the subject. "When shall I expect favorable results?" He stopped in front of the attendant, so close it felt the heat radiating from the First's body. The attendant cowered and tried to move away but was already backed against the wall. It pressed down its fight-or-flight reflex; either would be fatal. The other attendants ignored the interchange, their tasks encompassing the whole of their attention.

"There is no—"

"One Earth day," the First said, bending low enough to bite the attendant's head off. The First's beak parted slightly, his double row of teeth reflecting hints of light, trebling the attendant's terror. It would do as commanded—it must—and though the First had been warned, the attendant knew any resulting failure would fall on its head alone. The First drove that point home with a nip of one of the attendant's horns. He straightened and spat the short length of chitin to the stone floor. "One day," he repeated.

"It will be done." The attendant bowed, ignoring the pain. Its own mites would soon repair the damage, but it hoped they would wait until after the First departed. *He has indeed become erratic. Perhaps it is time for change.*

"I will return tomorrow. See that the animal is ready." With that he swept from the room, the door irising closed behind him.

Thirteen pulled the door open on crying hinges, throwing a rectangle of dull amber light into the room. The acrid smell of ammonia hit his nostrils all at once, and he looked down as his shoe splashed the puddle by the door. He almost laughed as he stepped over the accompanying pile of excrement. The woman had left the gifts for him just inside the door as protest, but her demeanor had changed since then, the long hours alone in the dark taking their toll.

Sergeant Clarke sat huddled in a far corner of the room, shading her eyes and blinking at the light. Her hair was in disarray and there were small scratches on her arms, but she looked otherwise whole. A single dead rat lay on the floor near her feet, its head smashed flat with the shoe still in her hand. Thirteen frowned and nodded his head, grateful he hadn't left her alone long enough for hunger to take hold. He pulled the device from his pocket, its green glow brightening toward white, filling the room with enough light to see by. He pulled the door closed.

Thirteen set the device on the table between them, then sat in the chair he'd left there the day before. "I see you survived the night." Clarke locked her eyes on the device, a silent and wild fear behind wide lids. "Don't worry. I still cannot use this to pry into your mind." He pursed his lips and peered into her eyes with a languid stare. "It does, however, act quite nicely as a lie detector."

She pulled the shoe back on her foot, stood, and wobbled toward the table. "I ain't tellin' ya nothin'." She stood before him like a cadet enduring a dressing down by an officer. *She puts on a brave front; I will give her that much. But she is unused to being on this end of an interrogation.* Harsh interrogation, the newest euphemism for torture, was the only arrow in his quiver, and he intended to make it count.

"Are your masters my masters?" It was the most obvious question, but he didn't expect an affirmative response.

"Don't know what your talkin' about." The device's glow held steady. *The truth.* "I can't even *answer* certain questions without dying, never mind digging into my skull."

He wanted to tell her he had done this many times, and that she could not hide anything from him, but that wasn't the truth. He had questioned no one with *nanites* before, and certainly none with a suicide imperative. It added a layer of difficulty, but that only made the task novel—not impossible.

"Then by all means," he said, spreading his hands in a welcoming gesture, "feel free to lie."

She stared at him like someone had asked her to multiply two eight-digit numbers in her head, then cackled a grotesque laugh. She found a second chair, pulled it up to the other side of the table, and sat. "All right, Lurch. Shoot."

"You told the truth earlier, but that may be only because you do not know my masters," he said, leaning on his elbows. "Are your masters Zzkritti?" It made no sense that they would be, but he must eliminate every possibility for the answers to be valid.

Clarke's eye twinkled, and she shook her head. "Never heard of 'em," she drawled.

The pulse reaching out to his mind from the device was pure Zzkritti, unfiltered and untranslated, but he'd become familiar with many of their words and phrases over the long years. *Lie*, it said, a phrase more metaphor than a single defined word. It was clear. It was concise. And it rocked him on his heels. His head reeled from the implications.

Why do they work at cross purposes? His mind raced, and the device responded to the unspoken request, scrolling backward through mountains of data, pouring knowledge into his mind in a torrent, large chunks of which were nothing more than white noise. *Redactions.* The bits and pieces he was allowed to view were a history of their species he already knew. An Earth history, separate from the hive's greater body.

His hands trembled, and he clasped them together to still the tremors. When he looked across the table, Clarke was still smiling, her face twisted with a look of satisfied triumph. *She knows.* Her eyes widened, the smile frozen for perhaps a second before it faded and her spine stiffened. Thirteen watched her topple, the chair spilling out from beneath, the glassy stare now unfocused and vacant.

She was dead before her head hit the floor with a wet smack.

185

October was always a busy month in American politics, and Dieter meant to ensure the next was no different. He'd seen more than a dozen presidential elections, but this cycle promised something special. Both sides always fought like the mortal enemies they never were, with little of it having anything to do with reasoned arguments or moral standing, but *this* one...

Dieter had ridden this train before—saw where the tracks led and who laid them; he had lived this nightmare, then as now maneuvering to land on the winning side. He knew which outcome was necessary for his plans, though he still didn't know the ultimate prize. *No matter*, he thought. *That will come soon enough.*

He checked his watch and looked both directions along the street outside the courtyard cafe. The big Russian was late again. "They are always late," he muttered. "Even sixty years ago they were late." He reached inside the leather satchel and patted the envelope filled with American dollars. Every Russian had a weakness for American currency, and he hoped there was enough for the inevitable upward negotiation from the agreed-upon price.

The disk in the envelope was the real package. Dieter didn't know where his skills as a programmer sprang from—either Evan or the nanites themselves—but they were prodigious. It was as if every time he sat at a keyboard, he opened a vein and just *bled* the code.

Sometimes he worried if *he* were nothing more than bits of code cobbled together for a greater purpose. Evan barked a hollow laugh from deep inside his crumbling fortress.

"So serious, my friend." A meaty paw clapped Dieter on the back, and Gregori flopped into the chair across the table.

"You're late."

"Bah! In Russia, late is on time." He said *Russia* expansively, pronouncing it *RrrOOsha*. Dieter had known many Russians, and none of them spoke the way this man did. It was as if he was an actor acting the part of what he thought a Russian *should* be. Dieter had thoroughly checked out the man's background, and he indeed worked for the Russian government—though in what capacity wasn't clear. He assumed the act was a character the man played to mask his deadly intelligence and chose not to call him on it. "Is program in bag?" He pointed at the satchel in Dieter's lap. Dieter nodded. "And money?"

"As agreed," Dieter said.

"Ah," Demetri said and crossed one leg over the other, holding his hands out as if in supplication. "About the money..." He sighed and shook his head sadly. "There have been a few minor complications."

"No."

"No?"

"No, Demetri. As in not one penny more." The dance begun, Dieter waited for the other man to bluster, feign non-complicity, then reluctantly suggest an amount lower than they had told him to take, though still much higher than agreed. He could compel the man's compliance, but where was the fun in that?

"My superiors—their words, not mine of course—they worry your program is Trojan Horse." He spoke the last as if it pained him to say it, when it was more likely he had raised the concern. A good operative laid out the downsides of any operation; the better to cover themselves if things didn't pan out.

The truth was Dieter's program *was* a Trojan Horse. It would work as advertised, but it would also give him unprecedented access to every Russian government system it touched. It was also both undetectable and untraceable by any human programmer.

The Russian checked his watch with a quick glance and lowered his hands.

Dieter arched an eyebrow. "Do you have a pressing engagement?"

"I have other friends in Washington besides you, *tovarisch*," he said, shrugging. "Some of them I owe money." He narrowed his eyes at Dieter. "Some will worry if I am late."

"Get to the point." Dieter sighed and waved his hand in a come-along gesture.

"You Americans," Demetri said, shaking his head. "Always in such a hurry."

"I'm not the one checking my watch."

"Fine. I must, as you say, grease a few more palms than usual." He gave Dieter a crestfallen look, one of resignation. "The price is now doubled I am afraid."

"Double..." *The idiot should be afraid.*

"If you want program to reach proper hands, yes."

He'd expected as much as a fifty percent increase, but even that much cash required another day to accumulate, and he told Demetri as much.

"Timing is, shall we say, critical. I must have both money and program when I leave, or I am to leave empty-handed." He watched Dieter for fifteen seconds while the latter simply stared back. "Bah," he said at last. "You win. I can accept... one hundred and fifty." His voice rose at the end as if asking a question, but Dieter knew there was none. This was the man's final offer.

After a reasonable play at stalling, Dieter took the envelope from his satchel and laid it on the table. "Deal," he said. Demetri placed a heavy paw over the envelope, pulled it into his lap, and barked a hearty laugh.

"Bah! You knew how much I would ask before you came, did you not?"

Dieter smiled, the motion staying well away from his eyes. He stood and pulled a twenty from his wallet and set it on the saucer beneath his coffee cup, then gathered his things. He turned to leave, hat in hand, and Demetri grabbed his arm and held him back. Dieter looked at the Russian, an odd and questioning look on the man's face.

"Why?" he asked, his bushy eyebrows meeting in the middle.

There were any number of meanings hidden in that one word, but Dieter knew exactly what he meant. He grinned with genuine humor, tugged the red ball cap with the dumbest campaign slogan in history onto his head, and pulled his arm away from the Russian.

"Let's just say I'm a true believer."

CHAPTER 16

SOHRAB LEANED BACK AGAINST THE SIDE OF the truck, cherry lollipop is his mouth, and scanned the highway beyond the expanse of broken concrete. Grasses and moss had taken hold in the abandoned parking lot, breaking the surface into ever-smaller pieces in a process as old as life itself. A hundred years from now, there would be little left; not even the empty husk of the K-Mart behind him would remain. Time was a ruthless bitch, and no one survived its ravages for long.

Clouds piled up south and east casting a dark shadow over the landscape, but none appeared ready to dump their treasure of water anytime soon. They drifted west, a lazy sloth climbing a steep hill. The sky was purpling to the east, and a hot, damp wind blew over Sohrab, reminding him the dog days of summer were far from over.

He checked the time on his new phone, then snapped it closed. Technically, the Shadowman wasn't late—he'd given no ETA—but as the minutes stretched into hours, Sohrab's initial irritation morphed into worry.

How long does it take to drive ten miles? He knew how long *he* would take, but most didn't have his knowledge of the city. The Shadowman had seemed preoccupied, and no matter how much Sohrab probed, he'd gently but steadfastly refused to discuss it over the phone. The only thing he *would* say was that Dieter was not involved in Jack's disappearance.

How does he know? He'd accepted the information, and the knowledge had even calmed his nerves a bit about his friend's well-being, but the more he thought it over, the less sense it made. *Who* else *would go to so much trouble? What is their motivation?* The questions would pile one atop the other for hours if he didn't control himself.

"Eliminate the impossible," he muttered, pulling the lollipop from his mouth, then chuckled. A time-worn problem-solving technique, it was less than useless when the problem included nano-machines and super-advanced aliens.

Sohrab itched to contact Amber but resisted. *She is smart enough to have discarded her phone by now, and if not, others may be listening.* The only method possible for reaching her now was through Maribel, and for that he needed the Shadowman.

"And even that only works if they are still together." He grunted and jammed the lollipop back in this mouth. There was no reason to believe they were, but even if he could speak to Amber, what would he say? *Sorry we can't find Jack, but at least he's not with Dieter?* Cold comfort indeed.

A dead-black sedan exited the highway, bounced over the pothole covered roadway, and drove into the parking lot. It slowed and rolled to a smooth stop beside the truck, the driver-side window sliding down.

"You are clear," the Shadowman said, still holding the wheel. "There are no records or video evidence of your escape from the jail." He tilted his head when no response came from Sohrab, pursing his lips and narrowing his eyes. "I have no further need of a driver, nor access to Jack. You are free to return to your home."

Sohrab, straightened, pulled the lollipop out of his mouth, and tossed it aside. "Now wait just—"

"However," the Shadowman said, short-circuiting Sohrab's instant ire, "I find I have need of your other skills."

Sohrab cocked an eyebrow. "And those being?"

"Get in." The Shadowman nodded at the passenger seat. "We will discuss it on the way to the airport."

"Airport?" Sohrab walked around the car and opened the door. He slid into the seat and closed the door again as the car lurched forward. "What is at the airport?"

"Nothing... now." The Shadowman drove the car out of the lot and onto the frontage road. "But it seems all four women have flown to Argentina."

"What is in Argentina?"

"Jack, according to the message Maribel sent."

A flood of questions crowded the front of his brain, each pounding to get out and join the conversation. *How did they find this informa-*

tion when even the Shadowman couldn't? was foremost, followed closely by *why go without us?* and *where did they get the money?* The one that spilled out of his mouth first surprised even him.

"Wait... *four* women?"

The Shadowman faced him, a thin, but amused grin on his lips. "It appears they have conscripted their Uber driver."

Sohrab wanted to laugh but couldn't. If Amber had found a lead to Jack in Argentina, the chances they were walking into a hornet's nest were astronomically high.

"So... if you know where they are going and why, why do you need me?"

"As I said, it is your skills—"

"No," Sohrab said, shaking his head. "That is not an answer. Everything I can do, you can do better—plus you have that device in your pocket."

"I only offer you the truth." He spun the wheel and entered the highway. "Your skills may be required, and I cannot go with you. Nor can the device."

"Something more pressing at home?" Sohrab said with a sneer.

"In a way, but that is not the only reason." The Shadowman slumped in his seat and sighed. "It is my belief the Zzkritti are involved in Jack's disappearance, and it is best if they do not know we have this information."

"Wait, wait, wait," Sohrab said, waving both hands in the air. "Didn't Jeff send you to enlist Jack in the search for Dieter?"

"Yes."

"Did he tell you Jack had been taken?"

"No. In fact I do not believe he knows even now."

Sohrab sat, his mouth hanging open, hands frozen in mid-air, and stared at the Shadowman with growing consternation. *How could he not?* He closed his mouth and lowering his hands to his lap. *What is going on here?*

"When I say the Zzkritti are involved, I do not mean my masters."

"Then... what?"

"You have heard of the war between the two factions of Zzkritti?" He slid the car into the HOV lane. Sohrab nodded. "They taught me the others were all destroyed before the end of 1942." He tapped the wheel with the fingers of one hand, the muscles in his jaw bunching. "They were not."

"You know this as fact." It was not a question.

"No, but it is the only premise that fits available information."

A second group of Zzkritti? Sohrab thought. *But they are a hive mind... how could his masters not know? And if they do, why allow them to operate freely? Why keep their enforcer in the dark?* None of it made any sense to him, and he stared at his hands. If he continued to apply human logic to an alien species, he would never comprehend their motives—even their mode of thought was alien.

"So why can't you go?" he asked at last. "It seems you are the perfect man for the job."

The Shadowman tilted his head and considered, accepting the compliment. "I have no evidence it involves others among my masters, nor if those holding Jack can track me as my masters do." He turned to Sohrab, a pained look on his face. "It is certain they will detect the device the instant I am in their midst. This, I cannot allow."

"Do they not have such devices of their own?"

He shook his head. "I do not believe they do. There would be no need to expose themselves as they have if they did."

Sohrab scratched his beard and considered... well, *everything*.

"Still," the Shadowman continued, "They will not act openly if they can avoid it. They must use their puppets as proxies, and enhanced or not, those will be formidable."

"And the women are walking right into it."

The Shadowman stared straight ahead as he drove, his silence all the confirmation Sohrab needed.

Maribel pushed past Amber and threw her bag on the bed farthest from the door. "Dibs," she called over her shoulder. She watched the others roll into the suite, each a different level of haggard, then turned a curled lip and squinted eyes to Janice. "With all your money, I don't understand why we all have to stay in the same goddamn room."

Janice didn't look up as she tossed her own bag to the nearest bed. "Safety, more than anything else." She sat on the edge and crossed her ankles.

"Safety?" Maribel said, her brow furrowing. "We're in a five-star hotel with security at every entrance... how much safer can it get?"

Janice shrugged and faced her. "This much, apparently."

Amber sighed and sat beside Janice, the strap of her small duffel still over her shoulder. She pulled it into her lap and tight against her belly. She hadn't looked well since the in-flight meal, as if she'd been ridden hard and put away wet, as Maribel's uncle used to say. Beth fairly bounced compared to the others and flopped onto the bed beside Maribel.

"I'm okay bunking with everyone. Kinda like a sleepover or a camping trip."

"Yeah, try hitting me with a pillow and see what happens," Maribel grumped, her eyes cutting at the young woman, more tense than anyone suspected. She hadn't really expected a reply from Josef, but Alberto should have contacted her by now. *At least a damn acknowledgment would have been nice.* So far, though, she'd heard nothing from either. Josef was a client, but Alberto was family; he had no excuses. Her last message to him had included the hotel and room number, and still nothing. *Never count on family.* Her father had drummed that one into her head, yet she never learned to heed it. "Friends are the family you choose," he'd said. "Choose them wisely and they will always be there for you. Family is undependable at best."

Granted, he'd learned that the hard way. She checked her phone again. *Just hope I'm not repeating his mistake.*

"Expecting a call?" Janice had watched Maribel with an intense interest each time she'd pulled the phone from her pocket.

"Yeah, actually."

"From?"

"If you must know, I messaged Josef before we left. Told him where we were going and what we hoped to find."

"You did *what*?" Amber said, suddenly alert. "How could you be so... so..."

"Stupid," Janice finished for her.

"Don't worry," Maribel said. "I routed it through our usual communication channels." She looked from Janice to Amber, each looking at the other with concern, then gave a flippant wave of her hand. "There's no way for anyone to trace the message."

Amber, her face turning from green to red, shook her head. "You don't really appreciate what you're dealing with here, Mari."

Taken aback, more by the diminutive used only by her father than the fact they now questioned her skills, she couldn't form a coherent response. *Of course I appreciate what I'm dealing with*, she wanted to say, but did she really? She still thought both women were crazy, but there were enough things hinky with this whole affair that she couldn't discount anything.

Maribel sneered. "So we're back to the whole alien thing again."

Janice's cheeks glowed hot. "We don't have to convince you of anything. You're hired help. Just do what I ask and nothing more."

Amber set her duffel aside and leaned closer to Janice, laying a gentle hand on her arm. Now that Amber had calmed, the green tint to her face returned, accompanied by a sheen of perspiration.

"No, Janice." Her voice was unsteady. "Mari's here for a reason greater than money—I'm sure of that." She mustered a smile at Maribel that became sad almost at once. *She may be crazy, but she's hurting—that's for sure.*

"I wouldn't be so—"

"You and I both know you didn't have to come." Amber waved her smartphone at her. "Argentina has the highest level of English proficiency in all of South America." She winked as if the motion pained her. "And surely anyone here could understand my rudimentary Spanish." She shook her head. "No, you're here for something else."

"Regardless," Janice said like an accusation, "she can't be sending messages without telling us." She faced Amber and looked hard into her eyes. *"They'll know."*

"Maybe." Amber's eyes never left Maribel's. "But what's done is done." She patted Janice's arm again, then sighed. "I think it's time Mari and Beth heard the whole story."

Janice tilted her head, her mouth a pucker. "Do you think that's wise? This woman already thinks you're crazy."

"She needs to understand the stakes and what we're up against." She pursed her lips. "They both do."

"More alien nonsense?" Maribel sneered. Amber smiled and wiped her forehead with the back of her hand, then propped a pillow against the headboard and leaned back, tugging her knees tight to her chest. Her calm was chilling, and Maribel felt that chill for the first time.

It wouldn't be the last.

"Yes," Amber said after an interminable silence. "But I'm not starting with them. The important part begins with an accident."

She reeled out her story in one long stream-of-consciousness telling, pausing from time to time for a sip of water from the sweat-beaded glass Beth filled and re-filled. When Amber reached the point in the story where she murdered Mason, it was clear that little fact had been left out when Janice first heard the tale, as was the mercy killing of Jack's brother.

She killed Mason. I should be angry—I should hate her—but all I feel is pity. She had more hatred for the way Sohrab had treated her friend's remains, even if she understood the necessity. It was Amber's admission, more than anything else, that convinced Maribel the woman at least *believed* what she said, but it was the facts surrounding the worldwide manhunt for Jack and how easily it all went away that sealed it for her. She'd watched the whole thing in real-time with great fascination, digging into reports not even congressmen had access to; each had dead-ended shortly after the events at the asylum.

When Amber finished, there were tears tracking glistening lines down her face. She wiped them away, neither angrily nor sadly. *She's seen too much—been through too much—to be sad or angry. How would I react?*

She saw exactly how... withdraw. *Run.* Hide where none could ever find her and live out her days hoping the monsters got to her last. *Maybe I should do that now.* She knew better. She'd hitched her wagon to Amber and the others knowing where it might lead, and for no other reason than curiosity.

And now the world's at stake. She scoffed. *Isn't it always?*

They all sat in silence—even Beth—the only sound in the room a chorus of breathing, Maribel pulled her bottom lip.

"So," Beth said to no one, her face scrunched in deep thought, "if the Zzkritti don't have Jack, then who—"

Everyone's head snapped toward the door, the lock rattling with the three sharp knocks on the dense wood. Janice, the closest, stood and smoothed her skirt, then looked down at Amber with fear-filled eyes.

"Don't worry." Maribel stood. "I've got this."

She walked across the room, and without checking, opened the door. A grin spread across her wide face. "Alberto!" she cried, letting out a breath she didn't realize she'd been holding. She threw her arms around his neck and stood on tiptoes to kiss his cheek. "Come in, come in." She pulled him into the room by the hand, watching with evil pleasure the shock and fear on Janice's face.

"I apologize," Janice squeaked out. "You are...?"

"This is Alberto, my cousin," Maribel said, hugging the tall boy. Both Amber and Beth got to their feet and stood beside Janice. "He's here to help."

195

Dieter closed the laptop on his writing desk and leaned back in his chair, vertebrae popping as he stretched. He'd been in the seat for well over twelve hours, and even with the control over this body's endocrine system, some physical realities were too urgent to ignore forever. He stood, stretched again, and walked into the bathroom. Dieter detested practically every aspect of physical maintenance, but bowel and bladder evacuation stood at the pinnacle of an extensive list of annoyances. He dropped his trousers and sat, then ignored the procedure as he pondered the last twenty-four hours.

His task had been simple in theory, but a rat's nest of tangled priorities in practice. The Russians already had a massive disinformation campaign in operation, and all Dieter had done was give them a nudge and a helping hand; the hard part was covering his digital tracks. There were still too many important men to meet to jeopardize his plans with a careless exposure. He grinned when he remembered how quickly Gregori passed along his program to the Russian team, ceding control of their systems to Dieter without ever suspecting he'd compromised them.

"And they never will." Dieter finished the distasteful activity, flushing as he stood. He wandered back into the main living area and considered the kitchen for a moment. He hadn't eaten in more than twenty hours, and his stomach rumbled a harsh scolding. Before, he'd been something of a gourmand—a *foodie*, as the Americans would say—but now the act of preparing and consuming a meal both bored and irritated him. He surveyed the empty takeout containers piled both in and around the trash can and sighed. *Another task I must perform.* He could easily afford a maid, but he must maintain the pretense of poverty; he also couldn't have strangers poking around his apartment.

He strode to the coat rack by the door and lifted the light jacket from its hook, shrugging it on as he grabbed his keys. *I will clean a bit when I return.* Evan snorted derision from inside his prison. *No, you won't.* Dieter grunted in frustration, took his fedora from the hook atop the rack, and jammed it on his head. There was a bar nearby that served a passable Reuben sandwich. He locked the door behind him, feeling suddenly nervous before tamping the emotion down.

"Curious." He tilted his head. "What is there to be nervous about?" He shrugged and turned toward the stairs. *Maybe I just worry that ham-handed piano player will sing again tonight.* The fat man was truly odious in his opinion, though he had to admit there was *some* artistry in his delivery.

He walked down the stairs to his car, never considering the feeble young man tucked in the back of his mind trembling in apprehensive anticipation.

Is this what Jeff looks like under his illusion? Jack supposed he did but couldn't manage enough interest to care. He stood in a wide circular room of stone, the wall reaching upward to form a cone far over his head. The monstrosity pacing back and forth in front of him was taller than Jeff, and wore an elaborate cape of scaly crimson hide, like polished alligator skin painted in blood. Its tail swished side to side as it paced, turning on a set of wickedly sharp talons to retrace its path. It looked like a general on an inspection tour, and the way it snapped at the smaller versions of its species only confirmed Jack's cold assessment.

Not cold, he thought. *Emotionless.*

Since waking on the stone slab, Jack hadn't felt, well... anything. Not frightened, or angry, or sad, or even mildly irritated. It was as if they had switched off his amygdala. The Zzkritti were clearly preparing him for something, and despite his prior objections to being altered, they had ignored them.

Where is Jeff? The smaller alien—still larger than those skittering about—had made no attempt to see Jack after he awoke. *Perhaps he is no longer in charge.* Without a clue how their society worked, or the sort of backbiting politics evident in any organization, he hadn't enough information to assume anything about their power structure.

The hulking Zzkritti stopped in front of Jack, one talon seizing his face, the sharpened claws surprisingly gentle, and turned his head this way and that. Jack stood perfectly still, not even his heart rate elevating. He had no choice, really. Every muscle locked, every emotion drained, he couldn't have moved even if he had the desire.

The insectoid snapped its beak at one of the others and spewed an odd series of clicks and hums as if an old dot-matrix printer had jammed. The smaller Zzkritti ducked its head and backed away, answering with the sound of a modem connecting to AOL. The first seemed to accept the response, nodded, and focused its attention back on Jack, releasing his face and stepping back.

"Tell me your name," it said in a passable, Spanish-accented English.

Until this moment, Jack hadn't realized it *could* speak, but he opened his mouth and croaked out "Jack Montgomery." He wanted to say more, but it was apparently all he they allowed him to say.

"Do you know what I am?"

"Zzkritti," Jack said, his voice stronger now, but his throat ached for water. He wasn't thirsty, though. *Odd.*

The caped Zzkritti nodded and spoke again to the smaller one, who straightened a little. *Can an animal with a beak smile?* It seemed as if this one could—at least with its eyes. It cooed a response and motioned at Jack. The two spoke to one another as if he weren't in the room.

What are they preparing me for? Why has Jeff not spoken to me? Or Thirteen, for that matter? Questions piled one atop the other, bubbling like a percolator. He still wasn't angry, but *something* rose in his belly, worked the muscles in his jaw, forcing itself up and out like water over a dam. When the dam broke, he was as surprised as anyone.

"Where is Jeff?" he boomed, blurting out the only question that mattered at this point. Every Zzkritti froze and the one with the cape—*Gonna call him Bruce, I think*—spun and narrowed its black eyes at him, a sharp buzzing emitting from its abdomen, the tail now whipping. It grated out something to the little one, its eyes never leaving Jack's.

"It spoke!" the First growled at the attendant. The animal should not be able to speak of its own accord. It wasn't impossible, but in his over twenty-thousand-year existence, he'd seen it but once. Curiously, that had also been a human. They had engineered its sacrifice soon after, but its message was much harder to kill. After two thousand years, the Zzkritti had finally given up and used the animal's followers instead.

"This one does not understand, First." The attendant stepped back. "The creature is fully integrated." It held out the scanner in its talon, showing the display to the First. "Observe... the mites still maintain control of its limbic system. Even its endocrine system obeys our commands." The attendant lowered its head. "This one assures you the human will obey."

"That may be true, attendant, but if it can ask its own questions, then it can speak the truth of what we program it *for*, can it not?"

"That is... possible, First," it said, lowering its head further. "The Hive released operatives before with rudimentary programming and nearly full autonomy." It spoke rapidly now, an obvious effort to avoid punishment. "In those cases, we gave imperatives on an as-needed basis." It lifted its eyes to the First. "It requires monitoring the animal more closely..."

"Yes," the First said, scratching the annoying patch of fungus on his flank. "I was once responsible for monitoring one of those." He shook his head in a human gesture of resignation. "Debilitating work, and quite tedious." He bent close to the odorous human. "I do not know what or of whom you speak," he said in English. The human showed no outward signs of surprise, but the flavor of its thoughts implied as much. It did not speak again, perhaps spent from its one attempt at autonomy. The First sniffed and spun to the attendant.

"Change the animal's programming if necessary, but it must be returned to its people soon." He glared at the attendant. "*You* will monitor the creature." He slashed the attendant's face once with a claw for emphasis. "The disease mites are ready, I assume?"

"Of course!" it said at once. "We implanted those after we completed programming."

"When you *thought* the programming was completed," the First corrected. He swept past the animal, making a final point with a swipe of his tail. His barb sliced through the human's leg almost to the bone, but the animal did not move. The First nodded approval and left. *The attendant must now contend with the damage, adding to its work.* Satisfaction bloomed in his upper thorax. *Perhaps next time it will remember and prepare properly.* For a moment he worried he had put the schedule in jeopardy but shook the notion away. The attendant could heal the animal while re-programming the nanites. *Regardless, the human must be moved to the training site a day from now.*

Drones skittered from his path as he strode the bore of smoothed rock, none coming within the radius of his tail's sweep; their survival imperative, honed by a half-billion years of evolution and genetic engineering, forced a buffer between them and the First's rising heat. He had always known they must use the mites but hadn't the power to order it until now; rarely employed to cleanse a planet, and *never* for the purposes he planned, but time had grown short.

One world, one Hive. It must be, or none survive.

CHAPTER 17

"WHO ELSE HAVE YOU TOLD?" Janice squared off with Maribel, and Amber noticed the younger woman refused to cower; whether that implied hidden steel in her spine or faith in the tall boy with the dark, smoldering eyes at her back, she neither knew nor cared. They must all show some steel in the face of what waited. *Odds are one will buckle and fold before this is over.* The thought tasted thick and bitter.

Maribel sneered back. "No one. Just Alberto and Josef."

"On your phone." Janice pursed her lips and narrowed her eyes. "On your *unsecured* phone."

Maribel raised her chin and sniffed. "Lady, nothing I use is unsecured."

Janice harrumphed, one eyebrow raised. "Against alien technology?"

"What's done is done," Amber said with a sigh, stepping between the women, separating them. "Welcome Alberto." The man had so far chosen not to speak. *He's at least smart enough to not get between two women in an argument.* "I'm not sure how you can help, but I appreciate your being here." She held her hand out for him to shake it. His eyes widened, then he smiled, took her hand, and bent low to kiss it. He looked up, holding her hand a little too long for her taste.

"The pleasure is all mine." He released her hand and straightened. His English was perfect, but the accent and baritone voice would have stolen her heart at once if she weren't already so focused on her mission. She smiled, maybe more broadly than she intended, and drew her hand back. Maribel watched them with unrestrained humor, then slapped her cousin on the back.

"Oh my God, Alberto," she said, her voice laughing. "I get it... she's fucking gorgeous, but you don't have to flirt with *every* woman you meet." She snickered and hit him again, this time with a fist to his shoulder. "You haven't changed a goddamn bit."

Alberto shrugged, and he faced Maribel. "I may not have to, but neither does one have to dance. These things are done for pleasure." He turned back to Amber. "We do many things for pleasure, no?"

Amber laughed. "You've got game—I'll give you that—but it won't play with me... or any mature woman for that matter."

"Speak for yourself, dear," Janice said, brightening. "You'll find the effects of flattery get stronger with age."

"Beautiful mature women are a special passion of mine." He swung his dark and deep-set eyes to Janice. Amber stifled a laugh when the woman blushed.

"All right," Maribel said, shaking her head. "That's enough, cousin. Can we get down to the business of the *actual* reason you're here?"

He nodded and leaned back against the writing desk, resting on his hands and crossing his ankles. "You are the boss," he said, smiling with perfect, straight teeth. Amber's eyes lingered on that smile, and when he looked at her, she shied away and spun to Maribel.

"Yes, Mari, why exactly *is* he here?" She sat on the edge of the bed near Beth, who had remained silent throughout the byplay. The only woman in the room not entranced by Alberto, she locked her eyes on Maribel.

"I told you... he's here to help."

"Well," Alberto said, "along with four of my best men."

Amber glanced in Janice's direction, then back at Maribel. "Four...? What's he talking about?" For the first time since she'd met her, Maribel looked abashed. She stared at her shoes for a second without a voice. Amber faced Alberto. "What are you talking about?"

"I am a construction worker," he said with a shrug.

"Uh huh," Amber said, drawing out the last syllable. "Go on."

"Ah, it is nothing. In construction it is easy to find large men willing to do what they are told to earn extra money." He crossed hard arms over a broad chest. "I work on the side providing security for visiting businessmen and certain foreign dignitaries."

"Does this include the use of weapons?"

"God, I hope so," Beth said, pulling her knees up to her chin.

"My men and I have trained—"

"How much?" Janice said, lowering herself to the corner of the other bed.

"We should first discuss your needs, then we—"

"How much is this going to cost me?" she said again, this time to Maribel.

Maribel glanced at Alberto, who nodded. "Twenty-five," she began. Alberto held up three fingers. "Sorry... three thousand a day." She looked at her shoes again. "But that is for all five," she added, glaring at Alberto.

Janice considered the sum, frowning. Her eyes drifted toward the ceiling as she thought it over. Amber knew the woman was not simply calculating the final cost, but what the service was worth to them. "I'll give him fifteen hundred a day, and he covers his own expenses," she said, looking directly at Alberto.

He grinned like a mountain cat, but Amber saw the pulse from his carotid quicken. It pounded as if attempting an escape. "Two thousand, and you cover expenses."

"Seventeen-fifty flat, and you'll take it and like it." Her eyes blazed, and everyone held their breath. Amber didn't care either way... she only wanted to begin; she saw no need for extra men, anyway.

Alberto looked from Janice to Maribel, the muscles in his jaw working, cheeks darkening; he looked like a teakettle ready to shriek. Instead he laughed. Loud and hard like Sohrab used to.

"I like this woman!" he boomed. "Your friends are as hard as my men."

Janice snorted. "Boy, you have no idea."

"Pull in over there," Sohrab said, pointing to the dilapidated row of storage sheds. "Third one on the right." The lot where the old sheds sat in shambled disarray was overgrown with weeds and thick clumps of grasses, and even the concrete between rows had succumbed to the decades of weathering and encroaching vegetation; cracked and crumbling, it made for a bouncy ride. *But it's cheap.* He'd purchased a long-term contract years ago—back when he still needed such things—and had forgotten it until last year when the contract came up for renewal. At the time, he'd regretted using the last of the money from Mason's wallet to pay the fee, but now he was glad he had.

"That one?" The Shadowman nodded at the small shed, its door painted a fading orange, large white numbers that may or may not have been *thirteen*.

"Yeah. Just park in front of the door."

The Shadowman complied, and the tires ground against the rough road. He pulled to a stop, the car's bumper less than a meter from the door, and he turned toward Sohrab. "Keep in mind we are on a schedule."

"This will not take long," Sohrab said, and opened the door and climbed out. He went to the door and lifted the combination padlock. The hasp on the garage-style door was mottled with rust, but formidable enough to keep anyone without a large bolt cutter on the correct side. The lock, heavy and expensive, was still in pristine condition. He spun the dial a couple of turns to clear it, then entered the combination: twelve, nine, two—the exact day, month, and year he had deserted his country's service and sought asylum in the US. If he hadn't possessed detailed information of Iraqi military assets and deployment, he likely would have been turned away; at the time, even the Bush administration was still a bit queasy about men who tortured their captives—especially if they worked for a foreign government.

Sohrab pulled the lock from the hasp and yanked up the door. He ducked his head and stepped inside, waving away the cloud of dust. A single set of shelves lined the three walls, each containing one or more footlockers and cases of varying sizes. None were labeled, but labels weren't necessary—he'd packed each one himself. The nearest held his go-bag. The passport inside was still valid, but the bundles of cash had dwindled over the years, used for more mundane purchases like shoes for the children. The clothing inside was serviceable, though he would have liked a Kevlar vest. He grabbed the bag by the straps, intending to turn and leave, but the small case beside it caught his attention. Sohrab raised one eyebrow and pursed his lips, then sighed and lifted the case as well.

Better to have it and not need it. It was a concept that applied to everything in the shed. He would never think to bring the case on a commercial flight, but the Shadowman had chartered a direct flight to Argentina and Sohrab was satisfied the man would get the case through the minimal security. *Things have certainly relaxed since the last major terrorist attack, but you never know when someone will actually do their job.* Any single item in the case, if discovered in-flight, would buy him a one-way ticket to Guantanamo. *Or worse... deported to Iraq.* A death sentence was a hard thing to ignore.

He stepped outside the shed, set the bag on the ground, and rolled the door down, then locked it once again. He tugged the lock twice for good measure and, satisfied it was secure, picked up the bag and strode to the car's rear passenger door. When he pulled it open and tossed both items inside, the Shadowman raised a questioning eyebrow at the case. Sohrab only grunted, closed the door, then opened the front and climbed in the front seat.

"Did you find everything you need?"

Sohrab grunted and patted twice on the back of the Shadowman's seat. "Let's just get this over with."

Dieter pushed the empty plate away and belched, then reached for the beer. He drank, wincing at the bite of the swill, then wiped his mouth with the back of his hand. *Americans know nothing of good beer.* He'd chosen the brew based on Evan's memories, but as he heard the soft chuckle deep inside his mind, he realized the remnant was playing with him. *Don't worry little man. I will root you out soon enough.*

Jimmy, the establishment's proprietor—a loathsome man in Dieter's opinion—towel draped over one shoulder, sidled over and snatched the plate, then pointed at the bottle. "Ready for another," he growled as if angry. Dieter guessed that was the man's default setting, since he hadn't heard him speak in any other manner.

"Thank you, no," Dieter said, his tight sneer doing its best to convey contempt for the horse piss labeled *Schlitz*. Jimmy grumbled something under his breath and wandered away. Dieter took out his phone and checked for messages again, frowning at the display. *Still no service?* "Why is it every time I come here there's no cell service?"

Jimmy grinned, grabbed a glass from the sink and wiped it dry. "Just lucky, I guess." He placed the glass on the shelf behind him and reached for another. His movements, while not exactly robotic, wasted no motion. To Dieter it looked like the practiced routine honed by years of labor; this was a man who had spent his life doing one thing, refining it day by day until nothing remained but the task.

Everyone should work like this. Do one job and do it well—cogs in a great machine. The Third Reich had, for some, worked that way according to the memories he'd recovered. The old Soviet Union was *intended* to work that way, but never reached its ideal. *Only the Zzkritti ever managed perfection. But even they devolved into chaos and internecine war.* It was his break from both sides of the conflict that marked his true path leading... *where?* That information, dangled at the end of a fishing rod, still eluded him.

A part of Dieter wanted to walk away from the whole affair, but the imperative woven throughout memories of his past life was too strong to ignore; it wouldn't allow him to quit now. Without knowing the goal, it reduced him to following a preset series of instructions in service to that goal. One instruction set, once completed, led to another, then another, and onward seemingly to infinity, the task never completed.

He had become the cog in his own meticulously crafted machine.

But that cog was one tooth short, each turn skipping over an important bit of machinery. He would forever spin in place, a gear failing to mesh until he either recovered the last piece of himself, or rediscovered the goal on his own. *Maddening.* He spun on the stool, ready to get back to prying the last bits of Evan from his mind, and was greeted by the smiling face of a waitress.

"Hey," she said to him, then placed the platter of dirty glasses on the bar, sliding it toward Jimmy. The man grunted and dropped the whole thing into the sink filled with soapy water.

"Goodbye," Dieter said, grabbing his hat and stepping off the stool.

Undaunted, she blocked his path and brushed long blond hair over her ear with delicate fingers. "Did you ever get hold of your friend?" she asked, eyelashes batting.

He furrowed his brow. "Excuse me?" Alarms shrieked inside his head, drowning coherent thought. His pulse pounded in his ears so loud external sounds barely had a chance. *Stop it, Evan,* he thought at the hitchhiker. *I can make your removal both long and painful if I wish.* The sounds faded, but only a bit.

"Your friend, Jack," she said, pouting and tilting her head. "Didn't Jimmy give you his information?"

"Um... I don't recall." He stared at Evan in his mind.

"Sure I did, buddy," Jimmy called out from the sink. He stepped closer, wiping his hands with the towel. "Told ya just a couple weeks ago Jack went to DC fer a new job."

"DC?"

"What are ya, bub... brain damaged or somethin'?"

"Jimmy, stop," the waitress said, touching his arm. "He's just confused."

Dieter ignored the girl. "Did you have an address or phone number?"

Jimmy shook his head. "Wouldn't'a given ya that even if I had it." He tossed the rag back over his shoulder. "B'sides, Jack Montgomery ain't the kind to leave a forwardin' address. KnowwhatImean?"

"Yes, I think I do." The two names came together in a shower of sparks in his head, and he could scarcely contain his glee. *Jack Montgomery. In DC.* The memories that name liberated led him down a deep well of recollection, and Dieter found a calm center then; for the first time since awakening in this body he had a purpose that *didn't* serve the machine. He placed the hat atop his head and tugged it into place, then turned to leave, new energy crackling.

"You gonna remember this time?" Jimmy asked with clear annoyance.

Dieter whirled, eyes filled with hunger. Both Jimmy and the waitress took a single step away. "Yes," he said to the big man *and* the cowering shade within. "I believe I will."

He spun crisply on his heels and strode from the bar with renewed energy, whistling *Die Wacht am Rhein* like a good little soldier.

A cog with a purpose.

Alberto pointed at the map he'd unfolded and smoothed out on the desk. "The truck offloading the plane drove to a warehouse at this location, departing minutes later."

Amber frowned at the map. "So, Jack is there?" Janice stood on her left and Mari on her right. Beth still hadn't moved from the bed, seemingly content to wait until given instruction.

"I do not believe so. An hour later, another truck departed and drove into the mountains near Villa Mascardi." He brushed a hand through his thick hair and sighed. "No one has seen it since, and there is only one way into the mountains on that road."

"What makes you think he was in that truck?" Amber asked, still peering at the map, tracing the road to Villa Mascardi with her finger.

"My men, um... *questioned* the driver at length once we found him. He had offloaded a tall box from his vehicle, and he swears he drove away empty."

"And you're sure Jack isn't in the warehouse?" Janice said, her eyes, like Amber's, glued to the map.

Alberto shrugged and held his hands out, palms up. "I am sure of nothing, but that warehouse is a common exchange point for drugs. Long-term storage of anything else is, shall we say, frowned upon." He straightened and crossed his arms over his chest. "The fact the second truck disappeared tells me there is a place it could hide... something not on the map. No one hides without a reason."

"Drug smugglers?" Mari chimed.

"Perhaps," he said, stroking his chin. "There were no other arrivals or departures that day."

"Could be your men simply questioned the wrong people," Janice muttered.

Alberto laughed, a harsh sound with no humor. "Not *my* men."

Janice chuckled and shook her head. "You still don't know what we're dealing with, son."

"The aliens Maribel told me of?" he said, eyes narrowing. "True, I don't know their capabilities... if they exist at all. I do know a truck is a truck, and a road is a road. These things do not change. If the truck had returned, my men would have found it." He shrugged again and lowered his arms. "They did not, so it has not."

Amber straightened, took a deep breath and exhaled in a whoosh. "So if we assume they hid the truck somewhere in the mountains, what's our next move?" No one spoke at first, and Amber assumed they had reached a dead end. *To come all this way. It can't end here before we've even begun.* If she knew why the Zzkritti wanted Jack, it would be easier to find him. *Probably not, though.* He wasn't dead—she was sure of that. They could have killed him at any time and going to all the trouble of bringing him here to do the deed was pointless. *He either has information they need, or...* She gasped and her hand flew to her mouth, eyes wide and wild.

"Goddamnit!"

"What is it?" Janice said, placing a hand on her shoulder.

"They're programming him." It was so obvious, the fact she hadn't realized it before only told her how much she'd been focused on just finding him. *Finding him is no longer enough, though, is it?*

"Wait... what?" Confusion twisted Mari's face.

"They're programming him for some task." All hope left Amber's heart in a rush. "It's the only thing that makes any sense."

"Can he be *deprogrammed*?" Mari said, disbelief creeping into her voice.

"Not by us." The finality of that statement hit her in the gut, punching the air from her lungs and the determination from her heart. *Even if we find him... what then?* Josef could maybe do the job—and if not him, his masters—but he would be more likely to kill Jack on the spot. He would be nothing more than a danger to sweep aside at that point, no matter how much his masters needed him for their purposes.

"How long would it take to program him, do you think?" Beth asked, her voice almost too soft to hear. Everyone stopped and turned to her. "I mean, either way we still have to find and rescue him, right?"

"I don't know." Amber sat next to Beth and faced her. "They may return him once they're satisfied the programming will work." She thought it over a moment, then nodded, agreeing with her own assessment. "In fact, I think that's the likeliest outcome."

"But he's *not* home yet, is he?"

Mari tapped a few keys on her laptop. "Um... not according to this."

"Then maybe there's still time," Beth said, her eyes full of hope.

I remember that look. I used to see that in the mirror every morning. Before the Zzkritti. Before Dieter. Before Jack.

"Perhaps," Amber said, drawing the word out, hope, despair, and resignation all fighting for a place in that one sound. "But how do we even find him?"

Beth pursed her lips. "Well... I'm no expert, but I think we should go to Villa Mascardi."

"The truck disappeared in the mountains," Alberto protested, shaking his head firmly.

"Yeah, but near the village, right?" She inclined her head thoughtfully and scooted to the edge of the bed, dangling her legs off the side. "It can't be very big, right? Not according to that map."

"No. It is a small village in population, but spread over a very large area."

"Either way," she said, waving the concern away, "someone has noticed comings and goings of a delivery truck. Surely we can narrow down a location for its hidey-hole."

Alberto worked the muscles in his jaw, arching an eyebrow, but said nothing. Amber wondered what was going on in that young but experienced head, then ignored it for more immediate concerns.

"She's right," she said, nodding at Beth. The young woman beamed back at her as if she'd won the lottery. "Anyone else have any better ideas?"

None spoke up, though Alberto grunted with what sounded to her like annoyance. *Don't like mere women showing you up, do you?*

"It's settled, then," she said and stood. "Gather what you need, people. Looks like the band's going on tour."

Jack fought. He fought for control, for sanity, and to suppress the pain in his leg, but to no avail; the pain was a flame consuming his flesh, his sanity slipping as he screamed inside his own head, and three words were all he'd croaked out to show for all his effort and agony. The smaller Zzkritti skittered closer, claws clicking on the cold stone floor. The air held an acrid odor, thick and moist, growing stronger the closer the creature came. It produced a small bulb of gleaming metal and waved the thing over Jack's leg, instantly dousing the searing pain. He would have heaved a sigh of relief if his keeper had allowed it, and for the first time since waking he could think clearly. Blood still flowed from the wound, but the throbbing hurt vanished. The Zzkritti buzzed and crackled at the others and each stopped their work to draw near. They lifted him gently and placed him on his back on a warm metal table, then scuttled back to their previous tasks. The one with the bulb bent over him, poking and prodding at the wound in his leg.

He'd understood none of what the aliens had said—no human could—but their intent was clear enough. *They're programming me.* He still couldn't understand why Jeff was doing this to him, but the Zzkritti spoke volumes simply by his absence. *Maybe he doesn't know.* Jack knew that was unlikely; hiding something like this from their nominal leader probably wasn't possible. Jack also had no illusions Jeff would save him even if he hadn't ordered the procedure. *They may have lived on this planet for millennia, but that doesn't mean they think like humans.* He thought of Thirteen. *They barely understand the humans who work and live with them.*

The heat in the room was oppressive. Jack wondered why he wasn't sweating and guessed they must control that as well. *Probably can't stand the stink of us.* The heat wasn't so bad he was in physical danger, but the discomfort was real enough. The other Zzkritti in the room responded to a series of clicks and clacks from their boss, ceased their work, and shuffled out the only exit Jack had seen. When they were gone, the lone remaining alien leaned close to Jack's face. It's chitinous beak snapped several times, clicking a staccato pattern as it examined him. Its eyes, round orbs of obsidian, were the size of golf balls—perhaps a bit larger—and they plumbed the depths of Jack's own. The thing's breath was hot—hotter than the room by far—and sweet, like rancid meat.

"This one will not reprogram you," it said in English with a cicada's voice—a susurration of sweltering air. "It would take too long, and the programming you have is sufficient." It looked behind and around, a film noir snitch ratting out his boss. "There are things you must do the First cannot know if this one is to survive." Jack heard the nervous tapping of the creature's claws, and it leaned closer. "It is imperative you not speak again unless directed. The First must believe this one has completed the task to his satisfaction." It checked the doorway again. "There is a message this one would ask you to deliver."

What message? Jack wondered. *And to whom?*

It told him, and Jack's eyes widened despite his programming.

CHAPTER 18

*V*ILLA *M*ASCARDI. S OHRAB TAPPED THE TINY BUD inside his ear, signaling receipt of the Shadowman's message. He had no idea how the thing still worked with the other half in DC, but accepted the magic and ignored it. He deplaned and stepped down the ramp to the tarmac carrying nothing. The bag and case were inside the terminal past the inspection point, held by a well-paid baggage handler. Sohrab had always loved taking assignments in South America, where the women were lovely, the food delicious and plentiful, and bribery was simply another recognized part of the economy.

Maribel was apparently still sending the Shadowman intel on the women's movements, and he wondered what sort of transportation was required; he hadn't thought past taking a cab to their hotel to surprise them there before they moved again. "Best laid plans, and all that," he muttered. The private terminal was modest, with little security—all the better to move drugs and other contraband in and out. He pulled the door open and stepped inside, frigid air blasting him in the face as he crossed the threshold. Outside the air was crisp, but inside was an icebox and far too bitter for his taste. The terminal was clean, everything shining, from the brass-trimmed front desk, to the marble-tiled floors. Sohrab knew from experience the main terminal was not so clean and richly appointed. *Drug money will do that.* He strode toward the desk.

"No need, sir." The baggage handler appeared at his side with his things in hand. He was short and dark-haired, with thick eyebrows hovering over dark, round eyes and a wide nose. While he couldn't be over fifteen, Sohrab suspected the boy was one of the nearby indigenous peoples. The handler saw him studying his face and beamed. "Guaraní," he said, hooking a thumb at his chest with pride. "Few work in the city. Most still farm." He held out the bag and case, still smiling, and Sohrab took them with a nod.

"Well..."

"Brian," the boy offered with a wide grin.

"Brian?"

"My father's idea of a joke."

"Yes," Sohrab said, grinning despite his mood. "Well, *Brian*, where can I rent a vehicle?"

"One is already waiting, sir." Confusion contorted his face. "Did you not see the Hummer outside?" The boy's eyes danced when he said the word. It was clear securing the vehicle was a special event in his life. Sohrab stifled the impulse to ruffle the boy's hair and instead looked through the wall of glass. Sure enough, parked at the loading zone was a large, matte-black Humvee, its suspension and knobby tires rigged for rough terrain.

Sohrab eyed the boy up and down, raising an eyebrow. "Did you drive that thing here?"

"Of course, sir." He grinned liked he'd won the lottery. "I have been driving since I was twelve. Nothing so big as that, though."

"I'm impressed."

"There is a map on the passenger seat, and a cooler of food and drink in the back."

"Now I'm more than impressed." Sohrab's stomach howled at the mention of food. He set his bag on the marble floor and dug inside his jacket for his wallet. Brian frowned and looked around the terminal, concerned. He reached out and placed a staying hand on Sohrab's arm.

"I have already been paid, sir."

"I know that, son. I thought a tip for the food and—"

"No, sir," Brian said firmly. He leaned in and whispered, "I am not allowed."

"Ah." Sohrab nodded understanding even though he did not. "Well, Brian," he lifted his bag from the floor, "I guess I must be on my way." He grinned at the boy, then swung toward the door.

"Sir?" Brian called before he'd taken two steps.

"Yes?"

"Please tell Josef my family thanks him for the gift." Brian looked decidedly less happy now, a hopeful sadness morphing the boy into a man. He shuffled his feet and averted his eyes.

"I will, son." Sohrab strode through the doors toward the truck. People passed by, some gawping at the great black behemoth dominating the loading area, but most ignoring it; vehicles worth more than a home were common around a private terminal. He tried to open the door, but it was locked, and he almost went back into the terminal building. "Boy thought of everything else," he muttered and unzipped a suspiciously bulging side compartment of his go-bag. He grabbed the remote key-fob from inside and unlocked the door, tossing both the case and the bag across to the passenger seat before he followed them inside. He settled in and started the Humvee, the sound of the engine in the plush compartment little more than a throaty, low-frequency rumble. Sohrab dug the map from beneath his bag on the passenger seat and opened it. "The boy did think of everything."

He put the beast in gear and pulled away from the curb, following the line on the map highlighted in yellow. "Too bad he didn't show me how to get out of the airport." Rather than stop and ask for directions, he followed the line of cars exiting the main terminal.

Forty minutes later, the city was behind him and he followed the yellow line, the terminus a location circled in red more than ten kilometers from Villa Mascardi proper. That was where Amber was headed according to the Shadowman's message. So why was the map taking him somewhere else? Sohrab had never been able to activate the ear bud on his end, so he couldn't just ask the Shadowman for clarification; he'd have to wait until the man deemed it necessary.

He grunted. *Just like every handler I've ever had.*

The women stuck out like four thumbs on a very strange hand. Alberto led the way, but it was Amber who was in charge. The tiny village on the shore of Mascardi Lake was little more than half a dozen small buildings and a few miserable shacks. One larger home stood out, but it was the view of the mountains surrounding the sapphire-blue glacial lake that took Amber's breath away. The only two not affected by the view were Alberto and Mari—one due to familiarity, the other the blindness of cynicism. She grumped and grumbled from the moment they got out of the car, and Amber had grown weary of it. She wiped sweat from her brow; even in the chilly air the sun beat against her skin bright and unrelenting. To her right, Janice dabbed herself with a handkerchief.

Janice smirked at her. "I think we made a few mistakes in our wardrobe choices." The shorts and light shirts she'd bought for them back at Pentagon City Mall were out of place in the crisp air; she,

Amber, and Beth were dressed for a safari. Maribel had opted for her usual rumpled look, choosing jeans and her ratty coat without explaining why. Janice sneered at the hacker. "You could have warned us, you know."

"Where's the fun in that?"

"Excuse me, ladies," Alberto said, then passed Amber on his way to one shack, his long strides widening the gap between them.

"Where's he going?" Beth asked.

"I'm more concerned with where everyone in this village is," Amber said. "It's like a ghost town."

"Most are off working somewhere, or in their homes watching us from behind their windows," Maribel said, stopping in the middle of the dusty lane. "We should wait here until he comes back."

Amber stopped and faced her, Janice and Beth stopping a step later. "Are they afraid of us?"

"No, but strangers aren't always welcome. Especially Americans."

I can understand that. To the rest of the world, it must look like we've lost our damn minds. Amber crossed her arms, watched Alberto greet a small old woman and disappear into the building, and waited. So much had happened in the news lately, she was grateful for any distraction. Jack's capture by the Zzkritti was no mere distraction, and that was what had happened—she was sure of it now. The war within the Zzkritti hive had not been as decisive a victory for Jeff's side as he had led them to believe. *Some must have survived, more determined than ever to complete their original mission.* Why they needed Jack for this was unknown, but working from that assumption might keep them all safe. Two incredibly powerful adversaries squared off in a battle with nothing less than the survival of the human species at stake, and like *Harry Potter*'s Dumbledore, one side just kept throwing children at the problem.

The thought sent a shiver down her spine; she felt exposed standing in the middle of the village, imagining a dozen pair of eyes on her, aliens of the human sort, each waiting for the proper time to strike. *That's just stupid.* The admonition did nothing to soothe her prickled nerves, and she squeezed her upper arms, hugging herself against the chill that felt more than simply atmospheric. There was danger here. She couldn't put a finger on what that danger was, but she felt it like the jangling bite of electricity. Suddenly impatient, she took a step toward the building Alberto had entered.

216

Maribel grabbed Amber's arm in a surprisingly firm grip. "Don't," she hissed. Amber stopped and stared at her, anger growing like a weed. "In case you haven't noticed, we're being watched." Maribel released Amber's arm and nodded slightly toward another building. "At least one is watching through a scope."

They're afraid. It wasn't anger or fear of the unknown, or the careless dust-up between locals and *crazy Americans*—this was fear of entanglement. The very real worry of being caught in no-man's-land between two warring adversaries. Their silence a cry of *keep us out of it.* Amber looked toward the building Mari indicated. *I know exactly how you feel, people.* Too late for her—too late even for the people with her—she now resolved to push beyond the village; give them room to breathe again. *As soon as we've learned whatever information you have.* That was it, though, wasn't it? Give me what I want and I'll go away. The demand of every thug, mafioso, or politician ever born. Amber suddenly felt sick, and this time it wasn't the airplane food.

Tension took hold of her back and neck, eating her resolve, and just when she was ready to scream, Alberto stepped through the doorway. He hugged the old woman, then pulled back slightly and said a few gentle words before releasing her. She smiled, broad and gap-toothed, and waved to the women as he strode away.

He walked straight to Amber, ignoring the others. "The truck passed through here, but did not stop. One of her sons saw it entering a small box canyon." He passed an odd look to Maribel, but said nothing to her. "I think I know this place, but it is difficult to approach without being seen. Perhaps my men and I—"

"Take us there," Amber said, her voice flat and demanding.

His eyes, so hard when focused on his work, softened. "This place has only one entrance." His voice was soothing, like speaking to a child. "If things should turn dangerous..."

"The others can stay if they wish, but I'll take my chances," she said, as firm as he was calm.

"I'm in," Janice inserted before he could protest. She stepped close to Amber and threw an arm around her shoulders. "I'd like to see this through."

He arched a thick eyebrow at Maribel. "And you, cousin?"

She shrugged and chewed her bottom lip. "Eh, I'm kinda stuck with the old broad here. She's payin' the bills, after all." Janice gave her an odd look. If Amber didn't know better, she might have called it respect.

217

"Beth?" Amber said, tilting her head at the young woman.

"Sure, why not?" she said, grinning. "I'm still your driver, right?"

Amber shrugged at Alberto. "That settles it. Looks like we're all in."

He cocked an eyebrow at her, then lifted one hand high and waved it in a circular motion. Amber furrowed her brow, wondering what was going on, when the underbrush behind them rumbled and a truck with four men—two in the cab and two in the bed holding weapons—burst from the trees.

"My men and I will follow close behind."

By the time Amber saw the first hints of the box canyon, the sun skirted the mountaintops, threatening to hide before the day was done. Dark green and foreboding, it looked less like a canyon and more like a giant salad bowl. The road dipped and disappeared inside the dense foliage, and Alberto steered the truck expertly over the muddy road—little more than a wide wagon track that twisted and writhed like an anaconda. Branches brushed the top of the truck's cab, a wet slapping of wide emerald leaves that left damp smears on the windshield. The tires slewed as they negotiated a turn and Amber gasped, her eyes wide.

"I will slow our pace if you like." Alberto looked at her with what she assumed was sympathy, but she waved him off.

"I trust you not to wrap us around a tree." She clenched the door's handle in a death-grip. "Ignore me."

He studied her a few seconds, then faced front in time to take another hard left. "That is most difficult."

Most women would have blushed—*Janice surely would have*—but Amber had simply been through too much in the last year. She no longer had the luxury. It wasn't only a lack of desire, but an abscess of the heart—putrefied flesh where a healthy organ should be. What the heavy muscle pumped no longer qualified as blood, hot or otherwise, and she fretted at the thought it would never heal; not even rescuing Jack would do the trick. Her soul was wounded in ways love couldn't salve.

Amber glanced in the side-view mirror at the jittering image; the truck bounced and bobbed like a pogo stick. Janice and the others followed close behind in the rented car faring no better, but Beth somehow kept up with Alberto's mad flight turn for turn. If the mud in the trail's ruts was any deeper, the car would have stalled out miles ago, but the plucky college student was doing her best to keep the wheels on the drier grass-tufted ground between. In the short time she'd been in Amber's life, the girl had both impressed and endeared herself to everyone but Maribel. *And unless I've misread the signals, she's the one Beth wants to impress the most.* Mari certainly hadn't noticed. *Either she's not interested or just plain clueless.*

The truck took a heavy dip and rebounded so hard Amber conked her head on the roof.

"Ow!" She rubbed the top of her head with one hand, the other still gripping the door handle. The men riding in the bed cursed through the open sliding window.

"Sorry," Alberto said with an uncharacteristic sheepishness. "The roads in the mountains are not so well maintained as in the U.S."

She chuckled and shook her head. "Clearly you have never been to the Ozarks."

"You must take me there sometime." His smile was blinding.

"Sure. The very next time you come to visit Mari." She cocked an eyebrow at him and he faced the road. The truck bounced again, but this time she saw it coming and braced.

The jungle canopy opened up a sliver overhead, offering a peek at the slope of the mountain, a flash of golden sunlight, then closed just as quickly. A canyon wall appeared on the right as they drove deeper inside, and Amber watched the slabs of rough rock slide past. For a second she was back inside the basement of the asylum with its walls of native stone, and she shivered. It had taken her the better part of a year to rid herself of the nightmares from that time, and all it took was a rock wall to bring it all crashing back. She shook herself and forced the thoughts down, compressing them into a tight ball of pain, regret, and horror—a mass so dense neither light nor love could escape the tug of its gravity. In time, without a counterbalance, she would collapse in upon herself, disappearing entirely. She glanced in the mirror again at the car behind and her new friends inside. *It's always about balance, isn't it?*

One of Alberto's men pounded three times in quick succession on the cab's roof, and he jammed on the brakes. The truck slid to a stop, brake drums squealing, and the men in back leapt onto the soft ground with heavy-booted thuds. Alberto rolled down his window and faced one of the men—Carlos, Amber recalled—his bald head glistening in the muted light of the jungle. The thick black mustache that dominated his face twitched when he stole a look at Amber, and his eyes flashed before he drew his attention to Alberto.

"Motion sensors and cameras in the trees ahead, *Jefe*." He pointed with the barrel of his rifle. "There... and there."

Alberto peered in the directions indicated, and his eyes narrowed. "I see them."

I don't, Amber thought with some annoyance. *How do they?*

"Scout us a path around them, 'Los." The big man shrugged one broad shoulder, waved at a second man, then both slipped silently away into the trees. Alberto sighed, opened his door, and stepped out.

"What are you doing?" Amber asked, brow knitted.

He bent and folded his seat forward. "Grab what you need." He reached behind the seat and lifted out a heavy and well-worn machete, inspecting the edge. "We're walking from here."

They had moved him. How far, or in which direction, Jack couldn't guess, since his eyes had been closed, and he'd lost track of time. Even the mere concept of time was meaningless. The Zzkritti switched him on and off like a radio, and he hadn't seen the sun since before entering the jail in DC. Whether two days ago or two years, he couldn't say with any certainty. Only that they *had* moved him was clear. That, and the pain in his leg was gone.

Jack opened his eyes and looked around, controlling his movements for the first time since his capture. He lay on a standard hospital gurney, institutional-grade sheets both beneath and over his body. The distinct odors of disinfectant and a room too-clean drifted in the air, and he wrinkled his nose. When he sat up, the top sheet slid from his chest, tickling his skin, and he saw the table with surgical instruments laid out and ready. For what, he shuddered to guess. The light fixture over his head was multifaceted and bright, and it was in that moment he realized he was in an operating room—not exactly primitive, but definitely third-world quality. Gone were the odd and indecipherable devices of the aliens, the stone floors, walls, and ceiling—even the Zzkritti themselves—replaced by walls of cinder block and a floor of worn linoleum.

Cold air blew in from a vent set in the wall's top and Jack shivered. With nothing covering him but a thin sheet, gooseflesh rose and the hair on his arms stood at attention. There was nothing else in the room he could use to cover himself, so he drew the sheet tighter and stared at the single door on the far wall. On another wall, a six-foot wide rectangle of glass was set in the center like a picture window. The space beyond the glass was dark, so he couldn't see through. *Two-way mirror?* The idea of someone watching through that glass angered him, and he stood, wrapping the sheet around him like a sarong. He shuffled to the window and cupped his eyes and pressed his face against it in a desperate attempt to see beyond. Stymied, he spun and stepped to the door. Testing the handle he discovered what he already knew. *Locked.* Trapped, maybe, but he wasn't helpless. He went back to the gurney and examined the tray of implements. Oddly, there wasn't a single scalpel among the lot, and he couldn't have named any of the others if someone had put a gun to his head, but there was one that looked like bigfoot's tweezers. Stainless steel and heavy, he carefully lifted the tool from the tray and hid it within the folds of the sheet.

As prepared as he could be, he sat on the bed and waited.

Dieter checked the hallway in either direction, then expertly picked the lock, straightened, twisted the knob, and scurried inside, closing the door softly behind. He didn't know where the skill originated, but like his programming acumen, he was glad to have it. He put the picks away and flicked the light switch by the door.

Jack Montgomery's DC apartment was not only in a better neighborhood than his previous, but was upscale by comparison. Real hardwood floors were a dead giveaway, and these weren't even scuffed. Dieter stepped to the granite-topped kitchen island and picked up the stack of mail laying there. He shuffled through, finding nothing but bills and sales fliers—certainly nothing indicating where the man had gotten off to over the last few days. He set the mail back atop the island, then fumbled the heavy snub-nosed revolver from his pocket and lay it beside. The kitchen sink was half-filled with dirty dishes, and Dieter pursed his lips. The apartment, other than the sink, was immaculate; someone who cleaned his home so well would never leave dirty dishes if he didn't expect to come home that night.

"So the trip was unexpected," Dieter muttered. "But not just that... it was urgent." He frowned and wandered around the living area before walking into the bedroom. The bed was unmade, but the room was otherwise as clean as the rest of the place.

He'd expected to surprise Jack in the apartment, watch the man's eyes when he explained who and what he was, then shoot him in the head, but plans never survived contact with the enemy. Dieter sighed and stepped back into the living room, unshouldered the messenger bag and set it on the sofa. He tossed the flap back and pulled out several tools. Killing Jack was one priority but not the most pressing; Dieter couldn't spend all his time waiting for the man to return. He dragged one of the island stools beneath the room's smoke detector, climbed up, and went to work.

⚭

"This one cannot allow you inside," the Zzkritti said for the fourth time with the exact same inflection as the first three. It barred the entrance to the outer cave, staring at Thirteen with those unblinking black eyes. Its tail swished back and forth over the sand, the only outward expression of its impatience.

"But—"

"What happens there is for Zzkritti only. Human *drones* do not witness." It spoke the word with all the contempt it could muster in a language it rarely used. *And it does it quite well.* The heat from the desert sun bore down on Thirteen's neck as if trying to chew through the skin straight to his spine. He stiffened that spine and crossed his arms over his chest.

"I have autonomy."

"To our utter shame," the creature spat. "But autonomy does not confer *authority*."

Thirteen narrowed his eyes. "I must speak with the one designated as Jeff. He does not answer my calls."

"Then that serves as your answer."

"Consensus." The Zzkritti could not refuse his request—it was hardwired into their genetic code. It straightened and hummed for a few seconds, a soft susurration like a chorus of distant cicadas. When it stopped, its eyes locked on his.

"Jeff cannot presently answer your call, and will not for another cycle."

Another cycle? Thirteen rocked back on his heels, his eyes widening. In the sixty-odd centuries on Earth, the Zzkritti had never adapted to the lunar cycle for their most basic biological rhythms, still adhering to that of their home planet. With three moons and twin suns, their cycles lasted anywhere from twelve to twenty-one days depending on the time of year.

"It is the directive of the Hive that the drone continue its path as directed. Infer further instructions from that to fulfill requirements."

222

"The Consensus rules from incomplete and faulty information," he said, hoping to at least argue his case.

"Irrelevant." The tail swished faster. "The drone has absorbed instruction. Adapt." It leaned forward, the tail stopping in ready mode. "Does it comply?"

Thirteen dropped his arms to his sides and sighed. "It does." He had *mother* in his pocket and could compel them to allow him inside, but if even one broke the connection for any length of time, he was a dead man. He turned without further comment and stalked back to the beige humvee parked downslope.

What could keep Jeff offline for so long? For the first time in his life, he was left entirely to his own devices. He didn't like it. Not one bit.

CHAPTER 19

"I MEAN... THEY DON'T LOOK LIKE ALIENS." Alberto had the binoculars up to his eyes surveying the non-descript little compound tucked up against the canyon wall. Two men armed with automatic weapons patrolled inside a fence, each pacing back and forth and scanning the road in front of the only gate in or out. A blocky out-cropping of three single-story buildings sat just inside, a single large Quonset hut located at the end of a paved road leading from the gate.

"They aren't," Amber sneered, taking the binoculars from his hands. "Doesn't make them any less dangerous." She crept back on her stomach inside the foliage, then stood and brushed herself off.

"What makes you think this is the place, then?" he said, standing beside her. He looked into her eyes with raw sympathy, edged with a twenty-something's lust.

"You see any other secret lairs around here?" She pointed through the fat leaves. "The big building in back seems like a good place to hide a truck, doesn't it?"

"Or bales of coca leaves."

"Touché." She peered through a while longer, then allowed the leaf to fall. "Still, it's our best bet."

"Agreed." He rubbed his chin thoughtfully. "If it's one of the cartels, they will be well-armed and ready."

"No more so than the Zzkritti." Amber chuckled. "At least drug dealers can't control your mind or zap you with a disintegrator."

"They have those?"

She shrugged. "Hell if I know." She'd seen no sign the Zzkrit-ti possessed such technology. What she *had* seen, though, was far worse. The memory of Bill dissolving in front of her threatened to send her mind gibbering, and she shuddered and hugged herself. She pushed the thoughts away, adding them to all the others. Jack was down there—somewhere—she could feel it, and the Zzkritti were doing God knew what to him. *Is he even still the same person?* She hadn't changed when Dieter had programmed her, but he'd been clumsy, careless... arrogant, and using a technology he couldn't fully understand; there was no way to know how deeply the aliens could dig into Jack's mind. *If a man loses a lifetime of memories—replaced with another—is he still the same man?* Was it the totality of a person's life experiences that made them what they were, or was it only the physical? The person whose mind Dieter had replaced—were they still themselves or now wholly Dieter?

And could such a person be made whole again?

All questions for another day. She turned and peered down the slope to the group gathered there. Janice and Mari sat on a fallen tree trunk while Beth paced in circles, chomping her gum like it fought back. Alberto's men stood nearby like beefy statues, weapons held casually. Each scanned the area with visibly heightened awareness. Each waited for her to decide. To make the call.

Carlos, Argentina's version of Mr. Clean, looked up at her and nodded. His neck was so thick it looked like his shoulders just melted into his head, and his arms bulged with heavy, if not well-defined muscle. There was a softness to his gaze, like he understood everything she'd experienced. He held her eyes for a few moments, time stretching between them, then shifted back to scanning for danger.

"Amber?" Alberto leaned over her, his voice a husky whisper. She shuddered and looked up at him.

"Hmm?"

"What do you want to do?"

"Oh, I'd like to go back a year and a half and ignore an old man when he offers me money." She said it as if in a dream.

"Qué?" He stared into her eyes with genuine concern, his head inclined.

She shook her head and met his gaze. "Nothing. Only a wish for retroactive good sense." She took a deep breath and blew it out in a heavy sigh. "Now, how do we get in there?"

"What... you?" He shook his head and wagged a finger. "Nooo, no, no, no. Only my men and me go in."

Amber placed a hand on his arm. "Of everyone here, I'm the only one with half a clue about what to expect. I've dealt with this before." She swung back toward the compound, a faint hum rising in her ears. "Besides, I have an ace up my sleeve."

The Humvee bounced, but the shocks took care of most of the motion and Sohrab barely felt it. He'd expected a much rougher ride when he left the paved road, though it shouldn't have surprised him the big truck rode so smoothly—this was no standard piece of battle-field equipment; they meant this for high-end customers who com-plained loud and long about any discomfort, real or imagined. The vehicle was as wide as the dirt road in places, and branches scraped both sides with ear-cracking shrieks.

"Hope the Shadowman paid for the insurance." Sohrab grunted as he spun the wheel hard to the left, negotiating another hairpin turn. He reached behind his seat with his right hand, grabbed one of the small sandwiches from the cooler, and shoved the whole thing in his mouth. He retrieved a can of soda while he chewed and took long gulps to chase everything down. Things weren't making much sense. There was a faction of Zzkritti that had taken Jack prisoner—what use he was to them, Sohrab didn't know—and it was clear at least the Shadowman had learned of them. Not only that, but their general location. The question now was why hadn't Jeff and his min-ions dealt with them already? And where did Dieter fit into this? Was he a part of their plans, or just an unlikely coincidence?

Everything about this was maddening.

He rounded the next corner and jammed hard on the brakes, sliding to a stop two meters from the rear bumper of a car blocking the narrow road. Ahead of that was a large four-wheel-drive truck with huge knobby tires. Both appeared empty, and there was no movement around them. Sohrab sat for a moment, lips pursed, eyes narrowed, and scanned the area. He found the answer to the mini traffic jam in the cloud of dust his tires had thrown ahead—three flickering beams of coherent light crossing the road ten meters ahead of the truck. Lifting his gaze to the canopy, it was even easier to spot the cameras hidden in the branches. Each was angled to catch the license of a passing vehicle. *You would think the Zzkritti would have something more sophisticated.* This was strictly government issue—se-cret base passive scanning 101. If this road led to Zzkritti facilities, they would cover the perimeter with better equipment.

"No," he growled and tugged at his beard. "Those were meant for discovery." The aliens surely knew someone had come call-ing. Sohrab sighed and entered the combination on the case in the seat beside him. The lid popped, and he opened it wide, revealing the weapon. He drew out the Glock 17L and the Trijicon RMR reticle sight and assembled the two, then snatched the four extra clips from their foam slots. Each contained seventeen 9mm armor-piercing rounds of depleted uranium, the cartridges custom-loaded for long-distance shooting; they were the last of those he'd smuggled out of Iraq when he defected. He ejected the clip in the gun and checked to make sure it was full, then replaced it. While he scanned for anyone lurking, he climbed out of the Humvee, stepped around to the rear and opened it, pulling the duffel close. He unzipped it and lifted out the lightly armored vest inside and shrugged it on, cinching the straps at his sides. He closed the doors and frowned at the road—he could trudge through the undergrowth as he assumed the others had, or he could saunter up the road and alert the Zzkritti of his presence. *Either they already know, or they don't. If they do, it doesn't matter what I do, but if they don't...* "Could draw them away and leave the place open for Amber and her crew." He scratched the side of his face and shook his head, then walked past all three vehicles, sticking to the road.

The door to the operating room swung open on silent hinges, and a small Zzkritti scrabbled inside. It was a ruddy brown rather than the deep blood red of the larger versions and was at least a foot shorter. Jack noticed the tail of this one sported a dull point instead of the dagger-shaped tip. A simple worker-drone, he guessed, and not the one that had spoken to him. It certainly wasn't the one with the cape, as it was too small by half. That one's color had darkened almost to black. *Perhaps this one is simply a juvenile.* He still didn't understand enough—nor did he wish to—about Zzkritti physiology or societal structure to make an informed guess; he recognized only that this one probably had limited authority.

The creature stopped in the doorway and cocked its head at Jack like a new puppy, then produced a small device and pointed it at him. All at once, Jack's muscles locked up tight like it had encased him in acrylic. He could still blink and move his eyes, but that was the extent of his control. The Zzkritti scrambled close, its claws clicking and sliding over the linoleum, and began to pose Jack on the bed like a Ken doll, laying him back and tucking the sheet around him. It peeled Jack's fingers off the large tweezers and lay them back on the tray, then methodically bound his wrists and ankles to the gurney with heavy leather straps. Jack squeezed his eyes shut against the harsh silver glare of the overhead surgical light and listened to the thing buzz and crackle as it worked; he had the impression it was humming a song to itself to pass the time.

If it starts to whistle—frozen or not—I'm gonna scream. His mind bucked when it inserted a needle into his arm and set up an odd IV device. Not a bag with fluids, but a foot-long cylinder of gray metal with a single long rectangle of a transparent material along one side and a small valve at the tube end. Something glowed with a greenish light within, pulsing and throbbing like a heartbeat. It, too, hummed. The tube leading from the cylinder to the needle in his arm was clear though, and frantic worry gripped him. *They've already got the nanites in me. What new hell is this?*

The Zzkritti nodded at its handiwork, stepped back from the gurney, settled on its tail kangaroo-style, and waved the little device at Jack. All at once he began to thrash against the restraints, his body suddenly his own again. The Zzkritti considered him with that puppy-like gaze, its own form otherwise frozen. Jack calmed and faced the creature.

"What now?" he growled. "Why am I here?" He narrowed his eyes. "What are you doing?"

"Waiting," it rasped.

Carlos found and deactivated three more sensors and two cameras before he, Amber, and Alberto reached a shallow gulley near the main gate. After a long argument, she agreed to leave the others behind in favor of a small incursion—so long as the list included her. Two men with weapons guarded the gate, and Carlos had spotted another in a tower. The fact it was so lightly defended gave them all pause, and she noticed both men remained vigilant while they made their approach; they had, in fact, grown more wary the closer they came. Alberto looked ready to jump out of his skin at the slightest provocation. Carlos though... Amber couldn't get a clear read on the man. He appeared as tightly wound as Alberto. His tension seemed to stem not from the worry of being caught, but a gathering potential energy, unleashed in a single spasm of action if the need arose. She noticed that, other than the perpetual shine on his head, the man simply didn't sweat—metaphorically or otherwise.

Neither of the men carried long-range weapons with them, opting for angry-looking handguns of matte black. The plan was to approach the gate in the open—three lost and harmless hikers in search of help. None of them sported a backpack or hiking gear of any kind, but they only needed the illusion to last until a guard came through the gate. Francisco, Carlos' younger brother, had taken a position above them where they'd first observed the compound, and likely already had the tower guard in the sights of his M110. It pained Amber to think they'd have to kill today, but if Jack was inside, there was no way to avoid it. *If I have a choice...*

"I still say this place belongs to one of the cartels," Carlos whispered.

Alberto shook his head. "Not enough guards. These depend too much on technology."

"But they—"

"The Zzkritti are here." Amber had said it so quietly, she wondered if she'd even spoken aloud.

Carlos looked at her with the agnosticism of a cat, but Alberto raised an eyebrow. "How do you know?"

She winced at the buzz tickling the back of her brain. "I just do." She'd known in an intellectual sense the nanites Dieter had placed within her were still there, but she'd hoped they were inert or at the very least inactive. What she felt was both alien and familiar, like the memory of an amputated limb... or the dream of a love that never was. The buzzing spoke as clear as a hive of angry bees, and if she'd never learned of the schism within the Zzkritti on Earth, she surely knew now; the others were behind those gates, and the nanites boiling her blood wanted them dead. *Can't say I disagree.*

Carlos stared at her for a few seconds longer, then faced Alberto. "You recognize this is a bad idea, yes?" His voice had a bored quality to it, as if it didn't matter either way what his friend thought.

"Perhaps." Alberto gazed beyond the wide leaves toward the gate, then faced Carlos. "Do you have another option?"

"Sí," Carlos nodded. "We go home, drink beer, and wait for things to work themselves out." It was half-hearted—joking, even—but Amber felt a kernel of truth in the man's plea. None of them wanted to be here; each was merely following her lead, and if it didn't get at least one of them killed, she'd be shocked. She had every reason to take Carlos' advice and retreat, and only one to press forward. It was enough. Enough, at least, for *her* to continue.

"Why don't you stay here and cover our backs," she suggested.

His eyes grew hard and narrow. "You think me a coward?"

"No!" She waved her hands at him. "I don't—"

"I do," Alberto rumbled, leaning in.

"'Berto!" Carlos' eyes widened. "You know me better than—"

230

"Then quit pretending to be the only one thinking clearly." Alberto grinned. "We both know you are the *least* likely to avoid a fight."

Carlos chuckled, a sound that came from somewhere south of his belly. "Sí. That is true."

Amber stared at them both, crossing her arms over her chest, and shook her head in mock sadness. "If you two boys are..."

Fifty yards away, the main gate rattled and creaked as the guard pushed it open. Before Amber had time to process the image, a large military-style truck rumbled down the lone road and through the gates out of the compound. A half-dozen soldiers in full gear and sporting assault weapons rode in the back in disciplined silence. The truck passed close enough she saw their determined faces, and she crouched lower in the broad leaves in the gulley. In moments the truck disappeared, swallowed by the jungle.

"Those men aren't going on patrol," Carlos whispered in the silence that followed. "They're going out to hunt." He turned a stone-faced gaze to Amber. "Something tripped their alarms."

Time's up, Alberto thought. He grabbed Amber by the wrist and pulled her close, Carlos huddling in to hear. The woman had the eyes of a cornered animal, but his friend had the look of a predator.

"We must move," he hissed. "Now."

"But they know we're here," Amber said, her brow furrowing. "They'll we watching for us."

"Which is why we must take them now." He pulled her along to the edge of the gulley and lined up his approach. "They believe they have time to ready their defenses, but we are here now. There is no fooling them anymore, so it is best if we take the compound before their men return."

Their plan was foolish from the start. They'd never have gotten the lone guard to open the gate, no matter their story. But it was open now, and that was an opportunity they couldn't waste. The guard casually shouldered his weapon and leaned into the gate to close it. Alberto pulled at his bottom lip. *Fifty meters.* He'd never be able to cross that distance unseen—not in a flat run—and that gave the guard plenty of time to close the gate or ready his weapon. He wasn't worried about getting shot. The guard was young and even trained men succumbed to fear when a man was charging—it would take incredible luck for the soldier to hit him on the run.

"'Los... count to five after I leave and follow with your weapon ready. Fire only if you have a clear shot." Carlos nodded, and Alberto turned to Amber. "Do not show yourself unless I call for you, and if I do not, make your way to the others and back to the hotel."

"No, I—"

"Do as I say!" He didn't wait for her to argue further but leapt from the cover of the leaves and sprinted toward the slowly closing gate. He was half-way there when the guard looked up with shock in his eyes, the shock turning to naked fear when Alberto heard Carlos emerge behind at a leisurely trot. The guard unshouldered his weapon and barely took aim before firing his first shot. Dirt explod-ed from the road ten meters to Alberto's left, and the guard aimed again. This time he waited for the intruder to close within can't-miss range. Alberto drew his handgun and fired from the hip, missing the guard by a hair. The guard grinned as Alberto ran, then a look of wild shock crossed the boy's face and a small circle of red appeared on his chest. The guard fell over as the faint *pop* reached Alberto's ears. An-other pop sounded simultaneously with the thump of the tower guard hitting the ground.

Alberto stopped the gate and stared at the dead guard, the boy's face still a grimace of pain and confusion. Carlos joined him, his weapon ready as he scanned the ridge to the east.

"That was no carbine, 'Berto."

"I know. You see the entry wound?" He knelt and pointed to the soldier's armored vest. "That's the hole of a nine-millimeter." He felt the edges, admiring the accuracy. "Look how clean." Carlos grunted, and Alberto rolled the body over. "Punched right through the vest and the heart. Through and through." He shook his head. "Francisco could not have made that shot."

"So... we have a guardian angel?"

Alberto frowned and pulled his bottom lip. "It would seem so." He stood and waved at Amber and called her over while Carlos did the same with his brother.

"We must hurry," Carlos said, dragging the body aside. "Even if there are no other guards inside, surely someone is calling the others back."

Amber joined them and looked down at the body, breathless from the short sprint. "Who shot the guards?"

"I do not know," Alberto admitted. "It was not Francisco." That man broke through the trees at a run, the others close behind. Alberto waved them toward the compound. "Everyone inside the gates." He grabbed Francisco by the arm as he arrived. "You take the tower," he said, then nodded at one of his men. "Julio... you have the gate. Carlos and Amber are with me. The rest of you take cover." He began to trot toward the first building.

Janice and Maribel both opened their mouths to speak, but Amber waved them off. "Where are we going?" She hadn't moved, but scanned the area with furtive glances.

"Search and Destroy." He stopped and nodded at Carlos, who nodded back. "There are certainly other armed men here—not to mention your spacemen—and I'd rather not be caught unawares." *There is no more time to talk.* "We must hurry. You can find your man?"

"I... I think so, yes." She showed no more confidence than the poor guard.

"Then we will start there." He waved her ahead. "Lead, please."

He, Carlos, and Amber ran from the gate, and while he saw no danger before him, he felt eyes on his back from the shooter on the ridge. *As long as that is all he puts there.* He surged forward to pace Amber.

CHAPTER 20

SOHRAB SCANNED THE COMPOUND THROUGH THE SCOPE on the Glock. Other than the men in the truck and the two he'd taken out with two well-placed shots, the compound appeared devoid of military presence. He had seen nothing that might be a Zzkritti either, but that didn't mean they weren't there—in fact, he fully expected they were. Schemers and manipulators, they'd never show themselves unless there was no other choice. All of which meant they felt protected, or at least hidden. Amber and her crew were either walking into a nest of rattled aliens, or a meat-grinder of human origins. Neither was good. Sohrab grunted as he stood, then began the long climb down from the ridge.

His placement had been ideal for sniping, but not so for joining in the coming fight. He figured he had less than five minutes to get into a new position—one that allowed him to engage the truck full of soldiers when they returned. That they *were* returning rather than investigating the tripped alarm was a foregone conclusion—someone or something had to have alerted them once he'd taken out the guard in the tower. They wouldn't return laughing and joking as they had going out, either. He'd watched them assemble and board the truck with military precision, their training obvious. What came toward him now was a force of ten men with the full knowledge their base was under attack.

Sohrab grunted again as he slid down the steep slope over damp green ground cover, balancing with his free hand. *I'm definitely getting too old for this.*

❦

The hum in Amber's head wasn't a directional indicator—there was no map with a blinking light that got brighter or dimmer with each turn of her head—but it lead her to Jack just the same. If pressed for details, she couldn't explain it even in the broadest terms. The closest she could have come to describing the sensation was a bright light calling to her across a crowded room, the way a child recognizes the sound of a father's sneeze or the way he clears his throat. It wasn't Jack's voice, or even the scent of his mind—it outlined his thoughts as distorted through a dirty and cracked window. The nanites placed in his body by the others broadcast his presence like a beacon, announcing for all who could hear, *I am here, I am here!*

Again, she wondered why Jeff's faction had never heard these others. *Is it because Dieter programmed mine specifically to react to the presence of other nanites?* She didn't know, but it would be the first question she asked if she saw Thirteen again.

The light in her mind pulsed, and she changed direction. "This way." She ran without looking back. The two pair of boots pounding the asphalt behind her were a comfortable presence, but neither man responded; they reserved their attention for the shadows at the corners of buildings or the few windows they passed. She sensed they were nervous no one else had challenged or attacked them, and if she spared a moment of thought for it, she'd feel the same, but that was their purview—hers was to find Jack.

She rounded a corner, her boots crunching on the gravel as she left the paved area, and hastened past a set of concrete steps leading from a steel door. Both men on her tail, they were passing the door when it flew open, the heavy metal clanging noisily against the side of the building. She spun, her eyes wide, in time to see the soldier brace and aim his weapon at her head. Carlos' handgun barked once before she even had time to process the image, and the soldier's head burst, bits of bone and brain splashing red against the institutional gray paint. Everyone froze in place as the limp form slid to the concrete, and they waited for anyone else to come through. After her heart slowed to a pounding *vivace*, Amber spun and left them staring after her.

He's close. I feel it. What she also felt was a gnawing, unrelenting, and wholly unreasonable anger, and it was directed right at Jack. She stopped and stared at the small gun in her hand. Alberto had given it to her in the gulley, more to assuage her fears than adding firepower to the group. *If I take this with me to find Jack...* Amber shuddered and she let the thing drop to the ground with a crunching thud. She doubted the nanites in her brain could force her to shoot Jack, but neither did she want to test that theory. Alberto scrambled to pick the weapon up, and he joined her at her side.

"Tell me which building. Carlos and I must clear the way if you won't carry the gun."

She stopped and spun in place, her head tilted as if listening, though what she heard was more color than sound. Everything around her was a bright blood-red, but there was a single mass of deepest black, and it was close... *he* was close. Amber pointed at a low building near the giant Quonset hut, and both men sprinted past her. The gap was wide—perfect for someone to pick them off one by one as they ran—and she left the shadow of the building and ran. Her legs pumped furiously, but she fell behind the longer legs of even the much heavier Carlos. They drove forward, determined to pacify the occupants of the building before she arrived, and they scanned left and right as they ran. She glanced up at the tower and saw Francisco sweeping the compound with his rifle, and she calmed a little. At least no one could sneak up behind them.

Alberto approached the steps, and both doors swung wide, two men stepping through, guns blazing on full automatic. They sounded like someone ripped a long sheet of burlap, and the guns walked up as the soldiers struggled against the recoil. Alberto was close enough they missed wide. Carlos wasn't so lucky.

The big man jerked violently as slugs of hot metal slammed into his body, stitching a line of crimson from hip to shoulder. His hand spasmed as he fell and his gun barked three times—two rounds burying themselves into the gravel at his feet, but one finding the meaty thigh of Alberto. He dropped at once to one knee, the fall saving him from the barrage of gunfire aimed where his head had been. Grimacing in pain and sorrow, he lifted his weapon and put round after round into the chests of the two soldiers, firing over and over until the clip was empty. When Amber reached him, he was still pulling the trigger on an empty chamber.

"Give me your belt," she cried, and he dragged his gaze away from the dead men and up to her, not a hint of understanding crossing his face. She reached for the buckle, unfastened it, and started pulling. "Your wound." She tugged harder, checking the wound with her free hand. She pressed hard, feeling through to the bone, and she felt him take over the job of freeing his belt. He was moving with more confidence, so she used both hands to apply pressure while he looped the belt around his leg and cinched it tight, grunting from the effort and pain. "The bone's not broken. The wound looks through and through." She looked into his eyes. "Can you walk?"

He grunted again, holding her eyes with his own and pointedly *not* looking at Carlos. "You lead, I'll follow," he said through gritted teeth.

"Hold on while I check on Carlos." She stood, but he grabbed her by the wrist and shook his head.

"Don't," he croaked. "One caught him in the head." He lowered his eyes. "You don't want to see what I saw." He held out her gun for her. "Take it. I don't think we're finished."

"I... I *can't*." Even if they had the time, she could never articulate why; if she tried, she'd vomit a steaming bolus of grief, regret, and pain. She clenched her teeth and tugged to free her arm from his grasp.

Alberto sneered up at her, then released her wrist and climbed to his feet. He wobbled a bit, but could stand on his own. He ejected the spent clip from his gun and pulled a fresh one from his pocket, jamming it in with an angry thrust. "Fine," he growled. "Let's finish this."

Jack heard the unmistakable pop and crackle of gunfire even through the heavy muffle of the thick walls, and he jerked against the restraints. The Zzkritti stood perfectly still. From the top of the twisted black horns to the tip of its barbed tail, the thing was a statue carved from darkest ruby. *What is it waiting for?* Jack thought. An alarm began blaring its rhythmic pulse, drowning the sounds of gunfire. It was too random and sporadic to be anything other than an attack on whatever facility they'd brought him to. *But who is attacking, and why?* The government would never bother with rescuing an employee from foreign soil, especially one so far down the org chart. *Doubly especially since no one seems to know I even work there.*

If the attackers were there to rescue him, the big question was *who.* Even if he'd been missed, who could have tracked him to wherever this was? He could only think of one person with the resources and skill, but Thirteen wouldn't need a gun. *He'd just walk through the front door and take me.* Three, maybe four men clomped in heavy boots outside the room, their footfalls fading down a long hallway he couldn't see. They spoke in loud and clipped voices in Spanish, and Jack listened intently. *Might be helpful if I understood a word of the language.*

The rapid pop of gunfire slowed, and somewhere a door squealed open. The Zzkritti had yet to move a single chitin-covered muscle, and Jack wondered if the thing was afraid. Other than when the big one had been around, he'd seen no indication the aliens even knew what fear was. Three more shots rang out—this time very close—and Jack struggled harder against the restraints. The heavy leather stretched tight but did not give. No matter who came through the door, Jack would be as helpless as a rabbit in a snare. Another shot outside the room, and something heavy fell against the door. A scraping sound followed, then a large arm pushed. Someone *not* attached to that arm shoved past, stepping into the steady glow of the surgical light, red light pulsing in the hallway bathing her back.

"Jack!" Amber cried and lunged forward, but the large man holding the door snatched at her jacket and held her back.

"*Madre de Dios!* What... *is* that thing." He held her fast with his right hand, boot holding the door open, and pointed at the Zzkritti with the gun in his left. The creature had finally moved during the minor chaos and now had both talons on the petcock for the tube attached to Jack's arm. It made to turn it, presumably allowing the green liquid to flow into him. Jack scowled. None of it made sense.

"Shoot it!" Amber yelled. The man didn't hesitate. He didn't even wait for her to get to the word *it*, and he fired three quick rounds at the Zzkritti. Two of the bullets ricocheted harmlessly from the alien's exoskeleton, but the third clipped one claw reaching for the tube. It scanned the intruders one by one, the man—boy, Jack realized—quaking in unrestrained fear. It released the petcock as the liquid began to flow and took one step toward Amber. The man steadied his aim and fired a single round directly into the Zzkritti's eye. The gun roared in the enclosed space, the eye exploded, and the back of the Zzkritti's head blew out in a shower of chitin and ichor, bathing Jack in red, black, and yellow. It took two more steps, then fell to the floor in a clatter of dropped stoneware.

"The IV..." Amber scrambled over the body, avoiding claws and tail, and ripped the tube from Jack's arm before any of the green glow reached the needle. Tears in her eyes, she loosened the straps and helped him sit up. "Are you all right?" She gripped his shoulders and peered deep into his eyes as he righted. "What did they do to you?"

Jack rubbed his head. He wanted to tell her everything—even what the other Zzkritti had told him—but the damn nanites wouldn't let him. All he could croak out was a weak "I'm fine."

239

"I'm fine?" Amber said, incredulous. "You've been missing for days, I risk getting arrested and killed to find you with a Zzkritti doing God knows what to you, and all you can say is *I'm fine?*" She pulled on his arms and helped him to his feet. He wobbled a little, and she held him up as best as she could.

"We must go." Alberto gripped the door frame and stuck his head into the hall, checking both ways. "Even if these were all the guards in this building, there are certainly others coming." He looked back at her and cocked a bushy eyebrow. "And there are still the men in the truck." As if to emphasize his point, three shots rang out beyond the walls of the building. Amber jumped, but Alberto gave her a knowing grin, waving her concerns away. "That was Francisco."

"How do you—"

"I know the sound of his weapon, and it's nothing like these." Alberto straightened and faced her. "He's keeping the area clear for our escape." He reached for her. "Which we must do. Now."

"The man's right." Jack no longer wobbled, but still looked weak. *What had they done to him?* She saw the green liquid oozing from the tube onto the sheets of the bed. *Whatever it was, it looks like we stopped them before they could finish.* Alberto knelt and began dragging the dead guard inside the room. Once inside, he started removing the soldier's clothes.

Amber frowned and furrowed her brow. "What are you doing?"

"He can't get far like that," he said, nodding at Jack's naked body.

"Oh," she said, cheeks flushing. "Yeah." Jack made a clumsy effort to cover himself with a sheet, but Alberto threw him a bloody pullover shirt. Jack poked a finger through the carbon-stippled hole, shrugged one shoulder, and tugged it on. Pants and boots came next.

"The boots are a bit snug," he said pulling them on.

"We'll stop by the gift shop on the way out," Alberto said with a slight sneer.

Jack angled his face up at Amber and grinned as he laced the boots. "I like him. Where did you guys meet?"

Alberto snorted. "In a hotel. She—"

Amber kicked him hard in the shin. "It's a long story, Jack. How about I tell it where there aren't so many guns around?"

Jack cocked an eyebrow and stood. He waved at Alberto. "Lead the way."

Alberto nodded, checked both ways in the hall, and gestured for them to follow. Amber pushed Jack ahead of her, and they both followed Alberto from the chamber of horrors. For all his earlier wobbling, Jack had no trouble keeping up with the young man, and Amber wondered how much of that had been an act—or maybe a result of programming. *But they didn't finish. Maybe he just recovers fast.*

They ran straight to the exit, Alberto kicking the door's bar before hitting it with his broad shoulders. He stumbled out into the light with what seemed to Amber as reckless abandon, Jack following with equal carelessness. When she exited, she saw both had flattened against the wall and Alberto swept the area with both his eyes and his weapon. The whole compound was strikingly quiet now, only a gentle evening breeze rustling the trees marring the perfect canvas of silence. Carlos still lay where they left him, the expression frozen on his face was more one of pure annoyance than pain or fear. Alberto crossed himself and whispered a few words as they passed the body. She refused to look too hard, but Jack stared slack-jawed.

"Was he... was he one of yours?" He stopped near the body, refusing to take another step, and looked into Amber's swollen eyes. She couldn't answer; she knew how she would feel if people died to save her. Francisco took the burden from her when he rounded the corner and slid to a stop in the loose gravel.

"*Dios mío.*" He dropped his rifle and knelt beside his brother. He reached out to touch his face, then pulled back, stroking the top of his head instead. Amber's eyes pooled. *He can't be over eighteen.*

"Francisco," Alberto snapped, and the boy raised his chin. "The tower. You are supposed to—"

"There is no one else." He looked down at the face of his older brother. "No one else."

Jack looked at Amber as if she'd killed the man herself, shaking his head sadly. His mouth worked like he had something to say, but no words came. He looked shocked and pained, and she could certainly understand; the thick stew of emotions running through her own veins was enough to give her pause. But they couldn't stop here. Not now.

"Alberto," she said. "We have to go."

"I know," he growled. He gripped Francisco's shoulder and sighed through his nose. "Come, Paco. There is still the truck."

Francisco sniffed, wiped his nose, and looked up at him, eyes narrowing. He snatched his rifle off the ground and stood, then

241

thrust the rifle into Jack's hands and turned back to Alberto. "Help me carry him."

"But—"

"I will not leave him here." He bent and lifted Carlos' shoulders. "I must bring him home."

Alberto's shoulders slumped, and he shoved the handgun in his belt, then bent and grabbed Carlos by the ankles. Together the two men carried him between them back to the main gate, Amber and Jack following in respectful silence. When they reached the gate, Janice gasped and Maribel broke into quiet sobs, Beth's arm around her shoulders. Julio and the other man took Carlos from them and lay him inside the little guard shack, wrapping him in a tarp they found there. Neither seemed pleased about the prospect of carrying the body all the way back to the truck.

The truck. Amber rounded when the open vehicle full of soldiers roared out of the jungle toward the gate.

Jack jerked his head toward the new sound while Alberto waved everyone behind the shack. He ripped the rifle from Jack's hands and thrust it out to Francisco. Jack watched the boy fumble with it a second before his eyes hardened, then he nodded and ran back toward the tower.

"He'll never get there in time to cover the gate," Jack said.

"I don't expect him to," Alberto said, his voice flat. He held out his hand in front of Amber. "Give me your gun."

"What?" She looked like someone had just peed in her cereal bowl.

"I need Jack to back me up." He said it as if the thing were obvious.

"Uh... I'm pretty sure she's a better shot than I am," Jack said. Alberto sniffed and looked at him with disdain radiating from every pore. He bent and plucked the cap from the body of the gate guard, then placed it on Jack's head, pulling the bill low. He handed him the man's rifle.

"Keep your face down and get out there." He shoved Jack into the open. "When they stop to wait for you to open the gate, get behind the shack."

Jack understood at once what the man wanted, and he waved Amber to silence before she objected. He noticed Mason's friend, Maribel the hacker, was among their group, but he didn't have time to consider all the implications. The truck was nearly upon them, slow-ing with a squeal of neglected brakes. He paced back and forth behind the gate, doing his best impression of a guard and hoping it was good enough. At least one woman sobbed behind the shack, snuffling un-controllably. *You should know what I know. That would sober you right up.*

He snapped an about-face and retraced his steps while the truck slowed to a stop. He glanced up, keeping his face down as instruct-ed. The driver seemed impatient, and a little confused, the men in back eyeing him with suspicion, and Jack realized the stupidity of Alberto's plan. Jumping behind the shack would only draw the sol-diers' attention—not away like a true diversion should. Without thinking—thinking would only slow him anyway—he sprinted away in the opposite direction. He heard the men cry out in surprise, fol-lowed by gunfire. Bullets spattered the pavement, but he made it to a small building on the opposite side of the road. A rain of gunfire erupted from the shack, and he watched as both Alberto and Amber stepped out of the little building's protection and began picking off soldiers one by one. It took less than a second for the men to recover and return fire, forcing the two back behind the shack. Two soldiers lay dead or dying on the road, while one slumped over the side.

Jack ached to step out of the shadow of the building and join the fight, but he knew he'd hit nothing but air. He watched in hor-ror as the remaining men stood to leap from the truck and swamp his friends. When the first man fell, Jack hadn't even registered the sound of the gunshot, but when he did, he saw neither Alberto nor Amber had fired. Two more fell in rapid succession, each with a clean bullet hole in their head. The rest had had enough, and they leapt from the truck and ran for the cover of the jungle. Sohrab climbed from a gulley beside the road and calmly picked them off as they ran.

Silence—marred only by the sounds of sobbing and the cries of the dying. Sohrab lowered his weapon, then spun and stalked toward the gate. Jack wasn't the least bit surprised to see him, but a little confused why it hadn't been Thirteen who rescued him. The nanites coursing through his system were wild with desire at his thoughts of Thirteen; their need moved him to ache for his presence. He was the one man they both needed, and the one man Jack knew *shouldn't* be here. As Sohrab approached, something between joy and sadness in his eyes, Jack wanted to tell him what the little Zzkritti had revealed to him... but couldn't.

The mites to destroy the others are within you, it had said. *You must only give them to Thirteen and he will spread them to the hive.* It had leaned closer and hissed, *this you must not do. Instead you will find Dieter and reveal to him the location of what he needs.*

That was when the thing told him Dieter had survived by transferring his consciousness to another through the nanites. But the device Jack had held disrupted the process, and it had split the man into many parts in many hosts. Dieter had recovered almost all of himself, lacking only one final piece, and it was the one with information needed to complete the mission these Zzkritti had programmed into him so long ago.

And that piece was inside Amber.

PART THREE

I once was lost,
but now am found,
was blind but now I see.

— John Newton (1725–1807)

CHAPTER 21

THE LEAD TRUCK BOUNCED ON THE ROUGH road, but the two men in back were barely jostled. They sat with their backs to the cab, eyes lowered and hooded. They had laid the body wrapped in the tarp with great care into the bed, then climbed in with a somber silence. Everyone, it seemed, was trapped inside their own head during the drive out of the mountains; none more than Jack.

Argentina? Thirteen told him the original Zzkritti base had been there, but he couldn't imagine the sheer stupidity of the other faction remaining after their split. *Maybe they had imagination itself engineered out of their DNA.* It was clear their technology had stagnated; Thirteen said the design of the device he carried hadn't changed in over a million years.

He rode with Sohrab, concluding after seeing the faces of his rescuers warranted a bit of distance. Janice—*And how did she get involved?*—rode behind in a big car with Maribel and a young woman he recognized but couldn't place. Amber rode in the truck driven by Alberto. Part of him thought he should be jealous, but the nanites had greater control of his emotions than he expected. He marveled at first that at no time during the rescue had he felt a hint of fear. *Though knowing the whole setup was a sham might have more to do with that than the little machines in my bloodstream.* The Zzkritti may control his actions, but they couldn't—or wouldn't—control his thoughts.

"Do you remember anything?" Sohrab gripped the steering wheel like it would start thrashing at any moment.

"A little." That was a lie. He remembered all of it. "I'm pretty sure they didn't get the little buggers inside me." Another lie. Sweat beaded on his temples as he fought for enough control to tell the truth, but the programming wouldn't allow it. Even if he had managed, the nanites would only kill him for his trouble. *And that would be better, wouldn't it?* He asked the question of no one but himself, but he had the odd impression they were shaking their little heads in disagreement.

Sohrab looked at him askance. "You were there for days, Jack." He didn't complete the thought; they both understood the question that lay beneath his words, and it would pain Jack to argue either side. *Literally.* "Amber may believe she stopped them in time, but I don't."

Good for you. Jack saw a ray hope. "Does it matter?"

"Of course it does!" Sohrab grunted and shook his head. "You could be a time-bomb just waiting for the right moment to trigger." He pulled at his beard and pursed his lips. "Our first order of business is to get you to the Shadowman. He can at least scan you with that thing of his, right?"

No, no, no, no, no... Jack gibbered internally. Outside, he was the very epitome of calm, but inside he fought like a demon for control. *Thirteen is the one person I can't see.* The Zzkritti doctor had been clear on that point. The nanites would invade Thirteen's body and lay in wait until he traveled again to the hive. Once there, they would quickly infect and eradicate Jeff's faction. The alien was defying his own leadership by trying to ensure that didn't happen. *Yet, it still strives to aid Dieter.* That Dieter had survived was enough of a shock, but that what he needed to complete his mission was inside Amber almost drove Jack over the edge into madness. The war between the two factions had touched the people he loved, killing four already, and it felt as if it would never stop. *They won't stop until all my friends are dead.* And it was his fault. *He'd* placed each of those dead directly into the path of the battle.

"I... don't... think he can detect them... even if they are inside me," he said with some difficulty. Both sides of the battle now raged within him—two different imperatives warring for supremacy. One drawing him to Thirteen, the other pushing him away.

Sohrab peered at him with both concern and suspicion. "Is that so?" He frowned and grew silent again, staring through the windshield at the fading light.

"It's a possibility." Jack shrugged one shoulder. "It's also possible there's nothing there to see." He grinned half-heartedly. "Not sure there's a discernible difference."

"Uh-huh," Sohrab intoned, his voice low and resonant. He hooked a thumb over his shoulder. "There're sandwiches and drinks in the cooler if you're hungry." Until that moment, Jack hadn't bothered to think about food, but his stomach took the cue to register its complaint to the management. Sohrab turned and grinned. "Guess that wouldn't happen if the machines were controlling everything."

Jack chuckled, but inside he was screaming.

Amber huddled against the door and wondered how things had come to this. It was odd... she had found Jack through her nanites, the little machines guiding her every step like sweeping a metal detector, but from Jack himself she felt nothing. Of all the noise and chatter of the various nanomachines in the building, Jack was a silent black hole. At first she'd decided that meant there weren't any in him, but now she wasn't so sure. There should have been—*images* was the only word—at least passing through him, but like a black hole, not a single signal escaped. In the end she found him not so much by a signal emanating from him, as by finding the place where he was not.

She glanced at Alberto and the scowl permanently affixed to his face. He clutched the wheel with an aggressive anger, grinding the plastic under strong fingers, and leaned forward like his posture might spur the beast to run faster. He drove as fast as anyone dared on this road, yet he seemed to want more. She looked behind at the inscrutable headlights of the Humvee crawling up their back, groping for Jack's presence and still finding nothing. The unreasonable hatred she'd experienced when entering the compound was gone. Whatever had raised those hackles was not present in him. *At least not anymore*, she thought.

One man—*probably Julio*—thumped a fist on the roof of the truck and Alberto slowed. The man, not much older than Francisco, poked his head inside the back window.

"Main road ahead."

"I see," Alberto growled. He allowed the truck to slow, then climbed the steep embankment back to the paved road.

"Can Janice's car make that?" Amber asked, looking back past the Humvee.

"If she cannot, we will just leave it here," he said, not looking at her. "There is plenty of room in the vehicle with your boyfriend." Any other time she might have considered he was jealous, but the way he spoke was more like an accusation. She wanted to tell him that wasn't fair, but she knew better. One of his friends was dead because of her and Jack, and there was no way around that.

Sohrab followed them without effort, and even Beth found a way without too much trouble—though they all had to wait in the middle of the road while she slowly worked her way back and forth until the front tires were firmly on the pavement. That problem overcome, the caravan continued its journey back to Bariloche. The trucks knobby tires hummed a low tune on the road, and would have lulled her to sleep if she could have slept at all.

"Carlos was the main source of income for his family," Alberto said without preamble. "It is a large family."

"I'm sorry," she breathed. If she could have thought of more to say, she would have, but in such cases—and she'd seen far too many of them—short and simple was best.

"Is that all you have to say?" He looked at her, hurt in his eyes.

She wanted to snap back at him it wasn't her fault, but she bit down hard on the rejoinder. Nothing good ever came of an argument borne of grief. Instead, she waited for him to calm, and he did so in stages, finally heaving a long sigh.

"I always knew this could happen, but..." He took another deep breath and let it out slowly. "Until today, it had never been so dangerous." He faced her and peered deep into her eyes. "I also did not believe you about the... *things* holding your friend." Alberto crossed himself, looking back to the road. "Dios mío," he whispered. "Jack said there was once an entire hive of them in my country. Is that true?"

"I don't know their history as well as Jack... but I believe what he says."

"And they are still here."

"Not so many as before, but yes."

He lapsed into silence for a while, pursing his lips and rubbing his chin. In her experience, that meant he was considering something crazy, dangerous, or both.

"I must root them out," he said after a long pause.

Yeah... both.

"That's... probably not a good idea."

"Why?"

She sighed. Nothing she said now would change his mind now he'd decided, but she had to try, regardless. "They've been here for over six thousand years and have puppet strings tied into practically every government on the planet." She shook her head. "Take them head-on, and even your own government will be against you."

He chuckled and shook his head. "That is not a new development." After a few more moments of silence, he looked at her again,
his face softer. "Perhaps you should sleep. It is a long drive."

"Bariloche is not that much farther."

"We're not going there."

Janice slammed the car door behind her and stalked over to the
truck. Alberto was waving the men out of the bed, Amber moving to
intercept her.

"Wait, Janice," she said, interposing herself between the two.

"Why are we here instead of the hotel?" Janice demanded, stepping around her. She wasn't really as angry as she sounded, but the
man was still her employee. If there was one thing Paul had taught
her, it was to maintain the pecking order.

"We must take care of Carlos." He lowered the tailgate for the
others to lift the body out. "Even in my backward country, the police
notice when a body is full of lead." The last he said low and only to
her. Francisco stood near the road, away from the others; her heart
went out to him. She turned and gestured at the building.

"This is a veterinary hospital."

"It is." Julio and the other man took Carlos' body away, carrying
him between them to the back of the building. The road was quiet and
empty, and there were no street lights on this corner; the only light
came from a gibbous moon, its cold white glow leaching color from
the landscape. A door creaked open in the back, and glaring artificial
light spilled into the alley. Muffled voices reached around, but she
couldn't make out anything they said. Alberto lifted the tailgate and
slammed it closed. "After..." He choked and cleared his throat. "After
the bullets are out, they'll take him to... eh, *la funeraria*." He stepped
close. "It will cost a lot of money."

Janice raised an eyebrow at Amber, who shuffled one foot and
looked away. "Fine," she said at last with a heavy sigh. "I'll take care
of it."

"And who will pay our family's bills?" Francisco hollered. He
strode to them out of the darkness, his eyes swollen and angry. "Mother cannot work, and the bonaerense killed our father when we were
boys." He walked directly to Amber, poking a finger at her. "*You*
got Carlos killed. He has a wife and three children." He stopped, his
hands clenched into tight fists. "*Had...*" Francisco lowered his chin
and stared at his feet. "What will the woman do for them?"

251

Janice's first thought was to offer money, but she was sure—even though it was both needed—the mere offer would offend him. *Besides, I can't take care of everyone.* Paul had stretched that concept into taking care of *no one*. He'd come from old money, while she had not, and his idea of pulling oneself up by their bootstraps was a far cry from hers. Still, she was responsible—regardless of how the man felt about Amber's culpability.

"I can—"

"Hold, woman," Sohrab said. He strode toward them out of the shadows where he'd parked the large truck. Jack stood beside his open door, watching with something approaching interest. *He doesn't look right. And not just because he was kidnapped and experimented on.* She couldn't put her finger on it—and she didn't really know him as well as Amber—but something wasn't right about him.

Sohrab stopped in front of Alberto, ignoring Francisco altogether. "You see the vehicle back there?" He hooked a thumb over his shoulder. "That's a Mil-Spec Humvee. All the bells and whistle." He nodded to Alberto's truck. "I'll trade you straight up for yours."

Alberto rubbed his chin, eyes narrowing. "That is worth over a quarter-million American dollars." His face was dubious, but the voice held pure awe.

Sohrab gave him a lopsided smile. "I no longer need it, and the man who gave it to me won't care." The smile widened into a feral grin. "And if he does?" He shrugged. "Fuck him."

"You would just hand it over. Here. Now."

"Of course." Sohrab chuckled. "Anyone who saw us leaving that place will remember *my* truck, not yours." He caught Janice's eyes. "This serves my interest and yours." He placed an ursine paw on Alberto's shoulder, nearly swallowing the bulge of muscle. "Sell it the first chance you get and give the money to Carlos' family."

"But..." Alberto choked and said no more.

"And I only need yours until we're safely away from here," Sohrab said, lowering his hand. "You can pick it up at the hotel in a day or two."

"I... I don't know what to say."

Sohrab held out his key fob. "Say it's a deal."

Alberto nodded and traded keys. "We should part ways here. There is no need for us to follow you to the hotel, nor should we be seen together."

Sohrab nodded. "Agreed."

Janice wrapped Alberto in a hug. "I'm sorry about your friend. Thank you for all you've done."

When she released him, he stepped back, a profound sadness in his eyes. "You hired us to do a job." His tone was all business, now. "We did the job. There is nothing more to be said."

She looked up into those dark eyes for a long time, gave him a sad smile, and turned to Amber. "You ride with us." She waved her toward the car. "Sohrab and Jack can take the truck."

"That is for the best," Sohrab grumbled under his breath as he passed her on his way back to the Humvee. He gathered his things into a duffel and walked Jack back to the truck. Julio and the other man returned from behind the building and everyone climbed into their respective vehicles in sullen silence.

Beth started the car and shoved a stick of gum into her mouth, chewed thoughtfully for a moment, then put the car in gear and followed Sohrab and Jack back onto the road. Janice stared out the window, watching the world slide by, and the car was miles down the road before she realized what it was about Jack that bothered her.

He was sweating. The air was cool... and he was just standing there sweating.

"The tall guy sure travels in style." Beth beamed as she buckled her seatbelt, and stared out the window at the Gulfstream's engines as they spun up, their whine rising in pitch. Sohrab closed the door and secured it, locking out most of the noise. Sohrab patted her on the shoulder when he passed, then settled into the seat beside Jack. Their seats faced those Amber and Janice strapped themselves into, but Maribel sat alone in the back of the cabin. She had her legs curled beneath her and her head down.

Janice saw Jack looking at Maribel. "She hasn't said much of anything since the compound." She glanced at the woman. "Do you think she's all right?"

Jack snorted. "Are any of us?"

Janice raised an eyebrow. "The verdict's still out on you."

He recognized she meant it as a joke, but felt the sting regardless. Everyone here held varying levels of suspicion about him. *Hell, Amber won't even look at me.* He wasn't sure he wanted her to. Every time they locked eyes the urge to tell her everything rose like hot magma, and every time the imperative to remain silent locked his jaw as tight as a bear trap. The pain of the two conflicting impulses bubbled through his veins like a bad case of the bends. It wasn't like he had no free will—he just couldn't do anything with it that challenged his programming. *Is this what Thirteen went through all those years?* Jack suspected it was. If that man had never broken his programming, what chance did he have? *He had nibbled around the edges, though. Bent the directives in such a way as to follow the program while serving his own purposes.* But how could he do that here?

"You really don't remember anything?" Janice asked.

He hesitated while his mind fought with itself. "Not much." He shrugged. "What day is it?"

"Um... Monday, I think." She nudged Amber.

"Yeah," she nodded, "all day."

"And it'll be Tuesday before we're back home," Maribel piped up from the back of the plane. Everyone turned and looked at her. Jack was just the first to speak.

"What was that?"

"It's a better than a ten-hour flight, so..." She shrugged and lowered her chin again, dismissing them.

Jack looked around at everyone in shock, and they peered back with sympathy. "Damn... I guess the whole Argentina-thing didn't register until now." He frowned and settled back into the seat anticipating a long flight. The engine whine grew, and the plane lurched as it began to taxi toward the runway. Within minutes the plane sped over the blacktop and lifted smoothly into the air. It banked sharply left, then straightened as the lights of the city fell away beneath them. Amber unbuckled her seatbelt and stood, then strode toward the front of the plane.

"The head's in back," Jack said as she passed.

"Yeah, but the galley's up front. I'm gonna see what's available. Anyone else hungry?" Four hands immediately went up, then a reluctant fifth in the back. Jack unbuckled and stood.

"Hang on. I'll help."

"It's okay, Jack," she said, the barest hint of a smile forming. "It's what I know."

Smile notwithstanding, the statement sounded sad to him.

Evan shivered on the cold cement floor, his teeth chattering. The monster controlling his body had left him alone for so long, he couldn't decide if the prison he'd made for himself were real or if he'd gone mad and was locked in a padded cell somewhere. The last clear memory he had from life was cleaning the bus. How long ago was that? A week? A month? Years? What was real? Everything anyone thought of as real was nothing more than a construct within their own minds. Touch a rock, feel the rough and gritty surface. Every person might describe it the same, but was the experience really identical for each? There was no way to know. Just as there was no way for Even to know what was real and what wasn't.

Everything real is still an illusion. Did he say that out loud? He guessed there wasn't much difference when everything that happened only happened inside his head. What was real didn't really matter anymore. He wondered if it ever did.

"Let's play a game, shall we?" His voice didn't even echo from the walls or floor. "How many times have I taken a shit since I've been here?" The answer, he realized, was none. Not one. Not even the pressure that came with the urge. "That's fair, I guess, since I haven't eaten anything either." Hearing his own voice, real or not, cheered him for reasons he couldn't explain. *What I wouldn't give to hear another's.* "Even Willie's," he said with a soft chuckle. Not that he'd want to listen for long; the man had a way of wearing out his welcome. Fast.

Evan rose to his feet and paced. The room had shrunk since he'd first sealed himself inside, now only requiring four steps to reach the far wall rather than the previous six. It didn't matter; pacing was like NASCAR—the road was infinite as long as you kept turning left. He was never getting out of this place. He recognized that the same way he knew the other had stopped trying to get in, and it was those realities that shrank his prison. Soon he'd be entombed like Fortunato, with neither a cask of wine nor a torch for comfort.

For the first time, he looked up at the ceiling quizzically. *Where does the light come from?* There were no light fixtures or wall sconces, no buried can lighting. The ceiling was as smooth as the floor and walls. The mirror along one wall where he'd often seen the monster peeking through from the other side reflected only his surroundings. So... whence came the light?

"There is no source. The room is just... lit." Of all the things that made no sense, this was the most obvious, and he wondered why it had taken so long to notice. It was fair to assume that, being a mental construct, there needn't be a source. It was also fair to assume the monster didn't provide any for his captive. That would require a level of empathy Evan hadn't seen from the thing. "The light, then... is mine." The last syllable rang from the cold, hard surfaces. "It's

255

mine, and he can't take it." More importantly... it was Evan's, and what was his, he could control.

Fear gripped him; if he tried and failed...

He concentrated, staring at the wall. *There... did it get a little bright-er?* It could just have been his imagination. He slapped his forehead and smirked. *Of course it's my imagination. Everything here is.*

The room brightened further, warming. Evan grinned, the ends of his mouth curling in grinch-like satisfaction.

"Let's play a little game, shall we?" he said with growing cour-age. He raised the goblet of wine to his lips and sipped. It tasted con-siderably better than nothing.

CHAPTER 22

BETH SET HER TRAY ASIDE AND STRETCHED in the low-ceilinged cabin, her back popping like bubble-wrap. Janice gave her an amused look but said nothing, engaged in sipping her wine. They had been in the air less than two hours, and all during that time disturbing thoughts ran through the young woman's head. The problem was she couldn't talk to any of the four nearby about her concerns. She needed an outsider's viewpoint, and the only one that fit that bill was Maribel. *Sure. That's why I'm going back there.* She took the first step before she could talk herself out of it, shuffling past Jack and the others toward the back of the plane. Maribel glanced up at her as she approached, then quickly back down at her tray. The woman looked as if she'd eaten, but all she'd really done was push the food around the plate. Beth frowned, then pasted a plastic smile on her face and plopped into the seat beside Maribel.

"Don't like airplane food?" She did her best to keep her voice normal and only succeeded in sounding desperate.

"I'm really not up for company." The way Maribel spoke, it was a clear dismissal. Beth ignored the warning.

"That's okay. I'm really not here to chat you up."

Maribel raised her chin, turned to Beth, and cocked an eyebrow. "That's good. I'd hate to have to shove this fork in your ear." She brandished the utensil like a switchblade. "Or mine, for that matter."

"Funny." Beth watched as Maribel's face softened before turning sorrowful. "You should eat. It's actually pretty good."

Maribel's eyes narrowed. "I thought you said you weren't here to chat me up." She frowned, looked at her plate, then stabbed a piece of the steak and shoved it in her mouth, ruminating. "Happy now?"

"Yeah, actually," Beth said, brightening. She watched her eat for a while, unsure how to raise her concerns. Maribel, rumpled and disheveled, didn't seem to notice. She'd pulled her dark hair back in a messy ponytail and didn't wear a hint of makeup; although, Beth had to admit, none of them would pass for a model right now—not even Amber. The woman's musk after their adventure was strong, but not unpleasant. Beth suspected her own wasn't exactly of the come-hither variety.

Maribel stopped chewing and gulped, then took a slow sip of wine, watching Beth with a sidelong gaze. She set the cup down and the tray aside and turned her upper body toward Beth. "Okay... out with it."

Beth pursed her lips, glanced at the others, then leaned closer and whispered, "Didn't it seem... well, a little too easy?"

"What are you..." Maribel's dark eyes widened. "*Easy?* A friend of mine *died* back there." Her voice was harsh and angry, and Beth was grateful she also kept it low. Sohrab glanced toward them, frowning, then turned away.

"I know, I know," Beth said, placating. "But..." She tilted her head and screwed her mouth up tight. This wasn't going as she imagined at all. "From what Alberto said, there were something like twenty trained soldiers inside that compound... and another bunch in the truck." She shook her head. "And four people took them all out without hardly breaking a sweat." She leaned closer. "How do you explain that?"

"I don't know. We had surprise and luck on our side, I guess." Maribel's face fell into a mask of sorrow, her shoulders slumping. "Except for Carlos."

"That's what I'm saying. His death sounded more like an accident than anything." Beth couldn't get the scene out of her head; one of the soldiers in the truck had a clean shot at Jack, tracking him with his rifle, neither firing nor taking cover before Sohrab shot him in the head. It had only been a matter of seconds, but even she could have fired off a couple of rounds in that time.

"You... you think it was all staged?"

"I don't know. That's why I'm asking you." Beth frowned and sighed. "You saw everything I did—what do you think?"

Maribel peeked up at the others for a brief moment. "To what end?"

"Do you think any of them are asking these questions?" Beth shook her head. "No... they're just happy they got Jack back, and they all got out alive."

"So you think they staged the whole thing to make us think... what?"

"You heard Amber. She thinks we got to him before the aliens could finish whatever it was they brought him there to do."

"And you don't."

"I'm just saying it was too easy, is all."

Maribel raised an eyebrow at that, then huffed and faced forward, drawing her legs up beneath her in the seat. "Doesn't matter. Once we hit the ground, I'm out."

"But—"

"Nope," she shook her head. "I got paid to do a job, and I've done it. I'm going home, getting a hot shower, and going offline for a week." Her face was stern and hard. *She means it.* "If Jack's been compromised, Josef can handle it."

"The tall guy?"

"Yeah. Josef, Thirteen, the Shadow Man." She waved her hand in the air. "Whatever they're calling him today."

Perhaps I should let it go. Mari may be right. I'm not suited for this stuff, anyway. Perhaps not, but it seemed she was the only one thinking clearly right now, and if that didn't draft her into service, she didn't know what would. Her mom always told her *If you can change things, change things. Sitting on the sidelines ensures nothing changes.* It was especially true, she guessed, if she was the *only* one who could change things. She could, at the very least, bring her concerns to the tall guy... Josef.

"And what about this Dieter guy they keep referring to?" she said at last. "He's supposedly responsible for a string of murders, and he's likely out to kill Jack from what Amber says." She bit her bottom lip. "He doesn't sound like the kind to leave loose ends." *Neither does Josef, apparently.*

"Then he solves the problem of Jack for us," Maribel said, shrugging one shoulder.

"And maybe he follows that with taking care of the loose ends that are us." Beth wanted to say more—wanted to ask how Mari could be so callous—but let it go. There was nothing else she could say that might change the woman's mind.

Maribel sat stone-faced for a minute or more, huffing through her nose, lips pursed. *Quite beautiful lips, actually. Too bad they're at-*

259

tached to such a hard woman. Ever since meeting her, Beth's emotions had see-sawed with every turn and reveal of Mari's character and background. If it were purely physical, she would have approached her already, but the woman both attracted and repulsed her in turns. *At least she's not boring.*

"So," Maribel breathed, one eyebrow arched, "what do you have in mind?"

Jack wasn't right, and Amber knew it. Not just because her nanites couldn't sense him, but because he'd become taciturn to the point of brooding. The first time she met him, she'd seen he was a world-class brooder, but this was another level. The grin he kept attached to his face like a fake mustache never quite reached his eyes. Considering what he and everyone else had just been through, it was out of place as well. He'd eaten in silence, occasionally making yummy sounds to show his appreciate of her ability to heat things in a microwave, but his eyes monitored everyone within his field of vision, like a pilot doing instrument checks. It was too methodical. Too mechanical. The only thing that seemed purely Jack-like was the constant bouncing of one leg; he always did that whenever he was nervous or lost in thought.

Janice gripped Amber's arm and squeezed. She inclined her head toward Jack as if trying to call Amber's attention to something out of place. *Of course there's something out of place. Everything about this is wrong.* Amber looked around the cabin. It seemed as if everyone had something bottled up inside desperately seeking release. Of them all, only Sohrab appeared content to just relax and enjoy the ride... though he spent most of his time staring out the window. Now and then he touched his ear, frowned and sighed, then focused again on the window. The night sky was clear beyond that window, and Amber saw a staggering array of pinpricks of light shining through. *Around one of those the Zzkritti homeworld orbits.* If only they'd kept to themselves.

"Still haven't heard from Thirteen?" Amber asked Sohrab, tapping his leg with the toe of one boot.

"What?" His head jerked away from the window. "Uh... no. Nothing so far." He looked at her quizzically. "How did you—"

"You keep tapping your ear." She tapped hers to demonstrate. "I figure he gave you a communication device of some kind."

He looked around, saw Jack observing him, and straightened in his seat. "Yes, he did." He tapped his ear again and shook his head. "I just cannot make the damn thing work when I want. It only seems to work when he wants to call me."

"Sounds like Thirteen," Jack muttered.

Sohrab grunted. "Indeed." He pursed his lips and pulled at his beard. "So... what are we to do about Dieter?" Jack stiffened at the name.

"I'm more concerned about the breakaway faction of Zzkritti," Amber said. "They are still following the original plan to lead humans astray, right?" She nodded at Jack. "And they obviously had something in mind for you as part of—"

"One disaster at a time, please," Sohrab said, waving his hands in the air. "With Argentina behind us, Dieter becomes the more immediate problem."

"Do you really buy that story Thirteen gave you?" She'd found it hard to believe at first, but the fact the nanites were still active in her system gave her pause. *Still... that's a long way from transferring consciousness.*

"Well, either the Shadowman is telling the truth, or there is a vampire draining its victims of blood all over the world." He turned to Jack. "You're the one who found the connection. What do you think?"

Jack opened his mouth, stopped and closed it, then repeated the process two more times before saying, "I don't know." The words came out as gravel dumped from a truck. Amber stared at him for a few seconds, then addressed Sohrab.

"Fine. We'll stick with vampire."

"Have any of you considered the possibility the two are connected?" All three turned their attention to Janice, looking at her as if she'd just appeared out of thin air. "I mean, other than the obvious one, of course."

Amber frowned, her brow knitting. "What do you mean?"

"Am I the only one who noticed Jack was taken by the Zzkritti *while* interviewing a possible witness to Dieter's crimes?" She looked at each of them. "That can't have been a coincidence, right?"

Now they looked at her as if she had a foot growing out of her ear. *How could I have been so stupid?* Amber mentally slapped her forehead. *Of course they're connected.* It was all of a piece somehow, and she'd missed it. *What else have I missed?* She glanced at Jack. *Everything.*

CRITICAL

The apartment smelled like new paint and chemical cleaners. Dieter closed the door behind him, flicked the light switch, and set the bags from Home Depot on the kitchen counter, then tossed his key to rattle beside them. He'd been lucky—this place was on the same floor as Jack's, but around the corner and closer to the stairs. While most in DC would walk the thirty feet to the elevators, Dieter would spend his time trudging up and down the steps where other feet rarely tread.

With this most recent trip to buy supplies, and the deliveries he expected in a day or so, he had almost everything he needed. What it all was for was still a mystery, but the information he needed was still out there for him to find.

"First things first, though," he spoke into the silence. He sat on the only chair in the room and lifted the bag from an earlier shopping trip into his lap. Digging inside, he drew out the box with the brand new Glock 9mm and opened it, lifting the weapon out and setting it in front of him on the table. Next to that he set the oil and cleaning kit he'd purchased with the gun. Within seconds, he'd expertly disassembled the handgun and began the task of cleaning and oiling everything. He whistled while he worked; it was a habit he'd picked up long ago. The process was neither long nor laborious, but he took his time. *It wouldn't do for the gun to jam just in his moment of triumph.* He'd briefly considered a revolver for that very reason, but ultimately rejected the idea for reasons other than utility or aesthetics—Jack had murdered him with a revolver, and while using one to kill *him* in return lent a modicum of closure, he just hadn't been able to even touch one.

Once the weapon was cleaned and oiled, he began the process of reassembly. It felt good to work with his hands again; he had done little of that in a very long time—his work with nanites notwithstanding. This was a more basic type of work—more primal—and he reveled in the mundane nature of the task. His fingers moved with a practiced precision that came from a place other than life experience. Dieter had long-since dismissed the question of where these abilities came from or how he acquired them, simply accepting them as gifts from the nanites.

The world stuttered, like a fleck of dust on an old vinyl record, and he cocked his head and pursed his lips, looking down at the fully assembled gun in his hands. Dieter didn't remember performing the last few steps and considered taking it apart again. His watch chimed. He frowned at the timepiece and lay the gun down; it was time for another dose of Adderall. *I guess I'm just tired.* He walked into the bathroom to retrieve the medicine, forgetting all about the gun.

Fighting the programming was getting Jack nowhere, and rather than lock himself into an endless loop of struggle and failure, he elected to watch and wait. His time would come. The window would be small, but it would be there. The only questions were would he recognize it and would he be able to act? *Save your energy and find out, Jack-o.* Even the thought of betrayal caused him pain, and he flinched.

"Are you okay?" Amber leaned across the space between them and had laid a hand on his knee. Soft and gentle; the caress of a cloud.

"I'm fine." He didn't dare look her in the eyes when he said it. She opened her mouth to say something else, and he turned to Sohrab. "Do you have any idea where Dieter is?"

"Ah... no," he admitted, shaking his head. "But I have an idea how we might find him." He studied Amber when he said it, and she scrunched up her face. Jack always loved it when she did that.

"Um..." she began, tilting her head.

"Do you think you can detect him? Like last time?"

Last time she was nearly catatonic. The nanites were possibly the only coherent voices in her head at the time. Like a homing beacon, the little machines had detected the man with disturbing accuracy. They had also been programmed to do so. *Little did he know when he wrote their code we would use it to kill him.*

"I don't know." She frowned, her gaze wandering miles away. Jack thought it was less that she didn't know, and more that she feared trying. "The last time it wasn't so much I was finding *him*, but the place where he held me." She pursed her lips and squinted. "Like the location was a saved map point in a GPS."

Sohrab shrugged and sighed; the sound a deflating bellows. "If the Shadowman cannot help, then you are our best hope."

No she's not. He'll come to me. It was the one thing he was sure of, and one of the many things they had forbidden him to say. The Zz-kritti had told him as much. It counted on it... because they couldn't find Dieter either. *And when he does come to me, I'm supposed to tell him—*

"I'll do my best." Amber cast a furtive glance at Jack when she said it, and he wondered what was in her head. *Does she know I'm compromised?* Her nanites had known at once about those inside his brother,

263

Bill. So far, she'd shown no indication they detected Jack's. *Do hers see mine as kindred spirits, both in service to the same goals?* He almost hoped they did; it would be at least one thing the two of them had in common. As commonalities went, the destruction of the human race was an odd one to have, but it was something.

"That's something, at least," Jack croaked, wondering if she heard both meanings. *If only she could read my thoughts...* It was difficult even to speak in oblique code; his nanites knew what he meant even if others didn't. He contracted in upon himself, a controlled implosion of his presence, both within and without, and he shrank by degrees. The more he fought, the harder it became to think clearly. His heart pounded in his chest like a chick struggling to break through its shell. He rubbed his sternum and lifted his gaze to Sohrab. "What are our options if she can't?"

Sohrab pulled at his beard a moment, his eyes drifting to the window. "I do not know." He took a deep breath and sighed through his nose. "Perhaps there is some way to discover the body he inhabits."

Jack knew there was—the search program Maribel had written for him might do the trick given the right parameters. If only he could tell them. He checked the young woman curled up on her seat in the back of the plane. She was doing her best to ignore Beth, but he could almost hear the wheels turning inside her head—or, as his father used to say, *I can smell the wood burnin'*. She would come to the same conclusion soon, if she hadn't already, but she seemed no longer invested in the problem.

He wondered what he could do to change that.

Thirteen remembered being a child. He remembered his mother, sitting on her knee and listening to her sing; her voice was so clear and pure, like the tones came from God himself. He remembered his twin, saw him every day in a mirror. What he didn't remember were the days between the joy and the pain, washed away in the years of training to become a weapon of the Zzkritti. His life, filled with death since, was a blur of directed violence. He'd done his best to mitigate the collateral damage, but the Zzkritti were often indiscriminate; they saw humans as less than themselves, even while understanding the need for their help. Now his masters had cast him upon an ocean of possibilities, with no direction and no clear objective. It was as when his mother had been taken from him, ripped from his grasping fingers and shoved into the rusty old cattle-car. To a little boy of six, it didn't matter his captors fed him sweets and gave him a soft bed—they had taken his mother.

The flight back to DC wasn't long, but by the time he deplaned, his feet itched to feel solid ground beneath his shoes. He stood at the top of the steps just inside the door, wiped cold sweat from his brow, then placed the fedora on his head and tugged it low in the front. He scanned the tarmac with mismatched eyes, half-expecting an attack, before stepping down and striding away from the plane. In days past, a car would be there to take him to his next assignment, but with autonomy came responsibility for his own transportation. Especially now Jeff was incommunicado.

He needed to call Sohrab to check on his progress, but he dare not until he was alone in his car. Though the small staff on the private jet left him mostly alone, nothing was as secure as the car he'd left parked in the satellite lot. The lamps of the lot, dull and yellowed with age, flickered and buzzed. Insects swooped and dove in and around the cone of light, and damp, sticky fog blurred each lamp into a fuzzy ball of probability; no single photon shared either location or speed. The soles of his shoes tapped a lonely beat on the asphalt, and he approached the only car within sight. It sat directly beneath a darkened lamp, exactly where he'd left it, and he tapped the device in his pocket, directing its energies with a nudge of his will. The car's door locks clicked, and the engine thrummed to life. Thirteen afforded himself a satisfied grin as he opened the door and climbed inside.

He tapped a nodule behind his right ear and it pinged in response. "Are you otherwise engaged?" No salutation was necessary; there was no other the man could hear.

"Shadowman?" It seemed Sohrab hadn't grasped the obvious.

"What is your status?"

Sohrab shushed someone on his end. "We have Jack and are on our way back to DC now." The man sounded annoyed. "Where have *you* been?"

"Unimportant." Thirteen gripped the wheel and pulled out of the lot. "What is your ETA?"

"Uh..." he spoke to someone else in hushed tones, "between four and five hours."

"Good. I will meet you at the airport." Thirteen frowned, and he tapped the turn signal to change lanes. "Did everyone survive?"

"Yes, but—"

265

"Excellent. We will speak more when I see you." He tapped the nodule, and the connection died. He allowed himself the luxury of a chuckle. *Everyone survived.* Thirteen would have wagered everything Sohrab owned that at least one wouldn't have made the return trip. *Even the old woman.* He chuckled again and shook his head.

CHAPTER 23

"**L**OOK, GUYS... I JUST WANT TO GO home and lay my head on my own damn pillow." Jack's voice could have come from the throat of a pack-a-day man, and he coughed up a mass of phlegm. The jet taxied toward the private hangar, light spilling out the huge door like trapped sunshine. The arguing over what to do next had begun on approach and hadn't let up since. Most, like Jack, wanted to go their separate ways and either start fresh in the morning or quietly go about their lives. Amber, though, insisted they stay together and plan. Janice appeared willing to go along with whatever Amber decided, a budding friendship between the two forging a nigh unbreakable bond—*that's a story I want to hear*, Jack thought—but Maribel stayed pointedly out of the discussion. She sat curled up in her seat, Beth hovering like a bodyguard.

Sohrab pursed his lips and tugged his beard. "I must agree with Amber, Jack. We don't know where, or even *who*, Dieter is, and it is a fair assumption he means to settle accounts with you."

"The man is mission-oriented," Jack said with a weary sigh. He yawned wide, covering his mouth. "I'm sure I'm not even fourth on his to-do list." He surprised himself with how sincere his words sounded even to his own ears. Amber seemed unconvinced.

"Isn't it better to be safe than sorry?" Pity—an emotion he'd come to despise during the flight—softened her face. *She assumes they programmed me, regardless of the little stage play the Zzkritti provided.* The worst part was he knew that if she were sure, she'd still do everything she'd done—and everything she planned.

"Even if he's looking for me, what do you suggest I do about it?" He narrowed his eyes, but tried to take the edge out of his voice. "If he has half the resources of Thirteen, he'll find me."

"Not necessarily," Sohrab said. "He does not know me. We could go to my—"

Jack cut him off with a chop of his hand. "No!" Amber, Sohrab, and Janice stared at him as if he'd beheaded a kitten, and even the conversation in the back of the plane stopped. He sighed and slumped in his seat. "Do you want to bet the lives of your family on that, buddy?" Sohrab's eyes rounded and widened. He closed his mouth and frowned.

Amber raised an eyebrow, glancing from one man to the other. "Maybe Thirteen has a place in mind."

"And do you trust him to do what's in everyone's best interest?" Jack shook his head. "He's as single-minded as the other, and he'll put all of you in harm's way to get to Dieter." The words poured out of his mouth as if they were his own, but he trusted them just the same; given free will, he might have used those very arguments. They were all best served by distancing themselves from him, and he would have said it himself if given the chance. It should have been all he had to say, the discussion ending there. Instead, Janice cleared her throat.

"Um... I see no way he knows about *me*." She raised her chin as if her point were obvious. When no one spoke, she pressed on. "There's plenty of room at my house for everyone, and I have no family close by to endanger."

Jack's blood ran cold. "Janice... I can't let you—"

"No," Amber muttered. "She's right. Dieter can't know she's helping us; it's too big a leap of logic." She flashed a smile at Janice and gripped her hand. "I think it's a perfect idea."

Jack wanted to argue further, but couldn't come up with a plausible reason—for good or ill, his friends had stuck by his side. The plane rolled to a jerky stop, punctuating his frustration, and Sohrab opened the door and lowered the stairs. Everyone else stood and stretched aching muscles, joints popping softly up and down the cabin. Beth hurried to the front and leaned in to speak, her eyes down.

"Janice... if you don't mind... after I drop you guys at your place, I'm gonna drive Maribel home." Her brow furrowed, and she frowned. "She says she's out."

"Sure, dear," Janice patted her arm and gave her a sweet smile. "You should probably go home as well. There's no need for either of you to be involved in the rest of this."

Beth rocked back as if Janice had slapped her. "But I thought..." She stood processing everything for a moment, then scanned the faces before her. "Okay," she muttered, her face slack.

Maribel closed to within a step of Beth's back and tapped her on the shoulder. "Hate to burst your bubble, but I ain't goin' home."

Beth turned, her face puckered. "But you said—"

"I know what I said, but listen to what I'm saying now." She straightened and looked Jack directly in his eyes. "I've got some payback to dish, and right now the only target in front of me is Dieter." She narrowed her eyes and leaned closer. "I think I know how to find him."

Every muscle in Jack's body tensed, and the urge to kill her flooded his mind like a tsunami; it took everything he had to fight it back, and he felt his control slipping. Sweat beaded cold and damp on his brow and his arm lifted of its own accord, ready to strike, and he turned it into jerking wiping motion over his forehead. He couldn't understand why the nanites wanted him to keep her silent—they wanted him to find Dieter, after all—but wave after wave of urgent need crashed against his psyche, battering his will into submission.

"Must I send an invitation?"

Jack spun, all the restrained energy redirected, and he stumbled like a toddler. Thirteen stood halfway in the doorway, watching him with curious interest. Competing directives within Jack's programming fought for control of his body, and gradually, his muscles relaxed. The message he must deliver to Thirteen took precedence, and his nanites temporarily forgot all about Maribel's revelation.

"We were just deciding on where to go next," Jack said, still shaking.

Thirteen nodded understanding. "I suggest the widow's home. There is little chance Dieter knows of her."

Everyone froze for almost two seconds before they all burst out in nervous laughter—even Jack.

"What is wrong with you, Jack?" He and Amber were alone in Janice's kitchen; she leaned her back against the island while he sat at the table. She had her arms crossed over her chest like his mom used to do when scolding him after a late night with his friends. The rest of the crew had tacitly agreed to give them some alone time, but he wished they hadn't—his whole body itched to speak with Thirteen. He, however, was huddled with Sohrab and Maribel around her computer. The urge to kill her had died the instant she told everyone about the search program. *I guess there's no point now the cat's out of the*

bag. "You're acting very strange, and if I didn't know better, I'd say they *had* programmed you."

I have been! He wanted to scream it like a banshee, but didn't have enough control over his body to even nod. "I just need to speak with Thirteen." He gritted his teeth and completed the scripted response. "I overheard some information he may need."

Amber pursed her lips and considered him, dubious. "You said you didn't remember anything."

"I didn't... I do. It sort of just came to me when I saw him. Things kind of fell into place." He was saying too much and too little all at the same time, and the words spilled out of him like yolk from a broken egg. "It's important."

"What is it?" Her face was full of earnest hope and empathy, and his heart swelled. He didn't know what they would be to one another afterward, but he could only hope she would look at him the same way again. Considering the information he must deliver to Dieter, the odds were increasingly slim.

"It has nothing to do with Dieter," he said, deflecting. The instant anger flashing in her emerald eyes told him it worked.

"When will we be rid of him?" she growled, shoving her hands in the pockets of her jeans. "You would think a bullet in the head would do it." She shook her head and ran a hand through her hair. "I'm tired, Jack." They all were, each for different reasons. "I've been living with this for over a year, and it feels like it will never end." She looked into his eyes, her own damp and reddening. "When will it end?"

There were a thousand answers to that question, none of them satisfactory—least of all to her. He'd considered the same question for just as long, and the answer kept coming back *never*. It would never end. The Zzkritti didn't care about the human cost, waging their hidden war amongst themselves for the fate of humanity. It. Would. Never. End.

"Soon," he said with a sigh. "Dieter won't be a problem much longer. I promise."

It was the one promise he knew he could deliver. Either Thirteen would kill Dieter, or Dieter would succeed. Both outcomes resulted in Dieter leaving them alone. *Well... the others, at least. He wants to kill me, and he'll likely do it, too.* Jack had no plans to even protect himself; he was also tired. If he could work events to allow Dieter to kill him before Jack could deliver his other message, all the better. And if he could have told her that, he still wouldn't; she looked at him with too much sympathy and worry as it was. *Hell, they all do.*

"Don't promise, Jack." Amber lowered her arms; defeat hung around her shoulders like a shroud, weighing them down, rounding them. "There are no guarantees in any of this." Her voice broke as she spoke, and she stopped, took a deep breath, and gathered control over her emotions. She raised glistening eyes to him, lines at the corners where he hadn't seen them before. "More people are going to die, aren't they?"

He clenched his jaw, and ground out words the nanites allowed as if taunting him. "Not if I can help it."

Janice emerged from her bedroom and pulled the door closed behind her. She sniffled softly and wiped at her eyes with a handkerchief. Beth watched with growing concern as the woman—now looking elderly and frail for the first time since they'd met—shuffled across the room and sat opposite from her on the sofa. The cushions accepted her spare frame, wrapping her in a light embrace. She settled back and crossed one ankle over the other.

"Is everything okay?" Beth asked.

"Oh, sure, dear." Janice waved one hand like shooing a fly. "Just had to take care of some business."

"Business? It's the middle of the night."

"You'd be surprised how many people adjust their work hours when money is involved."

"No... I wouldn't." Beth *was* one of those people, never having had the luxury of ordering others to do her bidding. *Well... other than a waiter.* Other than telling her where and when to drive, the woman had actually treated her more as a friend than the help. They'd even listened to her suggestions and acted upon them. Not even her family did that. Not since she'd come out. It wasn't like they'd disowned her, just that things hadn't been the same since. These people, though... *They accept me for what I can do for them.* For who I am, not just what I am.

"Don't worry your head over it, dear. It's nothing to do with any of," she waved her hand again, "this."

"Well... *that's* comforting," Beth said with a grin. Janice chuckled in response, but it was a hollow sound, with none of the humor Beth had already come to expect. *Yeah... in the whole three days I've known her.* Now would be the perfect opportunity to excuse herself from this nightmare, but she was no longer sure she could. There was something about this disparate group that was more of a family than hers had ever been. Jack, Sohrab, and Amber had apparently gone through fire together, but they had accepted the newcomers almost without question—as if everyone here were meant to be together. A team. Something more than a Scooby-gang, but less than Power Rangers.

Janice sighed and glance toward the staircase. "What's taking them so long?"

"To be fair," Beth said, "Maribel said she only *thinks* she knows how to find the guy." She fidgeted in her seat and pulled her legs up beneath her. "Somehow I don't expect it's gonna be as easy as tracking Jack to Argentina."

"You call that easy?" Janice grimaced and snorted. "Twenty hours in the air is a young woman's game. Personally, I could have done without the shooting."

Beth shuddered at the memory. "I'm just talking about the computer search. That was the easy part... at least for Mari." Janice raised an eyebrow when Beth said the name, a faint smile tugging the corners of her mouth. *Holy shit... have I been that obvious?* She was rusty in the whole flirting department—ever since leaving her first love behind after high school. *Heather was never gonna stick around, anyway.* She wondered if that were true, or if she just told herself that to calm her guilt for leaving. *Doesn't really matter, does it? Works out the same either way.*

"Well," Janice inclined her head, "after she finds him—if she finds him—I want you two to go home. Get as far away from this as you can."

"But—"

"You remind me of my oldest," Janice said, as if that were the next logical step in the conversation. "She always wants to do more, even when she's already done all she can." She leaned forward and winked. "Pretty sure she got that from her father." Her eyes twinkled, and she gave Beth a warm smile. "He never knew when to give up, either."

Beth tilted her head and considered Janice through a squint. "And I bet that's how he got you to marry him."

Janice froze for two or three seconds, then her smile grew. "You're good." She gave Beth a shallow nod. "Yes, as a matter of fact, he *was* a tad persistent." She stared a moment, peering deep into Beth's eyes, then took a long breath and let it out in a whoosh. "I'd like at least one of us to survive this, Beth. You've got a lot of life left in you—there's no point in wasting it on this."

Beth hadn't really considered it in those terms. Death—even in Argentina—had never seemed a near thing. "Kids think they're indestructible," her mom had always said, and her words held a lot of truth. *I think it's more we just don't understand the idea of death. It's too far on the horizon. Worrying about it is for people with one foot in the grave.* Still, there was no point in tempting fate.

"All right. If Mari finds this guy, I'll take her wherever she wants to go before heading back to my place." She cocked her head and gave a lopsided grin. "I've gotta get ready for this semester, anyway."

"Take my car when you do." Janice gave her an odd look when she spoke, but it was fleeting. "The police might still be looking for yours."

"You think?"

Janice shrugged. "No way to know. Better safe than sorry."

"I'll get it back to you as soon as I can."

"No hurries, dear."

"Anyway... we're probably stuck here for quite a while. I don't expect Mari—"

"Found him!" a husky voice called out from above, and both women craned their necks to look up. Maribel leaned over the railing. She waved a printout in her hand, and Thirteen snatched it from her on his way down. "Hey!" She followed him down the staircase as Jack and Amber rushed into the room. Sohrab followed Maribel down the stairs, his face gruff and dark.

"You have a list of possibilities," he said, trotting past her.

Maribel sneered. "More than either of you have done."

The seven members of their fellowship gathered in the conversation area where Beth and Janice sat, each waiting to hear what Maribel had found. Thirteen scanned the page, running one thin finger down its list of names and their accompanying data. He paused three times, frowning.

"It appears you have identified *three* people," he said, grumbling like a rock crusher. "Each must be investigated."

"Faster if we split up," Jack mumbled, taking the page from Thirteen's hand. He scanned the paper, lingering on one. "Amber and I will take this one. The guy has installed himself in my old apartment in Atlanta, of all things."

Sohrab pulled his beard. "It could be a coincidence." He squinted. "Better if I go with you, though."

lifting her feet to the coffee table. "You boys go battle evil while we cook and clean."

Thirteen stared at her without reacting, his face placid as always. After a few seconds, he nodded, then dipped one hand into his jacket. He withdrew a small oblong device about the size and shape of a used bar of soap, a green crystal dominating the upper surface; tiny lights pulsed a slow and random rhythm inside. He held it out to Jack. "Take this. You may have need of it."

Jack reached out, hesitated, and shook his head. "No. I've already turned down Jeff's offer." He blew out a long breath. "I haven't changed my mind." The look he gave said there was something more to his refusal, but Amber couldn't imagine what it was. "If we decide this guy is Dieter, we'll call you."

Thirteen gave him a dubious stare, then placed the device back in his pocket. "Very well, but understand—if this is Dieter, and he sees you, he will kill you." It was as close to a *please be careful* Amber imagined he was capable of uttering.

"Do not worry," Sohrab said. "He will not see us."

"Great," Maribel said. "Everything's all worked out." She stabbed at each person with her glare. "Can I go home now?" Without waiting for an answer, she threw on her rumpled jacket and lifted her messenger bag. She tossed the strap over one shoulder and turned to Beth. "You're driving me to my car, right?"

Beth shrugged. "Yeah, I guess." She stood, pulled a stick of gum from her pocket, unwrapped it, and folded it inside her mouth. She chewed for a moment, an eyebrow raised. "We should probably get these guys to their respective cars first, right?"

"Transportation will arrive for me shortly," Thirteen said. Amber hadn't seen him make a call since they'd been there.

"Uh huh," Beth said, chewing. She pointed at Jack. "Okay, how about you guys."

"Just take me to my apartment," he said. "I need to pick up a few things," he sniffed the borrowed uniform he still wore, "and maybe change my clothes."

Jack's eyes were cold and dull, and the sight sent a chill up Amber's spine. Her daddy had taken her with him when the vet put down her dog. The dog's eyes had looked like that.

⳩⳩

Dieter lay in the darkened room inside the bundle of blankets and sheets he'd fashioned into a makeshift sleeping bag, one arm thrown behind his head as a pillow. Sounds of the street, dull and muted, filtered through the window; the noise of car stereos mixed with distant sirens, squealing tires, and honking horns. The body he inhabited rebelled with little aches and pains from such deprivation, but he'd had a lot of practice sleeping this way—first in the camps, then later in Argentina. His life had never known comfort, not even before the war. It wasn't something he fretted over. It was what it was.

He stared at the ceiling, followed the contours of the textured plaster, breathed in and out, and counted the minutes from dusk to dawn. He hadn't had a decent night's sleep since he began taking the Adderall, and as it had forced him to increase the dosages, the insomnia had only gotten worse. A lesser man would have already gone insane. He hadn't started hallucinating, but he heard voices. One of those had been with him from the beginning. That one no longer bothered him. It was the unfamiliar—the *alien*—voices that frightened him the most. Like listening to a radio signal just out of range, they whispered to him in broken sentences. Most days he pushed them away. The *bad* days... well, then he doubled up on his meds and hoped for the best.

A light little giggle escaped his throat, and he clamped down on it hard, nearly choking. He was burning this body up from the inside out—nothing could be more clear, but it was all he had, and it had to last. *It will last.*

Will it? the old familiar voice whispered. That one had grown bold of late, but there was no power there, and Dieter laughed. No giggle this time, but a pure belly laugh.

When I have the last of me, Dieter told it, *I will at last be done with what is left of you.* He almost pitied the former owner. There was a time he'd known pity, though that particular emotion seemed to be among the bits of himself he hadn't found.

Dieter turned his head and stared at the harsh glow of the little green light on his receiver, willing it to turn red. It occasionally flickered, but never changed.

He would eat, sleep, and wait until it did.

CHAPTER 24

JACK RESTED HIS HEAD AGAINST THE WINDOW and watched the street-lights flash past as Beth drove; the damp asphalt glistened as if made of obsidian. The Bel-Air was a tank and exquisitely restored, but there was no joy in it for him. Riding with the top down might have been better, but a light drizzle fell; it mirrored the damp, moldy presence in his heart. As soon as he found Dieter, Jack would be forced to tell him about Amber, and his only hope was the man would kill him on sight or Sohrab would take Dieter down first. And Jack was certain the man in his old apartment was the bastard—the coincidence was simply too great. Evan Barrow had disappeared—just walked away while on the job—the same day Dieter died. He'd cleaned out his savings and bought a bus ticket to DC, leaving the day after the murders Double-D had been charged with committing. He'd disappeared again for a while, finally ending up in Atlanta and Jack's apartment. Dieter/Evan had moved openly at first but hid his activities soon after.

It was almost as if he realized Jack knew he was alive.

Or he's just getting smarter. What Jack couldn't understand was why Dieter hadn't attacked him as soon as he'd been resurrected. *Is that the right word? Maybe reincarnated.* He'd risen from the dead like the fallen angel Azazel, a being with no form, doomed to walk the earth in the body of others. *But that was from a movie. The real Azazel is the leader of the Watchers, teaching man to make weapons of war—teaching us to destroy ourselves.* As everything else in Jack's life, the revelation always connected to the Zzkritti. They'd been on earth since before the written word and had shaped history and religion in ways he couldn't even fathom. Azazel had likely been a real person—either a disguised Zzkritti, or one of their emissaries like Thirteen.

The knowledge didn't soothe him in the slightest... but it got him wondering. Was Dieter acting on his own, or in concert with the faction still trying to exterminate humanity? At least one alien was trying to help him through Jack. *Did Dieter know he may be nothing more than a puppet?* He sighed through his nose. *Does it even matter?*

"Okay over there?" Beth snapped her gum and faced him, concern radiating. Sohrab snored noisily in the back seat. They'd already dropped Maribel at her car, and he'd taken over the whole back to get comfortable.

"Sure. What's not to be okay about?" His tone was sharper than she deserved. She'd been a champ, as far as he was concerned, putting her life on hold to help people she didn't know—even placing herself in considerable danger. At least Janice was an acquaintance, if not a true friend before this began, and Maribel had known Mason, but this young woman was something else. She was a bystander, willing to risk life and limb for a cause she didn't fully understand. *Just like Mason and I were once.* The memories of Mason bubbled and frothed in his head, and his heart ached from the loss. Unlike with the loss of his wife and daughter, Jack really *was* responsible for Mason's death—regardless of who pulled the trigger. It was but one more thing he'd never said to Amber... the one thing filling the distance between them, pushing them apart.

"I don't know you, dude, but... you really don't seem right."

He pulled away from the door and settled against the seat's back. "A lot of people would agree with you."

Beth snorted and popped her gum a few times. "That's okay. Plenty of people say the same about me."

"They're wrong." He saw the difference, and she was as good as, if not better than, most people he knew. In a weird way, she reminded him of Mason. He cocked his head and considered her with an appraising eye. *In another life, she'd probably have made as good a wingman.* She slowed the car and steered it to a stop beside the curb outside his apartment building. The lumbering monster of a car rocked back and forth while the brakes squeaked and the shocks complained.

"This is your stop." Her smile was somber. "You guys okay from here?"

"Yeah, we can take a cab to the airport." He reached back and slapped Sohrab on the shoulder. "Wake up. Hibernation season is over." Sohrab grunted and stirred, rubbing his eyes.

"That was fast," he muttered. He grabbed the strap of his duffel with one hand, and the handle of the little black case with the oth-

coffee while the program chugged through mountains of disparate data looking for connections.

The coffee, strong and black, tasted like warmed-over death, and she was grateful to have it; she hadn't a decent cup since... *well, since the last time I stood here.* She leaned against the counter and sipped, doing her best *not to think. Argus has the right idea—don't leave home unless it's on your own terms.* She chuckled at the thought of him and laughed harder for thinking of him at all.

The program pinged. She took her cup and walked back to the desk, set the cup down and leaned closer to the monitor. She frowned at first when she saw the data displayed; her eyes widened and her hand flew to her mouth.

"Son of a bitch!" She reached for her phone.

I love this song! Beth turned the old radio up and drummed her fingers on the steering wheel as she drove. The streets were crazier than usual, even for this time of night, but she expected that with an election around the corner. A tight group of people stepped off the curb and crossed in front of her and she laid on the horn, missing a straggler by inches. She never considered the brake. After her last few days, she decided people could look out for themselves; she'd had enough saving others to last a lifetime.

"Not everyone chooses their destiny," her father had told her. That was the day she came out to her family, and he'd been the only one to accept it without a *discussion.* She'd countered with "no one gets to choose who they love." He'd accepted that with as much grace as she could hope for. Her mother, on the other hand...

"You just need to find the right guy." Her mom had looked at her with hopeful concern—no mean effort, that, and had prompted a quick exit. Beth hadn't had a meaningful conversation with her since.

May be why I like Janice so much. The woman was older than her mom—from another, less forgiving, generation—and could teach a course on acceptance. Beth hadn't wanted acceptance in years. She wanted more. *Someone to love and grow old with would be nice.* She winced, then laughed at herself. *Hell, I'd settle for a good lay.*

She took the next corner like steering a boat, the turn much wider than she was used to. She patted the dashboard like the flank of a horse. *I'm think I'm gonna miss you most of all, girl.* If the weather had been better, she'd have put down the top and enjoyed the drive. The traffic light ahead changed from green to yellow and she slowed to a stop, much to the consternation of the driver behind her. The black Mercedes inched so close the two cars almost kissed bumpers. Beth flipped the driver off through the rear window. He took it with all the grace of someone whose job was to ferry around the rich and powerful—that is to say, not at all. He lay into his horn as if kneading bread dough. Beth grinned at him through the rear-view mirror and when the light changed, she pulled away like a battleship taking up anchor. The Mercedes zipped around her, nearly clipping her bumper.

"Asshole," she muttered. Sure, she was responsible for at least *some* of the encounter, but... Her cell phone chimed and she drew it from her pocket. "Hello?" she said, wondering who'd be calling her at this hour.

"Beth, we've got a problem."

"Mari? What are you—"

"Yeah, dumbass. Just shut up and listen. It's wrong... just all wrong, and I don't have any number but yours, and..." Maribel's words tumbled through the air like a troupe of trapeze artists; they came out so fast Beth had trouble believing it really was Mari.

"Take a breath, girl. Tell me what's wrong." The woman on the other end breathed heavily for a moment before releasing a heavy sigh.

"The guy Jack and Sohrab are looking for? He's not where they think he is."

When the light turned green, Dieter didn't notice it at first—even though he'd been staring right at it—and when he did, he had trouble believing it had changed. He spent a few seconds reminding himself what the colors meant, then sat up like a meerkat, head darting from the door to the kitchen counter and back again.

He's home, he's home, his mind gibbered. *Home, home, home...*

Dieter stood, the thin sheet sliding from his body, and he bounded to his door, opening it a crack to peek into the hallway, watching the door to Jack Montgomery's apartment click shut. He closed his door silently and practically danced back to the kitchen counter, then drew the weapon from its case. The handgun gleamed in the harsh fluorescent lighting, and he stroked it like a pet.

"We will do great things, you and me," he whispered. "Terrible, but great." He wondered who he'd just quoted, then shook it off. Perhaps when it was all over, his mind would allow him to sleep again; it had been so very long. A part of him realized it was the drugs, but another part recognized it as the fire of his mission. "Soon," he slurred. "Soon I'll have everything." He stifled a yawn and skipped back to the door.

He'd planned and schemed for this moment since his rebirth and worked it into his mission whenever possible—whenever his imperative allowed. He'd imagined a thousand times how this moment might play out, but it always came down to a simple head-shot. As much as he wanted Jack to realize who murdered him, telling him was neither necessary nor wise. *No one will catch me monologuing.* Dieter opened his door a sliver and checked the hallway. The building was as quiet as a tomb, but people often surprised him; he never really understood what went on inside most heads.

His hands shook—*the drugs, the drugs, the drugs*—as he pulled the door wider and took a sliding step out of his apartment, the gun held behind his back. The only other thing behind him was the stairwell, and he was the only one who used those. *Close, close, close.* His brain writhed and squirmed like a ball of mating earthworms, and he shuffled closer to Jack's door.

Jack left Sohrab mining the depths of the refrigerator while he went straight to the closet in his bedroom. He should have returned the handgun to Bill's wife, but he'd never gathered the courage. After his brother's death, seeing his widow and kids had fallen far down his list of *very important things to do*; it didn't help she still blamed him for everything. *And rightfully so.*

He opened the closet door and reached up to the shelf, grabbing the box with the Sig Sauer and its clip. Without lifting the lid to check inside, he tucked it under one arm and left the bedroom. Jack didn't know why he kept it—he never planned to fire it, in anger or otherwise—and the weight of it seemed to double as he stomped back toward the living room. He entered, intending to join Sohrab in his search for edible food, when three sharp raps rattled his door. Sohrab pulled his head from the fridge, straightening and looking confused.

"Probably one of the women," Jack said.

He reached for the knob and yanked the door open just as Sohrab hollered, "*Wait.*"

The man in the doorway grinned like a snake, but Jack barely glanced at his face. His eyes locked on the gun in the man's sweaty hand, and he backed away, dropping the box on the floor. It burst open, and the contents clattered out and onto the floor, but the man with the gun never wavered or even looked down. Sohrab joined him at his side, gripping his elbow, ready to pull him out of harm's way.

"Stop where you are!" the man Jack realized must be Dieter snapped. Sohrab froze but didn't release Jack's arm. Dieter stepped into the room and closed the door behind him without taking his eyes from the two. "You don't know how long I've waited for this."

Jack's first thought was to rush him and take his chances or drop to the floor and get Bill's gun—if he were very lucky, there was still one round in the chamber—but what he did was nothing. He wasn't afraid. He wasn't anything. And no amount of effort from his brain caused so much as a single twitch of any muscle in his body. The Zzkritti programming wouldn't allow it; he was a stone statue, and soon to be just as alive.

"Very good," Dieter said, a greasy sound. "I wanted to be sure you learn who is pulling the trigger before you die." He raised an eyebrow as he spoke, as if it were a question.

Jack answered. "You are Dieter." His tone was flat—mechanical. "I killed you."

"Yes, and I'm here to return the favor." He didn't wait or signal his intent further, and without a change in his expression other than a widening of his eyes, he pulled the trigger.

The gun clicked, and Jack winced, but there was no explosion, no bullet flying from the muzzle to tear through his flesh. And still he couldn't move. Sohrab's grip loosened and fell away as he lunged for Dieter. Dieter pulled the trigger again and again as Sohrab flinched with each empty click of the gun. He fell upon Dieter as on the sixth attempt the firing pin remembered its function and struck home. The gun roared and Sohrab grunted as he drove Dieter back against the door, then dribbled off him and fell away to the floor. Dieter kicked him hard in the side once for good measure and turned his attention back to Jack.

And try as he might, he could do nothing more than watch.

☙❧

Dieter kicked the large man a second time and stepped closer to Jack, curiosity clouding his plans. "Why do you just stand there?" He snapped his fingers in front of Jack's unblinking eyes, and a smile crept across his face. "You've been programmed, haven't you?"

"Yes."

282

"But who? Thirteen and Jeff surely want me dead." Doors in the outer hall opened and slammed shut and questioning voices whispered. Time was short.

"The other faction." Jack's eyes flitted from the man on the floor and back to Dieter.

"The other...?" *Does he mean those Jeff's group destroyed during their civil war? But...* He grabbed a handful of Jack's hair and jerked his head back, placing the hot muzzle of his gun beneath the man's chin. "How is this possible?" he growled.

"I do not know. The attendant did not explain. He only gave me a message for you." Jack said this through clenched teeth, as if trying to keep from speaking.

Dieter released the shock of hair in his hands and stepped back, eyebrows furrowed. "And what message could they possibly have for me?" Someone approached Jack's door.

"The rest... of you... is... within... Amber Riley." Sweat poured from Jack's head, some rising in tiny wisps of faint steam.

Dieter recoiled, and spots formed before his eyes. They sparkled and danced as his head reeled. *Of course! She was the closest, and her nanites must have been downloading me when...* He bored a hole through Jack's head with his glare and shoved the gun against his sternum. *I'll take what I need and leave her empty husk for Jack to grieve over.* The thought cheered him. *Then I'll kill him.* "Where is she?" he hissed.

Jack told him.

A woman with a phone glued to her ear barreled past Beth as she walked down the hall toward Jack's apartment; she said something into her phone about an ambulance. Other than that and the noise of people milling in the hallway, the place was eerily quiet. Distant sirens wailed, splitting the night in two—one peaceful, the other tragic... for someone. She pushed past the residents gathering around Jack's door, and her heart climbed up her throat. Sohrab lay on the floor just inside, a pool of blood spreading beneath him; a stranger—*a resident*, she thought absently—knelt beside him, checking his pulse and screaming for help. She stepped around them both, her shock blocking every sound but her own breathing and the blood pounding in her ears. Jack stood across the room, wide eyes leaking tears, like a pillar of salt, no other sign of emotion on his face. She rushed to him and gripped his shoulders.

"What happened?"

He fought with his own mouth like he chewed a large wad of gum, then squeezed his eyes shut. "Dieter," he spit. "Came... to... kill me."

Everything was going to hell around her, women now gasping outside the door, the sirens getting louder and rising in pitch. People crowded around the doorway, and the man beside Sohrab waved them away. Focusing her thoughts, she asked, "Why aren't you dead?"

Jack chewed and his lips squirmed. "Going after... Am... Am... Amber."

Her eyes opened wide, and she searched the apartment with them, the lights suddenly brighter. "Where is your phone?"

"The ambulance is on the way, Miss," a voice behind her said.

She ignored him and shook Jack's shoulders as if she could rattle the words from his mouth. *What is wrong with him?* "Your phone, Jack."

"Gone. No landline."

She turned to the man beside Sohrab. "Give me your phone," she said with an intensity that tore at her throat, and she held out her hand. His brow furrowed, but he must have seen something fearsome, because he dragged his cell phone from a pocket and tossed it to her. She caught it deftly with one hand and turned back to Jack. "I need Amber's number." It was a sure bet he didn't have Janice's, and she had neither.

"Fu... fu... four... sev... seven..." He breathed heavily and sweat streamed down his face.

She punched the keyboard on the screen as he spoke and prayed there were no repeated digits.

CHAPTER 25

WATER SLUICED OVER AMBER'S SKIN. It was as hot as she could stand, and steam clouded the glass of the shower, covering the world outside in fuzzy white gauze; if she tried really hard, she could imagine there was nothing beyond. That wouldn't be a bad thing at all, in her opinion. *Maybe that's what heaven is—a clean white space where you can hurt no one but yourself.* She doubted humanity could be so lucky. Hell was doubtless the same thing; it was only a matter of perspective.

She reluctantly shut the water off and stepped out, lifting the fluffy peach-colored towel from the heated rack. This was the first chance to get really clean since she was last here—a lifetime ago. She toweled off lazily, enjoying the luxury and comfort of the warm terrycloth. *I could get used to this.* That assumed her life allowed her time to get used to anything. When she was dry, she wrapped the towel around herself and snagged another. She took the towel and used it to squeeze the water from the thick tresses, then brushed it back. Even the simple act of brushing her hair felt like an indulgence.

Amber left the bathroom, a cloud of steam following her out, and sat on the bed and began to dress. She had gotten as far as pulling a shirt over her head when she noticed her phone was lit. As its glow faded and the lock screen returned, she checked it with a frown—there were a dozen voice-mails filling her inbox. She set it aside, pulled on her underwear, then lifted the phone again and unlocked it. When it vibrated in her hand, she almost dropped it in surprise. Before she could even say hello, Beth's breathless voice bellowed.

"Amber? Thank God you finally answered. I've been calling for twenty goddamn minutes. Sohrab is, is… *shit*, and Jack can't *move*, and the cops won't come over there without a—"

"Slow down, slow down," Amber said, soothing. "Just tell me what's wrong."

"It's Dieter." She seemed to gather for another onslaught of words, but stopped and took a long breath. "He's shot Sohrab, and he's coming for you."

"Wait... Sohrab's been shot? Is he alive? What do you mean Jack can't move?"

"I... I don't know how Sohrab is. I left as soon as I realized I couldn't get hold of you. An ambulance was coming, but... it... didn't look good."

Amber bit her lip and set the phone aside and pressed the speaker-phone button. "And Jack?" she said as she pulled on her jeans. "What do you mean he can't move?"

"Just that. He's a goddamn statue. He couldn't even tell me what was wrong."

Programmed. Shit. She'd been too late. Worse, the Zzkritti had fooled her into thinking she'd gotten to him in time. *Why would they need to do that?* Virtually immortal, she knew they ran the long con; she wouldn't see all the pieces until they'd assembled it into a whole, and then it'd be too late.

"Amber... you and Janice need to get out of there."

"Where is Jack now?"

"Still in his apartment. He was, I don't know, *thawing* when I left, but he hadn't gotten farther than the sofa.

Twenty minutes. How far is Jack's apartment from here?

"Shit, Beth, I've got to go." She hit the end call button before Beth could complain, jerked on her boots sans socks, and dashed out of the room. Her first instinct was to call Thirteen, but only Sohrab had a way to contact him. *No help there.* She pounded down the stairs, nearly tripping—*and wouldn't that be lovely; break my neck and do the bastard's job for him.* "Janice!" She reached the bottom and yelled again. "Janice, we've got to go!"

"Jesus, dear, you'll wake the dead," Janice said, entering from the kitchen.

"Dieter is on his way here. *Now*." Amber gave Janice two whole seconds to process that. "We've got to go."

Janice's eyes flew open wide and one hand flew to her mouth as she gasped and turned back toward the kitchen. "Stop standing around, then. I'll get the keys and we'll—" An alarm hooted, and she froze. "God *damn* it!" she hissed. She ran to Amber, grabbed her by one arm, and turned her around. "This way!"

"Where—"

"Bless that wonderful husband of mine," she whispered. "He built a panic room, the dear." She ran to a door and opened it. Steps led down toward a darkened basement. "Thought it was stupid at the time." She chuckled, the sound rising into a manic titter. Glass shattered, and Amber spun her head around to see a wild-eyed man coming through a patio door, waving a gun, and grinning like a maniac.

"Hello, Amber," he said, the voice of a long-lost uncle. He walked toward her, not a trace of hurry in his stride; Amber spun and ran down the stairs. The gun in his hand boomed, and wood trim exploded over her head, but she was already too far ahead for him to get a good shot without coming through the door.

"This way," Janice said, grabbing her hand in the dark. "Not far."

Amber followed, accompanied by the sound of Janice's hand sliding along the wall. Feet clumped down the steps.

"Oh, Amber. This can go easy or hard." His voice rang from the close stone walls. "Personally, I prefer hard. How about you?" He cackled at his own joke.

"Found it," Janice whispered. She hit something on the wall and a door ahead of them slid open, a dull red light spilling out. Amber opened her mouth to tell her to hurry, but Janice shoved her through the opening. Her eyes adjusted to the dim light, and she reached for Janice, when the woman's head was jerked back. Dieter had her by the hair and he pulled her close.

"Come, come, Amber," he hissed. "No one has to get hurt." He sniffed Janice's hair. "Well... no one *else*."

"Hit the red button!" Janice screamed and elbowed Dieter in the ribs. Amber found the glowing button beside the door and pressed it without considering what it was Janice had planned. Janice took precisely one step before Dieter snatched at her hair and drove her head into the stone wall. Amber watched the woman crumple to the floor as the door slid shut, sealing her inside.

Dieter screamed his rage, the sound reverberating from the walls and floor and ceiling like an echo chamber. The door, smooth and dull, looked heavy, and even in the faint light from the stairway, he saw it was metal. There was no mechanism on his side other than the button, and he slammed it again and again with the butt of the gun.

"Won't work," the woman croaked weakly. She chuckled and coughed. "Once that door's closed, the only way to open it is from the inside."

Dieter pressed the muzzle of the gun against her head. "Tell her to open it," he growled.

"No." There was no grand defiance in her voice, only simple denial.

He wanted to shoot her and be done with it, but that was throwing away his only bargaining chip.

The woman coughed and rose until she sat with her back against the wall. "You've got about two minutes until the cops arrive. The system called them the moment I pressed that button." She laughed again, softer this time. "You hitting it again probably sped them up."

"The police are no worry of mine," he sneered, but inside his head Evan laughed. *You can't handle them all. Give it up. She's beat you.* "No!" he cried. "Can she hear me through the door?"

"I doubt it," she said, but there was something hidden in that statement, and he caught her glancing toward the door. He studied the door in the gloom, then stepped closer and found the grill and button for an intercom. Dieter grinned at the old woman and pressed the button.

"Your friend doesn't look good." His voice resonated with mock concern, then he released the button and waited.

"She's smart, she won't—"

"Janice," the little speaker crackled to life. "Are you okay?"

Dieter pressed the button again. "She is alive. For now. Would you like to keep her that way?"

"Dieter... the cops just told me they're on their way. It's over."

"*Nothing is over*," he spat. "Not until I deem it." He calmed himself and tried to seem reasonable, though he wasn't sure he could. "Amber... I can take what I need from you through the door, but that takes time, and I'm not sure how much longer your friend has." He wasn't sure he could, but she didn't know that. *You can't*, Evan goaded.

"Take what?"

"Your nanites, of course." He reached out and grabbed Janice by her hair, the strands wet with blood, and she screamed in pain, clawing at his arm with bony hands. "I really don't want to hurt anyone." He shoved her head against the wall, and she screamed again. "Come out and give me what I want, and you both shall live." He repeated the motion and her response was weaker. "Give me what I want, and I'll leave you alone." He released the button.

"Stop it, stop it!" Amber's voice overloaded the tiny speaker, transforming it into the growling roar of a wild animal.

Amber's hand trembled on the intercom button. "Stop it, stop it!" she yelled, straining her throat. "Let her go." She took a long shuddering breath. "I'll come out." She hadn't a clue how the door worked, but it couldn't be that difficult, and she searched for a way to open it. The lights had flickered to life as soon as the door closed, and she now searched for a button or mechanism.

"The officers are two minutes from your home, Mrs. Watson. Stay calm and do not open that door." The 911 operator had stayed on the line throughout, and Amber saw no reason to tell her that Mrs. Watson wasn't in the room.

She found a panel on the back wall, and a single red button in the center. What she really needed was a weapon, but if there was one in the tiny room, she couldn't see where it might be hidden. All she had was a sink, a toilet, and a small refrigerator filled with water bottles and a shelf with a short stack of protein bars. Clearly the room wasn't meant for long-term occupation. She ignored the operator and pressed the intercom button.

"Okay, Dieter. I'll come out." She bit her lip, but squared her shoulders. "Now let her go."

"I have already, Ms. Riley, but I fear she is in no shape to walk," he oiled. "You'll have to support her—*after* you give me what I need." He sounded like a man running out of time. *And patience.* She wiped sweat from her brow. But she had run out of options. If she walked out, he would likely kill them both, but if she didn't, he would *certainly* kill Janice out of pure spite before he left, and he would *still* be out there somewhere waiting to catch her off guard. If not today, then the next. *Jack's not gonna rescue you this time.* He hadn't the last time, either, but that was irrelevant. What had to be done, she must do for herself. Herself and no one else. She took a long breath and let it out with deliberate calm, then pressed the button to open the door.

It slid to the side with glacial slowness, revealing Dieter in the room's light an inch at a time. He stood before her with a look of casual indifference on his face, and she had the urge to leap and claw it off him. The gun, however, he kept pointed at her chest, wiping the thought from her mind. An odd calm settled over her, a realization the end was near shoving all her cares aside.

"Finally," he said with manic energy, his eyes wide and wild, "I shall at last be whole again." Dieter panted like a cougar stalking its prey, and he stepped past the insensate Janice as she sat on the floor. His face split, revealing white teeth. "Stand still Amber. This won't hurt much."

He extended his arm toward her and she felt an odd tugging sensation that tingled over her whole body. It began as a swarm of ants crawling over her, graduating to searing flame licking her skin. She grimaced in pain but refused to cry out. The air between them sparkled, and the light dimmed.

"*Get down!*"

Amber recognized Beth's voice, and two things went through her mind at once: *why is Beth here?*, and *I should get down*. She dropped to the floor as Dieter turned and the sparks between them died. The gun in Beth's hand barked once, twice, three times with a sound Amber knew all too well. Dieter's body jerked from the impacts, and a flower of blood and bits of bone bloomed from his back and shoulder. Beth stood at the bottom of the stairs in a wide-stance, holding the gun in a two-handed grip. She fired a fourth time for good measure before Dieter finished falling, and his stomach spurted blood in a fountain. He lay beside Amber, a questioning look in his eyes, and the gun he held slipped from his fingers.

She watched as the light leaked from his eyes, and then something strange and wonderful happened—his face softened, taking on a normal appearance, and the eyes twinkled for a fraction of a second before closing. He took a ragged, stuttering breath, and whispered in a voice altogether unlike the one before. "He's gone." He smiled. "I won." The man who had been Dieter, was Dieter no more, and he breathed his last as Amber wept.

"Drop the weapon," the voice of authority bellowed behind her, and Beth, no fool, complied at once. The gun clattered to the ground, and she knelt and clasped her hands behind her head.

"I had to," she said, choking. "He would have... would have." She broke down and sobbed as the police officer cuffed her and stood her up.

"Let her go!" Amber cried, clambering to her feet. "This man," she pointed at Dieter's body—*the man I just murdered*, Beth thought—"broke in and tried to kill us. Beth stopped him."

"Doesn't matter, Miss," the cop said as another walked past. "It'll all get sorted out by people higher on the pay-scale than me."

"Can you at least get a paramedic down here for Janice?" Beth nodded to the limp woman on the floor. Drying blood matted her hair, and a smear of crimson painted the wall above her.

"I'll be fine," Janice croaked. Beth couldn't help but notice she hadn't moved when she spoke.

Amber knelt before Janice and touched her face. "Idiot. Never be brave when someone's pointing a gun at your head." She wiped tears from her eyes, then brushed the hair from Janice's. "You're gonna have a hell of a headache."

A pair of EMT's rushed down the stairs and past Beth and the cop. They set their gear beside Janice and began to work. Amber stood and walked to Beth, a huge smile on her face.

"You're a better shot than you are a driver, you know."

Beth shrugged. "Daddy wanted a son." She chuckled. "I guess he sorta got what he wanted."

Amber reached out to hug her, but the cop intervened. "You'll have to come downtown to answer a few questions, yourself, Ma'am." He looked down at Janice and nodded. "She the owner?"

"Yes, officer," Amber said with a hint of impatience.

He nodded at Dieter. "And who's he?"

"I have no idea," Amber said while looking Beth in the eyes. *Yeah, I get it. It'll probably make more sense if we* don't *explain everything.* "He just broke in and threatened to kill us both." She waved at Janice. "It was a good thing she had the panic room."

"But you weren't in there," he said, frowning.

"Janice pushed me in and closed the door. I came out because he threatened to kill her if I didn't."

"Stupid move."

"That's why we're lucky Beth came along when she did."

The cop pushed the bill of his cap up and scratched his forehead. "Yeah... like I said, I'll let the higher-ups sort this out." He turned Beth around and guided her up the stairs.

Good luck with that. I still don't know what's going on.

CHAPTER 26

His eyes were gummy, his head filled with cotton, but he clawed his way to awareness millimeter by millimeter. Sohrab squeezed his eyes tight, then forced them open, though they merely fluttered. Bright light flooded his retinas, and he closed them again. Somewhere far away, someone squeezed his hand. His chest was tight and on fire.

"It was touch and go there for a while, buddy." Jack... it was Jack's voice. "The bullet nicked the aorta, and they lost you twice in the wagon on the way here." He leaned closer and tilted his head. "Your wife and kids have been here most of the time, but I sent them home to rest about an hour ago." He snorted. "Lucky me."

Sohrab opened his eyes a slit and Jack's haggard and stubble-covered face hovered over him. "Can you dim the lights," he said, voice crackling. "And get me some fucking water?"

Jack grinned, left his field of view, then returned with a water bottle with a tube on the end. Sohrab took a sip. Not much—he knew better. *Not my first time.*

"Amber?"

"She's fine," Jack said, but there was something else behind his smile that said all was not truly well.

"Dieter?"

Jack's face fell at once, hardening. "Dead."

Sohrab took another sip while Jack held the bottle. "How long have I...?"

"Three days." Jack took the bottle away and set it aside. "The doctors weren't even sure you'd wake." He chuckled, a sad sound. "I guess you're tougher than they thought."

"Not my first rodeo, as you Americans might say." He started to laugh, then thought better of it given the pain in his chest. "I'm just glad everyone's okay."

Jack winced and looked away.

"What happened to you, Jack?" When his friend turned back, his eyes were red and damp, but his face was hard. "Why didn't you—"

"They programmed me," he said. "They wanted me to *help* that bastard... and I fucking *did*." He shook his head and his eyes grew cold. "And if Beth hadn't stopped him..."

"Wait," Sohrab tried to push up on his elbows, then gave it up as a lost cause. "Beth?"

"Yeah," Jack nodded, brightening. "Took my... *Bill's* gun and drove over there. Shot him three or four times while he was trying to drain Amber."

"Drain?"

"Her nanites. She carried the last piece of him. The piece he needed to get back to destroying humanity. It was why the other faction wanted me to help him—they're still trying to kill us."

"I thought he only wanted to take over." Sohrab relaxed into the soft bed. It called to him, inviting him to sleep. He planned to Rsvp at the first opportunity.

"And we both know how well *that* always turns out." He shook his head. "Nope. He'd have ended up starting World War III."

"Probably," Sohrab slurred. He had other questions, but the bed said they could wait, and he agreed and closed his eyes. Something nagged him, but sleep took him before the thought could form.

Jack left Sohrab's room and wandered the hospital for a while; he still had time. He hadn't heard from Thirteen, and that was good; his programming was still in effect, and as soon as the two got within the nanites' range...

"He'll never be able to go back," he muttered to himself. The Zzkritti faction had loaded Jack up with nanites intended to kill Thirteen's masters, ensuring a clear playing field as they destroyed humanity. Once the nanites made the silent leap to Thirteen's system, the first time he visited Jeff he'd spread them throughout the hive like a virus. There was nothing Jack could do to stop himself, either. He'd certainly tried, going so far as attempting to purchase a ticket to Germany—perhaps getting Rutger to hide him. It was a stupid plan, but he had nothing else. The programming and the nanites wouldn't allow it; he hadn't even gotten as far as searching for flights.

Jack wandered far and wide through the hospital, even venturing into places he shouldn't go, and presently found himself in the exact place he didn't want to go. Janice's room. Her daughters had both flown into town to be by her side, and they stood over her now. She had fallen into a coma shortly after arriving at the hospital—an aneurysm had burst, the doctors said—and she'd fallen into a permanent vegetative state. Her brain was gone. *She* was gone.

He stood outside the room, allowing her daughters their grief in solitude, and fighting against his own. That battle was lost before it was begun, just as Janice's. Machines wheezed and beeped, and the odor of antiseptic drifted over him, both flooding his mind with memories he wished weren't there. A doctor breezed past him and entered the room carrying a clipboard with papers to sign, his shoes clicking on the floor with purpose. The two women signed, then sat on either side of their mother and waited; it didn't take long. The doctor wrote on the paper for a moment, then signed it himself. He stepped close to the machines keeping Janice's body alive, and flipped a few switches, just as Jack had done for his daughter.

Tears spattered the linoleum floor in front of his shoes, and he lowered his head. He didn't believe in God, but Janice had, so he said a quick prayer for her journey, then turned and shambled away.

Thirteen stood before Jeff—and he would always think of her as Jeff, no matter the form—and waited for the Zzkritti to adjust her newly shaped body into the birthing seat. The anointed First Among Equals sat to her right, the cape of office flowing over the sides of the seat. Jeff made several clicking and grinding noises, and a new egg— the first for this hive—slid out of her ovipositor into the claws of a waiting attendant. It scrabbled away with its prize and disappeared through an opening into the hatching chamber.

"How many so far?"

"Only six," Jeff said. "It is a slow and taxing process."

"It surprised me to hear they had selected you to become a queen... or even that the hive chose to *have* a queen."

"We have too long been out of contact with Home." Jeff made a gesture that Thirteen interpreted as a shrug. "It is unusual, but not unheard-of to create a queen in these cases."

"My congratulations, then," he said with a slight bow.

"It is a job. Since my individuality had already expressed, I was the obvious choice." She looked to her right. "Most are ill-suited for this."

That was as close to a rebuke as Thirteen had ever seen one Zzkritti give another, and he wondered what prompted it—not to mention what was so profound it cause her to do it in front of a *human*. Zzkritti kept their conflicts private.

"I came to report that Dieter is dead. There is no longer a threat from him or any humans he may have controlled."

"By the mites, you mean." Jeff leaned forward. "Humans have other means to control one another."

"You speak truth. I will monitor."

"But we already knew of his death," Jeff said, black eyes focused on him. "You did not come to tell us this."

"No. I came to tell you the other faction survived." Jeff leaned back at this news, and her First swiveled his head from side to side as his tail lashed. *Someone is nervous.* "I believe they may have a queen of their own and are rebuilding their numbers." He hesitated. "They may have also grown a Mother." Every Zzkritti in the chamber hissed, and a few skittered from the chamber in fear.

Jeff's voice crackled a sharp and short phrase, and the others stilled. She swiveled her head back to Thirteen. "This is not unexpected. There is a contingency." Her gills along her abdomen sighed with a soft sizzle. "This, too, you shall monitor. I presume you have a method in mind."

"Jack Montgomery was in their possession for a time," he nodded. "He may have useful knowledge. It is clear they programmed him, based on his actions with Dieter."

"Explain."

He did, and at length.

❧

"How did you get my number?" Maribel sat at her desk, feet up and coffee in hand, waiting for a program to finish compiling.

"You called me, remember?"

Shit. I didn't mask the number. Stupid, stupid, stupid. She didn't believe Beth would go spreading it around; it was the principle of the thing. You can't be some super-secret super-hacker if you go around giving your private phone number out. She wasn't exactly upset about it though.

"So, what's up?"

"I thought you'd like to know the funeral's tomorrow," Beth said. Silence stretched for several moments while Maribel chewed that over.

"And?"

"I thought... you know... you'd like to come pay your respects."

She snorted. "It wasn't like we were best buddies."

"But we went through a lot together."

"That doesn't make us all friends." What did it make them? She hadn't had many real, in-person friends for a long time. And one of those was dead, now. *Face it, Mari... your down one friend. Wouldn't hurt to reload.* The thought surprised her.

"I guess not," Beth said, her tone defeated. "I'll let you go."

"Hang on. I didn't say I wouldn't go."

"Really?"

"Sure, why not? Besides, the old bag still owes me a bundle."

"*Mari,*" Beth chided. "Don't be disrespectful of the dead."

Yeah, that probably was a step too far. Janice had paid up front for most of it, anyway. It wasn't as if her bank account was hurting.

"So, what time are you picking me up?"

It was a beautiful service, and on a beautiful day at that. The sun beat down on their shoulders unobstructed by a crystal-clear blue sky. Most of Janice's friends from the office attended, though her arch-nemesis, Mary Hopkins, was notably absent grave-side. The church had been full, and most made it to the cemetery. When the service was over, everyone passed by her daughters and their families to offer condolences, but Jack hung back, Amber, Beth, and Maribel doing the same. As everyone including family filed away and strolled back to their cars, the four gathered and stood before the casket.

"It's more than she would have wanted," Amber said, placing her hand on the ornate casket, her voice breaking.

"But it's what her girls wanted," Jack muttered. "Funerals aren't really for the dead."

Everyone nodded and sniffled, even Maribel. Beth reached a hesitant arm around her, then pulled her in and hugged her. To Jack's surprise, Maribel accepted the gesture and even returned it. He reached for Amber, but she glided away, pretending to examine the grave.

"Mr. Montgomery?" A tall man, not unlike Thirteen, strode up to the group. He wore a suit that looked as if it cost as much as all their clothing combined, his shoes probably worth more than Jack's furniture. He styled his hair like a corporate poster model, though his age would have precluded such a career. A stylish pair of glasses completed the look.

"Yes?" Jack said. The man stuck out one hand and Jack took it, the man giving it a firm shake.

"I'm Mrs. Watson's attorney, Wendall Holman." He waited as if everyone should recognize his name. When no one reacted, he released Jack's hand, coughed once and held up his leather brief case. "She said you'd probably all be here, and the last to leave, but I didn't believe her." He looked at each of the group. "You must be Amber," he said to her. He shook her hand, though not as firmly. "Maribel... Beth," he nodded to each.

"I'm sorry," Jack said, squinting. "What is this about?"

"Ah, yes..." He opened the case and pulled out a large manila envelope and set the case on the ground. "Mrs. Watson's last will and testament will be executed tomorrow in my office, but she asked me to, ah... present these *off* the books." Jack tilted his head, brow furrowing, and Holman added, "So as not to offend her daughters, you see."

"No, not really," Jack said.

"Well, regardless..." He pulled a smaller envelope from the larger and held it out to Maribel. "First, she asked me to present this check to you Ms. Vargas." She hesitated, then took it from his hand. "The amount should cover the balance of her expenses, plus a bonus." Maribel tore the envelope open and looked at the check. One corner of Holman's mouth tugged upward a tick as he watched her eyes goggle. "To Ms. Riley," he pulled out another small envelope. "This should cover the remainder of your school expenses. She was adamant you use the funds for that purpose only." He adjusted his glasses. "Though propriety forces me to add there are no *legal* constraints." He turned to Beth and fished around inside the envelope, rattling something there before pulling out another thin envelope and handing to her. "This is the title to the 1957 Chevy Bel-Air that I believe is still in your possession." He dragged a key from the large envelope. "This is the second key." He handed to her as she stared, her mouth agape. He lifted his case and placed the empty envelope inside. "Well, that would seem to conclude my business here." He smiled at each member of the group and turned to leave.

"Wait," Beth said, stopping him mid-turn. "Nothing for Jack?"

He looked pained for a moment, then gave Jack a wan smile. "No, she left nothing tangible, but said if asked, to tell Mr. Montgomery he has everything he needs right now... in this moment." He raised an eyebrow. "She said you would understand." He cocked his head, frowned, then nodded sharply once and walked away.

And Jack *did* understand... at least he thought he did. He didn't need money, or a car, or even further education. What he needed more than anything was a friend—a connection to the world he'd walled off from himself. *Friends*, he corrected, looking at each of the women in the group. He wished Sohrab could have been here to complete the picture, but he was busy recovering. His eyes pooled, and he wiped them dry. "Who's up for lunch?" he said. "I'm buying."

Sohrab winced as Marie helped him from the wheelchair. Simon, his oldest son, supported him on his right while Marie rolled the wheelchair back inside the hospital. When she returned, she levered beneath his left arm.

"I am not an invalid," he said in a raw grumble. He did his best to show no weakness, but ten days in the hospital weakened even the strongest of men. *And after, they clean out your bank account.* He shuddered to think what this would cost them; even with insurance, the bill would bankrupt them. *Americans* choose *this ridiculous system.* For such a smart people, they could be incredibly stupid and stubborn. *Not the people.* He shook his head. *It's the damnable politicians.* He grunted at the irascible nature of the American male, and Marie stopped.

"Are you in pain?"

He looked at her like she'd lost her mind. "Of course I am, woman!" He snorted. "I've been shot." *And I'm bankrupted by a profession that won't tell you up front what they charge. If only doctors were as honorable as a shade-tree mechanic.*

She began to walk again, and he shuffled to keep up. "Don't be such a baby about it." She was putting a brave front on for their son, and he knew it; even Simon, but the boy also knew better than to shatter her finely crafted illusion.

"I apologize," Sohrab said as they turned toward the parking lot. "I am worried about our finances, and the effect of this stay."

"Oh," she grinned. "I wouldn't worry about that." Simon chortled beside him, still working to support his weight.

"And why is that?"

"You'll see," she said, a twinkle in her eye.

They walked in silence until she brought him to a black Mercedes–Benz SUV. She stood there grinning while he considered the scene.

"What is this?"

"It's our new car," she said as if it should have been self-evident. "Your tall friend brought it over a couple of days ago." She gripped his arm tight. "He said the hospital bill is taken care of, too." Her eyes were bright, and they danced as she spoke. "He's still creepy as hell, but..." she waved one hand at the car like Vanna White. "He said you earned it."

Sohrab wanted to cry; he would have if Simon weren't standing at his side. *With this I can drive for premium fares.* With that, he just might dig his family out of the financial hole they'd fallen into.

Marie rose on her toes and kissed him on the cheek, then whispered, "Don't tell the kids, but our savings account is heavier, too." He turned to her to see real tears in her eyes.

"How much?"

"A little over a million." She opened the passenger door for him.

His knees buckled, but Simon held him steady.

"C'mon, pop," he said, laughing. "Let's go home."

After all morning in the sun, and a lunch with more alcohol than food, Amber opened the door to her dorm room and stumbled inside, her head pounding. She stripped off her jacket and shoes as she walked toward the bed, then fell into it without removing anything else; she was too tired and in too much pain. *I should take something before I pass out.* But now she was horizontal, her body refused to return to vertical.

That's right. Sleep. Everything is easier when you sleep.

"Who said that?" she mumbled, unable to open her eyes.

I am you, the gravelly voice said, soothing. *Or will be soon.*

Her eyes snapped open at once and she sat up. She recognized that voice. It had haunted her for more than a year. She searched the room for the source, but there was no one. Her heart raced, pounding against her ribs, and threatened to burst through when the walls of her room began to melt. She screamed and leapt to the door, her head pounding with the beat of her heart, and she ripped open the door, its cracked, dry-rotted surface covered in paint that curled and flaked.

She ran into the hall and froze. What she saw was not the clean paint and quaint molding she'd passed a hundred times, but the crumbled plaster and stone of the *asylum*—the place where Dieter had kept her. Where he had programmed her to kill.

Tears welled, and she forced down the lump in her throat, then ran for the exit. Her bare feet slapped against rotted flooring, and she felt hot breath on her neck. The smell of putrid flesh chased her down the hall, and with every turn the hall narrowed. The last turn brought her to a dead end punctuated by a wall of cinder block. When she turned, Dieter bore down on her, his eyes wild and rabid.

Without thinking, she threw her hands up to protect herself, and the feral thing with Dieter's face screamed. She dropped her hands and opened her eyes. Beyond a wall of iron bars, Dieter paced, his eyes flaming with pure hatred.

Bitch! he said, streamers of drool dripping from one side of his mouth. *Evan tried this, too.* He stopped, narrowed his eyes, and clutched the bars with both hands. *It did not work. I still took him.*

Amber's heart slowed, and she controlled her breathing. She straightened, crossed her arms, and stared hard into the thing's burning eyes. *This isn't a dream. It's in my head, but...* A final cruel thrust of the knife, he'd slipped inside her with no one suspecting. *Not even Thirteen.* Trapped inside her own mind, she was alone and without a weapon. She narrowed her eyes. *But I won't make it easy. Dead things just lay there.*

"All right old man," she growled, a furious, spitting cat. "Let's play."

www.ingramcontent.com/pod-product-compliance
Lightning Source LLC
Chambersburg PA
CBHW031109030726
47496CB00002BA/452